WHAT PE

David and ... n

Both a wise reading and a wild reimagining of the Bible's most fascinating personalities and most memorable single clash. Philistines and Israelites, their gods and loves and struggles, spring to dramatic life in *David and the Philistine Woman*.
David Wolpe, "America's Most Influential Rabbi" - *Newsweek Magazine*, author of *David: The Divided Heart*

King David is revered by more than half the population of the planet, yet he has never been more real and knowable than he is in Boorstin's breathtaking novel. Here the man God called "Beloved" is utterly, unforgettably human. I couldn't put this book down.
Reza Aslan, author of #1 *New York Times* bestseller *Zealot: The Life and Times of Jesus of Nazareth*, and executive producer/host of CNN's *Believer*

In *David and the Philistine Woman*, Paul Boorstin creates a remarkable new kind of narrative voice, at once mythic and insightful. His radiant David is a rare hero who feels as relevant as tomorrow.
Bill Blakemore, ABC News Middle East Correspondent

A compelling account of the fierce struggle of rival gods and their followers. A major achievement, gripping and finely wrought.
Nicholas Clapp, author of *Sheba: Through the Desert in Search of the Legendary Queen*

Leave it to this documentary film maker to conceive this richly imagined story. Boorstin has created the page-turner that book

clubs have been waiting for since *The Red Tent*. Storytelling at its best.
Judy Kancigor, *Orange County Register* columnist

Boorstin dazzles with razor-sharp insight as he focuses on characters who leap from the pages of history with rich and newly defined clarity. Be prepared for surprises at every turn.
Lionel Friedberg, *New York Times* bestselling author

A page-turning, action-filled novel that is both harrowing and fulfilling. Boorstin's poetic prose reimagines a world so long ago it might as well be mythical, but which resonates with eternal human truths.
Mary F. Burns, author of *Isaac and Ishmael*

With vibrant color, Paul Boorstin paints a wholly new portrait of one of the Bible's most enigmatic figures. *David and the Philistine Woman* is a welcome addition to the rich tradition of Jewish historical fiction.
Emily K. Alhadeff, editor of *Jewish in Seattle Magazine*

A stunning expansion of the Biblical tale of David. Boorstin vividly imagines an archaic world of ritual, intrigue and sacrifice. The writing is so gripping and intense you can smell the ancient cities of Gath and Gibeah.
Stephen Kitsakos, author of *The Accidental Pilgrim*

Paul Boorstin's *David and the Philistine Woman* is an exciting rendering of the Biblical story with compelling relevance for today. The dialogue sparkles with wit, and the ingeniously constructed plot leads to an unexpected and inspiring climax.
Joseph Schraibman, Professor of Jewish Studies, Washington University in St. Louis

David and the Philistine Woman

David and the Philistine Woman

Paul Boorstin

Winchester, UK
Washington, USA

First published by Top Hat Books, 2017
Top Hat Books is an imprint of John Hunt Publishing Ltd., Laurel House, Station Approach,
Alresford, Hants, SO24 9JH, UK
office1@jhpbooks.net
www.johnhuntpublishing.com
www.tophat-books.com

For distributor details and how to order please visit the 'Ordering' section on our website.

ISBN: 978 1 78535-537 0
978 1 78535 538 7 (ebook)
Library of Congress Control Number: 2016954756

A CIP catalogue record for this book is available from the British Library.

Design: Stuart Davies

Printed and bound by CPI Group (UK) Ltd, Croydon, CR0 4YY, UK

Contents

For Sharon

PROLOGUE

*

David had not yet seen Goliath. Though he had lived almost seventeen years, he had been spared the sight of the enemy and the blood of dying men.

His father, Jesse, had forbidden him from herding the flock close to the field of battle with the Philistines—for his safety, Jesse said—though David suspected it was only for fear his prized flock would be slaughtered. His mother, Nitzevet, had her own reasons to keep David out of harm's way: He was her youngest, the one closest to her heart. He was different from his brothers and she knew they had no fondness for him. They would not weep if while David visited the battlefield, a stray Philistine spear took his life.

Though he was now old enough to fight, David had not followed his brothers off to war. It was not for him to see Goliath or face the enemy as other Israelite men must. As the youngest, it fell upon him to be the shepherd of his father's flock. There was no glory in that. But he found no shame in it either. In fact, David took pride in the task.

He had not yet seen Goliath. But before he could face him, David's path would be a perilous one.

*

"Not a blacksmith could be found in the whole land of Israel, because the Philistines had said, 'Otherwise the Hebrews will make swords or spears!'"
—Samuel, 13:19

"He chose five smooth stones from the brook, and put them in his shepherd's bag; his sling was in his hand, and he drew near to the Philistine."
—Samuel, 17:40

PART I

Chapter 1

Through the tips of his fingers, the warning came.

The taut strands of sheep sinew allowed David to sense what would take place before his eyes could see it or his ears could hear. Sometimes there was a sweetness in the notes, like turtle-doves at dawn, which filled him with hope. At other times, the notes stung like thorns, announcing that a dust storm was brewing or that a pack of wolves had cornered a ram in a ravine.

In the unforgiving heat of the day, he watched over the sheep grazing on the hillside near Bethlehem and ran his hand along the strings of his lyre. The notes hovered uncertainly in the air to foretell something looming over the horizon. He sensed a mighty force, though whether for good or evil, he did not know.

He lifted his fingers from the strings and rested the cedar yoke of the lyre on his knee. All his life, he had waited for the Almighty to speak to him. He had listened for His voice on the wind and in the gruff crackling of the hearth fire. He had listened for Him in the roll of thunder and in the chirping of crickets. He had never heard Him.

And yet, for days, David had sensed that something momentous was about to take place. Only the night before, he had the dream, the one that had haunted him for as long as he could remember.

In the dead of night, he was standing outside a cave. He knew that a treasure was hidden inside it, but a giant boulder sealed the cave mouth shut so that the treasure was beyond his reach. Then, as he watched, by some unearthly force, the giant boulder began to move, revealing a glow from within the cave like a secret promise. From the unseen source of the radiance, he heard a voice speaking with solemn authority, but the words were muffled. Before he could understand their meaning, he awoke.

The vision of the cave had come to David on so many nights,

he doubted he would ever understand its meaning. But last night, it had been more vivid than ever. When he awoke, his heart was pounding, whether from excitement or terror, he could not say.

The dream told him that this day would be like no other. And so, that morning, he allowed fate to guide him. Usually, he led the flock, but today he followed them. It was the way of the sheep to trail after the oldest ram, even if it was senile and useless, and today the flock followed a lame old one with yellow horns warped by time. So it is with my people, he thought. The Israelites follow the ancient paths, while a young leader could guide them in a bold, new direction.

At first, the sheep moved as they always did, from the darkness into the light, leaving behind the shadowy ravines near home and setting out for the sunshine of familiar pastures. But today, he noticed they ignored the path of the feeble ram. Left to themselves, they did not proceed north toward Saul's city of Gibeah, where there was water from streams and ample pasture. Instead, the flock veered west, past Beth-zur, almost as far as Sochoh. He followed the flock of thirty ragged wanderers as they picked their way over the flinty hills.

Keeping an eye out for stragglers among the thornbushes and thistles, he realized they had strayed dangerously close to Philistine territory. David had hoped the sheep would be guided by the Almighty to a place where he would receive a sign. Instead, they had led him to a desolate spot with more nettles than grass, a brackish rivulet for a stream and one miserly terebinth tree that gave no shade. My sheep are lucky that I watch over them, he thought. Left to their own instincts, they would all starve to death.

But what if I am wrong? What if they were led here by a Higher Wisdom beyond my understanding?

Perhaps, here, in this desolation, he would hear the voice of the Almighty at last. He held his breath and listened: only the wind. It seemed that today the Most High had better things to do than speak to a mere shepherd who was the youngest son of Jesse of Bethlehem. The heat that had punished his flock was fading at last, but the boulders and brambles clung to the warmth like a grudge against him. And yet, the sheep were content to stay there and forage what little they could. He thought it was like every timid creature, man or beast, to nibble the meager meal in front of him, rather than risk setting out for unknown pastures with greater promise.

As he had countless times before, he studied the flock with a practiced eye in search of a sign from the Almighty. As always, the meekest of the sheep kept to the center of the flock for protection in case the outliers were attacked by wolves.

He noticed that a pregnant ewe, her black fleece flecked with white, had moved away from the others. She had not been eating, and now he saw why. A dark stain in the dust beneath her told him that her waters had broken.

She was about to give birth. Had the Almighty sent him a sign at last?

He took pleasure in bringing new life into the world, even though he knew that in the eyes of his brothers this made him no better than a woman. The ewe was young. This would be her first lamb. David felt compassion for her. He knew it would take her longer to give birth than an older ewe, and it was more likely that her lamb would be stillborn. She had never suffered through the ordeal before and needed more help than older ones in the flock that had borne many.

He eased the ewe out of the sun, beneath the shade of a boulder. She breathed fitfully. He picked up his lyre and began to play. He had found that music from the strings could calm the rapidly beating heart of a ewe and ease the delivery. Today, the gentle notes did no good. Pawing the ground, she bleated and ground her teeth. Sheep gave birth standing or kneeling on their front legs, but this one simply lay down, a sign something was wrong.

Jesse, his father, had told him, "Animals have no souls, so they cannot feel pain." David knew Jesse was wrong. A sheep was no less in the sight of God than the wisest priest. When he knelt down beside it, the ewe's eyes were open. He saw the suffering in them.

The lamb slowly emerged through the translucent membrane. First came the two front feet, then its nose was visible between them. The creature was pink and pale and, for the moment, blind. He saw the legs were pointed downward as they should be—this would not be a breech birth. But the lamb was too big. It could not escape its mother's womb. Gently but steadily, David pulled its legs down toward him. The ewe groaned.

He placed the palm of his hand on her taut belly to feel the contractions. With each spasm, he tried to ease the lamb further out. His hands slippery from the bloody fluid, it was difficult to keep his grip on its legs. He struggled to move the glistening, sodden flanks from side to side to guide them out. He had to be careful. If he pulled too hard, he would break the lamb's ribs.

At last, wet and shining, the creature slipped free of its mother. He cradled it in his arms, a bundle of gangly legs, and gently lay it down on the parched grass. The lamb was terribly thin, as all newborns were, and David knew it needed to drink its mother's milk immediately.

But all was not as it should be. The newborn's eyelids were closed. He leaned closer to its mouth to detect a flutter of breath on his cheek. He felt nothing. The lamb had not yet taken its first breath. Perhaps it never would.

In that tense moment, David did not pray to the Almighty. There was no time for prayer. It was his way to act quickly and let the work of his hands serve as prayer enough. He hastily wiped the mucous from the lamb's nostrils with his tunic, to make it easier for the creature to breathe. Then, snapping off the end of a thistle, he tickled the lamb's nose. If this made it sneeze, he knew it would start breathing.

But the lamb still lay motionless. He had to try something else. He lifted the gangly creature by its back legs and rubbed its sides, massaging them with both hands. The creature still did not draw breath.

At this moment, he knew other shepherds would abandon the newborn. And yet, David refused to give it up for lost. Tenderly, he took hold of the slippery creature by the hind legs and swung it in a slow arc through the air. Responding to the movement, the lamb's chest fluttered once, then again. Haltingly at first, then more strongly, the newborn started to breathe, settling into a regular rhythm.

David nestled the lamb beside its mother. The ewe was so exhausted that at first she barely noticed her offspring, but soon she began to lick the newborn clean. David eased the moist pink nose closer to her. The mouth of the newborn groped blindly. With his fingers, he helped the lamb to lock on a teat and suckle. The small mouth pulled at it weakly at first, then more eagerly. Milk flowed.

This time, he had saved a life. Too often, he could not. Why would the Almighty allow a lamb to be born, yet smother it at birth? It baffled him how the Most High could create life with one hand and then, a moment later, crush it with the other.

David's mother, Nitzevet, was a midwife. "It is upon women like me to stand guard at the threshold of life," she had told him. "We are the gatekeepers." But even a midwife could only do so much. She had told him that human infants, perfectly formed by God's hand, were all too often stillborn.

He knew that dreams could also die, killed at the very moment they took their first breath. He feared that now, when a new day was coming in his own life, the Promise would perish at dawn, smothered at birth.

The relentless sun overhead had not yet begun its retreat toward the horizon. To allow his flock the most time to graze, he seldom returned them to their pen outside the family dwelling before dusk. But today, a premonition told him he must take them home at once.

Chapter 2

Following his instinct that this would be a day of wonders, David guided his flock toward his father's dwelling near Bethlehem.

It was hardly a dwelling. Two years before, a Philistine raiding party had torn down their family home so that not one stone rested on another. Jesse and his sons had hastily rebuilt it as best they could without mortar, by stacking flat rocks. But the makeshift walls could not keep out the heat of the midday sun or the chill of the night wind. David had worked hard with them to construct it, but his toil did nothing to endear him to his father or brothers. Their hearts were hardened against him.

Now, as the sun descended over the western hills of Judah, he caught sight of the wood smoke billowing from the mottled clay dome of the bread oven behind his father's dwelling. As she did each afternoon, his mother Nitzevet busied herself there, kneading barley dough on a flat stone.

David caught sight of her face and remembered her as she was once, a plump, cheerful woman with a curly tempest of hair and an impudent laugh. Now her face sagged with sorrow from the death of two of her sons in battle. She wore only the black of mourning, as if each day that her remaining sons set out to fight the Philistines, she might be forced to grieve for another.

She slid the barley dough deftly into the oven with the strong but gentle hands of a midwife. After struggling to help with the birth of the lamb today, he respected Nitzevet's skills all the more. It was said that her gift had been passed down in her family ever since the time of the Great Enslavement. She had taught him that the ruler of Egypt had once ordered the Israelite midwives to kill at birth all the male infants born to their people. The midwives disobeyed the command, and so Moses the Lawgiver survived to lead them to freedom.

When David was a child, Nitzevet would embrace him and

say, "My beloved, you will be as Moses to our people in our time of need." She always smiled playfully when she said the words, but he knew she believed she spoke the truth: "Moses they revered, Moses they respected, but you, my son, our people will *love*."

Once, his father overheard her telling David this. "Your mother fills your mind with blasphemy!" Jesse shouted, and beat her with his staff. Now, as every day, while Nitzevet busied herself kneading barley dough by the bread oven, Jesse remained in seclusion inside their home. No doubt, he was chanting ancient incantations in the shadows to win the favor of the Almighty, David thought.

As he walked closer to their dwelling, his father rushed outside in his musty black robe, blinking in the late afternoon glare. Jesse shunned the sweat and filth of worldly toil. He did not plant barley or shear sheep in the harshness of the sun. His face was as sallow as sour goat's milk, his eyes weak and his lips parched from murmuring prayers in the stifling darkness. He wears his pallor as proof of his righteousness, David thought, evidence of how much time he spends consumed in prayer. But worship that does not spring from a compassionate heart is hollow.

He saw now that Jesse had not come out to greet him, but to welcome his three oldest sons: Eliab, Abinadab, and Shammah. Soiled with the dust of battle, they approached from the direction of the Valley of Elah. Their beards were as ragged as their tunics, and with each step, they leaned wearily on their spears.

Nitzevet stopped kneading the dough to murmur a prayer of thanksgiving. David was happy for her sake that her sons had come home alive. He feared she could not endure the loss of another.

Seeing his three brothers, shoulder to shoulder, David was struck by how different he was from them. With russet hair and a ruddy complexion, he was fair and lean, while they were dark and heavily muscled. He looked so unlike them that they sneered that he was not Jesse's child at all, that he did not belong to the tribe of Judah. They said that the blood of a heathen tribe flowed in his veins. David's mother had taught him to take pride that he stood apart from his brothers. When she prophesied, "Moses they respected, but you the people will *love*," he doubted he would ever count his brothers among his admirers.

As they did every time they returned from battle, his brothers shouted out to their father, "Once more, we have escaped death at Goliath's hand!"

David had never seen Goliath. But when his brothers returned from the field of battle, he saw the shadow of the Philistine on their faces. He heard the dread in their voices and observed how their terror sapped their strength. I have witnessed what Goliath has done to them, he thought, and I know what evil lurks in his heart. I need no more view the Philistine with my own eyes to judge his wickedness than I need to stare into the sun to know of its power to blind me.

Goliath afflicted his brothers as he afflicted every Israelite who had ever heard his name. David knew that to them, the Philistine was part man and part god. "I cannot protect you from his wrath," his father had warned them. "All I can do is pray for you to survive." David saw that his brothers feared Goliath as they feared Death itself.

"You return to me through the grace of the Most High!" Jesse warmly embraced his three eldest sons. He scuttled back into the dwelling and returned with a jug of barley beer. Jesse never offered any to David because, as he liked to say, "Drink only rewards manly deeds."

His father turned his back on him to face the others. "Tell me how my valiant sons have spilled Philistine blood!"

Abinadab held up his ox-leather shield. "Goliath himself tore these holes with his spear, but I escaped. Then I killed two of his bravest men!"

David was weary of such deceit. Yesterday, at dawn, he had seen Abinadab tear those holes in the shield himself. He knew that in their cowardice, his brothers stayed well clear of the Philistines' swords and spears, but he kept their secret. He forgave them for inventing false exploits, because he saw how his father drew strength from hearing their lies. After the Philistines had destroyed Jesse's dwelling and murdered two of his sons, he hungered for vengeance.

While David guided the sheep toward the pen, Shammah eyed him with contempt. "You have brought the flock home early. Why do you shirk your duty?"

Eliab spat in the dirt and laughed. "You are as shiftless as your sheep!"

David was tempted to reply, "You boast of brave deeds, though I do not see a drop of Philistine blood on your sword." But he bit his tongue and said nothing. No good would come from petty insults. Besides, his brothers had already forgotten him. As usual, they had slumped down together on a bench in the shade of their dwelling while Jesse passed around the jug of barley beer.

David's mother joined him at the sheep pen. She ran a hand tenderly along his cheek. "The time will come, my son, when all your brothers will bow down to you, just as, long ago, Joseph's brothers bowed down to him."

"Seeing how my brothers hate me, I fear that day will be a long time coming."

She patted a little straggler entering the pen. "You have a newborn lamb."

David watched it tag along after the ewe on wobbly legs. "Already it can tell its mother from the others in the flock." He frowned. "It was a difficult birth."

"If only it was as easy to bring new life into the world as it is to bake a barley loaf!" she said. They shared a gentle smile of understanding. He did not confide his disappointment to her.

Was I wrong to come home today expecting a revelation? Or is the revelation that there is nothing more than this, merely to survive from one day to the next, one year to the next?

My cowardly brothers will march off to more defeats in a war the Israelites can never win. My mother will toil as a midwife in Bethlehem, baking bread until her fingers are too frail to knead the dough. My father will drown his fears in prayer. And I will be fated to live out my days herding a dwindling flock, playing my lyre to the wind. My mother might weave fanciful stories of how I will someday be more beloved than Moses—she has many dreams for me and for that I love her—but they are as remote and unattainable as the morning star.

He glanced into the pen at the newborn lamb suckling from its mother. In that moment, he took pride in the simplest of things: He had helped one more creature to enter the world.

Suddenly, his father let out a yell and clapped his hands together. It was the way Jesse scared off stray mongrels that came scavenging for scraps. But he saw that his father was not trying to scare away a dog.

Jesse was shouting at a man.

Old and bent, with a ragged beard, the stranger was cloaked in the black sackcloth and ashes of mourning. He carried no sword or spear, bore no staff. He had only one good eye, the blind one as clouded as a divining stone.

No wonder my father is determined to be rid of this stranger, David thought. It looked like this lost soul had wandered for so long, alone in the blistering heat of the sun, that his mind had succumbed to demons. The intruder shuffled slowly but steadily toward Jesse and his three eldest sons, who lingered in the shade of the dwelling. David expected his father to offer the stranger a sip of rainwater from the gourd at the cistern, as was the custom of his people. Instead, Jesse squinted suspiciously at the unsavory visitor.

"Why do you dress in mourning, old man?"

"I mourn that the spirit of the Lord has departed from Saul, our king." The stranger spoke loudly—whether from righteous fervor or madness, it was impossible to tell. "I lament that Saul no longer follows the righteous ways of the Law!"

"It is not for you to say such things," Jesse snapped. "The king's men will cut out your tongue for such insolence."

The stranger's one good eye skewered Jesse with an unforgiving look. Once again, he raised his voice in righteous indignation: "I am Samuel of Ramah, prophet of the Almighty. This is not *my* judgment of Saul. It is the judgment of the Most High!"

Jesse sized up his decrepit visitor, unconvinced. "All have heard of Samuel, wisest of the prophets, who anointed Saul to be the first king of our people. Since then, I have seen many lost souls like you wander out of the Great Desolation." He pointed at the barren hills in the distance. "None of those who have come here are prophets, though all claim to be."

Could this really be Samuel? David wondered. It was said that the prophet delivered the word of God as readily as a servant delivers messages from his master. David had always imagined Samuel cloaked in radiant white robes, with a noble profile and a flowing silver beard befitting an emissary of the Almighty. And yet, whether or not this shabby derelict was the prophet, David found something oddly familiar about him.

It was not his craggy features or his threadbare robe. It was his voice, as harsh as wind through the branches of a dead oak. Yes, he understood now. He had heard that voice in his dream, echoing from within the cave, a voice muffled by the boulder that blocked its mouth. Under the spell of sleep, David had struggled in vain to understand the words. Today, he vowed to listen to this visitor from his dreams and learn the truth.

"I come here with the blessings of the Most High," Samuel said to Jesse. "I come here to anoint the Chosen One who will be king of the Israelites after Saul."

"Then you are mad," Jesse said. "Our king is Saul and the

next king will be his son, Jonathan, because Saul's blood flows in his veins."

Samuel shook his head. "Jonathan will never be king. The Lord has sent me here to anoint the next king from among your sons."

"My sons?" Jesse stared at him in disbelief.

David saw that his father longed to believe the stranger's words, but that he was torn between hope and suspicion. After a moment's hesitation, it seemed that Jesse decided to accept this astonishing stroke of good fortune on the remote chance that it might be true. "For a father, there can be no greater honor." Like a miser eying a heap of gold, he rubbed his pallid hands together. "I have eight righteous sons, but Eliab is my firstborn. Of them all, he is the most worthy."

He pointed proudly to his tall, broad-shouldered eldest, who slouched in the doorway with the jug of barley beer resting on his hip. "Eliab is brave and noble." He nudged his son forward. "I can think of no finer choice for one to lead our people."

Samuel sized Eliab up with a hasty glance. "He is not the one."

Jesse recovered quickly. He grabbed the arm of his second son, whose beard was sodden with barley beer. "Then here is Abinadab. His spear can kill a Philistine at a hundred paces. Our enemies flee at the sight of him."

Again, Samuel shook his head. Jesse pressed ahead. "And this is my third, Shammah." He pointed with pride to the last of the brawny young men. "He is righteous and has tasted battle. Like all my sons, he loves the Almighty more than he loves his own life."

Samuel did not deign to cast a look in Shammah's direction. "None of them is the one I seek." He glanced around him. "Where are your other sons?"

Though David was nearby, shutting the gate to the sheep pen, his father turned his back on him. "My younger sons are away performing their lowly tasks. So, you see, the Almighty could only have brought you here for one of my three eldest."

David knew now why he had been compelled to return early with the flock. He felt his mother watching him from beside the bread oven and realized she knew it, too.

"I am the one you seek."

David walked boldly toward them. He saw astonishment on the prophet's face.

"Who is this?"

"My youngest." Jesse dismissed David with a wave of his hand. "Pay no heed to him. He is a simple fool, his mind addled by dreams."

David stood before Samuel. "I am the reason you have come."

"Leave our sight," Jesse growled. "No one summoned you."

"You did not summon me," David said. "But I have been summoned."

"You are a shepherd?" The prophet asked.

David nodded. Samuel scowled, tilted his head and examined him closely with his good eye.

Will he judge me as my father judges me?

Unlike the others, David had not been scarred in war. He knew that Jesse had always disapproved of his unblemished good looks, calling it a sign of feminine weakness. While his brothers had the brawny, muscular bodies of warriors, he was slender and agile. Under Samuel's unsparing gaze, David felt like a goat being examined in the market.

Will he find me unfit to lead our people?

Samuel blinked and leaned closer. He pressed his thin lips tightly together in a scowl, peering deep into David's eyes as if probing the depths of a chasm.

Beneath the boldness of my gaze, the prophet detects something else, something he has never seen before: a promise beyond my understanding.

"What is your name?" the prophet asked.

"David."

"David." Samuel repeated the word slowly, his head cocked to one side to analyze the sound of it, as if the name held a secret meaning. Then, like a weary traveler whose journey has finally ended, he let out a long slow sigh of relief.

Fearing the prophet had fallen under David's spell, Jesse broke in: "He is only a callow shepherd who has never seen battle."

"A coward," Eliab muttered.

"He has never shed Philistine blood," Shammah added.

"One need not shed blood to have courage," David said, stifling his anger. "Sometimes, it takes courage to *not* shed blood."

Samuel had stopped listening. He had closed his one good eye and retreated into himself. The prophet's spindly legs wobbled, his knees unsteady. He had drifted into a trance so deep that David feared he might collapse before them.

Suddenly, Samuel's eye flashed open, blazing with fervor. "David, son of Jesse, the Almighty has sent me to anoint you to follow Saul upon the throne of Judah."

Nitzevet had pulled a barley loaf piping-hot from the bread oven. David saw that when she heard Samuel's words, her hands trembled and the loaf fell into the dust.

"This cannot be!" Jesse choked on his outrage. "I have introduced you to my three eldest! How can *he* be the Chosen?"

Samuel hunched forward and raised his bony shoulders, like a dog whose hackles were bristling. "You dare to question the will of the Almighty?" He spat into the dust at Jesse's feet. "You may as well ask, 'Why did the Most High choose drunken Noah to build the Great Ark?' or 'Why does He now choose so unworthy a servant as Samuel to speak His word?'" Impatient, he turned back to Jesse's youngest son. "Kneel."

"Stay on your feet!" Jesse snapped.

David knew that to follow Samuel's command would enrage

his father, that he would never forgive him.

"Obey me!" Jesse growled.

But David knelt before the prophet.

Abinadab nudged Shammah and Eliab. "David has spent plenty of time on his knees like a maiden, milking the ewes of the flock!" The brothers smirked.

Samuel fumbled in the folds of his sleeve and pulled out a cracked, yellowed object. At first, David thought it must be the bone of some ancient creature. Then he recognized it: a ram's horn, the brittle relic warped by time. Samuel removed the wooden plug from the tip of the horn. David inhaled the scent of olive oil mixed with myrrh and cinnamon, along with sweet fragrances unknown to him.

With trembling hands, Samuel raised the ram's horn over David's head. The prophet spoke in a clear, strong voice: "It is the will of the Almighty that David, son of Jesse, be king of the Israelites after the reign of Saul. May David be unifier of the twelve tribes and defender of the tomb at Machpelah, resting place of Abraham, Isaac and Jacob. May he preserve the Ark of the Covenant. May he lead his people on the righteous path of the Almighty."

The words cascaded over David, overwhelming him. But Samuel had not finished. His voice grew tender, as if he was about to utter both a prophecy and a prayer: "In distant days to come, from the House of David will rise the Messiah, the one who will at last bring peace to this weary earth."

David struggled to make sense of the prophecy, but it was beyond his understanding. How could such wonders ever be, distant miracles that he and his children would not live to see?

How does the blood flowing in my veins make me worthy of such a destiny?

But the time for thinking, for questioning, was over. Samuel's hands stopped trembling. With a single decisive flourish, he tilted the ram's horn, sprinkling the shimmering holy oil over

David's brow.

At first, the liquid caressed him with the gentle warmth of a summer dawn. Then it grew as hot as bread baking in his mother's oven. From somewhere deep within him came a joy too absolute for his mind to grasp, a joy too complete for his lips to shape into words. In that giddy moment, he discovered a place at the core of his heart that he never knew existed, a hidden wellspring that connected him to all things that had unfolded in the past, and all things yet to come.

David's face was flushed, his heart pounded and his breath came quickly, as if he was climbing a steep mountain. He was ascending at such a dizzying pace now that his feet left the earth and he flew, soaring all the way to the summit. From there, he was poised to enter a realm beyond imagining. He blinked, but he could no longer see. It was as if the holy oil had blinded him. Only now did he realize that the sacred liquid streaming down his brow had mingled with his own tears.

David rubbed his eyes and looked around him, slowly returning to his senses. At first, as he knelt in the dust, it seemed that nothing had changed. Once again, he was Jesse's youngest son, a humble keeper of sheep, doted on by his mother and despised by his father and brothers.

And yet, somehow his world had been transformed. He felt the Promise of Samuel as both a burden and a gift. A voice in his mind cautioned, *"You have been Chosen for a purpose that is impossible to achieve."* But a voice from his heart replied, *"Are not all miracles impossible until He makes them come to pass?"*

With startling suddenness, Samuel's voice that had been so pious, hardened into a command: "Jesse, you and your eldest sons must take a blood oath. Swear you will keep David's anointing a secret." Resentful, they avoided the prophet's gaze as he continued, "In His good time, the Almighty will reveal the truth to the world. Until that day, Saul must not know of this. No one can know! The king believes his son Jonathan will follow him on the throne. He will put to death anyone who thinks that is not God's will."

David saw the bitterness on his brothers' faces. Eliab muttered, "Why should we obey this old man? We owe him nothing."

Jesse winced as if he was forced to swallow vinegar. "We must do as he says. If David's anointing is revealed to Saul, he will have our heads."

Samuel reached into a fold of his robe and pulled out a twig with a barb curved like the talon of a hawk. David recognized that it came from a blackthorn tree. The prophet pierced Jesse's forearm with the barb, then pierced the arms of his three eldest sons. As he pricked their flesh, drawing beads of blood, not one of his brothers flinched. By their stoic bravery, David thought, they intend to show Samuel that he anointed the wrong son of Jesse to lead our people.

The prophet had them repeat the words: "If I reveal what I have seen today, may the wrath of the Almighty strike me down."

David saw in his brothers' eyes how much they hated him. For the first time in their lives, the youngest and lowliest son of Jesse had been given a gift they coveted. He knew they had sworn the blood oath not out of respect for Samuel, but out of obedience to their father. Would they keep their promise? Trust among brothers, he knew, crumbled as easily as a crust of barley bread.

"The road to Ramah is long," Samuel said, and abruptly turned to go.

David stopped him with a hand on his arm. "You have told me my destiny. Now I ask for your blessing."

"My blessing?" Samuel tilted his head and met his gaze with his one good eye. Whatever warmth David had once found there had been replaced by stony indifference. "You are the Anointed. The Promise has been given to you. But to become king, your way will be a path of thorns. It is the path you must take."

He pointed a bony finger toward the desolate hills. "A great obstacle lies between you and your destiny. The boulder will not move itself. You will not see the glory that lies beyond until you alone have moved it."

Chapter 3

The blade glowed an angry red under her blows, stubbornly refusing to yield. Her hammer pounded the iron relentlessly, spewing sparks, shaping it into a point. She plunged the newly formed blade into the cooling bath. It hissed like an adder, steam rising.

For Nara, it was a day in the forge like any other. She could not have known that this was the day her secret would be revealed.

Above the ringing of her hammer on the anvil and the roar of the furnace, she heard the gruff voice of her father, Ezel, master blacksmith of the Philistine city of Gath, in the adjoining chamber. He bellowed out a bawdy song as he sharpened the cooling sword blades and spear tips on a whetstone. She knew he only sang when he had been drinking, and the more honey wine he drank, the more he needed her help.

She sweated under the heavy goat-leather apron that she wore in the sweltering heat. Struggling each day with molten metal in the forge, others would have found much to complain about. But for Nara, this harsh life was a blessing. In her sixteenth year, she asked nothing more than to toil here at the furnace, with the ruby glow of iron and the tenderness of her father's love.

Her life had begun in tragedy. Her father told her she had been so large an infant that the ordeal of birth killed the gentle woman who gave her life. Without a mother's love, she had looked to her father to care for her, to protect her. After so much sorrow, she took comfort that here she was secure, shielded from the world.

At bedtime, Ezel would tuck the wool coverlet tightly under her chin. Her father smelled of charcoal and molten iron, his brawny shoulders stooped by years toiling before the furnace.

Each night, he pressed his heat-cracked lips against her forehead and whispered the words she longed to hear: "There is nothing on earth as eternal as the anvil of a blacksmith. There is nothing on earth as eternal as my love for you." Harsh as thistles, his unkempt beard brushed against her face. To Nara it felt like a caress.

To have brought about the death of my own mother is disgrace enough for any woman. But it was only the beginning of the shame I brought on my father, one who did nothing to deserve it.

As if to lash out at her fate, Nara pounded her hammer fiercely against the scorching iron. The din could not drown out the question that haunted her.

Why did Dagon punish me with my affliction?

It was not that she was ugly. Viewing her reflection in a polished oval shield hanging on the wall, she beheld a beauty that she believed other young women might envy. But the charm and grace of her countenance, her lithe, supple body, did not matter. I might as well be a leper, she thought.

"You are not like other women," her father had told her on the day when he could no longer ignore her transformation.

* * *

When she had lived only thirteen years, on the brink of womanhood, she grew.

She grew taller than the others her age, taller than her father could understand. And she kept growing until she was taller than he was. Soon she was not only the tallest woman in Gath. She imagined she must be the tallest woman in all the five great Philistine cities, perhaps the tallest woman who had ever lived.

Awkward and clumsy, she dreaded stepping out of her father's forge into the world. The boys and girls her age laughed at her when she stumbled on the stairs in the alleyways, taunted her when she blundered into the walls of the narrow stone passages of Gath. They jeered at her, confident that even though she was much stronger than they were, Nara would not fight back. She knew she could never hurt them, for fear of dishonoring her father.

Then came the wound that would never heal. On that day, the body of Jadan, her brother, was carried back on his shield into Gath through the Gates of Eternity. A javelin of crude Israelite copper had pierced his throat.

For her father, Jadan's death was a terrible blow, and not just because he had lost his only son. She realized that without Jadan to serve as his apprentice in the forge, Ezel could never keep up with the Philistines' relentless demand for blades of iron. And so, the day after her brother died, Nara knelt before her father to comfort him in his sorrow.

"At last, I understand why the god Dagon made me so much mightier than other women." She enfolded his hand in hers. "Dagon gave me the strength to take my brother's place. I will work beside you at the anvil."

Ezel buried his face in his hands and wept. "You know that can never be. Women are forbidden to work in the forge under pain of death. The priests say a woman's hand on an iron blade weakens it, just as a woman's touch on a warrior's body weakens him before battle. The priests say that because a woman bleeds at her time of the moon, she is unclean, unfit to make a sword of the purest iron."

Though he recited the reasons why she was unworthy to work in the forge, it seemed to her that he spoke without conviction, as if in his heart he knew they were lies. "You need my strength, father. There is no other way to complete all your work for the warriors of Gath. If you do not satisfy their demands, they will make you suffer for it."

Ezel gazed into the palms of his blackened, callused hands as if searching for an answer. Finally, he sighed. "Yes, I must do as you say. But it means defying the priests."

"We will keep it a secret from them, from everyone in Gath."

"Forgive me for putting your life in danger," he said.

"It will be my honor to work at your side."

He gazed up gratefully at his daughter, who stood head and shoulders above him. "My beloved Nara, I will make you my secret apprentice. I will teach you to be my trusted right hand."

"I will not disappoint you." Joyfully, she wrapped her powerful arms around him in an awkward embrace.

After that, Ezel cleaned the stacks of firewood out of a musty storeroom adjoining the forge. He lovingly fashioned a frame of sturdy cedar planks to hold straw-filled bedding generous enough to support her. In that makeshift bedchamber, she lived contentedly, nurtured by the warmth of his affection and the purring of the furnace.

At first, his commands had been simple. "See to it that the belly of the forge is fed," he ordered, and she ran off happily to fetch armloads of charcoal. Then he instructed her to sweep up the foul-smelling slag with a broom made of green acacia twigs. Soon, she was fetching the hammer, tongs and pincers, learning to step nimbly to avoid scorching her legs on the coals spewed from the mouth of the furnace. Ezel taught her when to plunge the red-hot blade into the saltwater bath to cool the iron and when to remove it; when to use the pincers and when to use the tongs; how to temper the black metal by throwing a handful of rock salt into the seething vat.

At last, the day came when he bestowed on her the highest honor of all. From its hiding place in the forge, he removed a strange-looking contrivance of bronze tubes, leather bladders and wooden levers, which was the size of a bellows. "This is the Serpent's Tongue," he explained. "It allows the Philistines to craft blades of iron that vanquish the Israelites' crude copper. I will teach you its secrets." He told her how the priceless device offered the only way to melt iron so it could be shaped into deadly weapons. Yes, she thought, my father even entrusts me with this, the secret known only to the master blacksmiths of Gath, the secret they guard with their lives.

She took pride that the blades she forged were straighter and stronger than those any man could make. Even her father knew this, but she forgave him for being too proud to admit it. Though working in the forge was forbidden to women, she believed she was serving the needs of Dagon and the Philistine people. She told herself that she had the gift to do what no other woman in Gath dared.

In the days that followed, when the commanders made relentless demands on the handful of master blacksmiths in Gath to fashion deadly swords and spears, Ezel's forge turned out more than all the others. No one knew it was because Nara worked at his side. But the constant danger weighed on her father. She saw how he feared she would be discovered working in his forge and swiftly put to death.

To protect Nara from being found out, he had hung an ox-hide from hooks in the ceiling to shield her from prying eyes. On one side of the makeshift curtain, she secretly toiled at the anvil by the furnace. On the other side, Ezel sharpened the cooling blades on a whetstone and dealt with the Philistine men-at-arms who came for their weapons.

Nara was grateful for her secret life, grateful she could serve her people as other women of Gath could not. And yet, as time passed, she felt pangs of longing. She wished she could someday be like the young wives of Gath, loved by a husband, bearing him children they could cherish together. But she knew no Philistine would ever take her as his bride. What man would marry a woman taller and stronger than he was?

* * *

Today, the awareness that she was doomed to live and die alone stung her like the barbs of iron that flew from the furnace. The only way to fight off the sadness was to work. She returned to hammering the iron blade on the anvil, striking it so hard that sparks flew. Instinctively, she glanced over to make sure the ox-leather flap had been lowered to conceal her from any visitor who entered through the door to the forge.

She was alarmed to see that today her father had forgotten to lower the ox-hide. He is drinking too much honey wine, she thought. It makes him careless about even the most crucial precautions. But there will be no harm done, so long as I quickly lower the hide to shield myself from view. She reached up to unhook it from the smoke-blackened ceiling.

Too late. A man, visible only in silhouette, had entered the forge and was speaking to her father.

Startled, she dropped her hammer. It clattered to the ground. The noise drew the visitor's gaze. For a panicked instant, she thought of ducking behind the clay-brick dome of the furnace, but she was too tall to hide there.

There is no escaping it now. My secret is revealed.

But who had caught her? She strained to peer into the shadowy threshold. If it was one of her father's friends, he might be persuaded—or bribed—to keep silent.

But no, she recognized the one who had seen her: the high priest, an ominous presence in his heavy white robe. He was the most unforgiving of men. Dalziel's haughty eyes gleamed in the light of the furnace, judging her. His long pale fingers were clenched together tightly before him, the way they must clutch a knife at the altar, she thought, when he slits a bull's throat.

He has witnessed me hammering out an iron blade on the anvil. That alone is enough to condemn any woman to death.

She felt his severe gaze play over her, but in the flickering light of the forge, she could not read the priest's expression. When, at last, Dalziel spoke to her father, she could not hear his words over the roar of the furnace.

The priest pointed a sharp, bejeweled finger at her. Her father bowed to him and nervously wiped his grimy hands on his leather apron. He gnawed his lip. She saw that he feared for her life.

The priest hurled his words at her, shaping them precisely with his thin lips: "Approach me, daughter of Ezel!"

Nara's mind told her to follow his command, but her legs refused to obey. She held back, dreading his punishment.

"Come at once!" her father shouted.

First, as Ezel had taught her, she slipped the precious Serpent's Tongue into its shadowy hiding place in the niche beside the furnace. Then, as quickly as she could in the bulky sandals that protected her feet from slivers of molten iron, she approached the high priest.

Her heart pounded like a hammer striking an anvil. Her mouth was too parched to speak. She knew it did not matter that a massive bronze idol of Dagon with its upraised sword of fire stood outside their dwelling as proof they were true believers in the vengeful god of the Philistines. She knew it did not matter that Ezel paid generously to buy fattened rams for sacrifice on the high altar of Dagon's temple. None of those things would save her now. As a woman who had dared to work in the forge, who had defiled it with her touch, she would surely be put to death. The high priest would force her father to watch her die, and then take his life.

Until this moment, she had only glimpsed Dalziel from a distance, a fearsome presence looming on the highest parapet of Gath, exhorting the Philistines to slaughter the Israelites without mercy. She had always imagined him as a mighty figure. But now that she stood before the high priest, she found she was the mighty one who towered over him.

Nara thought she must look monstrous to Dalziel, her hair wiry and wild from the blistering heat of the forge, her face smudged with charcoal dust, her hands scarred from shaping the black metal. In her own eyes, her shameful, unwomanly appearance made the splendor of the high priest—the rubies and sapphires sparkling on his fingers, the opulent gold pendant around his neck proclaiming his power—all the more intimidating.

She stood close enough to him to smell the frankincense from the temple of Dagon that permeated his elaborately embroidered brocade robes. In the radiance of the furnace, Dalziel's flowing white beard glowed the fierce orange of molten iron. At any moment, she expected him to bare his teeth like the cruel idol of Dagon on their threshold and announce her fate.

She struggled to purge the fear from her voice: "I am your servant." She held her breath and waited for him to pass judgment.

The old man gazed up at her towering over him. For the first time, she could see into his eyes. She expected to find hatred and vengeance there. Instead, she discovered something even more unsettling.

The high priest looked up at her in awe.

His brittle lips cracked like dry wood and the corners of his mouth rose to shape an expression that looked disturbingly like a smile. The high priest's eyes sparkled with an emotion that did not seem to belong on his pitiless face: pure joy. He reached out his bony right hand, the palm raised in blessing.

"Nara, daughter of Ezel of Gath, kneel before me."

Fearing the worst, she did as he commanded. Even on her knees, she was as tall as he was. She bent closer to him and felt the tips of his cold, bloodless fingers touch her forehead.

"Nara, daughter of Ezel, you are chosen for an honor greater than any Philistine woman has ever received. This honor can only belong to you."

His words mystified her, but she bowed her head in gratitude. Somehow, for a reason she did not know, Dalziel forgave her for working in her father's forge. She had been spared. "You are chosen for an honor," he had said. She wondered what that honor could be.

In that giddy moment, such questions no longer mattered. She felt the warmth of her father's gaze upon her. All her life, she feared he had been ashamed to have an outcast, a misfit, as his child. Now, with the high priest's blessing, she saw that Ezel took pride in her as his daughter, pride in her as a woman.

Chapter 4

"Men have come for you!"

Her black cloak billowing behind her, David's mother ran toward him at the sheep pen, where he was opening the wooden gate to take the flock out at first light. Nitzevet was pale with fear, breathless.

"There are three of them."

David caught sight of the men standing before Jesse's stone dwelling: two brawny young Israelites with spears and shields, and their gaunt commander, his face badly scarred, his hand on the pommel of his sword. The men wore embossed helmets and breastplates of polished bronze. Their spearheads and swords of heavy copper were more finely wrought than his brothers' crude weapons.

"They belong to the palace guard," he said. Their reason for coming must be important, he thought. They must have marched through the night to arrive now.

His mother's eyes widened in fear. "Your father and your brothers have betrayed you. They have told Saul that Samuel anointed you as the next king."

"It does not matter who told him," David said calmly. "This was meant to take place." He closed the gate of the pen behind him. "They are bringing me to Saul because he wishes to see the one Samuel anointed instead of his own son."

She studied his face. He saw she was puzzled by what she found there. "You act as if you welcome this!" she said.

"It was meant that I should meet the king face-to-face."

"David, son of Jesse!" The commander called out to him. "May it please you to come with us to Gibeah."

He had seen Saul's men before, when they came to collect taxes from the farmers of Bethlehem. The soldiers treated his people brutally, spoke to them arrogantly, as city dwellers from

Gibeah talked down to simple peasants. Not today, he thought. The king must have told them to treat me with respect. How much more had Saul told them?

He said to the commander, "I am ready."

"Do not go," Nitzevet whispered. "The king will have you killed!"

He looked into her troubled eyes. "If Saul wanted to do away with me, these men would have done it already." He embraced her tightly, her hair smelling of cumin and barley dough from the bread oven. He felt helpless to comfort her. She tried to turn away to hide her face from him, but he saw that her eyes were filled with tears.

David slung his lyre over his shoulder. He carried it with him on its worn leather strap as others carried a sword, to face the unknown.

* * *

Two of the palace guards flanked him while the commander led the way down the dusty road to Gibeah. David took one look back: Nitzevet stood alone beside the bread oven, watching him, her hands clasped tightly before her, as if she feared she would never see him again.

The men marching at his side said nothing, staring straight ahead. They do not prod me with their spears to walk faster, he thought. They do not treat me as an enemy, but as their guest.

Once the king meets me, once he looks into my eyes and into my heart, he will accept it is my destiny to follow him on the throne. He will understand I wish him and Jonathan no harm. Then Saul will find the right time to announce it to the people, so they will accept that he has passed over his warrior son to crown a shepherd.

In his eagerness to reach Gibeah, David walked more rapidly than the guards who escorted him. He felt the lyre swinging on his shoulder. Even now, did he hear faint music rising from it?

He felt as if his lyre was eager for what would come, impatient for him to touch its strings and rejoice.

* * *

At dusk, they reached the battle-scarred ramparts of Gibeah, Saul's royal city. To David, the cracked and pitted granite walls looked worn and weary, the haggard fortress unworthy of a king who was the Chosen of God. A banner stitched with the Lion of Judah drooped, lifeless, from a staff above the battered main gates of tarnished bronze.

In the failing light, David noticed a handful of peddlers hawking their last basket of lentils, their last ephah of barley, before nightfall. Hunched on benches outside the walls, three toothless old men grumbled bitterly to each other. David heard them complaining about the Israelites' latest defeat, grieving for their sons whom the Philistines had slain. He recognized some of them from his last visit to the market. Each day brings more misfortune, he thought, more dead to be mourned, and the anguish does not fade. When he walked past, the elders fell silent and gaped at him. He knew they must wonder why a harmless-looking young shepherd arrived here with his own escort of palace guards.

Three ragged boys ran up to him, their palms outstretched. The guards shoved them roughly out of the way. These are the sons of men the Philistines killed in battle, he thought. When I am king, I will see to it that no more urchins with empty bellies beg in the dust. Hunger is a pestilence I must banish from our people. When I rule, I will serve the poor and hungry and they will love me for it.

But what of the warriors? He glanced up at the wary sentinels on the parapets. Why should they accept me as their king, one who is only a shepherd, a youth untried in battle? "Someday they will all bow down before you," his mother had said. "Moses they respected, but you, my son, the people will love." Looking up at the hardened faces of the sentries, David thought it would take a miracle to win them over.

The guards escorted him through the weathered city gates, into the shadows gathering within the walls. David came here often on bustling market days, when this square was packed with merchants and peddlers, the stalls echoing with haggling voices, the clucking of chickens and the braying of donkeys. But now, at dusk, the square was deserted. The cobblestones were as cold underfoot as the windswept battlements that loomed above him.

They stopped before a brass-bound door blocked by six guards with spears. He had heard that this was the entrance to Saul's palace, where only members of his inner circle were allowed. A sentry nodded to the commander of his escort, as if he had been expecting them. The guards stepped aside and pushed open the heavy doors, which yawned wide.

David felt blessed to be the first member of his family ever to enter the king's palace. He expected to be dazzled by royal splendor befitting the ruler of God's Chosen People: grand hallways glittering with brocade tapestries and polished inlaid marble. Instead, he followed the guards down a murky corridor where flickering torches left the cobwebbed ceilings swallowed up in darkness.

Gradually, his eyes adjusted to the gloom. He noticed that the walls had been stripped bare. Copper hooks hinted at the ornate tapestries that he imagined had once decorated the halls of the king. Now all such treasures were gone, bartered away by Saul, he guessed, to buy the loyalty of his fickle commanders. This palace of shadows is unworthy of a monarch who serves the Almighty, he thought. When my time comes to rule, I will exalt Him with a glittering palace that reflects His glory.

Their footsteps echoed hollowly through dim pools of torch-light. The soldiers and servants they passed in the hallway lowered their eyes to avoid his gaze. He saw the shadow of fear on their faces, as if all of them were afflicted with the same terrible pestilence.

At the end of the gloomy corridor, the guards halted before doors intricately adorned with lions in gold leaf. David wondered, is this all that remains of Saul's splendor?

A bald, portly man rushed toward them out of the darkness. Though his fingers glittered with gold rings, his amber-studded robe looked faded and worn. David detected the same shadow of fear on his face that oppressed all the others.

"I am Tobiah, counselor to Saul," he said in a tremulous voice. With a wave of his hand, he dismissed the guards, then let out a weary sigh of defeat. He looks more like a condemned man than an advisor to a king, David thought. He felt Tobiah studying him, and sensed the king's advisor was surprised at what he saw: David's young, open face, his threadbare tunic and rough sandals, his simple cedar lyre. "So you are the son of Jesse they have brought from Bethlehem . . ."

"The king has sent for me," David said.

"The king did *not* send for you," Tobiah corrected him under his breath. "He does not even know you are here!"

David stared at him, speechless. He was certain Saul had summoned him because of his anointing by the prophet. If that was not true . . .

I have dangerously misread the king's motives. If I could be so mistaken, perhaps I understand nothing, least of all my own destiny.

He fumbled for the words to shape a question. "But if Saul has not sent for me—"

A woman's voice interrupted him: "My father did not send for you. I did."

Chapter 5

A pale, slender young woman in a purple robe stood in the doorway to the king's chamber.

"This is Michal, beloved daughter of Saul," Tobiah said, bowing his head in respect.

Her eyes were red from weeping, her face ashen, her cascade of raven hair unkempt. And yet, in her profound sadness, David found a stark beauty. She dazzled him like sunlight striking the purest water from the deepest well.

"I am David, son of Jesse. I will serve you as I would serve your father."

He had heard his brothers speak of her in whispers. Though she had an older sister, Merab, it was rumored that Michal was Saul's favorite. They even said Michal was as beloved to Saul as his eldest son, Jonathan.

David's brothers had led him to believe that the privileged women in the palace were selfish and idle, consumed with petty gossip. But the young woman who stood before him seemed anything but frivolous. She did not paint her lips with the juice from crushed pomegranate seeds or darken her eyes with kohl powder, as he had been told was the practice of the vain women of the court. The bracelets glittering on her wrists were of plain silver instead of bejeweled gold.

"We have tried potions and healers," Tobiah said. "We have tried prayers and sacrifices from the priests. All of it, in vain." He threw up his hands in frustration. "I know it is not seemly for me, Saul's most trusted advisor, to follow the counsel of a young woman, even if she is the daughter of a king, but—"

"It is right for the daughter of a king to help her father," Michal broke in, with a boldness David had never seen in a woman. "And it is right that others should obey her."

In someone else, David might have found such daring rude

and unbecoming, but it only enhanced her grace in his eyes. "I am here to carry out your wishes."

"My father is possessed by demons," she said. "He will not sleep or eat. He sends for neither his wife, Ahinoam, nor a concubine to share his bed." She met David's gaze. "I pray you can help."

"How can a shepherd help the daughter of a king?"

"I have heard you play your lyre . . ."

"How can that be? I have never set foot in the palace before."

"More than once, I have passed through the spice market in Gibeah with my handmaidens," she said. "You were playing your lyre in the sheep pens."

"It calms the flock before they are shorn," he said awkwardly. I am a fool, he thought. How could I have been so blinded by my playing that I did not notice her?

With the tip of one finger, she touched the cedar instrument hanging from the strap on his shoulder. "Your lyre looks like any other. But your music . . ." She hesitated, searching for the words. "It is different from the other music I have heard, both in the market and in the palace."

"Different, because all I know of the lyre, I have taught myself."

She dismissed his modesty with an impatient shake of her head. "I have heard the sorcery in your music. It is the reason I summoned you."

He was about to object that his music held no sorcery, that it was as ordinary as the strands of sheep sinew on which he played it. But he did not want her to think she had made a mistake to bring him here. Above all, he wanted her to believe in him.

"Whatever power there is in my music, I offer it to you now."

* * *

Michal beckoned David to follow her into the king's darkened bedchamber. Heavy brocade drapes smothered the windows. Slowly, his eyes grew accustomed to the gloom, noticing the dull luster of an unsheathed sword with a bejeweled pommel lying discarded on the floor. On a table, a platter of lamb, seemingly untouched, had attracted a swarm of flies.

A crumpled figure lay curled up on the bed, shrouded in shadows. At first, David refused to believe that this husk of a man could be Saul. He had glimpsed the king a few times before, standing on the ramparts of Gibeah, a tall, heroic leader in glittering armor, exhorting the Israelite host to victory. But the face of this specter was waxen and ravaged, his beard veined with gray and matted with spittle. He wondered, can this really be the one chosen by the Almighty, the one anointed by Samuel to be the first ruler of our people?

Saul's voluminous gold-embroidered robe seemed to swallow up his frail, shivering body. With his eyes shut, he wept softly and muttered meaningless words to himself. David saw that the king's suffering brought tears to Michal's eyes.

She feels her father's anguish as her own. She loves him so much more deeply than I love my own father. For Saul to inspire such devotion in Michal's gentle heart, there must be great goodness in him.

Tenderly, Michal reached out to touch Saul's sallow cheek with her fingertips. He flinched as if she had struck him. "Leave me!" he growled and turned away.

She withdrew to David's side. "See how my father is tormented by demons. Though he struggles against them, he cannot defeat them."

David watched the king's eyes dart back and forth beneath his closed eyelids. Was his soul locked in battle with phantoms even now? At last, Saul opened his eyes. They were a watery gray, empty as a cold sky before dawn. They told David nothing.

"You see, my father does not even know we are here," she said. "Soon the evil spirits will destroy his soul and he will be lost to me forever." She turned to David. "I implore you . . . heal him with your music."

"I have never used my music for healing," he said. He did not tell her that he believed it was blasphemy to claim such god-like powers of enchantment. The only magic he had experienced was the spirit that possessed him when he played the lyre, something beyond himself, something beyond his power to control. He wondered whether it was the part of him that was closest to the Almighty.

"You must do what you can," she said. It was both a command and a plea. He knew he could not refuse her.

I play to calm my skittish sheep in a hailstorm. I play to calm my flock when a pack of wolves lurks nearby. I have never played to comfort a king afflicted by demons. But is there so great a difference between a king and the humblest of creatures? All living things suffer. All living things seek solace from their fear and loneliness.

He knelt down beside the ornately carved bedstead and slid the leather strap off his shoulder, cradling the simple cedar instrument in the hollow of his hip. His fingers stroked the strings, rippling a cascade of notes.

The music echoed off the walls of the cold stone chamber, swirling in upon itself, thick as frankincense. It felt unnatural to David to play indoors. His father did not allow him to make music inside their dwelling, thinking it pagan and unholy. David only played the lyre outdoors with the flock, his music drifting up to the heavens.

Now he chose the sweetest melody he knew, notes woven from strands of tender memories. This melody had come to him at an unlikely moment: Once, in a sudden downpour, he had crouched under the branches of a terebinth with his flock. When it seemed the rain would never end, the sun burst through the storm clouds and arced a rainbow from horizon to horizon. The sight had kindled a melody, pure and vivid as a holy vision. His mind could not recall it, but his heart remembered it now so that his fingers could find the notes.

David's music filled the room. It pleased him to watch Saul's daughter listening, her eyes closed, lips parted as if breathing in a heady fragrance. But her father? David searched for some flicker of emotion on the king's face: It was as unyielding as granite. He played until his hand ached, until his fingers throbbed, as stiff as an old man's. He leaned closer to Saul, as if his lyre was a torch that could warm him to the bone.

Slowly, almost imperceptibly, the king stopped shivering. His eyes and mouth shut and his rigid jaw relaxed. He lay perfectly still.

Tears glittered in Michal's eyes. "He is at peace. You have rid him of his demons."

"The Almighty has done this," David said. "I am only His servant."

"Then He never had a more worthy one." She met his gaze with a fondness that David knew was forbidden between a king's daughter and a shepherd. And yet, it seemed to him that she felt no shame in it.

He saw now that Saul's chest was gently rising and falling beneath his robe, his breathing slow but regular, growing stronger as he was embraced by sleep. David wondered whether it was time for him to depart. But Michal did not ask him to go. And above all else, he wanted to stay.

* * *

David awoke to the sound of coughing. He realized he had dozed off on the floor beside the king's bed, with his lyre in his arms. A shaft of morning light pierced a gap in the heavy curtains, revealing that Michal had curled up on a cushion a modest distance from him. Her eyes were open. She too had been awakened by the sound.

The king wheezed and spat out yellow bile. Stretching his stiff arms, he slowly sat up. He breathed in deeply, as if savoring each mouthful of air. Rubbing his eyes, he blinked and looked around him, squinting in the dim light. He ran a hand along the silken coverlet, seemingly surprised to find himself in bed.

The spell is broken, David thought.

Saul caught sight of Michal and broke into a broad smile. "My beloved daughter..." He lifted his trembling arms to her.

She rushed over and embraced him. "You have come back to me!"

Moved by their tenderness, David began to play again. As his fingers raced across the strings, he saw that the king drew strength from it. The pace of the music seemed to quicken Saul's pulse and revive the spark of life within him. Soon, roused by the melody, he summoned the will to pull himself out of bed. He had been lying down for so long that his knees were weak and, at first, his legs struggled to support his weight.

Michal gripped Saul's arm and gently helped him to stand up, his bare feet unsteady on the cold stone floor. Suddenly, he tore his arm from her grasp. David feared the demons had seized hold again. It looked as if Saul was lunging for his sword, which lay on the floor within reach.

Instead, the king took a few determined steps over to the heavy drapes that smothered the windows. He grasped them with both hands and tore them aside, flooding the chamber with daylight. The king raised his face to drink in the warmth of the morning sun and Michal hugged him in its radiance. As one, father and daughter wept for joy.

David considered withdrawing from the king's chamber to allow them to be alone together. But he decided that he must stay.

Saul must know who has done this. It was meant that I should heal him. It is the first step toward the day when he will accept me as the one anointed to follow him on the throne.

"I thought the Most High had abandoned me," the king murmured to Michal. "Instead, my God has freed my soul from its torment."

"The Most High did it through His servant," she said, "David, the son of Jesse of Bethlehem, a shepherd . . ."

Saul smiled weakly at David. "With your lyre, you performed the work of the Almighty." The king's eyes were brimming with tears.

"May I serve you even as I serve Him," David said.

He no longer saw Saul as a king, only as an old man who had suffered, an old man he had helped to heal. He stepped forward, hoping for the king to lift his hand and bestow his blessing. Instead, to his surprise, Saul clasped him in his arms, holding David so tightly that he could feel the king's heart beating rapidly against his.

My own father never embraced me with such affection. Despite all that I have done for Jesse, my own flesh and blood, he has never shown me such gratitude.

"David," Saul said, speaking his name for the first time, "You belong here, serving me in the palace, not in Bethlehem tending sheep!" He looked around him impatiently and clapped his hands together. "Tobiah!'

The king's advisor opened the door a crack and peered in on them with amazement. "My king, you have returned to us!" He wiped his sweaty jowls with relief and summoned two male attendants to follow him inside. One held cloths of fine linen, the other an onyx vessel. Tobiah directed them as they removed Saul's robe and purified his body with fragrant myrrh.

While the king was being cleansed and dressed, David found he was standing closer to Michal than he had intended. In the unexpected intimacy of the moment, his eyes met hers and she graced him with a smile. David knew that healing Saul had been God's miracle. But he took secret delight that despite his protests, she seemed convinced the magic was his.

Moments later, Saul stood before them in a clean white robe shimmering with silver threads. Tall and clear-eyed, he seemed to David a man transformed, a commanding presence.

"Play for me now and every night, son of Jesse." He smiled benignly. "Your music is touched by the Almighty."

"It will be my honor."

Saul turned to confer with Tobiah. David felt Michal watching him and took up his lyre once more. In that moment, he was no longer playing for the king. He played for her. He rejoiced that each time he returned to the king's chamber, Michal would be here to greet him. He was only a shepherd, while she was the favorite daughter of a king. He knew it was forbidden for their hands to touch. But with his music, he touched her.

Chapter 6

"One step closer and we die." Hafaz spoke half-heartedly, expecting his impulsive master to ignore his warning.

Crouched on a hill behind a sparse stand of oaks, Jonathan, eldest son of Saul and heir by blood to his father's throne, gazed down, unruffled, at the Philistine city of Gath. His seasoned bodyguard feared they were vulnerable in their precarious hiding place, that any moment, a sharp-eyed Philistine sentinel would spot them.

Jonathan smiled at him. "You cluck over me like a fretful crow."

"Your father, the king, made me swear on my life to watch over you." Hafaz did not dare repeat Saul's exact words: "Protect my son. His recklessness endangers his life." And so it endangers mine, Hafaz brooded. That day, when he had bid farewell to his family in Gibeah, he had hugged his wife and two small daughters tightly, fearing the worst.

What would his master do next? Jonathan was brash and unpredictable. Trying to guess his next move, Hafaz studied him. The king's son was tall and lanky like his father, but unlike Saul, he had not been bowed down by defeat. Jonathan hungered for battle. While the king turned his anger inward against himself, his son took his fury out on the Philistines. Jonathan's sharp, angular features were quick to show rage; his bold black beard came to a point beneath his chin like a spear tip. With darting, deep-set eyes that flashed from an insult—real or imagined—Jonathan was notorious in Gibeah as one whose hand was too quick to reach for his sword.

How do I protect a hot-headed young Israelite with neither judgment nor discretion? If Jonathan is slain while I am charged to watch over him, Saul will have my head.

Hafaz looked down at the towering gates of Gath, which

bristled with bronze spikes. He knew that for generations, this portal had been scourged by fires and assaulted by battering rams, but the gates had never been breached. The battlements glistened in the early morning damp and he recalled the Philistine boast: "The walls are wet with the tears of all the Israelite mothers whose sons Goliath has slain."

He murmured, "It is said that in the time of Joshua, seven priests sounding seven rams' horns marched around the city of Jericho with the Holy Ark for seven days. They let out a great shout and the walls of Jericho fell. But how would Joshua have fared if his priests had marched around *these* walls?"

Jonathan did not reply. Hafaz suspected that the king's son agreed with him. Even priests trumpeting the wrath of the Almighty could not topple these ramparts.

Hafaz felt compelled to add, "We must use prudence."

"*Prudence*? It has helped you survive many battles, my prudent friend, but not to win them. The only crime worse than caution is cowardice!"

Hafaz knew that Jonathan's last bodyguard had paid a high price for his master's recklessness, impaled on a Philistine spear while Jonathan walked away from the skirmish untouched. Hafaz blurted out the question that weighed on him: "Why have we come here now?"

"Najab, a cunning Nubian trader, tells me what I must know, for a price. He says all the Philistine forces have been recalled to the city. Something momentous is about to take place."

"Are they marshaling their forces for another offensive against us?"

"I fear it is something far worse. Things are not as they should be." He sniffed the air. "Usually, Gath smells of iron from the furnaces where their blacksmiths hammer out swords to defeat us. Not today."

Puzzled, Hafaz said, "I smell a sweet and holy fragrance."

"Frankincense. The priests are burning so much that it drowns out the stench of the forges. They are celebrating. Why?"

From their hiding place, they spotted the sentries on the parapet raising a golden banner on a high staff. "It is the flag they fly before they set out against us." Hafaz faltered, surprised by what was taking place before him. "Usually, they unfurl only one . . ."

Hafaz saw the Philistines were hoisting more banners, one after the other, until ten were flying. A fanfare resounded from the ramparts. The frankincense, the ten golden banners, the flourish of trumpets, heightened his foreboding. "If today the Philistines rejoice, tomorrow our people will weep."

A stern voice rang out from the golden tower of the temple.

Clad in a shimmering white robe, an old man, who Hafaz realized must be the high priest of the god Dagon, spoke to the people of Gath. Hafaz was too far away to understand the priest's words, and he could not see the restless multitude beyond the lofty city walls. But as the priest continued his announcement, Hafaz heard their shouts of jubilation.

Seemingly roused by the cheers of the Philistines, Jonathan stood up boldly from his hiding place.

"Master!"

In his purple tunic and bold golden sash, Jonathan made an easy target against the pale green of the barley fields. Hafaz grabbed his arm to pull him back to safety, but he tore free of his grasp. Is my master so in love with death that he must embrace it here and now? he wondered. Knowing it was impossible to stop him, Hafaz said, "May the Almighty watch over you."

"May He watch over *us*. You are coming with me."

Hafaz pointed toward the ramparts, which bristled with spears. "How can I protect you from *them*?"

"I do not need your protection. I brought you because you understand the Philistine tongue. Tell me what the high priest is saying."

"But to hear him," Hafaz stammered, "we must come within

range of their—"

"Yes, their spears may kill you." Jonathan drew his sword. "But if you refuse to follow me, I will make your wife a widow *now*."

With a sigh of resignation, Hafaz crouched low and followed his reckless master beyond the concealment of the oaks, down the hill toward the shadows cast by the ramparts.

"Take heart." Jonathan clapped him on the back. "Right now, the Philistines have their minds on more important things."

Hafaz saw Jonathan was right. On the parapets, the sentries had turned to face inside the city walls. From the tower of the temple of Dagon, the high priest issued a ringing proclamation in the Philistine tongue.

"What is he saying?" Jonathan asked.

When the high priest finished speaking, Hafaz turned back to his master, his eyes wide in silent wonder.

Chapter 7

I am drunk, David thought, and I like the way it makes me feel.

He had always looked down on his brothers for swilling barley beer. Their drunkenness made them sloppy and brutal, so they brawled with each other or lashed out at him. Once, out of curiosity, he had secretly tasted the thick fermented liquid. He had found its sour taste revolting and spat it out.

Tonight, instead of barley beer, I drink the king's wine at the king's table.

He dined alone with Saul in his royal chamber, which was illuminated with beeswax candles. Accustomed to the weak glow of oil lamps, David was dazzled by their radiance. Tobiah, the king's advisor, directed a procession of servants bearing platters with delicacies unknown to David, luxuries too costly to be sold to common people in the market in Gibeah: roasted quail and venison; walnuts glazed with date honey; bowls of quince and carob with sweetened fig cakes. For him, tasting this food was like hearing bold new harmonies played on his lyre for the first time. The flavors were sharper, sweeter, spicier than any he knew. They vary as sunsets vary, he thought, no two alike, each leaving its own afterglow.

In the flush of the moment, he allowed himself to drain another cup. He knew he was drunk on more than wine. He was drunk on Saul's praise.

"Nothing is too good for the shepherd who purged my mind of torment!" With the gold-etched blade of his dagger, the king carved a slice of venison and offered it to him.

"I have much to be grateful for," David said, taking the meat on his platter.

Saul cut an even more generous slice for himself. David noticed that tonight the king ate and drank heartily, with an appetite he had not shown before. "When I have *this*"—Saul lifted his goblet—"I do not need *that*." He pointed to the lyre at David's side. "But when I lie in bed tonight, I will need its sorcery to keep evil phantoms at bay."

"I am here to serve you."

He marveled at how the king had been transformed. His deathly pallor was gone and his cheeks were pink, his eyes sparkling. Now that he is free of his demons, David thought, Saul has returned to his true self. It seems he is a kind man with an easy laugh and a generous heart. How different he is from my own father, who is so quick to judge me, so miserly in his praise. If the Israelites knew the warm, benevolent nature of their king, he told himself, they would love him as his own daughter does.

In keeping with custom, Michal stood dutifully behind her father's chair, to refill his wine goblet. Though he sat across the table from them, David had tried not to look at her, for fear he would betray his feelings to Saul. But his eyes were irresistibly drawn to Michal. The shadow of dread had lifted from her brow and her pale skin glowed in the honeyed aura of the candles. After the king's recovery, she had changed into a fresh robe of sapphire blue. Though she had still not outlined her eyes with kohl, it seemed they shone more brightly than before. Her raven hair had been brushed so that it shimmered like a night sky after rain.

Michal met his gaze and a look passed between them. He felt that they shared a longing they could not put into words. He lowered his eyes. Such feelings must remain locked in my heart, he thought, until I fulfill my destiny.

"Bring me more!" Wine dripping from his beard, Saul pounded his empty goblet on the table.

Michal refused to pick up the silver wine pitcher, her hands clenched tightly at her sides. David suspected that she feared her father's drunkenness would once again spark his murderous rage.

Instead of lashing out at her for her disobedience, Saul roared with laughter. "My daughter thinks it is her place to tell a king when he has had enough." He winked at David. "Pour me more!"

David knew he could not refuse. Despite Michal's disapproving frown, he dutifully picked up the pitcher to fill the king's goblet to the brim. Then, on a nod from Saul, he refilled his own.

"Son of Jesse, you always give me what I need! Your talents are wasted herding sheep. From this moment, you will serve as my shield-bearer. After you have tasted battle, I will make you a warrior, and then a commander, to serve my son, Jonathan!"

"It will be my honor."

David ached to confide to Saul that his dreams were much grander than that. He longed to tell him of his secret anointing and how it would shape his destiny. But he was not yet ready to take the risk.

* * *

Late that night, the beeswax candles burned low, deepening the shadows. Saul waved his hand toward Tobiah, the servants and the guards. "Go! And do not hover outside my door. Leave us alone in peace!" He turned back to David and Michal. "I place my faith in the young. You, son of Jesse, and my beloved daughter . . . . If only my eldest son, Jonathan, was here with us, I would have all those I hold dear gathered around me. I trust no one else!" He beckoned David over to sit in the chair beside him.

Know that I will serve you better than you can imagine, David thought. I will learn all you can teach me, but as the next king of our people, I will follow a new path. I will build on your glory with my own.

"After all you have done for me," Saul said, "I feel we are as close now as father and son."

They were the words that David had longed to hear. He

decided this was his moment. "Then may I speak to you as a son speaks to his father?"

David had promised Samuel that he would keep their secret. And yet, his heart was full to overflowing, so that he could not hold anything back. He took the risk. "There is something I must confide to you, something you must know. I believe it is because I am your son in spirit, if not by blood, that it took place . . ."

Saul's drunken grin faded. His eyes narrowed with suspicion. "What took place?"

David came out with it: "The Almighty has chosen me."

"Chosen?" The king flinched as if David had struck him.

"Samuel, the prophet, has anointed me to follow you as king, to rule over our people."

Saul stared at him without uttering a word, his eyes unblinking. David had expected that the king's initial shock would be followed by acceptance and understanding. Now he realized that he had fatally misjudged him.

"Samuel told you this?" Saul's jaw tightened and his nostrils flared. "Then the old fool lies!" The blood drained from his face, his fury building. "You are only a shepherd, and a shepherd is all you will ever be! *My son Jonathan will rule after me!"*

His right hand shook uncontrollably, knocking over his goblet, spilling wine across the table. He turned on Michal. *"You* are the one who brought the shepherd here. Even my own daughter plots against me!"

Unflinching, she held her father's gaze. "I did not know of David's anointing."

Saul was deaf to her words, his mind fevered. "You would have this shepherd steal the throne from your own brother?" He shoved back his chair and stood up unsteadily, his hand clutching his dagger.

"I summoned David here for one reason," Michal said, her voice calm. "To rid you of demons—"

"Only to bring a demon into our midst!" Brandishing the

dagger, he lurched drunkenly toward her.

David stood up to block Saul's path. The king took another step toward Michal, staggered, and reached out to lean on the back of a chair for support. David wrenched it away. Saul stumbled and crashed to the floor.

Michal ran to the door and threw it open. David saw the hallway was deserted—the guards and servants had obeyed Saul's orders to leave him in peace. Following her out, David shut the door behind them. Through the thick oak, he heard Saul shouting with rage, then the clatter of guards running closer.

"There is one way out," Michal said, and led him down a narrow corridor.

"You must leave with me. He tried to kill you!"

"My father's rage is like spring lightning—a sudden fury that passes quickly," she said. "Tomorrow, he will kneel down before me and beg my forgiveness. That is his way." She sighed. "He does terrible things at night, but repents in the cold light of day."

"And his anger at me?"

"Samuel anointed you instead of his son. Some things my father will never forgive." Michal pulled a torch from a wall sconce and handed it to him, then led him behind a granite column to a hidden door. "Go this way. No one will see you."

He opened the door. In the torchlight, he glimpsed a narrow passageway that veered down steep, crumbling steps into the shadows. Rats skittered in the darkness. "I am in your debt." He turned and, holding the torch, started down the stairs.

The shouts of the guards and the rattle of their weapons in the corridor suddenly grew louder.

"May the Almighty bless you and keep you." Her words echoed hollowly down the narrow stairwell, so it was impossible for him to decipher the emotion in her voice. Before he could decide whether she had spoken out of simple decency or fondness, she closed the door and was gone.

Alone in the flickering pool of torchlight, David sensed the gulf that separated them, as great a distance as it was from his father's humble dwelling in Bethlehem to the palace in Gibeah. It was a gulf that he vowed someday to bridge.

Chapter 8

The stairway led down through the darkness to a musty door. David pushed and it creaked open. He found himself outside, in a corner of the main square of Gibeah. In the first light of dawn, the dusty expanse was already bustling with ragged merchants setting up stalls for market day, the braying of donkeys and the clucking of chickens.

He felt the lyre hanging heavy from his shoulder on its leather strap. Yesterday, it seemed to him that the melodies he coaxed from it had magic in them, the power to change his life. Now this raw piece of cedar with its strings of sheep sinew was little more than a plaything. Thanks to the honey wine he had drunk last night, his mouth tasted as foul as the wool of a sick ram and his head throbbed. All the king's delicacies had conspired to turn his stomach. All the promise of last night had soured.

I was a fool to let the wine loosen my tongue. I should never have told Saul of my anointing. I was hungry for a father to love me, but Saul will never see me as his son. I should have known he would never favor me over his own flesh and blood.

I have thrown my future into jeopardy. If this was a test of my worthiness, I have failed.

Eager to leave Gibeah behind, he plunged into the throng flowing out through the main gates. A vengeful sun was rising over the eastern wall of the city, punishing him with its glare. He did not allow himself to think of Michal, and yet her glittering eyes, the luster of her hair, the effortless grace of her every movement haunted him. He refused to accept that he had seen her for the last time. After all she had done to save his life, he was convinced that she was an essential part of his future.

But what does my future hold? Now that Saul refuses to accept my anointing, my path to the throne will be all the more dangerous.

He passed through the gates with the rest of the crowd,

leaving the city behind. But as the others continued down the dusty road, he struck out alone across the broken plain.

* * *

David walked until the distant walls of Gibeah shimmered like a mirage in the morning heat. He stopped and lifted his gaze toward the brightening sky. As he often had at times when he was afflicted with doubt, he decided to attempt the impossible. He pulled out the sling that hung from his belt. His mother had stitched together the two supple strips of goat leather, each the length of his forearm, with a pouch between them to cradle a stone.

His brothers would laugh at him if they knew it was their mother who had taught him how to use the sling, he thought. Women were forbidden to handle metal weapons, for fear they would defile them with their weakness when they shed their blood of the moon. But a girl was allowed to play with a shepherd's leather sling. His mother, Nitzevet, had confided to him that when she was a child, she had grown adept with it. She never told her husband or her other sons about this skill. It was one of the secrets she shared only with David.

The first day he had set out alone as a shepherd with the flock, Nitzevet gave him the simple strip of leather and said, "The lyre allows you to feel, but the sling allows you to *act*." He quickly learned that the sling was more than a shepherd's plaything to while away the endless hours of solitude. He could hurl a rock with it to scare away a jackal, but he was just as likely to use it to cradle a sprained arm, or to pull a stray lamb out of the brambles.

And he used the sling for something more—to reach beyond the defeats that surrounded him, to seek out clues to events to come. The sling was his link to the unspoken mysteries that lay beyond.

His mother had taught him: "When you feel cut off from the

Almighty, hurl your prayers to the heavens as you would hurl a stone at the sun. Each prayer you send to the High Places is like that stone. You do not know how far it will reach or how high it will soar, only that you must summon the strength of your faith to send it up to the Almighty."

David reached down and selected a smooth, round stone from the dust. With one hand, he placed it into the pouch of the sling he held with the other. For a moment, as his fingers touched, it seemed they were clasped together in prayer.

"Farther than the eye can see, the heart can reach," his mother had said. "If you succeed, the stone will fly out of sight and vanish into the wellspring of the sun. It will mean that the stone has reached its mark as a prayer reaches Him. If you fail, the stone will fall to earth like a dead sparrow. And yet, the simple act of throwing it will bring you a small, precious grain of wisdom."

David swung the sling swiftly around his head until the whoosh of the leather through the air sounded like the beating wings of eagles. Then he thrust out his arm for the sharp instant of release.

He squinted into the dazzling sky to watch the stone arc toward the sun, and tried to lift his thoughts up to the Almighty. He longed to gaze into the inscrutable future, to discover what promise lay there, to learn where his destiny would lead him. Perhaps, he thought, at the moment the stone reaches its highest point, the revelation will come.

The stone fell to earth.

Despite what his mother had taught him, today the act of throwing it had not brought him even one grain of wisdom. As he always did, David walked toward the spot where the stone had landed. This time, it had fallen near a withered acacia. But when he approached the tree, he could not find his stone among the countless hundreds scattered in the dust at his feet.

Only then did he notice a small bird, no larger than a sparrow, which fluttered down to land on a branch of the acacia. Stepping closer, he saw it was a sand-colored shrike with a red tail.

His father, Jesse, had taught him only to look for holy signs in mighty things: the blinding flash of a thunderbolt, the howl of a whirlwind. David knew Jesse was wrong. As a shepherd, he had learned that the Almighty was a God of small things as well as great ones. The gathering of a flock of starlings meant an approaching downpour, alerting him that he must seek shelter for his flock. A swarm of flies hovering in the still air foretold the coming of a sandstorm. Often the humblest signs held the deepest meaning.

The shrike perched nearby looked like those he often saw while tending his flock. This lowliest of birds survived by catching insects stirred up by the hooves of sheep in the dust. He noticed something remarkable about the one before him: Instead of holding a cricket or a beetle in its beak, this shrike clung to something unexpected—a twig from a thorn bush.

For David, as for every shepherd, thorns were a common nuisance. When he was not combing them out of the matted wool of a stray lamb, he was freeing a ram's horns entangled in brambles. And yet, for this bird to hold a thorn twig in its beak struck him as remarkable, because there was not a single thorn tree in sight.

Why had the shrike brought the twig here? The bird did not flutter off with it to build a nest. Instead, it dropped the twig on the ground at David's feet and darted away.

Picking it up with care, so the barbs would not prick his fingers, he examined the twig more closely. It was different from those he was used to seeing, curved like the talon of a hawk.

A blackthorn twig.

The shrike must have flown a great distance with this in its beak, but why? David's father had told him how the Holy Scrolls recounted that at the end of the Great Flood, a dove flew to Noah on his ark, bearing an olive branch, a message of hope. Today, a shrike brings me a barbed twig, he thought. What message does it hold?

It struck him: When Samuel made his brothers swear a blood oath to keep his anointing secret, the prophet had used a blackthorn twig to prick their fingers. That the shrike came here is no accident, he thought. It brought the blackthorn twig to summon me into Samuel's presence.

He knew of only one thicket where blackthorns grew, so harsh a place that shepherds with their flocks went out of their way to avoid it. For that very reason, he thought, it is a place where Samuel could find seclusion and peace.

He remembered the prophet's words: "To be king, your way will be a path of thorns. And yet, it is the path you must take."

Chapter 9

Half a day's trek from Bethlehem, the blackthorn thicket loomed before him. The twisted branches formed a seemingly impenetrable wall. Pointed leaves sprouted among the brambles, but David knew that few birds dared to dart among the bristling spines to pick at the black berries hidden there. Though the thorns flashed in the glare like daggers, in this harsh, inhospitable place he found something to admire.

On arid land where the sun is cruel and other plants die, thorn bushes take root and thrive. My people are like these brambles. We Israelites are prickly and difficult to embrace, and yet we survive in places where all others perish.

From within the depths of the thorn thicket, he heard a cry. The sound was so shrill that at first he thought it must be a bird.

"Speak!"

It was Samuel's voice.

David's eyes probed among the branches to discover its source, but found nothing but a dense web of brambles. "I must talk with you, Samuel of Ramah."

Through the tangle of thorns, he glimpsed a blur of movement. The voice cried out, "Son of Jesse, I do not need ears to hear the Almighty. But for me to hear a mortal man, you must come here and stand before me."

David realized the prophet's invitation was a test. The maze of brambles seemed too dense to penetrate. He noticed the carcass of a jackal impaled among the spines like a warning. The animal must have become hopelessly entangled and starved to death, he thought. Its belly was crawling with maggots.

Searching for a pathway among the brambles, David noticed a narrow gap between the branches. It might offer an opening, but he doubted how far it would lead. Not knowing whether he could find his way to the prophet—or find his way out again—he took the first step inside the labyrinth of thorns. The tortuous trail grew ever narrower as he walked deeper into the thicket. A barb hidden in the dust pierced the thin leather of one of his sandals, drawing blood.

The mesh of brambles grew thicker above him, blocking out the sunlight. Overhanging thorns forced him to shield his eyes. The curved barbs clawed at his arms, tore at his neck, as he threaded his way among them. He knew he was lost, and yet, it was impossible to turn back. He pressed forward blindly, step by step.

Just ahead, a pale brown shrike darted among the brambles to a scorpion it had left impaled on a spine. The bird seized its prey in its beak and gulped it down. David realized that the thorn bush where the bird had perched opened into a narrow clearing.

He took a cautious step inside it and found himself facing Samuel. The prophet sat cross-legged on the ground, clad only in a loin cloth, so gaunt that his shoulder blades jutted out starkly beneath his pale, mottled flesh. Samuel looks more like a beggar than a prophet, he thought. On one side of the cramped enclosure, he saw a pottery cistern to collect rain water; on the other side, a cracked clay bowl held what looked like parched grain, no doubt the prophet's only food.

"You have summoned me and I have come," David said.

"Yes, I summoned you!" Samuel lashed out. "To chastise you . . . to reprimand you!" He leveled a piercing glance at David with his one good eye. "After what you have done, you will never be king!" He snatched a brittle, yellowed relic from the dust. David recognized it as the horn that held the holy oil. "I regret that I anointed you. I erred with you as I erred with Saul."

"No, you were right to anoint me. I know that now."

Samuel spat on the ground in disgust. "Son of Jesse, you should never have healed Saul of his affliction! By doing so, you only lengthened his time on the throne!"

"I could not leave him to suffer in his madness," David said without shame.

"Let him suffer! You will never be king if you are weak. To heal him was an act of weakness!"

"Compassion is not weakness," David said. "If I am to be king, I will be king on my terms, not in the old ways. I will follow my own path."

"*Your* path? Your path led you to defy me, to tell Saul of your anointing!"

"Because I had freed him of evil spirits, I thought he would accept me."

"Folly!" In his fury, Samuel turned over the brittle horn and pointed the spout at the ground. "Look! The horn is empty!" He squeezed it so tightly between his fingers that it crumbled. "I squandered the last of the holy oil on you!"

"You have not squandered it. I will be king."

Samuel knelt down and picked up the cracked clay bowl that David believed held grain. A closer look told him that it was filled with dried locusts the color of flax seed. The prophet selected a plump one, popped it into his mouth and chewed it thoughtfully, the insect crunching between his toothless gums.

"The Holy Scrolls tell us that in the time of our enslavement, locusts were the eighth plague that the Almighty visited upon Pharaoh. Locusts can be a plague or locusts can be a banquet. If you are to become king of the Israelites, you must learn—"

"To become king, I must learn to thrive on a feast of locusts," David said, understanding. He took the bowl from Samuel, and as the prophet watched, David ate a handful of the dried insects, one by one.

Chapter 10

He had to speak to his father at once.

Saul was not inside his chambers, so Jonathan walked out onto an adjoining parapet that led to a balcony. He found the king slumped, asleep, in a chair covered in peeling gold leaf. Jonathan saw that it overlooked the empty palace courtyard below. Once, he thought, this courtyard was packed with Saul's men cheering him as he rallied them for battle. Now the sunbaked expanse was empty, except for a handful of black-cloaked widows crouched in the shade. A few crows perched on the edge of the balcony beside his father. Once, Saul soared with eagles, Jonathan thought. Now he dozes among crows, napping in the heat of the day, basking in the warmth of bygone victories.

Today, Saul cannot afford to see things as he dreams them to be. He must see things as they are.

Jonathan studied his father's face and perceived that in sleep he was not finding comfort in dreams of long-lost glory. Saul was stricken with terror, his brow shiny with sweat, his eyes darting fitfully beneath closed lids. His breath came quickly and he whispered fearfully to himself.

"Father . . ." Jonathan knelt down and gently touched his trembling hand. "I must speak with you . . ."

Saul's eyes blinked open. "Jonathan, my son!" He took in a deep breath and let it out with a sigh of relief, then wiped the sweat from his forehead with his sleeve. "Thank God you have rescued me from my dream!" He rubbed his bloodshot eyes with trembling hands. "Each day, it comes back with a vengeance."

Jonathan saw the fire smoldering in his father's eyes. "What is it that afflicts you?"

"I dream of the day of our destruction. A day when there is not one Goliath . . . but a legion of them!"

"A legion?"

"A host of Goliaths invading our land of Judah, an army of Goliaths marching on Gibeah to destroy us . . ." His voice drifted off.

With a tenderness that did not come easily to him, Jonathan clasped his father's hands in his own, to steady him for the pain that he knew his words would cause. "I have returned from Gath, city of our enemies. And from what I learned there, I know that your dream is not a mere phantom of your mind."

His father stared at him in bewilderment. "How can that be?"

Jonathan suddenly felt trapped in the confines of the balcony, vulnerable under the gaze of the sentries on the ramparts. He helped his father up from his chair and led him out of the glare, into the shade of a secluded corner.

"I stood outside the walls of the Philistine city. On the battlements, I watched our enemies raise not one golden banner, as is their custom, but ten. I heard the clamor of war trumpets . . ."

Saul's eyes narrowed. "They are marshaling their forces . . ."

"It is worse than that." He clenched his hands into fists, reliving the moment. "The high priest made a proclamation to the Philistine people—"

"But you do not speak their tongue," Saul interrupted warily.

"My comrade-in-arms, Hafaz, translated the words."

"Bring Hafaz before me!" The king's voice was sharp with impatience. "I wish to hear this from his own lips!"

"That cannot be. A Philistine spear cost Hafaz his life. But what he told me made it worth his sacrifice . . ." He hesitated, then came out with it: "My beloved father, your dream of a legion of Goliaths . . . It is a prophecy of what will come to pass." He leaned over and grasped him by the shoulders, forcing Saul to look into his eyes, to see he spoke the truth. "Goliath is betrothed."

Saul pushed him away. "Impossible! There is no woman on earth who is . . . as he is."

"There is one, a Philistine woman. She is as fearsome in size and strength as Goliath. When the high priest spoke to the people, he said she will bear warrior sons as mighty as their father."

"There will never be a woman fit to give Goliath sons." Saul said it resolutely, as if this undeniable fact was a pillar of the universe. "He can never bring forth more of his own kind . . ." But shaken by his son's words, his voice trailed off uncertainly.

"At first, I also refused to believe it," Jonathan said. "But the high priest summoned Goliath's betrothed. The Philistine woman stood beside him at the shrine on the high tower."

"You saw her?"

"They stood side by side to receive the priest's blessing. Goliath's bride is a fitting match for him in her strength and stature, as a wife must be to her husband."

"Their god Dagon . . ." Saul muttered. "*He* created her for Goliath!

"They are to marry tomorrow. They will lie down on the marriage bed tomorrow night."

The king spoke slowly, mindful of the weight of his words. "Then tomorrow night, the seed will be planted. It is too late for us to prevent it . . ."

"No!" Jonathan gripped Saul's arm. "Before the wedding night, before he can conceive a son, Goliath will die."

"Has the Almighty promised this to you?" Saul mocked him. "So far, the Most High has not helped me or my men to slay the Philistine. Too many Israelites have died trying."

"Goliath cannot be slain in combat," Jonathan said, turning it over in his mind. "But there are other ways I can destroy him, and without the help of other men."

Saul stared at him with dread. "My son, I command an army. Why must you attempt so dangerous a mission alone?"

Jonathan studied his reflection distorted in the gold signet ring glittering on his finger. He did not like what he saw. "When I returned from Gath, Michal told me of the shepherd's anointing . . ."

"Samuel is a mad fool!"

"I know I am not beloved by our people. If I am to surpass David, son of Jesse, in their eyes, I must earn their love. This is the only way."

His voice tinged with foreboding, Saul asked, "What is your plan?"

"I will not tell you. You will only tell me why it will fail."

"And if I am right to foresee the worst?"

"I will kill Goliath," Jonathan said, pushing ahead. "And when I lift up his head for all to see, it will not matter that David was anointed while I was not. The Israelites will hail me as the one ordained to follow you as king." He slipped an arm around his father's shoulder. "Or would you rather a worthless shepherd take what is rightfully mine?"

Saul stared down at his hands, as if something priceless had slipped through his fingers. "I know it is beyond my power to stop you, but I fear for your life."

"I do not. Because I know I will prevail." Jonathan embraced his father, and walked boldly away from him along the parapet.

Saul called out, "May the Almighty guide and protect you!"

Jonathan turned back to face him once more. "I do not rely on His protection. For too long, the Almighty has abandoned us. But I will not fail you, even though our God has."

"I admire your bravery, my son," Saul called after him in dismay, "but to attempt such a reckless act . . ."

Jonathan looked up into the sky at a solitary eagle circling overhead. "It is from reckless acts that kings are made."

Chapter 11

What would my father say? What would Saul say if he knew that today his son Jonathan is about to gamble everything on a pagan who prefers the company of donkeys to men, an idol-worshipper who eats the rancid flesh of pigs?

I have no choice. Najab is the only one I trust.

The Nubian's face was black and lustrous as water in the depths of a cavern, his bald head shaved shiny and smooth as a glazed cooking pot. His eyes gleamed yellow as a leopard's. Jonathan lamented that of all men, Najab was the one on whom his plan—and his life— depended.

"Come, my flea-infested harlots, my lovelies!" In the livestock pen at Gibeah, the long-limbed young Nubian clucked to his beasts. Their coats ragged, their long ears notched and mangled, the donkeys snorted in the blinding glare. Najab offered one of them water from a leaky goatskin bladder. "Drink, Shaya, my beauty!"

Jonathan knew that the Nubian's black skin allowed him to pass freely back and forth across enemy lines, without being mistaken for either Philistine or Israelite. Najab played the foes off against each other, juggling them as deftly as a conjuror juggled pomegranates in the market square. And yet, he trusted the Nubian because his motives were so simple. Najab had no lust for power, no appetite for treachery, only the need to stuff the pouch on his belt with gold.

Disguised in a worn leather tunic, Jonathan frowned at the motley array of market stalls. Slabs of meat hanging from hooks had spoiled under the harsh sun and were thick with flies. Melons had softened with rot. The sorry sight brought home to him the plight of his people. Harassed by Philistine raiders, few merchants and peddlers from other tribes dared make the dangerous journey to trade with the Israelites. Spices were scarce, which made them costly. Toothless old women hawked meager piles of coriander, saffron and cinnamon, as if they were heaps of jewels.

Why wasn't Najab ready yet? Jonathan's face was flushed, his annoyance souring into anger. He longed to pull his sword, but resisted the temptation. They had to leave at once.

He scanned the shabby throng. In the shade of the stalls, gaunt, disgruntled men squatted together in groups, trading idle talk. This isn't a market for food, Jonathan thought, but for rumors, and the gossip is as stale as the bread. He watched the men barter with each other for magic charms to ward off evil spirits: a vial of powdered wormwood; a crooked mandrake root; the dried paw of a jackal. Of course, to worship amulets violated the Holy Commandments, but he knew these desperate Israelites feared the iron blades of the Philistines more than the thunderbolts of the Almighty.

There are traitors among these men who conspire to overthrow my father. He is right to be afraid. My mission must not fail. It is the only way to keep Saul in power and secure the throne that is my birthright.

"Najab!" He clapped his hands impatiently. The Nubian was still fussing over his beasts, and prodding him seemed as futile as goading his most stubborn donkey. Jonathan hated being at the mercy of this wily trader, but he could not do without him. The Philistines paid dearly for the iron ingots that the Nubian transported from the pits of the Timna Valley all the way to Gath. In the Philistine city, blacksmiths melted the ingots to forge invincible weapons, iron blades to defeat the crude copper swords of the Israelites. Though Najab helped the enemy, Jonathan knew the Israelites did not dare to kill him. In exchange for safe passage through Saul's kingdom, the Nubian offered them advance warning of Philistine troop movements, telling when the enemy would set out from Gath and where they might strike.

Prodding his donkeys with his ebony staff, the Nubian coaxed them out from under the meager shade of the date palms. The beasts groaned, then planted one weary hoof ahead of the other to begin yet another punishing journey. Jonathan joined Najab as he led his five stubborn beasts into the bustling market square.

The string of donkeys stopped in their tracks. A flock of sheep blocked the way. Jonathan caught sight of the shepherd herding them and knew instinctively who it must be. This ruddy youth with the friendly smile and the shrewd eyes was the one that Saul had warned him about.

"The shepherd is David, son of Jesse of Bethlehem?"

Najab nodded. "It is said that the music from his lyre rid your father of evil spirits."

When Michal had first told him about that supposed act of sorcery, Jonathan had heard the admiration in her voice. It had been enough to make him instantly dislike the shepherd. When she had gone on to speak of his anointing by Samuel, and David's belief that he was destined to be king—a callow youth to replace him in the line of succession!—Jonathan saw him as a mortal enemy. And yet, watching the young shepherd in the morning sunlight, it was hard to see him as a threat.

"His skin is as smooth and unblemished as a girl's," he confided to Najab. "He looks like a coddled mother's boy."

"That is so," Najab said, "but he has a gift with words. Look how he wins the hearts of the people."

Studying the fresh-faced youth as he chatted with the others in the market, Jonathan saw that Najab spoke the truth. David possessed an easy charm that seemed to endear him to everyone he met. At one of the stalls, a giggling maiden offered him a pomegranate. A mother introduced him to her two small boys. David tousled their hair and they all laughed.

Jonathan spat in the dust, disgusted that the shepherd so easily beguiled strangers, while he himself was often blunt and insolent. He turned to Najab and shrugged. "Honeyed words never chopped off a Philistine's head or won a throne. I doubt the shepherd even owns a sword."

"With so much meanness in this war-torn land," Najab replied, "some find it praiseworthy that David is so generous of spirit." He cleared his throat and hid a smile. "Though, of course, we are not so easily fooled."

Jonathan was ready to answer that the shepherd's sincerity was only a ploy, that cold cunning lay hidden beneath the surface. Instead, on impulse, he walked away from Najab and the donkeys. The time had come to face David.

It was meant that we should meet like this, so I can be done with him.

* * *

David instantly recognized Jonathan approaching him through the crowd. He had seen him before, standing beside the king on a palace balcony while Saul exhorted his men before battle. Today, Jonathan was clad in a shoddy leather tunic—David guessed it was to escape notice—but with the arrogant bearing of a prince, he gave himself away. Jonathan stood apart from the ragged common people, whom David knew he looked down on with disdain.

Suddenly, a young woman burst out of the milling throng and stood before Jonathan. Her face was hidden, so David pushed his way through the crowd for a closer look.

Michal. Clad in a bold sky-blue robe, she stood out from the somberly clothed handmaidens who escorted her. He watched brother and sister warmly embrace, and envied them their shared tenderness. David had feared he would never see her again, but the Almighty had brought them together once more. Seizing the moment, he made his way through the throng toward her.

"It is a blessing to see you again," he said.

"David . . ." Startled, Michal broke into a smile. For an instant, she blushed.

Jonathan stepped between them. "You dare to speak to the

daughter of a king?"

Michal hastily regained her composure. "We have already met. When David played his lyre to heal our father."

Ignoring her, Jonathan glared at David. "You cannot speak to my sister as if she is some peasant girl from your village."

"I will speak to anyone I choose." David boldly met Jonathan's gaze. "No doubt, your father has told you that Samuel anointed me to follow him as king." David regretted his boldness, but Michal was watching and he would not show weakness before her. He would face her brother as an equal. He saw that Jonathan struggled to control his fury, his hand flexing nervously on the hilt of his sword.

"Samuel, the raving prophet, has wandered in the desert mumbling prayers for far too long. It has turned his mind to mush." Jonathan lowered his voice so they would not be overheard. "Son of Jesse, you were anointed by the prophet in his madness. You will never lead our people."

"That is not for you to say."

Jonathan lifted his fist so that his gold signet ring etched with the Lion of Judah blazed in the sun. "Saul raised me from birth to rule over our people. So long as I draw breath, a shepherd will not take my place."

"In the eyes of the Almighty, it seems I already have." As soon as he spoke the impudent words, he saw Jonathan's arm tense to unsheathe his sword.

A donkey butted between the two men before the blade could clear the scabbard. "Forward, my toothless beauties!" Najab shouted, poking the other donkeys with his ebony staff so they jostled close together, forcibly separating David and Jonathan. He bowed his head respectfully and beckoned for Jonathan to join him. "Son of Saul, you said we must leave at once."

Jonathan swallowed his rage and stormed off through the crowd to join the Nubian. Taking long strides on bare feet thick with calluses, Najab drove his plodding caravan toward the outer gates of Gibeah.

David saw that Michal was walking back in the direction of the palace, surrounded by her handmaidens. He hurried to catch up with her. "I must speak with you."

She eluded his gaze, as if it might ensnare her. "We must not be seen together," she said. But after a moment's hesitation, she nodded for him to follow her behind a stall that would shield them from view.

"Your brother thinks I am his enemy," David said, "and yet I wish him no harm."

"He will never accept you as king."

"That is why I ask your help. Jonathan listens to you. Only you can convince him it is my destiny, not his."

"Convince him? My brother has protected me through all our father's trials, helped me as only one of my own flesh and blood can!"

David wondered whether he had misjudged her fondness for him. "But Samuel, who anointed your father, chose *me* . . ."

"Jonathan deserves the throne." Her voice hardened: "And Jonathan will have it. My brother has the courage to lead our people against the Philistines, while you"—she eyed the lyre hanging from his shoulder—"you cast gentle spells with your gentle music. That does not make you a warrior or a leader of men."

She nodded to her handmaidens that it was time to leave. "Forget your anointing by a mad prophet." Her voice sharpened to a haughty edge, as if she was speaking to a servant. "Forget your dreams of the throne. David, son of Jesse, you are only a shepherd. That is all you will ever be."

Chapter 12

"A husband's undying love is no more than a maiden's foolish dream."

Hada's cleft lip was split to the base of her nose. It gave her mouth a raw, unformed appearance, like the lips of an infant torn from her mother's womb. "I am an old spinster who has never seen the marriage bed and never will. But one thing I know: Better to be feared than to be loved. As Goliath's wife, you will be the most feared woman in Gath. All will court your favor."

In the cramped bedchamber beside her father's forge, Nara knelt before Hada in the dim light. It was barely dawn, but there was much to be done. Her aunt's fingers deftly braided Nara's auburn hair with fragrant crocuses and silver threads. Nara knew she would wear this elaborate style only once in her life. Today.

"Fate has brought you and Goliath together." Hada tugged a comb of carved ox horn through Nara's stubborn hair. "There is not a maiden in Gath, or in any one of the five Philistine cities, who would not joyfully take your place!"

"But how can I be a wife to him? I know nothing of the wifely skills."

"There will be more than enough servants to bake bread, sweep the floor, and work at the loom. All you must do is give Goliath sons!" To drive home her point, Hada yanked a braid so tight that Nara winced. "Whatever your failings, my beautiful niece, the priests will bless you. They know that you alone have a body created by the god Dagon to bring forth Goliath's heirs."

Nara heard the booming of the great drums from the temple citadel. In reply, trumpets of rejoicing blared from the ramparts.

"Come, my dove!" Hada beckoned for her to stretch out her arms and helped her into her bridal robe of pristine white linen. "Because you stand so much taller than other women, I had to stitch together two separate garments. And I had to weave two garlands into a single wreath." She laughed. "You are twice the bride of any woman who ever lived!"

As awkward as a small child trying to help her mother, the plump old woman stood on tiptoe to loop a fragrant chain of crocuses around Nara's neck. "You are not only the tallest and strongest woman in all of Gath, but also the most blessed, for you alone will bear sons for Goliath. They will have his courage. May they also have your generous heart."

Hada helped Nara slide her feet into her sandals. "I sewed these for you of the supplest leather." She kissed her niece's foot. "From the day you entered the world, you were different from all other women." Hada's eyes glistened with tears.

Nara hoped that today her aunt would not tell her, yet again, the tragic story of her birth. She had heard Hada recount it too many times—how Nara's unnatural size had been too much for her mother, how her mother had bled to death in Hada's arms.

"As I entered the world, I forced my mother to leave it," Nara said.

"No, my child." Hada stroked her hair. "Your birth did not kill my sister. Life and death are decided only by the gods."

Nara recalled how the other children her age had cruelly taunted her for her ungainly height, her awkward arms and legs, her absurd clumsiness. "As I grew to be taller and stronger than the others, why did they all hate me?"

Hada shook her head with disgust. "Among men, to be a giant is seen as godly and heroic. But for a woman to be taller and stronger than a man is viewed as a disgrace! To the frail and puny maidens of Gath, you were a freak of nature, like a two-headed calf, an accursed creature to be laughed at and spat upon." She stopped to examine a fresh burn on her niece's wrist.

"From the forge," Nara said.

"No one can know. That secret part of your life is over." Hada poured henna powder from a gourd into a small earthenware bowl, then squirted the juice of a lemon into it. She stirred the mixture, adding droplets of water until it became a russet paste.

Nara watched as, with the feather of a white dove, her aunt skillfully swirled the henna into intricate designs on her hands and arms, concealing the burn scars that betrayed her forbidden vocation.

As Hada worked, she sighed wistfully. "Long ago, I adorned your mother's hands for her wedding day."

"I wish she could be here with us now," Nara said, trying in vain to picture her mother's face.

"She is with us." Hada opened a timeworn acacia coffer and pulled out a finely wrought silver chain adorned with five indigo sapphires. "This was your mother's necklace. She would have wanted you to wear it today. But such is your size . . ." She fastened the necklace around Nara's muscular wrist as a bracelet, and held up a small mirror of polished copper. "Behold the bride! Goliath is the luckiest of men!"

Nara gazed at her reflection. Her eyes had been outlined with kohl, her lips reddened with pomegranate juice. She admired the henna designs on her hands and ran her fingers along the silver threads that Hada had woven into her hair. For the first time, she saw herself as a woman.

"How can I thank you?"

"It is for me to thank *you*," Hada said. "You have brought me as close as I will ever come to the delights of wedlock." She touched the gash that split her upper lip. "Alas, women like me are outcasts no man will wed. My beloved niece, we have both been shunned by our own people. That has been our bond from the start." She reached out awkwardly to embrace Nara, but her arms could not encircle her. "Now, as Goliath's bride, all those who once scorned you will shower you with gifts to win your favor."

Nara enfolded Hada in her arms and gently kissed her on the forehead. Then she slumped down on her bed. "If all the women in Gath envy me, why do I feel afraid?"

"Take heart, my beloved Nara! I am told that every woman dreads her wedding night." She dabbed at her niece's eyes with the swan-feather amulet that hung from her neck. "Whether Goliath is a man or a god, you alone among women will find out tonight."

Nara felt Hada's moist cleft lip pressed against her cheek. Its warmth had reassured her through many painful moments in her life, but today it brought her no comfort. She listened to the thunder of the temple drums proclaiming the wedding day, the trumpets of rejoicing echoing from the ramparts.

"I do not fear Goliath because he is a god," Nara said. "I see nothing godly in him. I fear Goliath because I know he is a man."

Chapter 13

"The wicked have gathered here from the four corners of the earth."

At dawn, Najab crouched down with Jonathan behind a windswept copse of oaks. They gazed down on the sprawling encampment. Row upon row of ragged tents sewn of goatskin and ox leather were spread out before the towering gates of the Philistine city. "They have descended on Gath to pay tribute to Goliath's marriage," Najab said.

From the crude ritual scars on their arms and faces, Jonathan judged they belonged to the most savage and warlike tribes. He smelled the bitter smoke rising from the fire pits for their morning meal. He knew these barbarians savored the roasted entrails of creatures unfit to eat. Acrid incense smoldered at makeshift shrines before their tents. He saw how each of them had brought an idol to his own pitiless god—a multitude of graven images shaped in wood, copper, or bronze. Some of the holy monsters had the forked tongues of serpents or the fangs of jackals, others the hooked beaks of vultures. How, he wondered, can my one invisible Almighty do battle with this vile legion?

"Heathens." He spat in the dirt.

"In their eyes, *you* are the heathen!" Najab chuckled. "Look at your barbarous ways! You cut off the foreskins of your sons on their eighth day of life. You refuse to eat the flesh of pigs, the most delectable of creatures. Worst of all, you take as much pleasure in smashing idols as all others take pride in creating them." He ran a hand along the twisted snakes carved into the flesh of his forearm. "The laws of your God are strict and unforgiving. How beneficent are my gods of prosperity and healing!"

"It is not for your god or mine to work miracles," Jonathan said. "It is upon me. If I do not end Goliath's life today, he will marry and spawn a dynasty of giants." He peered down at the tents below. "Then all the wicked of the earth will join the Philistines and destroy us."

A shrill fanfare rang out from the North Citadel of Gath. The bronze spikes that studded the massive Gates of Glory flared in the sunlight as the hinges creaked wide. Jonathan watched the impatient throng of heathens surge forward, jostling each other. Every one of them, he thought, seeks to be the first to present his offering to honor Goliath and his bride: clay jugs of wine; baskets of pomegranates; reed cages of chickens; and sacks of pungent spices.

"When Goliath is dead," Jonathan said confidently, "when I am king of the Israelites, these heathens will flock to my palace in Gibeah. They will bring gifts to win *my* blessing." He stood up and beckoned for Najab to follow him down the hill toward the crowd. "We can enter Gath now, if we lose ourselves among them."

To his surprise, the Nubian prodded his heavy-laden donkeys in the opposite direction. "Where are you going?" Jonathan shouted. "We have no time to lose!"

Ignoring him, Najab drove his donkeys off the trail into a narrow ravine, out of sight of the city walls. Jonathan ran to catch up with him. "The sentries at the gates know me," the Nubian explained. "They respect me because I bring iron ingots for the blacksmiths of Gath. But if they find out I bring an Israelite with me, they will kill both of us." He rummaged in one of the dusty goat-skin sacks on his lead donkey's back. "Cover yourself with this." He pulled out a threadbare cloak of the same faded indigo as his own, and threw it over Jonathan's shoulders.

"I smell like a dead donkey!"

"It will convince the sentries that you are my bondservant." The Nubian pointed to Jonathan's feet. "You must take off your sandals."

"A king's son does not walk barefoot!" he complained, but grudgingly removed them and handed them to Najab.

Sizing up Jonathan's transformation, the Nubian shook his head. "This is not enough. I must disguise your face."

"Disguise it? But how?"

"By revealing it!" The Nubian unsheathed his curved sword. "All Israelite men wear beards as proof of their manhood. You will not."

Jonathan struggled to pull away, but Najab gripped his arm. Holding the blade, the Nubian scraped the sharp edge against his face. In his haste to shave him, he nicked Jonathan's cheek, drawing blood.

"Look at yourself!" Najab showed him his reflection in the blade. "Your face is as naked as mine. No Israelite would shame himself to look like this. You may be a king's son, but the Philistines will think you are my slave!"

"A most unwilling one," Jonathan grumbled.

The Nubian clucked to his lead donkey and poked it with his ebony staff. The animal lurched forward and the others plodded after it toward the city gates. Najab sighed. "Alas, I cannot rid you of all proof you are an Israelite."

"What proof is left?"

"You are circumcised, as is no other tribe on earth. If the Philistines lift your cloak and find that out . . ."

Together, they shoved their way into the unruly throng streaming toward the gates. To Jonathan, the barbarians around him smelled as foul as goats. There can be no doubt that they hate the Israelites as much as the Philistines do, he thought, all of them bent on the destruction of my people.

They approached the Gates of Glory. "It is not enough to look like a slave," Najab whispered. "You must walk like one. Slouch forward and lower your eyes to the ground in shame."

Ahead were the gatekeepers, hardened Philistine guards wielding spears. They eyed each one entering the city with suspicion. Nearing them, Jonathan hunched over as Najab had instructed. He felt a painful jab in his ribs from the Nubian's staff, forcing him roughly ahead.

The guards waved them past. They were swept along with the throng pouring into the city.

* * *

Jonathan took his first breath inside the walls of Gath. A pungent odor stung his nostrils. "The noble creatures most despised by your people," Najab explained. "They are roasting pigs for Goliath's wedding feast." He licked his lips at the thought.

The hooves of the donkeys echoed harshly off the cobblestones as they threaded their way through the twisting alleyways of Gath. "In Gibeah, there are stray dogs scavenging for scraps," Jonathan said. "I see none here."

"The Philistine priests view mercy as weakness," Najab said with loathing. "All strays are destroyed."

After a few more steps, he murmured a command in his own tongue. Shaya let out a weary groan and the donkeys lurched to a stop in a narrow passageway. Jonathan took a cautious look around him. The walls of Gath seemed mightier than the crumbling battlements of Gibeah. He ran a finger along the edge of one of the massive granite blocks, impressed that it fit so perfectly with the one above it that a knife blade could not slip between them.

Najab noticed that the soles of Jonathan's feet were bloodied from walking on the sharp cobblestones. "You will need these." He handed his sandals back to him. "Your feet are as tender as a girl's."

Jonathan gratefully put them on. "Najab, I am in your debt for all you have done."

"I brought you into Gath. It will not be so simple for you to escape without my help."

"When word gets out that Goliath is dead, the city will be thrown into confusion. Escape will be easy."

"Easy?" Najab raised an eyebrow. "That is for the gods to decide." From the folds of his robe, he removed a small clay vial sealed with beeswax. "Use this as I have instructed you."

Jonathan took the vial from him. "I only wish I could slay Goliath with my sword, instead of with your treachery."

"The mind can conjure up many ways to slay Goliath," Najab said darkly. "Only one is the death that fate has chosen for him."

Jonathan removed three shiny lumps from the pouch tied to his belt. He pressed them into the Nubian's hand. "For all you have done for me, my Almighty will shower you with blessings."

"I did it for your gold," Najab replied, biting one of the nuggets to test its worth. "Not for your God."

Chapter 14

The High Priest Dalziel led the wedding procession, his flowing white beard shimmering in the morning sunlight like a breastplate of beaten silver. Nara walked beside him in her delicate white robe, followed by the lesser priests and acolytes. Despite her size, she did her best to move with a grace worthy of a bride, careful not to stumble in her delicate sandals on the uneven cobblestones. She feared embarrassing herself at the very moment when all eyes were on her.

The Great Market was packed to overflowing with excited onlookers. In keeping with Philistine custom, Goliath awaited his bride before a marble obelisk honoring past victories. It was the first time she had seen him since the high priest formally announced their betrothal at the temple citadel. When Dalziel had blessed them, she had lowered her eyes modestly, not daring to look upon Goliath's face. Now she studied him closely. There was something crude and unfinished about his features, as if they had been hastily chiseled in anger from a massive block of granite. His nose was blunt and wide, his chin jutting forward like a clenched fist. His eyes were concealed beneath the ridges of heavy brows, guarding their secrets.

At the citadel, Goliath had been dressed for battle. Now he wore a robe of the same pristine white linen as her own. With his face scrubbed, his hair and beard neatly trimmed, and a ruby the size of a ripe olive in his right ear, he looked to her more like a prosperous spice merchant than a warrior. On a nod from the high priest, Goliath took Nara's hand, which was almost as big as his own. He did not squeeze her fingers, perhaps because he knew his grip might crush them, and instead gently cupped her hand in his. To Nara, his thick fingers felt as cold and dead as those of a stone idol.

The crowd burst into cheers, a roar that shook the cobblestones beneath her feet. She breathed in the myrrh that perfumed his beard. Hada had told her that the priests believed a seductive fragrance would yield more sons from a bride than the sweat and stench of battle. Goliath bared his jagged yellow teeth in a smile for the joyful crowd. His breath reeked of decaying meat. The illusion that the beast in Goliath had been tamed dissolved before her like smoke.

Surrounded by the jubilant multitude, Nara felt utterly alone. She scanned the crowd for a familiar face. Hada was nowhere to be seen, but she caught sight of her father, beaming with joy. Ezel's hands were still black from the charcoal of the forge, the stains too much a part of him to ever be scrubbed away. But he had changed from his soot-smudged leather blacksmith's apron into an immaculate white ceremonial robe tied with a purple sash. To her, his shouts of rejoicing sounded the loudest of all. She was thankful that her father, who had for so long looked on her with shame, took pride in her at last.

Holding hands, the betrothed couple set out through the market. Eight burly guards escorted them, shoving aside all those who, in their fervor, pressed too close. These same people once laughed at me, she thought. I was a pathetic outcast whose height and strength were unseemly in a woman. Now they gaze up at me in awe, as if, like Goliath, I have the blood of gods flowing in my veins.

Walking at his side, she saw Goliath lick his lips greedily, as if devouring the adulation of the throng. In the frenzy to fight their way closer to the betrothed couple, the mob knocked over the poles that supported the market stalls. They crashed to the ground, shattering wine jugs and smashing melons.

Frantic wives elbowed each other out of the way to stand in Goliath's shadow. Nara knew the women believed that this assured they would bear male children. To her amazement, the wives of Gath were fighting to stand in her shadow as well, as if she shared the magic of her betrothed.

"Bless us!" they shouted, "Grant us sons!"

Hearing their ecstatic cries, Nara wondered, why do I not feel their joy? Hada had warned her, "On your wedding day, evil spirits will try to turn your heart away from your betrothed." She thought, it is just as my aunt said. Now, when mothers hold up their infant sons for Goliath to bless, the demons speak out against him.

Why should Philistine boys grow to become men if only to be slain in battle? Why should Goliath bless these women now, only to lead their sons to violent death?

She strained to peer into his eyes, but they were hidden beneath his heavy brows. A young mother thrust her baby up toward Goliath. When he pressed his coarse mouth to its tender skin, one of his jagged teeth nicked the infant's cheek, drawing a drop of blood. The little one cried out in pain. Cupping the baby in the palm of his enormous hand, Goliath awkwardly returned it to its mother. She wept with gratitude, as if the wound her child had suffered was a gift. Nara imagined that in years to come, this woman would point to the scar on his face and boast how Goliath himself had bestowed his holy mark upon her son.

In the mounting hysteria, all the Philistine women clamored for this mark of blood from Goliath. Nara saw that they all wanted proof of their bond with a leader they believed was more god than man.

Chapter 15

The frenzied drums, the strident trumpets, told him there was little time left. Clutching the clay vial that Najab had given him, Jonathan quickened his pace down the alleyway. In Gibeah, Najab had made him memorize a map of Gath that he had drawn with a stick in the dust. Jonathan knew exactly where he must go.

Cheers rang out from the multitude gathered before the temple of Dagon, alerting him that the high priest was escorting Goliath and Nara inside. He heard the thunderclap of the massive doors slamming shut, then a clank as they were bolted from within. Najab had warned him that a detachment of Philistine soldiers would block the temple portals, and that no one would be allowed to enter.

At any moment, he knew the wedding ceremony would begin, but he did not panic. As Najab had predicted, the procession had entered through the great doors at the front of the temple. Now he followed the Nubian's instructions: "Livestock are penned in back. Go there."

He heard the braying of donkeys, the bleating of sheep, and followed the noise around a corner. The pens behind the temple were as Najab had described them. The Nubian had explained that he always gave grain and water to his donkeys here before setting out for the smelting pits of Timna. Jonathan passed a fenced enclosure holding a dozen donkeys, all younger and fatter than Najab's scrawny beasts. Beyond them was a pen for sheep and another for goats.

All the men who cared for the animals were gone. He guessed they had joined their friends on the streets, impatient to celebrate the glorious event with flagons of barley beer.

"Make your way past the animal pens to the sacred enclosure," Najab had said. "There you will find a creature like no other, the only one the priests deem worthy for Goliath's marriage sacrifice."

He stood, now, before an imposing enclosure of sharpened cedar posts. It towered above the other pens, too high for him to see what it concealed. From within, he heard the snorts and heavy footfalls of an enormous beast. He pressed his eye to a crack between the posts and peered inside.

A white bull.

He thought, this creature dwarfs all other bulls as Goliath dwarfs all other men. The pointed hooves of the beast were as sharp as axe heads and its horns jutted out like javelins. Its white flanks had a ghostly pallor, so that Jonathan thought he could see the hot blood coursing beneath its hide. To restrain the bull, two ropes as thick as his arm were knotted around its hulking neck and lashed to iron rings imbedded in the temple wall.

Jonathan had heard of this rare breed, too fierce to raise for any purpose other than sacrifice, a creature endowed with an all-consuming hatred of men. It was said that the priests believed the very ferocity of this bull imbued its blood with powerful magic when spilled upon the altar. Yes, he thought, the priests have chosen a creature to offer the gods that is as mighty as the Philistine himself.

Najab had told him, "Goliath is both a man and a beast, so it will take both a man and a beast to kill him." For the plan to work, Jonathan thought, this beast must be my accomplice.

* * *

Her ears ringing from the joyful tumult in the streets, Nara suddenly found herself entombed in silence, the eternal stillness of the innermost sanctuary in the Temple of Dagon. She heard only the ponderous breathing of Goliath at her side. Dalziel stood nearby, as haughty as the massive gilded image of Dagon that gazed down upon them. Flanking the idol were fierce guardian deities wrought in silver—part lion, part serpent—which, she had been told, protected Dagon in his palace in the High Places.

A frail priest shuffled over in musty robes, his gossamer beard as translucent as a moth's wings. Hada had explained that this venerated servant of Dagon, Uziel, would be the one to unite her with Goliath. His bony fingers clasped an ancient iron dagger. From the crudeness of the blade, Nara guessed it had been hammered out in the Dawn Time, when the gods first bestowed the gift of the black metal on mortal men.

Uziel nodded for them both to kneel. Nara stole a look at Goliath beside her, his mighty hands piously clasped before him. For that moment, she could imagine him capable of humility, even kindness. When Uziel lifted his hand, Nara and Goliath repeated the most sacred words a Philistine man and woman could speak:

"I swear to obey the will of Dagon and his celestial legion of gods.

I swear to worship and protect all their graven images, for they are as holy as Philistine flesh.

I swear never to worship the wrathful and invisible God of the Israelites.

I swear never to circumcise my male children as do the Israelites, for what the gods have created in perfection must not be mutilated by men.

I swear to obey the priests of Dagon in all things."

Dalziel stepped forward to join Uziel, then beckoned for Goliath and Nara to stand. The high priest clutched Nara's arm so tightly that his fingernails bit like teeth. She knew that the time had come to utter her final vow, the promise that she must keep above all others.

"I swear to bring forth sons to lead our people, sons who, like their father, Goliath, are mightier than all other men. May the seed planted within me on this, my marriage night, fall on fertile ground."

On a glance from Dalziel, Goliath grabbed Nara by both arms and pulled her roughly to him. She felt a jolt of panic. No one had warned her of this. Goliath's face, coarse as ox hide, chafed her cheek. For the first time, he kissed her. His lips felt as slippery as a calf's liver and his breath reeked. His sharp teeth did not cut her face as they had cut the face of the infant in the crowd, but what Goliath did now distressed her more than if he had shed her blood.

Pressing hard against her lips, his mouth smothered hers. The act said that he was taking possession of her, that for the rest of her life, she belonged to him. It said she must yield to him in all things or die.

The high priest beckoned for the couple to turn away from the altar and kneel to face a shadowy archway of beaten gold. Beyond it, Nara saw only a black void. "Through this portal," Dalziel said, "the final offering will be brought forth for sacrifice."

* * *

Crouched in the shadows outside the wall of cedar posts, Jonathan listened to the white bull snorting and pacing restlessly inside the enclosure. He heard voices. Two brawny acolytes in crimson robes rounded the corner of the temple, striding closer. He hoped they would be in too great a hurry to notice him.

The men swung open the heavy gate to the holding pen, stepped hastily inside, and shut it behind them. Najab had alerted Jonathan that it was the acolytes' duty to lead the bull up the ramp into the inner sanctum for sacrifice. Now, through a crack between the posts, he watched them struggling to unknot the two thick ropes that secured the beast to the massive iron ring on the wall.

The bull fought back, bellowing and pawing the ground. Each acolyte clutched a rope, too focused on keeping clear of the thrusting horns to notice the stranger in an indigo cloak who opened the gate and entered the pen.

Jonathan unsheathed the copper dagger hidden in his sleeve.

He edged closer, a skilled hunter of men. On the field of battle, he would never stab a Philistine in the back, for he took pride in letting the enemy look his killer in the eyes. But today, too much was at stake to quibble over honor. He struck hard from behind, stabbing the man closest to him between the shoulder blades.

As the acolyte toppled lifeless to the ground, the other spun around quickly, drawing his sword. Jonathan dropped to one knee and thrust his dagger upward beneath the Philistine's ribs. Again and again, he plunged the blade into his chest until the acolyte fell with a groan.

Now that the men had loosened the ropes tying it to the wall, the bull tore free. Bellowing, it charged across the enclosure, hooves trampling the bloodied bodies of the acolytes lying in its path.

The bull veered toward Jonathan.

He reached down and snatched up one of the two ropes knotted around the animal's neck. Before its horns could reach him, Jonathan lashed the rope back onto the iron ring on the wall and knotted it tightly.

The beast snorted and threw all its weight against the rope, threatening to tear free. Jonathan saw this was his moment. He slid his hand into his sleeve and grasped the clay vial.

The bull flailed its horns, the points narrowly missing his chest. Forced backward, Jonathan found his shoulders pressed against the wooden posts of the enclosure. He could not escape. Another sweep of the horns narrowly missed his throat, the immense weight of the bull slamming into the heavy timbers.

Jonathan tightened his grip on the clay vial, but the beast was coming toward him too fast. He was powerless to use it. The curved horns hurtled back at him once more.

For a fleeting instant, Jonathan seized hold of the bull's foam-flecked muzzle with one hand, clutching the vial like a dagger with the other. Najab had told him, "A plant grows in my land that brings forth the bitter seeds of rage. Once a beast swallows them, it will kill any living thing in its path."

A swift shake of his wrist emptied the bile-colored seeds into the bull's upturned mouth.

But did the beast swallow them? It happened so quickly, Jonathan could not be sure. For good luck, he rubbed the gold signet ring on his finger and murmured a hasty prayer: "May the Almighty judge me worthy to slay Goliath, worthy to lead my people." He doubted that the Most High would accept his clumsy plea—prayer was a task for priests, not warriors—so he bargained with the Almighty: "Help me kill the Philistine and I pledge to devote my life to serving You."

With a suddenness that astonished Jonathan, the seeds of rage inflamed the beast. Its eyes widened and its nostrils flared. Bellowing, the bull tossed its head, horns thrusting, hooves stabbing the ground.

One final lunge and the beast tore the rope free from the iron ring that held it. Swinging its massive neck like a battering ram, it slammed blindly against the temple wall, struggling to break out of the enclosure.

Jonathan hastily unbolted the gate to the dark passageway leading into the temple, then leapt out of the way as the beast's powerful haunches hurled it forward. As swiftly as a javelin flung through the air, it charged out of the enclosure and into the depths of the tunnel. Long after the bull had vanished, Jonathan heard the sharp clatter of its hooves echoing off the stone walls.

What happens now is beyond my control, he thought. To commit this murder, to kill a warrior who is more than human, is too daunting a task for any mortal man to perform alone. But if the Most High created one beast on earth mighty enough to kill Goliath, surely it is this one.

Chapter 16

Nara and Goliath knelt side by side, facing the mouth of the darkened portal, with Uziel and the high priest standing behind them. She had overheard them whispering about what would happen now: Two acolytes would lead the bull from the holding pen, up a ramp that led through a tunnel, to be formally presented for sacrifice. She listened for the echo of measured footsteps.

Instead, from deep within the passageway, she heard the rumble of thunder. The marble floor trembled as if it might yawn open beneath her feet.

With the helpless confusion of the very old, Uziel's legs quavered and his palsied hands shook. Beside him, Dalziel seemed stricken. His eyes were filled with dread, as if his warrior god had betrayed him.

The thunderbolt struck.

At first, Nara did not recognize it as a creature of flesh and blood. Anything so filled with fury, she thought, must be a god that has come to wreak his revenge.

The bull hurtled from the mouth of the tunnel. Nara dived out of the way, but Goliath was caught directly in its path. She feared the horns would gore him, but he nimbly stepped aside. The bull charged past Goliath, its sharp black hooves scarring the marble floor.

Uziel was paralyzed with fear, powerless to escape. Nara watched, helpless, as the bull's left horn impaled his chest, crushing his brittle ribs. The priest crumpled without a sound. The sacrificial dagger slipped from his fingers and clattered to the floor, lost in the blur of hooves.

Goliath seized the moment to pounce. With both arms, he grabbed hold of the bull's head behind its massive horns, tightening his embrace into a death grip.

With a sudden vicious twist, Goliath wrenched the neck of the beast.

Nara heard a loud crack, like the trunk of a great oak splitting, and realized the spine of the bull had snapped. Its legs buckled. The beast collapsed with such force that it cracked the marble floor.

Temple guards poured into the chamber. Nara folded her arms before her, so they would not notice that her hands were trembling. Only when she saw that the bull was dead, did she realize how long it had been since she had taken a breath.

The guards knelt down beside Uziel. Nara saw that the old man was clutching his gashed chest and coughing up blood. Enraged at the sight, Dalziel leaned down and snatched the sacrificial knife from the floor. He tilted back the lifeless head of the bull and slashed its throat, again and again. It seemed to her that he was avenging himself, punishing this creature that had fought so fiercely for its life. Blood spurted from the bull's throat into a golden bowl held by a young acolyte.

"An evil spirit possessed this creature," Dalziel announced to Goliath. "You have vanquished it!"

Goliath drew himself up to his full height so that his head almost touched the ceiling. "No demon can kill me," he said with unwavering conviction. "The god Dagon will always protect me."

Dalziel raised the glistening bowl frothing with warm blood. "Man and woman, you will drink from the same cup of life. You will taste the bitter with the sweet." He held it out to Nara. "You will bring forth sons for Gath."

With unsteady hands, she lifted the rim of the golden bowl to her lips. The vile black liquid tasted harsh as rusty iron. Though she knew this was the highest honor that the high priest could bestow upon her, she could only force herself to take one sip. If she drank another, she knew she would vomit.

Goliath snatched the bowl from her and drained it in a single hearty gulp. The ease with which he swallowed the foul liquid told Nara this was not the first time he had tasted blood. With the crimson droplets trickling from his beard, his teeth stained red, he reminded her of a lion at a fresh kill.

She felt that this was a time for rejoicing, but Dalziel did not rejoice. It seemed that he was afflicted with doubt. Lifting his robe so that the hem would not be stained with blood, the high priest knelt down beside the carcass of the bull. With bejeweled fingers, he turned over the bloated tongue, which lolled from the side of its mouth. The high priest scowled. It seemed that he had found something that outraged him. He muttered a torrent of words, but Nara realized that he was not praying to the gods. He was spewing curses.

She took a wary step closer and saw what he had discovered: The tongue of the bull was coated with a thick green froth. The priest leaned over cautiously to sniff it. He nodded, as if his suspicions were confirmed.

"The beast was not possessed by a demon." His voice trembled with fury. "This was the act of an assassin. Find him."

Chapter 17

For Ahinoam, wife of Saul and mother of his children, the Mikveh harbored unholy secrets. Here, cloaked in the mist, she hatched her schemes safe from prying eyes. The holy bath was reserved for the privileged women of Saul's court who came to cleanse themselves after their blood of the moon flowed. Here, immersed in the twilight where no man was permitted to enter, Ahinoam found she could plot court intrigue and enlist accomplices, shielded from the palace infighting that embroiled her husband.

She sank to her neck in the sacred waters of the Mikveh and the warmth soothed her, an embrace. Scorning the vanity of other women, Saul's wife wasted no time admiring her reflection in the shimmering water. She knew her face was too unsettling to be beautiful—her chin too angular, her nose too sharp— but her black eyebrows, which met in a point above her nose, gave her gaze a piercing intensity. Saul believed that she could cast a spell over a man, even steal his soul, and blamed her wicked female instincts for bewitching him. She wanted him to think that. She drew power from his fear.

After bearing the king six children, Ahinoam's hips had thickened and her breasts sagged. She realized she had lost the allure to seduce him—Saul had not taken her to his bed in years—but she had learned his weaknesses. She knew how to use them as weapons against him.

Today, she had sent her attendant, Cael, who was loyal to her as no man could be, to gather the latest tidings from her spies in Saul's palace. Awaiting Cael's return, she had ordered the outer doors to the Mikveh shut to exclude all others. Ahinoam hoarded the sacred pool to herself, luxuriating in its healing warmth. Only her young handmaiden, Talitha, remained with her. The graceful young girl was barely strong enough to perform her one simple duty, pouring water from an alabaster pitcher onto hot stones to produce dense, enfolding clouds of steam.

Soon, Cael will return with the latest tidings from the palace, Ahinoam thought, and my plans will move forward. But for now, she reveled in this moment of solitude. The reflections of the pink marble walls in the water shimmered with rosy visions of her future. She closed her eyes and imagined how her life would be transformed when Saul was dead and her beloved son, Jonathan, ruled. This was more than a daydream. It was a plan she vowed to bring to pass.

When my son is king, I will no longer sit here in the holy bath, but on a golden throne at my son's right hand. Jonathan will treat me with the love and respect worthy of a true queen, something his father, Saul, has never done. And it will be for me to select a suitable bride for my son, one from a powerful tribe, to forge an alliance to crush our enemies.

Before that day of betrothal comes, I will serve as Jonathan's most trusted advisor, using his power as king to settle old scores with all who have wronged me. I will watch my enemies suffer and die . . .

Her vengeful fantasies faded. She opened her eyes. Something was not as it should be. The cloud of steam that had swirled around her in the sacred pool was starting to dissipate. She needed its protection to filter out the world. She did not like to see life too distinctly, with all its warts and wrinkles, least of all her own sagging flesh. She preferred the blush of the hazy future conjured up in her mind.

"Pour more water on the hot stones!" Her haughty voice echoed hollowly off the high ceiling.

Talitha, her handmaiden, did not reply.

Ahinoam clapped her hands, but there was still no response. Annoyed, she climbed out of the sacred pool and hastily pulled her robe around her. She thought, Talitha deserves a whipping for this.

She heard a voice, one that was unthinkable here.

A man's voice, calling her name.

This cannot be, she thought. Men are forbidden to enter the holy Mikveh under penalty of death. But yes, it was a man, taunting her. The awareness came over her that a male intruder dared to set foot here. Her heart pounding, she slid her hand inside the pocket of her robe and pulled out the dagger hidden there. With the blade pointed before her, she padded barefoot through the mist.

Her foot struck something. A body sprawled face-down on the tiles.

Her handmaiden.

She knelt down and turned the girl over onto her back. Talitha's eyes were wide open, unblinking, her lips parted as if to scream. The silken cord of her robe had been knotted tightly around her throat.

Beside Talitha's body she found a drawstring pouch, too finely stitched to have been sewn by an Israelite craftsman. Its soft leather was dyed the crimson of the Philistines' battle standards.

With dread, Ahinoam picked up the pouch and fumbled with the leather thong that bound it. When she saw the object that it held, she knew she could not keep the revelation to herself. She must immediately bring it to the king, her husband, the father of her six children.

The man she hated. The man who despised her.

Chapter 18

"The king would not have summoned us to Gibeah merely to announce another defeat," Jesse said, with hope in his voice.

But David feared the worst. He had experienced Saul's fits of madness, narrowly escaped his murderous rage. Now, standing beside his father and brothers, he had joined the restless multitude waiting in the sunbaked courtyard of the king's palace. He felt like an outsider, as if he did not belong among these men. All the others wore makeshift armor and carried swords forged of crude Israelite copper. He was the only one who was unarmed, the only one who had never risked his life in battle against the Philistines.

Though I am different from all the others, my fate, like theirs, hinges on what will happen here and now.

Sensing the importance of this convocation, even his father had interrupted his daily prayers to come with his sons. "When the king appears before us," Jesse whispered excitedly, "I will look at him and know if the demons that possessed him have finally departed. I will know if the spirit of the Lord has returned."

The bronze doors of the palace balcony creaked open. Escorted by Tobiah and six palace guards bearing spears, the king stepped out into the sunlight. No cheers welcomed Saul, but the wary silence told David that his people still viewed him with grudging respect.

The king was clad in glittering battle armor. The beaten bronze of his breastplate, emblazoned with the lion of Judah, bore the scars of Philistine iron, proof of old battles fought and won. His hand resting proudly on the gilded pommel of his sword, he lifted his arms to greet the Israelite host that packed the square before him.

"This is the Saul we lost!" Jesse whispered excitedly to his sons. "The evil spirits have left him. He has come back to lead us at last!"

My father's eyes are weak from years of praying in the shadows. All Jesse sees is a tall leader in gleaming armor, but I notice details that my father overlooks. Saul's weary eyes betray a profound sadness. His bronze breastplate weighs heavy on his shoulders, as if the burden is too great for him to bear. It seems Saul's strength has dwindled along with his royal power.

The king spoke: "By now, you all have heard the tidings from Gath. The Philistines have proclaimed to the world that the marriage of Goliath has taken place today." His voice wavered. "They say that once Goliath's seed is planted tonight, it will spawn a dynasty to rule over us for all time."

David thought, the Philistines made sure that their triumphant message reached us, to crush our spirit. Now what will Saul offer his people to bring us hope?

"My son . . ." the king began. At first, David thought that he was introducing him. He expected that the door would open and Jonathan would step out onto the balcony, clad for battle, as he had so many times before.

The crowd was hushed, expectant. But the balcony door did not open. Jonathan was nowhere to be seen. An uneasy murmur swept through the crowd.

"My son, who will rule after me, was determined to prevent the calamity of this marriage from taking place. And so, he set out for the Philistine city on the most noble of missions . . ." Saul took a deep breath and said, "To slay Goliath."

The assembled multitude fell silent in disbelief. David knew that they realized it was an impossible goal, and yet, they did not laugh at Saul's words. It was as if they clung to the fragile hope that by some miracle beyond their imagining, such a heroic act might be possible.

For an uneasy moment, Saul turned away, as if he would rather flee into the palace than say what must be said. Then, at last, he turned back to them. "I had hoped that today my beloved Jonathan would return to me with Goliath's head. Instead, I received this."

Tobiah solemnly handed him a small pouch of red leather. The king removed a glittering object and held it up for all to see. David realized that it was Jonathan's gold signet ring, identical to the one the king wore on his right hand. "The Philistine priests sent me this as proof that they hold Jonathan hostage." Saul's brave front crumbled and the words poured out: "They say he will remain locked in the North Citadel of Gath until I pay the ransom for his life. It grieves me that the ransom they ask . . ." He raised his voice, revealing the anguish he had tried so hard to conceal. "The ransom is one I cannot pay."

David could not imagine what that ransom could be. He was certain that to save his favorite son, Saul would empty the coffers of his treasury. The king would even take his son's place in the dungeon in Gath, trade his son's life for his own. And yet, it seemed there was something that the king prized more highly than life itself.

The crowd waited restlessly, as if dreading to hear the price of Jonathan's head. Instead of telling them, Saul pointed to the back of the crowd and raised his right hand. From the direction of the city gates, six Israelite priests in white robes entered the packed courtyard. David saw that they carried a massive coffer covered by a thick white mantle woven with gold and silver threads. Supporting the heavy burden with cedar poles resting on their shoulders, the priests marched at a stately pace. The throng parted silently to let them pass.

"Amariah," Jesse whispered under his breath, pointing to the pale old man with a faded red beard who led the procession. David saw that as a sign of his authority, the high priest of the Israelites wore a gleaming silver breastplate set with twelve jewels, one for each of the twelve tribes. Such was the secret nature of his holy duties that David knew Amariah was seldom seen, but he had heard his father speak of him with reverence.

Bent over, as if from the crushing weight of his responsibilities, the high priest led the procession through the throng until they stood beneath the palace balcony. Slowly, carefully, as if their burden was a fragile living thing, the priests set it down.

On a nod from Saul, Amariah swept aside the white mantle to reveal the treasure it concealed.

"The Ark of the Covenant," Saul said, his voice breaking with emotion to see the coffer gleaming before him. "It holds the Tablets of the Law, the Commandments that the Almighty gave to Moses on Mt. Sinai."

Like his father and brothers, David had never seen the Ark before this moment. He stood motionless, forgetting to draw his next breath, enraptured by the sight. The acacia chest, covered with beaten gold, seemed to glow from within. Two delicately wrought golden cherubim knelt on the heavy lid, their exquisite wings curved to touch, as if to consecrate the priceless relics that the coffer held.

It seemed to David that the king drew strength from the sight, standing straight and tall, his eyes sparkling, his spirit revived to have it so close at hand. "To protect the Ark from being captured by the Philistines, I have it moved secretly, from one hiding place to another, under the watchful eyes of Amariah," Saul said. "It does not remain in each safe haven for more than one Sabbath."

Saul runs a terrible risk bringing this holiest of treasures here today, David thought. The king only would have done this if he feared his power was so threatened that he must show the Ark to the people, to prove he is their leader in the sight of God.

The blood drained from Saul's face. At first, he could not bring himself to speak. Then his words tumbled out, with what seemed to David like the fervor of madness. "*This* is the ransom the Philistines demand. In exchange for the life of my son, Jonathan, the Philistines would have us surrender the Ark of the Covenant!"

How cunning the Philistines are, David thought, and how cruel. They force Saul to choose between his beloved son and the Holy Ark—the two things he cherishes most—knowing that he can forsake neither.

David's gaze was drawn back to the glittering golden coffer surrounded by a sea of desperate men. He was struck by the conflicting ways his people reacted to the sight. His father's eyes brimmed with tears, while a few other old men Jesse's age clasped their hands in prayer and knelt before it. But the younger men did not pray. His own brothers stared impassively at the ground. It disgusted him that they did not pay homage to the glory of the Law preserved within the Ark. Instead, it seemed that they looked upon it as a tired old relic, a stale remnant from the past, not as their eternal link to the Living God.

It is not enough for the Israelites to possess the Tablets of the Law, he thought. They need a strong ruler who will embrace the Law and use it to guide His people down the path of righteousness. He saw the anguish on Saul's face, the creeping awareness that his people no longer believed in him. The king hastily wiped tears from his eyes with the back of his hand. David pitied him. Weeping is for women and old men, he thought, not for a monarch. My people will see his tears as proof of his weakness.

When Saul spoke again, his voice broke. "This is a ransom I will not pay. But I cannot, I will not, let my beloved son die. There is only one way to save him. We must free Jonathan through the force of arms."

David understood that Saul was not issuing a command. He was pleading with his people. His son's life was in their hands.

"We must attack the Philistine city of Gath."

"Attack Gath?" The words rippled among the men. From the terror on their faces, Saul might as well have asked them to storm the gates of heaven, David thought. He saw that the Israelites were no longer listening obediently to their king. They were passing judgment on him.

"I will lead you!" Saul said. "It will test us, but the Almighty has tested us before."

"The Almighty has tested us enough!"

David saw it was Shodok, a hardened veteran of many battles, who spoke out. Though he was no longer young, the gaunt commander wore the short tunic of a young man. His arms and legs were bare, as if to show that his taut muscles had not weakened with age, and that his battle scars had only served to strengthen him.

"I have faced Goliath on the field of battle and have paid a price for it." Shodok raised his right hand for all to see. It was missing three fingers, the scarred stumps as ragged if they had been chewed off by a wild beast. "I know Goliath is not like other men. Though some say he is part god, I would risk my life to face him again. But I will never attack Goliath's city. The walls of Gath will never be toppled. Their gates will never be breached."

"The Almighty makes all things possible!" Saul protested, but David saw that the king's forehead glistened with sweat.

"And if the time for miracles is past?" Shodok pointed scornfully at the Ark. "If the Tablets of the Law are truly a gift from the Almighty, why do they not bring us victory? The Tablets are worthless scraps of stone. Surrender the Ark. Buy your son's freedom. Buy all our sons long lives of peace!"

One of Shodok's men cried out, "Sacrifice no more of our loved ones in battle!"

"I have lost two of my sons," Jesse shouted. "Is that not enough?"

David watched his brothers join in with the rest of the crowd, roaring their agreement. He was dismayed at how easily their cowardice crushed their veneration for the Ark of the Law.

The king's face reddened, his fury building. He clenched his hands into fists. "So long as I am king, I will not betray our birthright! The Holy Ark is our link to Moses and the Almighty.

It is our shield against false gods and wicked men. Once the Commandments in the Ark are lost, once we no longer live by them, we are no better than our heathen enemies!"

David knew that Saul spoke the truth. But he saw how the king's words splintered the crowd into a clash of angry voices. Some wanted to give away the Ark to save their skins, while others vowed to keep the Ark at all costs. No one wanted to sacrifice his life in an assault on the Philistines' impregnable city to save Saul's son.

First one brawl broke out, then another. Men lashed out with their fists and unsheathed their daggers. Sickened, David wondered whether the fragile alliance of the twelve tribes in Saul's kingdom was shattering before his eyes.

The king gazed down on his people, humiliated that they had rebuffed him. He nodded abruptly to his guards. They escorted him, with Tobiah, back into the refuge of the palace. The bronze balcony doors slammed shut behind them. David thought, Saul cannot so easily escape from his own people. They fear that just as their God has abandoned their star-crossed king, so He has abandoned them.

In the crowd, the violence had dwindled into sullen looks and defiant words as the Israelites went their separate ways, more bitterly divided than ever. Emboldened, Shodok strode out of the square, surrounded by his men.

David noticed that only a handful of devout old men stayed behind, praying before the Ark. Amariah, the high priest, hastily raised his hands to bless them, impatient to leave with the treasure entrusted to his care. His acolytes gathered, ready to shoulder the cedar poles and bear the golden coffer back to its hiding place.

In that fleeting moment, David felt irresistibly drawn to the Ark. He knew this was as close as he might ever come to the holiest of God's gifts and longed to experience its full glory. But as he neared the gleaming coffer, he realized there was a much more earthly reason that he felt compelled to come here.

Michal. He understood that the turmoil of the crowd offered her a rare chance to worship before the Holy Ark. Since women were not allowed to approach the Ark, she had cloaked herself in a man's dark mantle, her face partially concealed beneath it. And yet, he recognized her eyes glistening with tears. Bowing her head, she clasped her hands tightly before her.

"Michal . . ."

She turned at the sound of his voice, flushed with anger. "You interrupt my prayers for my brother. He will not stand in your way now. Is that why you have come to me, to rejoice at his fate?"

"No," David said. "Please hear me."

"We have nothing to say to each other. My father is powerless to save Jonathan. My beloved brother will die."

"Jonathan will not die," he said calmly. He took a step toward her, closer than was seemly for a man to approach a woman who was not his wife. He did not know whether the urge that drove him was sacred or profane. Was it because he stood so near to the Holy Ark that he felt certain what he must do now? Or was it much simpler than that, as simple as the pale luster of Michal's skin, the fresh cinnamon scent of her hair, his need to ease the suffering in her eyes?

Are there rare moments in the human heart when both earthly desire and righteousness can speak with the same voice? If so, this is such a moment.

"Your brother will live," David said. "I will save him."

Chapter 19

Squinting through the rusty bars of his cell window, Jonathan traced the journey of the sun across the sky. The sight dazzled him, as if he watched the flight of a bright, exotic bird that he feared he would never see again.

The priests of Dagon had announced that Saul must pay his ransom before nightfall, and it seemed that the sun was descending with spiteful haste. He forced himself to peer down into the glare of the temple courtyard at the wedding banquet. A boisterous throng of drunken guests sat at the long oak tables spread with a sumptuous feast: fig cakes, dates, and pomegranates; sweetened bread from fine-milled flour; stewpots filled with freshly killed venison—all of it washed down with goblets of honey wine. Roasted pigs, their charred skin still sizzling from the fire pits, were carried in by servants on silver platters. The smell sickened him.

In massive oak chairs braced to support their weight, Goliath and his bride sat side by side at the head of the crowded banquet table. Jonathan saw that they towered over the other guests—priests, commanders, wealthy merchants and their wives—the elite of Gath. Concubines danced before them, to the pounding of timbrels and the tinkling of finger cymbals, their voices raised in shrill songs of rejoicing.

The Philistines had seized him soon after his failed attempt on Goliath's life. When the guards had lifted his robe and found he was circumcised, they knew he was an Israelite. Jonathan understood, now, why Dalziel had selected this cell for him. The high priest did not need a torturer to inflict pain. For Jonathan, the sight of the wedding feast from his cell window was torment enough.

If I had killed Goliath, this never would have come to pass.

Tonight, the marriage bond will be consummated, he thought.

Soon, the bride will bear a warrior son, first in a mighty dynasty of rulers with Goliath's blood flowing in their veins.

If only I had killed him . . .

He did not allow his mind to go further than that. The Philistines had told him they were demanding a ransom, but not the price they placed on his life. No matter how exorbitant the cost, he was confident that his father would pay it out of love for his own flesh and blood, his heir to the throne.

Dalziel, the high priest, had told him, "If you hear a trumpet sound three times from the ramparts, it will mean your father has paid your ransom. You will be set free. But if Saul has not paid for your life by sunset, you will hear the beating of a great drum. It will announce that at dawn tomorrow, after Goliath arises from the conjugal bed, you will die by his sword."

* * *

The trumpet did not sound. Jonathan heard only the raucous laughter of the drunken wedding guests, mocking him. The rays of the dying sun lengthened the shadows of the dancers at the banquet, transforming them into long-limbed giants. This foretells the day soon to come, he thought, when a dynasty of Goliaths will rule the earth.

In the deepening twilight, he watched as two acolytes carried a cask-sized drum to the high priest at the banquet table. Out of deference, the dancers lifted their hands from their timbrels and the boisterous guests fell silent. The high priest grasped a heavy ebony mallet with both hands. He looked up at Jonathan in his cell window in the citadel, as if to make sure he bore witness to this moment.

Dalziel struck the ox-leather drumhead three times, three blows echoing off the high ramparts. Before the sound faded away, the guests returned to their drunken revelry. Jonathan thought, now that they know the son of Saul is sentenced to die, the Philistines have even more to celebrate.

Why did Saul refuse to pay the ransom? What price could be so great that my father would not pay it to save his own son?

He knew that Saul would empty out the treasury for him, but he doubted it was as simple as that. He suspected that Dalziel had demanded something more. Overcome with despair, he turned away from the barred window. This was not as it was supposed to be. He had always imagined he would die a hero in the heat of battle, the sword in his hand dripping with Philistine blood. Instead, he would be executed like a common thief.

I have until dawn.

A cruel night stretched before him, a torment that he dreaded because it forced him back upon himself. For Jonathan, soul-searching was the most severe punishment. He could never be certain where it might lead, what faults he might discover lurking within his heart.

Is my execution the judgment of the Almighty? Is it His will that I die in disgrace so David can become king? Will a cowardly shepherd rule in my place? If so, my God is even more treacherous than the Philistine priests.

Without warning, the deadbolt of his cell clanked open and the heavy door creaked wide. A beardless young acolyte entered, flanked by two burly guards. The youth said something in the Philistine tongue that Jonathan did not understand, and, grinning, placed a covered copper platter on the floor. The guards smirked as they walked out.

The door slammed behind them and the bolt slid shut. This will be my final meal, Jonathan thought. Hungrily, he lifted the cover from the platter. A roasted suckling pig stared up at him, its eyes hollow sockets, its jaws open to reveal yellow teeth.

In revulsion, Jonathan tore the suckling pig apart and shoved the meat through the bars of the window. Chunks of the greasy carcass landed on a granite ledge below. With the rasp of flapping wings, ravens swooped down and tore at it with their beaks.

Soon, Jonathan thought, the ravens will be fighting over my own flesh.

Chapter 20

Goliath wedged his greasy thumb into the jaws of a roast pig large enough to feed six men, and tore it in half. Hot juices spurted, dripping from his fingers, staining his pristine ceremonial robe. Hunched over the banquet table, he stuffed his mouth with both hands, noisily chewing the meat and bones. Sitting at his right, in the place of honor, Nara nibbled on a pork joint that she held daintily between two of her thick, unladylike fingers, trying not to spill a drop onto her immaculate white robe.

Flanked by his priests, who primly sipped honey wine, Dalziel studied the bride from the opposite end of the banquet table. He watched with contempt as the wealthy women of Gath, in their glittering gold jewelry and ceremonial robes, crowded around Nara, showering her with praise, vying with each other to curry favor with the wife of Goliath. They are fools wasting their time, he thought. The bride is too shy to speak to anyone but her aunt, Hada, the plump old woman with a cleft lip seated beside her. Dalziel suspected that she was the only one whose counsel Nara trusted. Because Hada was not under his control, he saw her as a threat.

A fawning acolyte broke in on his thoughts. "If you had not discovered the daughter of Ezel, this glorious day would never have come!"

"She is a jewel," another chimed in. "The most precious gift of our god Dagon."

"The only one who can bear sons for Goliath," said a third.

Dalziel dismissed their shameless flattery with a wave of his hand, as if to rid himself of flies, but he took pride in the marriage that he had so deftly arranged. So auspicious a match could only have been ordained in the High Places. He felt confident that it proved the god Dagon was with him.

The Philistines of Gath did not know the truth—that he had

discovered Nara hammering out iron weapons in Ezel's forge, an act forbidden to women, a crime punishable by death. No one can ever know, Dalziel thought. The wife of Goliath, soon to be the mother of his warrior sons, must be pure and blameless before her people.

The priests droned on with their honeyed words, but Dalziel had stopped listening. He noticed that the guards had blocked the path of an outsider who had trespassed on the wedding celebration. The intruder was clad in a blood-spattered leather apron that protected his delicate priestly robe, his hands red as a butcher's. His deeply lined face was ashen with fear.

"Tamzin should be working at the altar," Dalziel muttered. "I did not summon him here." Sensing trouble, he beckoned to the guards to admit him. He wondered what calamity would compel this priest to abandon his urgent duties in the temple, to come here in such haste that he did not even wash off the blood of sacrifice.

Tamzin slowed as he approached him, fearing his anger. "Forgive me." He knelt before the high priest, eyes lowered in respect.

"Why have you come?" Dalziel snapped. "Unless you complete the sacrifices to Dagon, the bride will not get with child!"

"The offerings . . ." Tamzin whispered, then fell silent.

"The animals have all been carefully chosen," Dalziel said impatiently. "You must lose no time sacrificing them to Dagon, to sanctify our prayers on this most sacred day."

"The creatures placed before me . . ." Tamzin hesitated, but he could delay no longer. "When they were led to the altar . . ." He blurted out: "The calves are blind. Blood oozes from their hollow eyes. One ram has the stunted legs of a pig. Another, as it burned upon the high altar, reeked of excrement!"

Dalziel pressed his lips tightly together to keep from saying what they both knew: Such omens foretold a disaster beyond imagining. "And what of the bulls?" he asked. They were the most prized offerings, essential for winning the favor of the gods.

"When we slaughtered them and slit open their bellies"—Tamzin seemed to choke on the words—"their entrails crawled with maggots!"

The high priest's face showed no emotion—to reveal his alarm would be a sign of weakness—but he betrayed his thoughts: "What has brought this curse upon us?"

Tamzin summoned up the courage to speak. "Perhaps the God of the Israelites . . ."

"The Israelites?" Dalziel turned on him in fury. "Their toothless, invisible God has no power within our walls! Go back to the altar. Tell your acolytes to sharpen their knives. For every offering that is corrupted, ten worthy animals must be slaughtered!"

Tamzin pointed at the dim red tinge fading in the western sky. "But it is forbidden to perform sacrifices after sunset."

"You will continue the sacrifices into the night."

Although Tamzin had never heard this command before, Dalziel knew that the priest did not dare show his surprise. Tamzin nodded obediently, his eyes lowered in respect. Dalziel longed to leave the drunken foolishness of the wedding feast to join him at the altar and take part in the bloodletting. He would show Tamzin and his priests that the act of killing could be a sacred dance with its own fierce beauty—slashing the throat of the creature so swiftly that it could not cry out, then tilting its head back so the blood arced into the marble channel without a drop wasted.

"Work until your knives grow dull from slitting the throats of the offerings, until the acolytes drop in exhaustion from dragging away the carcasses," Dalziel said. "The priests must shed blood on the altars until it flows like a rushing river. Only then will Dagon smile upon Goliath and his bride tonight."

Chapter 21

The gates of Gath that yawned open in the distance were about to swallow the setting sun. David regretted that he had misjudged how long the journey would take.

I have reached the Philistine city too late. The gates are still open, but for how much longer? Here, as in Gibeah, they will be bolted at nightfall. The sentries will close them at any moment.

Ahead of him in the twilight, he saw two gangly Philistine peasants herding a handful of sheep into a crude enclosure of sharpened stakes. The men wore coarsely woven tunics and shabby sandals that David judged were no better than those of his own people. With their gaunt faces, blunt noses and doleful eyes, the young Philistines looked so much alike that he guessed they must be brothers. For the moment, in the fading light, a tangle of tall grass screened him from view. But he feared they would soon catch sight of him, and edged forward to take cover behind a granite slab.

Suddenly, both the young peasants looked up, startled. Had they spotted him?

No, they turned to face a heavy-set Philistine in a bronze helmet, wielding an iron-tipped javelin. David was surprised to see that the man striding briskly toward them did not come from the direction of Gath, but from the shadowy hills. The two peasants humbly bowed their heads before the soldier, as slaves bow to their master, he thought. David pitied them. He had heard how the Philistines oppressed their own people, collecting heavy taxes so that the priests could build idols of gold.

The commander barked orders at the peasants. David knew enough of the Philistine tongue to understand his words: "More animals for sacrifice." Two soldiers loomed out of the twilight, driving a dozen livestock toward them, prodding the sheep and bulls with the shafts of their spears.

"Whose animals are these?" the older peasant asked suspiciously.

"Your kinsmen in the outlying lands," the commander said, with a mocking laugh. "They are most generous."

David saw that the peasants did not believe him. To judge if any had been seized from their own farms, they knelt down beside the animals—three of them were older bulls, the rest ewes and rams—and carefully examined the marks of ownership scorched into their flanks.

Before they could finish checking, the commander growled, "You are wasting time. Choose those that are most worthy. Herd them into Gath as it is your place to do."

"But it is past sunset, the time when all sacrifices end," the younger peasant protested.

"Tonight they say the sacrifices must continue." The commander eyed the livestock. "The priests are sharpening their knives to cut their throats." He pointed his javelin at the peasants. "Hurry or I will cut yours."

The soldiers vanished into the shadows. From behind the granite slab, David sized up the animals with a shepherd's practiced eye. He knew he only had an instant to devise a plan before the peasants drove them into Gath. A childhood memory flashed through his mind: In his first days tending the flock, when his brothers were drunk and came to beat him, he hid from them by clinging to the belly of a sheep. Could he do the same now?

He needed a creature hefty enough to conceal him and strong enough to move while bearing his weight. Among these animals, there was only one that might do: a formidable ram that, no doubt, weighed as much as a man, with impressive curved horns that would make it highly prized for sacrifice. He judged that its mottled-brown wool, badly in need of shearing, was thick enough for him to cling to, so long as his strength held out.

He crept out of the shadows. Lying down on his back in the

dust, he slid beneath the ram. His fingers dug into the wool. The damp, filthy underbelly of the animal stank, but he forced himself to press his face against it and pull himself up. Unexpectedly, the ram took one step forward. David lost his grip on the moist, oily fleece, and fell backward into the dust.

He had to come up with another way. Pulling his sling from his belt, he looped the long leather strap over the ram's neck, pulling it snugly so the leather was hidden in the thick wool. He slid beneath the ram again. Gripping the sling, he hoisted himself up against the belly and hugged it with his legs.

He knew that like all old rams, this one would be skittish, quick to anger. His task now was to keep it from balking at its secret burden. With a practiced touch, he tried to calm it, stroking it gently along the flanks, as he had comforted the sheep in his flock. He ran his finger across familiar markings seared into the ram's right foreleg, proof that it had been seized from his people. This is as it was meant to be, he thought: A stolen sheep from an Israelite flock will be my key to enter the Philistine gates.

He heard the restless hooves of the other animals as they stirred and started to move ahead. The ram lurched forward to follow them. Clutching the leather strap cinched around its neck, he bent his head back and strained to look out between its front legs. But his vision was limited. He could only see an arm's length ahead into the shadows.

The clamor of voices, the orange flare of torches in the dust, told him they had neared the sentries stationed at the city gates. He heard sheep bleating as the men poked the slower ones with spears to hurry them along. The ram that concealed him trotted ahead to keep up with the others.

At last, a shadow swept over them. He knew it meant they had passed beneath the massive arch of the main gate. The hollow thud of hooves on cobblestones told David that he had made it inside the city.

For the first time in my life, I am in the Philistines' domain. I breathe the same air as Goliath. Our enemies say our God has no power within these walls hallowed to pagan deities, but I know they are mistaken. The Almighty rules the dark places as well as the light, just as He rules the heavens and the earth.

He whispered a silent prayer of thanksgiving to his invisible Almighty. And yet, he realized he was only here thanks to the cruel Philistine god. If the priests of Dagon had not prolonged their sacrifices into the night to slaughter more animals, shed more blood, the city gates would have been closed long before he could have entered.

Herded down the narrow alleyway, the sheep bleated frantically, as if sensing they were being driven to the slaughter. With mounting panic, they slowed their pace, balked, then were prodded and grudgingly walked ahead. David's arms and legs ached from clinging to the strap of his sling and the wool of the ram's underbelly. He knew that in moments, his strength would fail.

From his low vantage point beneath the ram, he saw the path shift from rough cobblestones to flagstones, and then to gleaming tiles. Drunken laughter, frenetic drums and the rattle of timbrels told him they must be passing the wedding banquet for Goliath and his bride.

His hands were sweating, making it even more difficult to keep his grip on the wooly underbelly. Ahead, between the front legs of the ram, he glimpsed the sandals of Philistine soldiers and the tips of their spears.

They must not see me.

He struggled to hang on. The men marched past and their voices faded away. He used the moment to slide out from beneath the ram, pulling the sling from around its neck. Crouched low, he crept among the sheep and bulls, across the cobblestones to the sheltering shadows of a deserted alleyway.

The last of the sheep crowded past, driven toward the temple and their own death, David thought. He caught one final glimpse of the Israelite ram that had brought him here, condemned, he knew, to have its throat slit on the altar of Dagon along with all the others. He whispered his thanks.

Now, before I can save Jonathan, I must find him. But what if the Philistines look at my shabby tunic and my wary eyes and guess I am the enemy?

Chapter 22

Goliath ran the tips of his fingers along the blade as tenderly as if he was caressing a baby's cheek.

Standing before the other guests, Nara's father, Ezel, looked on, his brow beading with sweat as if he was toiling in the blistering heat of the forge. His hands, so steady with tongs holding red-hot iron, trembled now, awaiting Goliath's verdict.

Watching from her seat beside him at the banquet table, Nara did her best to hide her fear. Ezel was presenting her dowry, weapons hammered out on his anvil. If Goliath found the gifts unworthy, she knew her marriage would be doomed, her father disgraced forever.

His broad forehead furrowed in concentration, Goliath nestled the massive hilt of the sword into his powerful grasp. He weighed the blade expertly in his hand and grunted with satisfaction at its balance and heft. Then he plucked a bristle from his coarse beard and with a swipe of the blade, sliced it in half. But she saw that he had not finished. He picked up the spear and grazed the iron point against his callused thumb, marveling at how swiftly it drew blood.

"Ezel of Gath, I accept your dowry," his voice rumbled. "I accept your daughter as my bride. And as she will bring forth my sons from this day onward, so you will serve as my blacksmith, to bring forth my weapons of war."

Ezel fell to his knees, speechless with gratitude. As the guests joined in the chorus of praise, Nara fought back tears of relief. With Goliath's blessing, the warriors of Gath would pay handsomely for the iron weapons that her father forged. His future was assured.

A battle-seasoned commander raised his goblet. "Ezel fashions wonders of the blacksmith's art!"

Another broke in, "His weapons are worthy of the gods!"

Her father basked in their flattery, but Nara saw he was too embarrassed to look her in the eye. Only she knew the truth: When the day had arrived for Ezel to hammer out her dowry, he had been stricken with panic. Late that night, she had found him sprawled unconscious in the forge, an empty jug of honey wine clutched in his hand. With time running out, she had been forced to finish the dowry herself. For two days and two nights, she had toiled alone at the anvil, until her fingers were blistered and her weary muscles ached. When, finished at last, she had examined her glittering handiwork, she knew that she had hammered out weapons surpassing any that her father had made.

And yet, as the wedding guests congratulated Ezel on what they believed was his craftsmanship, she felt no resentment. Her father had spent a lifetime laboring tirelessly in the heat of the forge for the good of Gath. How could she begrudge him his moment of glory? She would never reveal their secret.

While the others at the banquet table rejoiced and downed goblets of honey wine, it surprised her that the high priest ignored this triumphant moment. At the far end of the table, Dalziel was locked in intense conversation with a visitor whom she recognized, the same priest in the blood-stained apron who had visited Dalziel earlier, seemingly stricken with panic. This time, the terror had lifted from his brow.

She watched as the visitor completed his report and Dalziel nodded approvingly. The high priest rose to his feet. In deference, the musicians lowered their timbrels and the guests fell silent. "The sacrifices augur well," he said. "They will continue into the night." His thin lips broke into a smile of triumph. "Goliath and his bride need wait no longer."

The announcement sparked excited whispers around the banquet table, quickly building into a rowdy chant: "To the bed!"

All the guests took up the cry, pounding their fists on the table, rattling the silver platters of roasted pig, knocking over goblets of honey wine. The shrill voices of old women and the gruff shouts of warriors were echoed by the hundreds of onlookers gazing down into the temple courtyard from the parapets.

"To the bed!"

While the guests shouted themselves hoarse, Goliath stood up from the banquet table. With a drunken grin, he effortlessly swept his cumbersome bride into his arms and raised her before the guests, to wild applause. Nara was dizzy with excitement, overjoyed to see her father cheering along with all the rest.

Only her beloved aunt wept. Nara knew that for Hada, this was a bittersweet moment. Last night, biting her cleft lip, she had confessed, "I am wise in many things, but I know nothing of the mysteries of the wedding night. They are pleasures the gods have denied me."

Those pleasures of the marriage bed would have been denied me too, were it not for this miracle. I have wed the one man on earth for whom I was intended, the one man who will have me as his wife.

Goliath lifted her higher into the air and spun her around before the guests. She burst out laughing, giddy with joy.

Fear is for the weak, and I am anything but weak. Whatever the mysteries of the marriage bed, I will survive them. For am I not the mightiest of women?

With three long strides, Goliath bore her away from the banquet table and across the torch-lit temple courtyard. Guards swung the gilded doors wide. In the street, the cheering throng showered them with rose petals.

"Goliath's bride will give sons to Gath," they chanted, "Goliath's blood will flow in their veins!"

To escape the adoring multitude, he veered swiftly down a back alleyway. It gladdened Nara's heart to finally be alone with him, cradled in the arms of one even stronger than she was. As he carried her deeper into the shadows, she felt as if they were setting forth on a warrior's mission. It was an all-important task that he could only accomplish with her as his partner.

She realized now that Goliath was bearing her up a steep staircase, and she trusted him to guide her wherever this night of mysteries would take them. Climbing ever higher, he was breathing heavily and she smelled his sweat. It did not repel her. She told herself that lying down with him on the marriage bed tonight would be like entering her father's forge for the first time. Others might fear Goliath's passion as they feared the roar of the furnace or the heat of glowing ingots struck on the anvil. But she was drawn to his raw power as she was drawn to the radiance of molten iron.

* * *

Through the barred window of his cell, Jonathan glimpsed the shadowy figure of Goliath carrying his bride up the staircase to the marriage bed. It was the moment he had dreaded. Until the end of time, he thought, the chronicles will tell how on this night, Goliath spawned a mighty dynasty to rule the earth.

Will the scribes even mention my death at dawn tomorrow? Before my blood dries on the chopping block, I will be forgotten, a minor prince, son of a mad king who was the first and last to rule over a doomed people.

He despised soul-searching and viewed it as a sign of weakness. But locked in this cell, he could not escape the truth: He had courage, yes, but without prudence to temper it, his courage had proved reckless—he was bold, but without wisdom, his boldness had spawned folly. He admitted to himself that he had not come here to kill Goliath out of a noble motive. It had been a vain and selfish act, compelled by his hunger for glory and his ambition to rule over his people.

And what has come of all my foolish plans? I have burnished Goliath's legend and brought a callow shepherd that much closer to sitting on my father's throne.

He caught sight of them once more at the top of the stairs.

Goliath bore his bride past a towering stone idol of Dagon. It seemed to Jonathan that the graven image knew an Israelite was watching them and that it smirked in triumph.

My people are taught that Dagon is a false god. But what if our Almighty is the delusion? Though I am Saul's favorite son, it seems I am better suited to serve the Philistine god of war than to obey the invisible God of my people. The Almighty expects too much of me—love, justice, compassion—while Dagon demands only that I quench his thirst for blood. If hatred is the force that rules the human heart, Dagon will prevail.

And what of my own invisible Almighty? The God of my father and of my people is the only God I have ever known. I cannot deny that He alone has shaped my sorry destiny. At dawn, when the Philistines lead me to the chopping block, I will curse Him with my last breath.

Outside the barred window, Jonathan saw that an eerie hush had settled over Gath. Now that the honored couple had vanished in the darkness, the banquet guests melted away. He watched as servants silently cleared the tables and snuffed out the last torches still flickering in the temple courtyard. He knew it was unlike the Philistines to cut short their revelry—they were renowned for lavish celebrations lasting days—but tonight was different. He guessed that the high priest had decreed this early end to the festivities so Goliath could consummate the marriage bond without distraction.

Beyond the empty courtyard, on the roof of the temple of Dagon, flames leapt skyward as priests set fire to the carcasses of freshly slaughtered animals, one after the other. It surprised him that the sacrifices continued after sunset—this was neither the Philistine nor the Israelite way—but he reasoned that with so much at stake tonight, the high priest was determined to please Dagon at all costs. How many poor dumb creatures must the Philistines slaughter to appease their bloodthirsty god? He saw how the acrid smoke that billowed from the charred offerings stained the night sky a deeper black.

He peered down through the bars into the murky alleyways of the city. The men and women of Gath had not returned to their dwellings, but had gathered together in small groups. Talking excitedly to each other, they gazed up at the highest parapet of the temple tower. Through the narrow cell window, Jonathan could not discover what it was that held them spellbound. Whatever they waited for so eagerly, he feared it would decide his fate and the fate of his people.

Chapter 23

They glared down at him fiercely with onyx eyes and teeth of sharpened ivory, graven images of Dagon that stood even taller than Goliath. To David, looking up at them, they were dead things, possessing no more magic than a handful of dust. Though the Philistines who jostled past him in the narrow alleyways wore fine linen robes and carried iron swords instead of the crude copper weapons of the Israelites, he did not envy them.

The Philistines live in the shadow of their idols and are ruled by their fear of their gods.

Saul had announced to his people that Jonathan was being held in the North Citadel of Gath, but where was it? While he tried to figure out which way to go, he blended into the throng at the market square, where he thought he was less likely to be noticed. Though it was after nightfall, the stalls displayed delicacies for the feast day tomorrow celebrating Goliath's marriage. David saw that the luxuries spread out before him in the torchlight were too costly for his own impoverished people: clay jars of amber honey and the purest olive oil; almonds, dates, and figs; pungent heaps of spices and more varieties of melon than he had ever seen.

Walking among the Philistines, he realized they showed little interest in the goods on display in the stalls. They were not gossiping or bartering as they did in the Israelites' market in Gibeah. Instead, all eyes gazed upward in the same direction. Whether wealthy merchants or their matronly wives, delicate maidens or brash men-at-arms, all of them stared up at the gilded temple tower.

There, on the highest parapet, an aged priest kept a solitary vigil. David noticed that he clutched a crimson banner rolled up as tightly as one of the Israelites' holy scrolls. The Philistines watched the priest and waited, whispering excitedly to each other.

He understood now. When word came that Goliath's marriage had been consummated, the priest would unfurl the banner. All of Gath would erupt in rejoicing at this triumph for the Philistine people.

Beyond the ornate temple tower, an ominous structure loomed. David guessed this must be the North Citadel, a place that his brothers had spoken of in whispers. Unlike the glittering shrines of Dagon that were elaborately ornamented with gold, this leaden granite stronghold was as severe as a blade of Philistine iron. It was said that many Israelites had been imprisoned within these walls. None had come out alive.

If Jonathan is being held captive in the North Citadel, where in the tower are they keeping him?

He saw that two heavyset sentries blocked the brassbound door, swords unsheathed, eyes scanning the excited crowd that awaited the priest's announcement. To avoid them, he made his way out of the throng, circling around to the far side of the granite citadel.

The back of the tower was deserted and adjoined the temple courtyard. David realized that this had been the site of the wedding feast. The immense table had been cleared and the guests had departed, but the cloying odor of spilled honey wine lingered. Fate is cruel, he thought. This was the celebration of the marriage that Jonathan would have given his life to prevent.

David knew that the priests of Dagon were notorious for inflicting pain on the mind as well as the body. What better way to torture Jonathan than to force him to witness the marriage feast?

He gazed up at the sheer face of the North Citadel. There were three barred windows on the top floor, and one window that was not barred on the floor below. He concluded that Jonathan was most likely being held in one of the cells with the barred windows. He would have to enter through the open lower window.

"Climbing is a skill for cowards," his brothers had scoffed when they saw his talent for it. "Go climb a tree and escape the Philistines!" And yet, it was a skill that had served David well. As a shepherd, he had clambered up towering oaks on the lookout for marauding packs of wolves, and scaled sheer cliffs to recover strays.

He pulled off his sandals and knotted them to his belt. It would be easier with bare feet. He pressed his chest against the cold wall of the citadel. One foothold, one handhold at a time, he pulled himself up, feeling for a nub of stone that jutted out, a hidden crevice where he could wedge his fingers. For now, he was out of sight of the crowd, but how soon would he be discovered?

A loose rock gave way under his foot and plummeted downward, forcing him to lunge for a toehold. Slowly, methodically, he edged his way upward. The darkened window that was not barred seemed almost within his reach. A granite cornice jutted out from beneath the window. He reached up for it, but the ledge was too far away to grasp.

And yet, there might be a way. He slipped the sling from his belt and looped it over the end of the cornice above him. He did not know whether, stretched taut, the goat leather would be strong enough to support his weight. He tested it and the sling held firm. Clutching the leather strip, his shoulders straining, he struggled to pull himself up.

Something stabbed his hand: a raven, black as the night sky, its beak sharp as a dagger.

David raised his arm to shield his face. The bird came at him again, its beating wings a blur. Another thrust from its beak drew blood on David's neck. He flinched and lost his grip, off-balance, about to fall. Flailing out, he seized hold of the cornice with one hand. With the other, he swatted at the raven swooping down on him. Squawking, his attacker vanished into the night.

He pulled himself onto the narrow ledge. Balancing precariously, he saw that the raven had been gorging on pieces of roasted pig scattered across the granite. How had scraps of this vile animal ended up here? he wondered. He doubted the Philistine priests would place an offering in so unlikely a place.

He glanced up at the barred window on the floor above him. The scraps could have been dropped down from there. Had a prisoner thrown them out of his cell window in disgust? If so, David reasoned that it had to be one of his people, an Israelite who found the flesh of pigs repugnant. It would be like Jonathan to commit such an impulsive act.

Careful not to slip on the greasy ledge, he raised himself onto one knee and strained to peer through the citadel window. No guards were visible in the shadows. Struggling not to lose his balance, he pulled himself up—first one foot, then the other—and climbed through the opening into the tower.

He dropped down onto the cold granite floor. He realized that he stood in a darkened corridor with a flight of stairs at the far end of it. Mindful that a guard could appear at any moment, he untied his sandals from his belt, slipped them back on, and hurried through the shadows. Silently, he climbed the narrow stone steps. At the next landing, he hung back in the stairwell. This was the floor with the barred windows and, he hoped, the cell where Jonathan was being held prisoner.

Ahead stretched a hallway lined with bolted oak doors. Two Philistines with spears stood before the one farthest from him. Because none of the other doors were guarded, he guessed Jonathan was held inside this one. As long as the men were stationed before it, there was no hope of rescuing him.

The two sentries were talking excitedly. David guessed they were caught up in the suspense that gripped the city, waiting for the announcement that Goliath's marriage had been consummated. He knew that the moment the priest unfurled his crimson banner, Gath would erupt in rejoicing. For that tumultuous instant, all else would be forgotten.

The Almighty takes with one hand and gives with the other. The announcement that Goliath's marriage has been consummated will mean disaster for my people. But the chaos of the Philistines' wild rejoicing will be my only chance to save Jonathan's life.

Chapter 24

The trumpet sounded a piercing blast, sharp as a javelin. Crouched in the shadows near Jonathan's cell, David heard the stab of sound and knew the moment had come.

The Philistines proclaim that Goliath's seed has been planted, establishing his dynasty. Does the trumpet announce the end of my world?

Shouts of celebration erupted from the alleyways below. The two sentries left their post in front of the cell door and ran down the hall to a parapet, to see for themselves. The joy on their faces told David that the crimson banner had been unfurled.

In their excitement, the guards did not notice David as he dashed down the hall to the cell door. He grabbed the heavy iron bolt with both hands. At first, it resisted, but he wrenched it open. The door swung wide.

Jonathan was standing by the window, clutching the iron bars, his face lit by the flare of torches from the city below. He looks stricken, David thought, because he knows why the Philistines are cheering.

"Come with me!" David said.

Jonathan turned and saw him standing in the doorway. The blood drained from his face as swiftly as if he had been skewered by a Philistine spear.

"You?"

David ran over and grabbed his arm, but Jonathan stood rooted to the spot. The son of Saul would rather die in his cell than accept that I came to rescue him, David thought.

"We must go now!"

Jonathan would not move. A cry from the guards jolted him back to his senses. David saw his eyes snap back into focus. Jonathan squared his shoulders and lifted his head, the son of a king once more. Taking the lead, he ran out the door and down the hallway, with David close behind.

They scrambled down the stairway. From above, they heard a guard shout orders, summoning more men. When they reached the next landing, David glimpsed the look on Jonathan's face: His eyes blazed with excitement at the prospect of fighting his way out. Footsteps clattered down the steps after them, closing the distance.

They reached the bottom of the stairs and pushed open the citadel door. A flood of revelers choked the square before them. Some adorned idols of Dagon with garlands of thanksgiving. Others gulped wine from silver goblets or downed barley beer from earthen jugs. All lifted their voices in jubilation.

The guards burst out of the door to the North Citadel that opened onto the teeming square. Jonathan and David were swept along with the multitude before their pursuers could follow.

Suddenly, the frantic pounding of a drum cut through the din. "They see us!" David pointed out a detachment of guards clambering down ladders from the ramparts. The men rapidly fanned out through the crowd.

"Take this!" Jonathan snatched a torch from a wall sconce and handed it to David, then grabbed one for himself. "We must reach the gates of the city. When they send out messengers with the joyful tidings, we will escape with them."

"The gates are heavily guarded."

"By the time we reach them, all the sentries will be drunk. We will escape!'

David was not convinced. He saw that to reach the front gates of Gath, they would have to fight their way forward against the surging tide of the throng. When they tried to push ahead, they were quickly shoved aside, driven back into a blind alley.

Struggling to catch his breath, David watched as guards took up positions blocking each passageway, cutting off every path of escape to the city gates. He pointed in the opposite direction, toward a row of immense marble columns. "That way!"

Jonathan shook his head in disbelief: "You would have us take refuge in the *Temple of Dagon*?"

"Sometimes, to escape a wolf, one must hide in its lair."

"But the Philistine god dwells there!" Jonathan pointed to the roof of the temple, where robed priests kindled burnt offerings on an altar, black smoke billowing into the sky. "In his temple, Dagon is all-powerful—"

"No," David broke in. "The Almighty is Ruler of all places and all things. The Philistines cannot change that with a hundred graven images or the blood of a thousand bulls!"

"I will not go there."

David decided there was only one way to coax him to take refuge inside the temple. "How can so brave a man as the son of Saul fear lifeless idols of stone?"

"I do not fear them!" David saw that his ploy had worked. Now that Jonathan's courage was questioned, he had to prove himself: "I will go with you."

Rounding the corner, a guard spotted them and let out a shout. With their pursuers much closer now, they broke into a headlong dash down the alleyway toward the temple. This time, it was David who led the way.

Jonathan fears the hollow idols of Dagon inside these walls. I fear the daggers of the priests.

Chapter 25

They threaded their way between the immense columns that dominated the murky temple portico. It took a moment for David's eyes to adjust to the amber glow of torchlight within. He saw that Jonathan was awestruck by the ornately inlaid ceiling and mosaic floor, the gilded scrollwork cascading down the marble walls.

"There is more gold before me now than in all of my father's kingdom," he whispered.

"I see something more precious than gold." David pointed to a row of graven images of fierce sentinel gods, some with the sharp claws of leopards, others with the talons of eagles or the fangs of wolves. Each as tall as a man, they stood vigil in the dark temple antechamber. Jonathan saw now what had caught David's attention: the Philistines had bestowed on these idols the same iron weapons that they carried into battle.

Jonathan snatched a sword and spear for himself. Now that he was armed, it seemed to David that the son of Saul regained the proud bearing of a warrior. David pried a sword from the claws of an idol chiseled in the likeness of a winged lion. He held the weapon awkwardly. He had never been trained to use one.

"Come!" Jonathan whispered.

David glanced back through the colonnade at the temple entrance and saw the telltale gleam of swords and shields. "Soldiers are waiting to ambush us outside. They do not dare defy the priests and enter the temple. But the moment we leave here . . ."

Jonathan pointed out three priests entering the temple through the colonnade. He readied his sword, but David grabbed his arm. "They have not seen us yet." He beckoned for Jonathan to follow him away from them, beyond the temple deities, deeper into the temple.

They entered the cavernous inner chamber. Through a thick haze of frankincense, a towering idol of Dagon covered in beaten gold gazed down on them, its right arm raising a sword of fire toward the lofty ceiling. At Dagon's feet stood a high altar of chiseled porphyry, the stone veined the bright crimson of freshly spilled blood.

At the altar, five priests were consumed with their task of slitting the throats of bulls and rams. David heard an unseen acolyte pounding a great drum, the throbbing as persistent as a heartbeat, to set the pace of the killing. The priests labored in such a frenzy that David wondered whether they had absorbed the life force of each creature they slaughtered. Their arms drenched in blood, their eyes wild, the men looked to him like demons.

The bellowing of bulls in their death throes echoed off the lofty ceiling. David saw how after each animal was sacrificed, one acolyte flayed off its hide, while another chopped off its hooves and horns, as if ensuring that nothing corrupted by the outside world remained. The carcass was then dragged to the far end of the dais and placed on a platform.

Jonathan pointed to the open skylight above the platform. Through it, priests on the roof lowered ropes with barbed hooks. Acolytes below attached each flayed carcass to be hoisted up and placed on the pyre atop the temple, where it was burned as an offering. Once the priests unloaded the flayed bull onto the roof, they lowered the thick rope with its iron hooks once more, to await the next carcass for the pyre. The acolytes below walked back across the dais to the altar to obtain one.

Jonathan pointed at the rope dangling from the skylight. David understood. If they could pull themselves up from the platform to the temple roof, from there they could make their way across the rooftops of Gath to the outer gates. Then, if the Almighty smiled on them . . .

With the acolytes returning to the altar at the far end of the dais, their backs to them, David and Jonathan dashed toward the platform. Jonathan grabbed the rope that dangled above it and started to pull himself up, hand over hand. David admired his strength—Jonathan climbed so rapidly, he was soon within reach of the open skylight.

Suddenly, a priest's face appeared overhead, glaring down at him. Clutching the rope with one hand, Jonathan strained with the other to grasp the rim of the skylight above him. But the priest sawed through the rope with his dagger. It snapped, curling up like a dead snake as it fell. Jonathan clattered down hard onto the marble temple floor. David ran over to him and offered his hand. Jonathan refused it, doggedly scrambling back to his feet.

Through the skylight, javelins rained down on them, a blur of iron glancing off the marble, striking sparks. The clamor roused the priests and their acolytes at the main altar on the far end of the dais. David saw the men start toward them, clutching their bloody daggers.

Jonathan snatched his sword from the floor to hold them off. The Israelite priests were men of peace, David thought, but for the Philistine priests, shedding blood at the altar of Dagon heightened their ferocity. Untrained in combat, he felt powerless to help Jonathan resist them.

Samuel's words flashed through his mind, taunting him: "You must learn to survive on a feast of locusts." His eyes probed the shadows of the cavernous temple around him, searching in vain for a way out. All paths of escape were blocked.

I must find deliverance in the place where I least expect it.

He glanced down at the floor and noticed a small, seemingly unimportant detail: From the base of the sacrificial altar, copious amounts of blood and entrails from the offerings flowed along a sloping marble channel that ran the length of the temple dais. Without this channel, David realized, the priests would be working knee-deep in gore.

He did not know where this vile stream flowed, but realized it must lead out of the temple chamber. Eying the channel, he caught sight of the opening in the floor where the bloody viscera drained from the altar. The hole was little wider than a man's shoulders, but was it wide enough?

The wine-red current might sweep them away to their deaths—or carry them to safety—but he saw they had no other choice. Jonathan was steadily losing ground, backing away from the onslaught of the priests and their acolytes. He could not hold them off much longer.

"Look!" David pointed at the drain in the floor. Jonathan looked down at it and shook his head: Impossible. With the Philistines closing in, there was no time to persuade him. David grabbed Jonathan, snatched the sword from his hand, and pushed him, feet first, into the hole. Jonathan vanished from sight.

David held his breath, shut his eyes, and leaped in after him. The frothing crimson brew engulfed him, as warm as if he was swimming in his own blood. The flow swept him down the sluice in a swirling broth of entrails, the conduit winding deep beneath the temple floor. The channel suddenly shifted direction, hurling him from side to side, buffeting him against its walls.

Starved for air, he felt as if his lungs would burst. His mind grew numb, clinging to the edge of consciousness. He struggled to keep his lips pressed tightly together. If he opened them, he knew he would drown in the blood of the offerings.

Chapter 26

The flow of blood swept David ever deeper through the channel. In a final spasm, the surge spewed him out of the sluice and hurled him down onto his back. Gasping for breath, he wiped his eyes and looked around him. He smelled the night air and knew he was outdoors, but in the blackness, it was difficult to know more.

At first, he thought that he had been flung into a muddy trench. As his eyes grew accustomed to the dark, he discovered that the pit where he lay was outside the walls of Gath. When his mind cleared, he realized that he had been dumped among heaps of entrails. His stomach churned and he fought back a wave of nausea. He understood now: He lay in a charnel pit.

A vivid memory flashed through his mind: the moment, only days before, when his arms had cradled a newborn lamb still sodden with blood, its heart beating frantically in its joy to be alive. He had learned there was a holiness to the instant when a creature drew its first breath. Tending his flock, he had been fortunate to witness it again and again. Soaked in blood, he felt that holiness now, the miracle of his own heart pounding, each breath a blessing.

Giddy, he stood up unsteadily, the viscera slippery underfoot, and searched around him in the darkness for Jonathan. In the overflowing pit, all the blood and entrails seemed intermingled, death and life inextricably fused. He waded, sickened, through the foul-smelling mire, his mind numb, his task seemingly impossible.

At last, exhausted, he spotted an arm protruding from the heaps of viscera. Unsteadily, he made his way closer. Jonathan's motionless body looked like one more blood-spattered mass of discarded flesh. David struggled to pull him out and lay him down gently at the sodden edge of the charnel pit.

Jonathan's eyes were shut. Was he dead or alive? David knelt down and pressed his head against his chest, but he could not find a heartbeat.

I forced Jonathan to attempt this escape. If he dies now, it will be on me, not the Philistines.

Instinctively, he fell back on his shepherd's skills learned while bringing lambs into the world. Placing his mouth over Jonathan's nose, he sucked out the fluid that clogged it and spat it out. Then he pressed his mouth against Jonathan's, laboring to fill Jonathan's lungs with his own breath.

Once more, he listened, his head pressed against Jonathan's chest. He detected a heartbeat, faint at first, growing stronger. Jonathan's eyelids fluttered. He coughed, gagged, struggling for breath. David sat him upright and pounded him on the back until he vomited.

Jonathan took in deep gulps of air until, bit by bit, the pace of his breathing settled into a regular rhythm. David had saved the lives of sheep in his flock, but never before had he saved a human life. Watching Jonathan come back from the brink after he had seemed lost, filled David with wonder, as if he was bringing a newborn into the world.

Jonathan wiped the viscera from his face. "Am I in this world or the next?" He groaned, dazed to find himself drenched in blood. He vomited again.

David watched as he gradually came to his senses. "We are outside the walls of Gath." He pointed up at the towering ramparts, stark against the night sky, where sentries made their rounds, holding torches. "We must go, before they catch sight of us.

Jonathan avoided eye contact with him, seemingly distant and aloof. Even now, David saw that the son of Saul could not bring himself to express his gratitude, as if to do so would be to admit that his mission had failed. And yet, when David offered his hand, Jonathan grasped it firmly and pulled himself to his feet.

Wearily, they limped off together into the sheltering darkness. David realized that for the first time, the king's son did not seem ashamed to lean on a shepherd for support.

* * *

Their trek took them deep into the night. The two of us must look like doddering old fools shuffling in the dust, David thought, each feeling his way, each helping the other to take his next step. Finally, they heard the babble of water flowing over pebbles. They followed the sound and stumbled upon a stream coursing through a narrow gully, past a grove of acacias. Tending his flock, David had learned that rivulets like this arose when the flinty earth could not absorb the downpour from a recent cloudburst.

The sky flushed with the first glow of dawn. In the half-light, David realized they could not return to Gibeah looking as they did now, like bloody corpses. First, they rinsed out their mouths and scrubbed their faces. Then they removed their tunics and soaked them in the stream. David knelt down to help Jonathan wash the blood from his body. The son of Saul, in turn, helped to wash David.

The cold water revived them, but it stung their wounds. Jonathan examined the raw cuts and bruises on his arms and legs from their violent passage out of the temple. "These are hardly the wounds of heroes."

"That is true." David's eyes met his. "But shared wounds heal into friendships."

Jonathan nodded in agreement. It seemed to David that here, in their nakedness, the barriers between them had fallen. Under a brightening sky, they wrung out their moist tunics and pulled them back on. David knew that after the sun rose, the garments would dry on their bodies.

He felt Jonathan studying him closely. It seemed he had an

urgent question, but that he held back, fearing it would be perceived as a sign of weakness. Finally, he said, "No man ever risked his life for me as you have done. Why did you? I am your rival for the throne, your enemy. You had everything to gain from my death and nothing to gain from my safe return."

David struggled to understand his own motives. Had he come to rescue Jonathan for noble reasons, or out of raw ambition to prove himself deserving of the throne? Had he done it to prove himself worthy of Michal? Or had he journeyed to the Philistine city to find out whether, even there, the Almighty was with him?

Then he understood. "I had to rescue you. I felt that somehow by freeing you, I could free myself . . . to become the one I must be."

Jonathan shook his head in frustration, unable to grasp his words. David saw that such soul-searching was alien to him. The son of Saul shrugged, as if, in the end, David's motives were of little importance.

"What matters is, with a brave heart, you helped me to escape." Jonathan spoke with an admiration that David had not seen him show before. "You are untrained in the skills of battle, and yet you have a strength I lack. What a warrior could not do, a shepherd has done." He added warmly, "My friend."

David rejoiced in the bond that their trials had forged between them. He sensed that in the future, their lives would be intertwined as their lives today had been. For that, he was grateful. He pointed out a granite crag in the distance that resembled the head of a ram. "That marks the boundary of the Philistines' domain. Soon we will be back on friendly ground."

Side by side, in their stained tunics, they set out together on the path toward Gibeah. It was a demanding uphill journey over the barren no man's land stretching between the Philistine and Israelite kingdoms. And yet, David felt that the warmth of the rising sun eased their way. Each helped the other along the rugged, rock-strewn trail. They were both so weak, David knew that neither could have made it alone.

We have survived, but survival is not victory. Goliath lives. So long as he draws breath, our people will never escape from beneath his shadow. But I face a more immediate threat. What will happen to me, the one Samuel anointed for the throne, when the king is reunited with his beloved son and heir?

The outcome will be as dangerously unpredictable as Saul himself.

Chapter 27

"No Israelite taken prisoner by the Philistines of Gath has ever returned. Until today."

In the throng below, Michal watched her father address his people from the palace balcony. The Israelites had flocked to Gibeah to witness proof of the miracle with their own eyes, and in the heat of the day, they packed the courtyard to overflowing. To escape being recognized as the king's daughter, she had changed into the plain blue cloak of one of her handmaidens. It was better this way, she thought, better to bear witness from among the people. It allowed her to see her brother and Saul as the Israelites saw them, for these were the men who must be inspired to follow them into battle.

The sight of her father filled her with pride. Saul seemed transformed, standing straight and tall with his shoulders back, his chin proudly raised as befitted the ruler of the Israelites. From the faith she saw shining in his eyes, he no longer believed the Almighty had abandoned him. From the joy on the faces of the people, her father had won a victory at last.

Her mother, Ahinoam, stood beside Saul on the balcony to greet the cheering multitude. No doubt, she had forced her husband to allow her to share in this glorious moment, Michal thought. Her mother had refused to let her join them. Michal despised Ahinoam's jealousy, her envy of Jonathan's love for his sister, her determination to hoard her son's triumph to herself.

The door on the balcony flew open. Jonathan stepped out between his mother and father to face the throng below. In that moment, priests blew rams' horns from the ramparts in thanksgiving, and maidens scattered a flurry of rose petals into the wind. Mothers held up their infant sons on their shoulders so they could see the son of Saul for themselves. With one voice, the people roared their admiration, proclaiming their loyalty.

Michal saw that her brother had changed into the glittering trappings of a warrior prince: sword and spear, shield, helmet, and breastplate, befitting the heir to his father's kingdom. The Israelites beheld Jonathan with wonder, as if he had risen from the dead. With his arrogant manner and fiery temper, she knew he had never been beloved by the people. But today, his miraculous escape from Gath had made him more than human in their eyes.

Jonathan raised his hand and all fell silent. "Only a few days ago, my father stood here to plead for your help to rescue me from the Philistines. As ransom, the cowards among you were willing to give away the Ark of the Covenant, our priceless gift from the Almighty."

Michal realized that Jonathan's barbed words were aimed at Shodok, the commander she knew coveted Saul's throne. The king's rival stood with his men-at-arms on the edge of the crowd, his face ashen, stunned that the son of Saul stood alive before them.

"My father refused to surrender the Holy Ark to the Philistines," Jonathan continued. "Now the Almighty has rewarded him for it!"

The Israelites pounded their spears on the ground to hail Saul as their leader, their faith in him restored. Now that his son had miraculously returned, she saw that Saul had tightened his grip on power. In defeat, Shodok had no choice but to swallow his pride and cheer louder than all the others.

Jonathan unsheathed a sword that Michal guessed Saul had given to him only moments before. "With this copper blade, I alone defeated Philistines armed with swords of iron. For all his power, even Goliath could not hold me prisoner."

Michal was stunned by his words. She knew her brother was lying. Soon after his return, he had confided to her how David had risked his life to rescue him. Jonathan had seemed humbled by his admiration for the shepherd from Bethlehem, proud of his friendship with one more worthy than himself. It only made his lies now all the more hateful in her eyes.

"The Philistines now fear me as greatly as we once feared Goliath," Jonathan said, to the crowd's wild applause. Michal watched him bow his head with feigned humility, even as he basked in their cheers. No doubt, the people would have been happy if, at this very moment, Saul abdicated in favor of his son. But she knew that her father would never give up the throne, not so long as he drew breath.

Jonathan lowered his arms to hush the crowd. "I must admit to you that I was *not* alone when I fought my way out of the Philistine city. I did not free myself single-handedly from Gath. I had help . . ."

At last, Michal thought, the people will know the truth. He will praise David for his courage and affirm their friendship.

Jonathan's voice swelled with emotion: "I speak of the One who made this miracle possible. I was not alone, because the Almighty was with me. He brought my deliverance!" The people fell silent, moved by his piety, but it rang false to her. She doubted Jonathan worshipped anything but himself.

What of David, who risked his life to set you free? You told me you forged a bond with him that would last forever. It has not survived a single day in Gibeah!

On the balcony, Saul stepped forward, basking in his son's glory. He opened his fist to reveal a small golden object that blazed in the sunlight. "This is my son's signet ring. The Philistines sent it to me as proof they held him hostage."

He slipped the ring onto Jonathan's finger, raising his hand for all to see. "Now it is proof that my son will follow me as king!"

The crowd cheered, but Michal caught sight of one who remained silent. David, who had watched impassively from the edge of the crowd, now turned abruptly to leave. It seemed to her that he could not bear to see how Jonathan had betrayed him.

Chapter 28

Standing outside the walls of Gibeah, David heard the roar of the people like the crashing waves of a distant sea. He felt a gnawing awareness that by saving Jonathan, he had made it all the more difficult to fulfill the promise of his anointing, all the more difficult to fulfill his destiny.

The shouts of rejoicing faded away. The celebration of Jonathan's return had ended, but David did not feel ready to return to Gibeah. From force of habit, he resorted to the ritual that he performed when he was alone and afflicted with doubt. He pulled out the leather sling tied to his belt. He reached down into the dust and selected a smooth, round stone the size of a falcon's egg. He placed the stone into the pouch and whirled the sling around his head. The leather strips whooshed through the air with the roar of flames in a bonfire.

With a snap of his wrist, the stone took flight.

As always, his target was the sun. In its distant, blinding radiance, it was an impossible goal—unattainable, and yet, he always aimed for it, in the belief that the simple act would bring him a few grains of wisdom. Today, though he had hurled the stone with all his strength, he had no hope that it would soar into the heavens. As if the arc of its flight was bent by some unknown force, it plunged earthward.

The ritual of throwing the stone is an empty one. It has brought me nothing.

As was his habit, he walked toward the spot where the stone had landed, this time in the shadow of a crumbling mud-brick ruin. He knew that its two decrepit walls were the last vestige of a forgotten pagan shrine. The stone lay in the dust beside a long-abandoned well. He smelled the stench of rotting flesh that rose from its depths.

Like every shepherd, he had learned to avoid this place. Long ago, Philistine raiders had thrown the bodies of Israelite dead into it. The corpses had festered and decayed there, corrupting it forever. He knelt down to pick up the stone and thought, this befouled well stands as a testament to Philistine cruelty.

"David!"

He looked up, surprised to see Michal standing before him.

"I came to thank you for all you did for my brother."

In her eagerness to speak to him, she stepped closer than David thought she had intended. For an instant, perhaps only by accident, her fingers brushed against his. He knew it was not proper for an unmarried woman—much less the daughter of a king—to touch a man unless they were betrothed.

He politely pulled his hand away. "You need not thank me."

"On Jonathan's behalf, I ask your forgiveness."

"There is nothing to forgive."

Her eyes flashed with anger. "Today, my brother lied to our people. He claimed all the glory for his escape. But when he returned yesterday from the Philistine city, he told me the truth. He told me that you saved his life."

"We saved each other." David shrugged, making light of it. "Together, we forged a friendship."

"And now he betrays you!"

"I did not betray him."

David turned and saw Jonathan. He was breathless, as if he had rushed here from Gibeah. "I wanted to praise David for rescuing me," he said to Michal, "but he made me promise not to. I lied because he told me to lie." He embraced David like a brother.

She stared at them in amazement. "But why?"

"To protect me," David said. "If the people sang my praises for rescuing Jonathan, Saul would have put me to death."

Michal knelt before Jonathan. "I misjudged you, my beloved brother. I was wrong to suspect your motives."

"No, you were right to suspect them," he said with a wry

smile. Taking her by both hands, he raised her up to stand beside him. "All too often, you have been right. You know me better than I know myself."

He turned to David and removed the gold signet ring. "When I stood before the people today and Saul slipped this ring inscribed with the Lion of Judah on my finger, I realized you are the one who must wear it. It belongs to the next ruler of our people."

"I know it was always your dream to follow your father as king," David said, treading lightly.

"A false dream. I know that now." He handed the ring to David. "I know the throne is meant for you."

David pressed the ring back into Jonathan's hand. "Keep this. It was a gift from a father to his son. I have no use for gold. What does not lift me up, weighs me down."

"It is better this way," Michal said. "You must do nothing to make Saul suspect . . ."

Jonathan slipped the signet ring back onto his finger. "Then you will join me in supporting David?"

"Yes," she said without hesitation, and turned to David. "But it is not enough that my brother and I believe it is for you to be king. Saul will never accept it."

"If I have the support of the people, Saul will be powerless to stop me," David said. "And there is only one way to win that support." He looked at them with affection. "It was meant that the two people closest to my heart should be brought here for this moment. Because I know now what I must do." Michal and Jonathan waited in uneasy silence for what he would say next.

"I must stand alone before Goliath. And I must kill him."

David realized that, hearing this, his brothers would have burst out laughing. His father would have beaten him for his folly. Only his mother, Nitzevet, would have understood. But he suspected that she would have wept, certain that her youngest, her favorite, was lost.

Jonathan broke the stunned silence. "To kill Goliath . . ." He stopped himself, stifling his misgivings. David saw his friend was doing his best to imagine that such a feat might be possible.

Michal could hold back no longer: "They say Goliath cannot be put to death by a mortal man. They say he is part god."

"He is as mortal as any man," David replied calmly.

"You say this, but you have never seen him," Jonathan objected. "I have."

"I will see Goliath soon enough," David said.

PART II

Chapter 29

His long fingers crept across her belly, as loathsome to her as the legs of a spider. She did not flinch. Nara knew that everything depended on the high priest's verdict. Two times the moon had waxed and waned since her marriage night. Still her blood of the moon had not flowed.

"This may be what we have prayed for," her aunt Hada had said, lowering her eyes to hide her excitement. "We must summon him."

Now, while I lie on my marriage bed, he examines me, this man who is not my husband, lifting my linen shift as only my husband should, placing his hands in forbidden places where only my husband should be allowed to place them.

She feared what his decision would be. He could have requested a midwife, but Dalziel had told her that he did not trust a woman for so momentous a judgment. Only he could determine the truth and proclaim it to the world. He ran the palms of his hands along her belly, as if to foretell the destiny of the Philistine people.

Goliath stood apart, watching intently from the shadows of the doorway. Nara noticed how he clenched and unclenched his fists in a futile gesture, as though realizing that despite his strength, he was helpless now before female forces beyond his control.

At her side, Hada looked on anxiously. Nara remembered how, after her marriage, she had embraced her aunt and wept. "How can I be a good wife to Goliath? I know nothing of the womanly arts of cooking or weaving at the loom. I was raised to help my father with the man's work of the forge. I would rather pull molten iron from a raging furnace than slide a barley loaf into a bread oven."

Hada had laughed and squeezed her hand. "What does it

matter how artfully you bake bread or roast a suckling pig? So long as you bear sons for Goliath, your duty as his wife will be fulfilled. To conceive a son is a feat not even Dagon or his priests can equal. It is an act of magic only a woman's body can achieve."

Her nights with Goliath had held no magic, Nara thought. Every one of them had been a painful ordeal. In the marriage bed, he did what must be done, brutally, coldly, with neither tenderness nor passion. It was as if he was intent on performing his duty to the god Dagon and the high priest, nothing more.

But is my body, so different from that of other women, capable of a woman's sorcery? Or, by its sheer size, its strength, is it too much like a man's body to ever be fruitful as a woman is fruitful?

She saw that Hada was worried, biting her cleft lip. Nara felt the intrusion of the high priest's touch on her belly and dreaded what he would discover. Impatient for the verdict, Goliath tensed the muscles in his arm, as if ready to deliver a blow.

How terrible will his anger be if I disappoint him?

At last, the high priest turned decisively to Goliath. "She is with child."

The judgment was not yet cause for rejoicing. Nara knew that an even more important pronouncement was yet to come. Dalziel leaned over her and, once again, placed his right hand on her belly. His fingers spread wide, pressing down harder than before, so that it was all she could do to not cry out in pain.

Abruptly, Dalziel withdrew his fingers. She waited for the second half of his ruling, the one on which everything depended. The high priest opened his mouth to speak, but before he could say a word, he bent over and buried his head in his hands, overcome with emotion. He fell down on his knees before her, his eyes brimming with tears.

"You carry a son. He will be a great warrior, the first of many you will give to our people."

Hada wept with happiness. Goliath's mouth widened into a

grin and he clasped Nara in his arms. She remembered how, after the wedding feast, he had seized her lustily, then carried her off to the marriage bed. But in this triumphant moment, he embraced her with surprising gentleness, as if he knew that he must care for her and defend her above all else. She felt his heart beating against hers, not with a warrior's rage, but with a father's joy.

Blinded by tears, she heard Dalziel summon an acolyte into the room. "Send messengers to all the other Philistine cities: Gaza, Ashkelon, Ashdod, and Ekron. Tell them that the wife of Goliath is with child. Tell them she will bear a son. And send a messenger to the Israelites. Let them know our cause for celebration, and that even as we rejoice, they will be utterly destroyed."

* * *

Nara was amazed at how swiftly the announcement raced across the Philistine city. Dalziel commanded that Goliath carry her through Gath to celebrate their triumph, and when he bore her in his arms down the alleyways, the Philistines were waiting, crowding around her to shower her with praise. As they passed her father's forge, Ezel tearfully hugged her. His whispered blessing was drowned out by the cries of the multitude:

"Nara, bride of Goliath, may you bear a hundred sons!"

"May all of them be as strong as Goliath!"

Swept along in his arms, she recognized many of the faces in the throng. The same people who now sang her praises had jeered at her when she was growing up as an awkward outcast. A worshipful flock of women pursued her, even more of them than on her wedding day. And as she basked in their adoration, she felt her overwhelming new power.

At last, after the triumphal walk around the entire city, Goliath gently set Nara down at the threshold to their dwelling.

Offerings from the people were already piled up there: a wool shawl embroidered with golden threads; a jug of fresh goat's milk; a clay vessel of date honey; a vial of scented oil for the lamp beside her marriage bed.

Hada threw open the front door and stepped out to embrace her. "Nara, you are the mightiest woman in Gath, and the most loved!"

* * *

That night, and the nights that followed, behind the closed doors of their bedchamber, Nara discovered that Goliath treated her differently. When he lay down with her now, it was as if he feared damaging the delicate treasure she carried in her womb. He touched her with a restraint that, she hoped, might be his first clumsy attempt at tenderness.

It proves his new respect for me. Once our son is born, that respect will blossom into love.

Chapter 30

They set to work, concealed behind the crumbling walls of the pagan shrine. Here, David was confident that even the most sharp-eyed sentinel on the ramparts of Gibeah in the distance, could not see them. On his first day of training, he told Jonathan, "To face Goliath, to become king, I must fight as a king fights. And so you must teach me to kill with the weapons of a king."

Jonathan lifted his spear. "I have been tested in battle. I will teach you all I know."

He handed David a spear, then picked up a sheep skull from the dust and jogged over to a withered acacia tree, forty paces away. He wedged the skull between two dead branches.

"That is Goliath. Kill him."

David weighed the heavy weapon awkwardly in his hand and squinted at his target. The sun-bleached skull shimmered against the black branches. He pulled the unwieldy cedar shaft back and hurled it with all his strength.

The spear fell short, its copper tip thudding harmlessly into the dust.

Jonathan raised his own spear, balanced it deftly in his right hand and let it fly. His point skewered the skull, shattering it. For fear of discouraging David, he said, "You will learn how to use the spear soon enough." Jonathan handed him a sword. "This copper blade is no match for Philistine iron, but it is all we have."

"I will learn to make the most of it." Clutching the hilt of the weapon awkwardly, David thrust out the blade as far as he could stretch his arm. "Goliath's reach is far greater than mine."

"Yes, but if you move in quickly and come in closer than the Philistine expects"—Jonathan demonstrated with a skillful twist of his own sword—"you can catch him off-balance and drive the blade upward into his heart."

They faced each other, swords crossed. Reluctant to harm his friend, Jonathan made his first few thrusts hesitantly.

"Do not hold back," David said. "If your blade draws blood, that lesson is one I will not forget."

Jonathan took him at his word and lunged. He struck David's arm with the side of his blade, raising a welt, then nicked him with the tip of his sword, bloodying his wrist. Blow after blow, his weapon attacked David relentlessly, forcing him to block each thrust of the blade with his own, until he fell backward in the dust.

Jonathan pinned David's right hand to the ground with his foot, his sword pointed at David's throat. "If Goliath ever knocks you down like this, he will not bother to chop off your head," he said, pulling his friend up. "Instead, he will crush your head under his heel."

They went back to work, dueling in the harsh noonday glare. David struggled to learn, but he saw that it was a sorry, one-sided contest. And yet, each time he was knocked down, he stubbornly scrambled back to his feet again. Soon his knees were bloodied and his head rang from the blows.

He heard Jonathan mutter to himself, "To fight Goliath, why did the Almighty have to choose a shepherd?"

David made light of it. "I trained myself to play the lyre. Now you must train me to make music with a sword."

"It is the nature of a lion to go for the throat, and for a lamb to graze in the pasture," Jonathan said. "So it is with men. Some, like Goliath, are beasts that kill. And there are others . . ."

"It is not in my nature to kill," David said calmly, "but it is in my nature to do what must be done."

"Then know who you are up against. They say the infant Goliath had a war shield for his cradle. The sweet music you hear in a lullaby on your lyre, Goliath hears in the death cries of our people—"

He cut himself short. A toothless old woman in a ragged cloak was shuffling toward them. She held a cracked clay jug in her spindly arms.

"Water . . ." she said in a hoarse voice, and pointed at the decrepit well.

"Go away, old woman!" Jonathan growled. He turned back to David. "You and I must not be seen together."

"She means no harm." David walked over to her. "It is not safe to draw water here," he said gently. The old woman shielded her rheumy eyes against the glare, squinting up at him, bewildered. "The Philistines have poisoned the well with our dead. Take this instead." David grabbed his goatskin, which was hanging on a dead tree branch, and offered it to her. She held it over her toothless mouth with trembling fingers and gulped down a stream of water. With a nod of thanks, she handed the goatskin back to him and wandered away.

"The old woman is mad." Jonathan said.

"No, not mad." David followed her with his gaze. "Old age is her only affliction."

"May we live long enough so that someday that is *our* affliction!"

David frowned as he watched her vanish in the distance.

The people look to their king as a wellspring to sustain them. It will be upon me to assure my people that the well is not poisoned. Only then will all who come to drink from it draw life.

He picked up his sword and pointed it at Jonathan. "We begin again."

Chapter 31

The rising sun gilded the tower of the North Citadel, bathing the walls of Gath in a gentle radiance. In Nara's eyes, each morning glittered with the same bright promise as the day when the priest announced she would bear a son. The moon had waxed and waned once more, and her protruding belly proclaimed her new power and importance among the Philistines.

After the day Goliath had carried her through the city in triumph, she had not left her dwelling. It was enough, when she stepped into the sunlit courtyard each morning, greeted by the cooing of doves, to place her fingertips on her belly and feel the new life stirring within her.

She was grateful that her home offered a refuge like no other. Dalziel had commanded that it be constructed near the main garrison, on a grander scale than a dwelling for other Philistines. The ceilings of the spacious corridors were so high that Nara could walk from one room to the next without ever lowering her head in a doorway. The massive dining table was the length of three of Goliath's war shields, and the chairs were carved of solid oak, heavily braced with iron rods to support their weight.

Hada oversaw the servants. "You have accomplished the holy purpose for which the gods created you," she said. "You need not trifle with the foolishness of household chores."

Nara noticed that her aunt's favorite among the servants was Arjun. An orphan of sixteen, with eyes and skin darker than other Philistines, he was spurned by all. But despite his crooked nose and rotten teeth, Hada doted on him. Nara suspected it was because her aunt had suffered for her cleft lip, and knew the loneliness of being an outcast.

With Hada, Arjun, and the other servants to wait on her, Nara devoted herself to preparing the infant's chamber. Trained by her father to work with hammer and tongs in the heat of the forge, she was not by nature a dreamer. And yet, feeling her body magically transformed, she could vividly picture her son. She imagined that she had already given birth to him and that he was healthy and strong, gazing up at her with an all-consuming love. She longed to cradle him tenderly in her arms, to suckle him as her own mother had not lived to suckle her.

She stepped into the sunlit chamber where her young one would spend the first precious days of his life. To Nara, this was a holy place. On the far side of the bright room, beside fragrant baskets of white rose petals, was the crescent-shaped birthing stool, constructed of solid oak to accommodate one of her remarkable stature.

This is where I will sit when the hour comes. I will hold Hada's hand through the pain of birth as she helps me bring forth my son. Then, after he is born and cleansed, I will place him in the crib on a coverlet of the softest linen.

Her aunt had told her that the crib was three times the size of any built before, and was fashioned of the thick staves used to pen livestock. To honor the infant who would someday be a fearsome warrior, the cedar had been gilded and carved with scenes of battle. Beside the crib, the gifts for Goliath's firstborn were gathered together, playthings to train him for war: swords and spears carved of oak, javelins, and shields of cypress, all too heavy for any other child to lift.

And yet, Nara vowed, for her son, all this would not be enough. He deserved more. She took pride that the window beside the crib opened onto a lush garden where pristine white roses cascaded over limestone walls. Raised in her father's forge, feeding a furnace that reeked of charcoal and smelted iron, she had always craved the sweet scent of growing things. She resolved that the garden would be a sanctuary for her son, rich with the perfume of orange and pomegranate blossoms.

That is why I rejoice in looking out on this garden. Like the pomegranates that ripen in the sunlight, I feel the ripening within me.

* * *

On the day when it would all change forever, Nara breathed in the fragrance of the garden and imagined cradling her son in her arms, showing him the gentle wonders of the earth: shimmering butterflies and silken doves; bouquets of clouds in the sky like so many lilies.

"I must teach him that there are more important things than war," she said.

"He will be the strongest child in Gath." Hada kissed her hands.

She embraced her aunt. "May he also be the most beloved."

A sudden pounding shook the heavy front door to the dwelling. Arjun, Hada's favorite from the cooking tent, had been arranging an offering of fresh dates and pomegranates on the altar to Dagon in the entry alcove. He hurried over and pulled back the heavy bolt.

Dalziel, accompanied by four acolytes, crossed the threshold, his pallid right hand raised in blessing. Emerging from the infant's room, Nara was troubled by their arrival. A visit from the high priest was usually announced well in advance. Today it came as an unwelcome surprise.

So exalted was her position as Goliath's wife, even Dalziel courted her favor. She noticed how his harsh voice took on a musical lilt, and his usually scowling lips strained a smile. "Our god Dagon has sent me to see that all is well."

"I am honored by your visit," she said, concealing her misgivings.

He had paid such visits before and she knew all too well what to expect. Now, in the cool shadows of her chamber, she lay down on the bed and he placed his hands on her belly. Closing his eyes, he bent down until his ear rested against her womb, listening to the heartbeat of the son growing within her. He hovered so close to her that she could smell the frankincense perfuming his robes. Beneath it, she recognized the stench of the dead beasts whose throats he had slit on the altar of Dagon.

She knew she should respect and revere the high priest for all he had given her, but she loathed him. She resented how, on each visit, he spread his bony fingers possessively over her belly like a miser hoarding his gold. Did Dalziel hold some secret claim to her unborn child? she wondered. Would he someday steal her son from her? She swore on her life that she would never allow this to happen.

"All is as it must be." The high priest removed his hands from her womb and clasped them piously before him. "Now show me the chamber you have prepared for Goliath's son."

He spoke the words sweetly, but she heard them as a threat. Though the High Priest of Dagon had every right to enter there, she feared the sorcery he brought with him, and that he might cast a spell on her unborn child.

She led Dalziel across the sun-splashed courtyard, past the doves cooing in their cage of woven cedar twigs. They walked by the enormous cooking tent generously stocked to feed Goliath's voracious appetite: wooden tubs brimming with lentils and dates; whole pigs hanging on hooks; clay jugs filled with pungent barley beer and sweet honey wine. She knew that Hada took pride in the immense mud-brick oven that stood before them, spacious enough to hold an ordinary oven inside it.

At last, she opened a gilded door. "This is my son's chamber."

Dalziel stepped inside the sunlit room and walked over to the enormous crib. He gazed disdainfully at the gifts arrayed before it. "All these playthings are of no value. Today, I have brought you the one gift that will assure the health and good fortune of Goliath's son."

He clapped his hands. His four acolytes entered, carrying on their shoulders a massive object concealed beneath a cloth woven with golden threads. He gestured for them to remove the mantle, revealing a graven image of Dagon exquisitely wrought in bronze. As tall as the priest, it glared at her with cold ruby eyes. The idol was unlike the other images of Dagon she had seen. Instead of raising a flaming sword in its right hand, this one wore a black, crescent-shaped shield on each arm.

"Place it here." Dalziel beckoned for the acolytes to position the massive idol between the tall cedar crib and the window. She saw that it completely blocked the view of the garden with its roses, crocuses and lilies, its delicate perfume of pomegranate and orange blossoms.

"The boy must sleep in Dagon's shadow," the high priest said. "Dagon must be the first thing the son of Goliath sees when he opens his eyes in the morning, and the last thing he sees before he closes them at night."

"I am blessed by this priceless gift." Stifling the impulse to refuse it, Nara knelt before Dalziel to show her gratitude. To her eyes, the two black shields on Dagon's arms resembled the ominous wings of a vulture. Dalziel's gift spoke of cruelty and death.

Chapter 32

Moving the graven image would be no easy task. It was cast of bronze, so heavy that Nara doubted any man in Gath other than Goliath could lift it. And yet, she vowed to move the idol by herself. Was she not mighty like her husband? That she was with child made it more difficult, but it did not worry her. She told herself that it was because she carried a son that she must do this.

From the moment he enters the world, my son must experience the flowering abundance of life. That I am doing this out of love for him will only increase my strength.

Reaching down with her powerful arms, she clutched the base of the massive figure. She could not lift it, but perhaps she could drag it. Summoning all her might, she slowly pulled the idol away from the window, into a shadowy corner.

Once more, her son's crib looked out onto the sweet-scented garden. She felt no guilt at defying Dalziel's wishes. Her child would now be free to admire the green and growing things that flourished in the sunlight, free to inhale the scent of orange blossoms. Did her son not deserve the abundance of a bountiful world? She told herself that in this duel of wills with Dalziel, she had won.

Her joy was short-lived. As she turned away from the window, a sudden twinge shot through her belly. The throbbing tightened into a stab of pain. Cramps seized hold of her, growing more intense. With the next spasm, she staggered backward and collapsed onto the birthing stool. Though she knew that the bride of Goliath must never show weakness, she cried out.

Hada ran into the chamber. She saw Nara bent over on the birthing stool with drops of blood on the floor beneath her. "No one must see the blood," Hada whispered, and knelt down to wipe it off the floor with the sleeve of her robe. She seized one of the baskets of white rose petals placed nearby and hastily slid it under the birthing stool.

Nara glanced down at the petals in the basket beneath her: Blood was dripping onto them. "What is happening?" Tears filled her eyes.

"Be calm, my dove," Hada said.

The blood flowed copiously now, drenching her robe and the basket of flowers beneath her. "Why has Dagon done this to me?"

"It is not for us to know the will of the gods," her aunt said guardedly. "No god is more unforgiving than the god of the Philistines."

A violent spasm wrenched Nara's womb. She groaned. In the next contraction, she felt something expelled from within her.

On her hands and knees, Hada searched through the blood-stained rose petals in the basket. She found what she was looking for and cupped it gently between her hands. Nara forced herself to gaze down at this thing that had lived inside her, a twisted growth, a seedling of flesh and viscera.

Hada clapped a hand over her niece's eyes. "Such things are not meant for a mother to see." She removed a linen cloth from a pocket of her robe and carefully wrapped the bloody remnant in it.

Nara asked, "Was it a boy?"

Hada did not answer. Nara feared that her aunt did not want to tell her the truth—that the blood-soaked creature expelled from her womb was neither male nor female, that it was not human. And yet, she wept for the death of this living thing that would never grow to be her son. She wept for her father and for all the people of Gath who had placed their trust in her. "I have failed them!"

"No, my dear." Hada kissed her cheek with the warmth of her cleft lip. Nara felt her aunt's tears as they mingled with her own. "You have failed no one."

Nara drew no comfort from her aunt's words. That she might

be guilty of the death of her own son was a crime too terrible to forgive.

Did I bring this upon myself? By moving the graven image, by defying the wishes of the high priest, did I rouse Dagon's vengeance?

"Goliath must never learn of this—" Her aunt stopped. Arjun was standing in the doorway.

Hada's favorite gazed fearfully at the bloodstained white roses and Nara's tear-streaked face. "What has happened?"

"Something that men are forbidden to know," Hada said.

Arjun turned to leave, but she beckoned him closer. He approached cautiously, his eyes averted from Nara out of modesty.

Hada held out the folded cloth, which was moist with blood seeping from the thing hidden inside it. "Do not cast your eyes on what I give you. Ask me nothing. Only obey me." She placed it into his hands. "Go to the high rampart overlooking the charnel pit. Fling this over the wall, into its depths."

He nodded, clutching the folded cloth tightly between his hands. "I will do as you ask."

"No one must see you." She patted him fondly on the shoulder. "Hurry back to me."

Hiding the blood-soaked cloth beneath his robe, Arjun rushed out of the room.

"What is to become of me?" Nara murmured.

Hada removed a vial of myrrh from the folds of her cloak and sprinkled the sweet-smelling liquid on her niece. Nara knew it was to mask the scent of blood. "My beloved sister placed you in my care. I will see to it that no misfortune befalls you." She clasped Nara's large right hand tightly between both of hers. "Goliath does not dare harm you, for only you can give him a son."

"But I have failed!"

Hada pressed her cleft lip tenderly against Nara's broad palm. "Your body has the power to get with child again. And when you do, all will be well."

The youngest of the servants, a barefoot girl clutching a broom of bundled sticks, stood in the doorway, breathless with excitement. "Goliath, our master, has entered the gates of the city!"

Chapter 33

He did not greet Nara with an embrace. That was not Goliath's way. Standing before her in his torn, stained tunic, he boasted, "See the blood of the Israelites upon me. It is not thick like Philistine blood. It is thin, like the weak blood of women and cowards!"

Only moments before he entered the bedchamber, Hada had helped Nara to wash herself off and change into a fresh white robe. Now, like every good Philistine wife, she did what was expected of her and dutifully stripped off her husband's foul-smelling tunic. A servant girl carried over a pot of hot water from the cooking tent, and Nara scrubbed the rust-colored clots from Goliath's face, shoulders and armpits, his hairy back and legs.

She fought back a wave of nausea. The lingering odor of blood from her secret loss mingled with the butchery of war. Can he not smell it too? she wondered. How soon before he finds out the truth?

He had suffered a deeper gash than usual and his left shoulder oozed blood. She knew better than to mention it. To remind Goliath that an Israelite had inflicted this wound would only enflame him, and it was his rage that she feared most.

When she cleansed the gash with herbal balm, he winced and glared at her. "Your clumsy hands are shaking. Does the smell of blood sicken you? That is why women will never be warriors."

In this dangerous mood, she knew he might strike her. But Goliath's stomach rumbled loudly. Obeying its command, he pulled himself to his feet and strode into the courtyard. She followed close behind.

The heavy oak dining table groaned under the weight of a heaping platter of freshly roasted suckling pigs, tubs of lentil stew, and enough jugs of barley beer to satisfy ten thirsty men. He gorged himself and pounded his goblet on the table for more, sending the terrified servants scurrying. Nara stood at her husband's side. It was the place of a Philistine wife to look after his needs, but never to sit down with him at the table to eat. That honor had been hers only once, at her wedding feast. Tonight, if she had been allowed, it would have turned her stomach.

* * *

Goliath thumped his bulging belly with his hand. He leaned back in his chair and picked his teeth with his dagger, then wiped his greasy lips on the back of his arm. For the first time since his return, he looked her in the eye. It was the moment she dreaded.

"Tell me of my son."

He had asked the same question every evening since she was with child, and she always replied with the same words: "Your son grows mightier each day." His thick lips would then soften into a smile and he would touch her belly with surprising tenderness.

Tonight, his words hovered in the air like a threat. She felt his gaze rake over her, as if he sensed things were not as they should be. His jaw hardened and he leaned closer, sniffing her neck. "You wear a scent. You have not before." His nostrils flared. "What do you hide from me?"

Her mind scrambled for a convincing lie, but she had never been a skillful liar. Her voice wavered: "I thought the scent would please you."

She saw that he did not believe her. He lifted her robe and leaned closer to place the broad palm of his hand on her belly. "I smell blood."

In the ominous silence, she heard his labored breathing as his mind groped slowly, relentlessly, forward. His hands hardened into fists. Beneath the ridges of his brows, his eyes blazed. *"My son . . ?"*

She expected him to bellow in fury. Instead, when he caught his breath, he spoke in a hoarse whisper.

"My son is lost?"

She wanted to say, "It is a blessing." She wanted to explain that the creature she had carried in her womb was a thing too monstrous to live. Instead, she said softly, "The gods have taken him from us."

The words struck Goliath with their full force. He stood up from his chair and looked around him, dazed, as if he no longer knew where he was. His thick lips were too tight with rage to speak. As if his hands had a mind of their own, they seized the massive oak table heavy-laden with his feast, lifted it up and turned it over. The platter of suckling pigs, the clay vessels of barley beer, crashed to the ground.

He lunged for Nara. She ran blindly away from him, out of the courtyard. When she reached her son's room, she stepped inside, slammed the door and bolted it behind her. She knew it was madness, but even though her son was dead, she felt his presence here. Even though her son was dead, she felt compelled to protect him from Goliath's rage.

One kick of Goliath's foot splintered the door off its hinges. They faced each other with the tall staves of the empty crib between them like the bars of a cage. To defend herself, she said, "I can get with child again."

In his fury, he was deaf to her. She knew that all his life, he had seized everything he wanted, but now the prize was beyond his reach. "What god would do this to me?" he murmured.

"We can create a child tonight. A son!"

He ignored her, his mind lumbering ahead. "Who did this? Was it the Israelite God? No, Dagon did this thing himself!"

"But Dagon wants me to bear you a son!"

"You are not worthy to bear my son!" he bellowed. "That is why Dagon has killed him!" He lifted up the massive crib in both hands and threatened to bring it down on her.

"Take my life!" She met his gaze boldly with her own. "But where will you find another woman like me, created by the gods to bear your son?"

The heavy crib wavered in his grasp. The muscles of his arms twitched. She saw he was wrestling with himself, and knew his rage was the one enemy he could not easily subdue.

"Before you take my life, find another woman who can bear your son! What if I am the only one who can?"

As if to shake off her question, he moved his ponderous head from side to side. She saw he was cornered, that he did not see a way out. Grudgingly, he lowered the massive crib to the ground. He took a deep breath that filled his massive chest, then let it out.

For the first time, she saw terror on his face.

"If the priests find out my son is lost, they will think Dagon no longer smiles upon me. They will believe I am cursed!" Goliath spoke to her differently now, as his ally, his accomplice: "No one can know what has happened."

"I will get with child tonight and all will be well," she whispered, seeking to comfort him.

She doubted her own words. Though she believed her body had the power to bear sons, she could no more control its sorcery than she could turn night into day. The death of their unborn child was the only secret that she and Goliath had ever shared. She dared to hope that this unspoken bond would forge an alliance between them.

* * *

That night, they slept on opposite sides of the great bed. For the first time since their marriage, Goliath did not try to have his way with her, but she knew his restraint did not come from tenderness. He was allowing her body to heal, not for her sake, but because he knew his fate depended on it.

Goliath lay awake on his back with his eyes wide. She saw

that, like her, he too was vulnerable. At last, he spoke, whispering the words so softly that it seemed he had forgotten she was with him, as if he uttered his innermost thoughts.

"What if I do not have time?"

"Time?" she asked.

He licked his thick lips. Sweat beaded his brow: "They say I am part god. It is not so. Each day, I grow older. Each day, I fall prey to the perils faced by all mortal men. And one day, the Israelites will . . ." His voice faded, so faint that she could hardly hear him.

"What if, before you get with child, I die in battle?"

They were words she had never imagined he would speak. She knew what she must reply. "No Israelite can kill you. Their king knows it, and so does their invisible God."

He touched the raw gash in his shoulder. Blood seeped from it and he winced. "If I can bleed, I can also die." She watched the awareness creep over him: "It is easier to kill a hundred men, to chop off a thousand heads, than to create one new life." He said it bitterly, as if this was a cruel injustice, a terrible flaw in the workings of the universe.

* * *

The following night, it was as if Goliath had never confided in her. He took her to bed and used her cruelly.

More than he wants to conceive a son, he wants to punish me for failing him. He knows he cannot kill me—at least not yet—but he sees me as his enemy. He will make me suffer.

Chapter 34

The blood-stained rag held something unholy and unclean.

As the High Priest of Dagon, he was adept at divining the future in the entrails of slaughtered beasts: sheep, goats, bulls. But this dead creature that Arjun had brought to him in his musty chamber within the temple was unlike any Dalziel had seen.

Across the years, he had shed torrents of blood in countless sacrifices. The act of killing no longer enticed him with its mysteries. Death, delivered in copious amounts on the altar of the temple, was the price he paid to buy Dagon's favor. But this strange dead thing that might have grown into Goliath's son. . . . It forced him to ask questions he could not answer.

Was this the vengeance of the Israelite God or an act of Dagon himself? Dalziel feared that this malformed creature foretold his own fate. But he concealed his dread and smiled benignly at the young visitor who knelt before him.

"You have proved yourself to me." He placed the palm of his hand on Arjun's forehead in blessing.

The boy humbly averted his eyes. "I am your servant."

Dalziel traced a bony finger along Arjun's dark cheek. "I have no sons by blood. But in my eyes, you and the other young ones whom I have chosen are my sons."

Arjun was hardly Dalziel's only spy. In Gath, he had built a network of such novices. He had found that orphans made the best informers, boys without fathers to teach them right from wrong. This young one is no beauty, he thought. Arjun had a crooked nose and bad teeth, but that was what made him so useful. Hada, a barren, unsightly outcast with a cleft lip, would naturally take to this homely orphan. She would confide in him, trust him. Just as Dalziel had predicted, Arjun had won her heart. There was an art to treachery and the boy had mastered it:

to bow his head obediently before Hada, even as he betrayed her. And when he spoke to the old woman, Arjun could twist the truth to his own ends as skillfully as a blacksmith bends molten iron.

"Come. I will reward you for serving me," Dalziel said.

He led Arjun out of his chamber, down the narrow hallway into the high-ceilinged sanctuary of the temple. It was the first time Arjun had set foot here, and Dalziel watched as the youth stood open-mouthed before the ornate gold carvings, the pillars of porphyry, the inlaid floor of multicolored marble. The darkness resounded with the chanting of the priests, which magnified the glory of the immense graven images that gazed down upon them. Peering through the swirling smoke, Arjun was mesmerized by the blood sacrifices on the high altar, the frenzy of the knives.

"I see what is in your heart," Dalziel said. "You are drawn to this portal between life and death. You wish to take part in our sacred offerings, and you will."

Arjun bowed his head in gratitude. Dalziel knew how it began for boys like him. No doubt, Arjun had performed his own crude sacrifices in the dust, killing a sparrow with a broken wing, a lame dog. The suffering he had inflicted on these doomed creatures as he snuffed out their lives had been his first taste of pure joy. The high priest thought, how much more joyful, how much more powerful, Arjun will feel standing before the altar of the great temple, when the life force of each creature he sacrifices surges into his body!

"Now you must return to Hada," Dalziel said.

"Must I be a slave to the cooking tent?" Arjun muttered. "I despise the giggling of the servant girls and the braying of that foolish old crone."

"Soon I will free you from the tyranny of women. But for now, you must serve Hada, and Nara, her mistress. The wife of Goliath will be desperate. She may turn away from Dagon to false gods.

This must not happen."

Arjun knelt before him and kissed the golden hem of his robe. This servant boy deserves to be one of us, Dalziel thought. His fervor springs from a deeper place in the human heart than love.

Chapter 35

Their swords clashed, blade against blade, striking sparks. David spun around and caught Jonathan off-balance, knocking him backward into the dust. He stood over him, his blade pointed at his throat.

"For the third time in a row you have bested me!" Jonathan said, as David helped him to his feet. "You have learned how to take advantage of my weaknesses."

"You have no weaknesses!"

They laughed, but both knew that Jonathan was right. David had discovered that in his boldness, his opponent lowered his guard too quickly, seeking out an opening that wasn't there. So far, Jonathan's daring had allowed him to prevail against the Philistines. But David feared that someday that recklessness would kill him.

I cannot afford to be as reckless as my friend. I will only have one chance against Goliath.

Another face-off, the clatter of copper against copper. Again David forced Jonathan to his knees, a blade pointed at his heart. "We have practiced here for so long, I no longer notice the stench of corpses rising from the well," Jonathan said, climbing back to his feet.

"And yet," David replied, "it reminds us that death is close at hand, lying in wait."

They faced each other once more. David attacked decisively. His opponent struck back at him, but not fast enough. David lunged, inflicting a welt on Jonathan's arm. They stopped to share a goatskin of water. David thought, covered with dust and drenched in sweat as we are now, a king's son and a shepherd look like brothers.

Jonathan raised the goatskin like a wine goblet to salute him. "My friend, you have learned to fight as a king fights, with the weapons of a king."

"Are you saying I am ready to face Goliath?"

"No man can ever truly be ready to do battle with him. But I have taught you all I know. And if the Almighty is with you . . . I pray you will prevail."

They were the words that David had been waiting to hear. He embraced his friend warmly. But he wondered, was Jonathan's blessing just another case of his recklessness?

Ever since I rescued him from Gath, Jonathan believes blindly in me, as if no obstacle is too great for me to overcome. But as I approach the moment when I will face Goliath, my confidence flickers like a flame in the wind.

How can I know whether the Almighty is with me? I listen for His voice in the night, but I hear only the hollow beating of my heart. If the Most High forces me to rely only on the muscles of a young shepherd and a crude Israelite sword, Goliath will have my head.

As if to bear out David's doubts, in their next clash, his copper blade broke off at the hilt. "How can I defeat Goliath if I must pit Israelite copper against Philistine iron?"

Jonathan was deep in thought. Suddenly, he clasped David by the shoulders. "I have the answer!"

Chapter 36

Time had passed—one month, almost two—since she had lost the son who might have been. Still, Nara was not with child.

With open jaws, Dagon gazed down into the depths of the empty crib. It seemed to her that the hungry god had devoured her son. She had managed to drag the heavy bronze idol back against the wooden staves of the crib, exactly where the high priest had wanted it. With its two uplifted shields, the figure blocked out the splendor of the garden beyond, but she had no choice. She did not dare displease Dagon now, even if it meant shrouding the infant's room in shadows.

I have returned the idol to its rightful place. I have paid with the life of my unborn son. Is that not penance enough? I am ready to conceive again, but Dagon withholds his blessing.

"Each night, Goliath grows more vengeful." She sat in the dappled shade of the acacia in the courtyard while her aunt smoothed an aloe poultice over the fresh bruises on her shoulders. "Why does he hurt me if he still needs me to bear his son?"

"He no longer has faith in you." From the pocket of her robe, Hada removed a folded palm leaf that held fresh turmeric. "In the spice market today, the old women said the priests believe you have lost the child. I told them they are mistaken, that your son grows strong within you. For now, the women believe my lies."

"But the priests?"

"Somehow they learned the truth. It is said they have already sent messengers to the four other great Philistine cities and beyond." Hada shook her head sadly. "It may take weeks. It may take months. The woman they find may not be as tall or as strong as you. But make no mistake, the priests will not rest until they find a woman to take your place."

"Their search will take time," Nara said, seeking reassurance. "That gives me time to—"

"I fear not." With the tips of her pudgy fingers, her aunt applied a poultice to a bruise on Nara's right arm. "Goliath's rage is a beast he cannot control. I fear that long before they find another wife for him, he will kill you."

She stood up abruptly and beckoned for Nara to follow her across the sunny courtyard into the alcove with the door leading into Hada's bedchamber. After checking that no one was watching them, her aunt hastily opened the door and nudged her inside.

"Why have you brought me here?"

Hada did not reply, but bolted the door behind them. Nara had never before been allowed to enter here. The air in the cramped space was stifling, the ceiling so low that she had to crouch down. She peered into the shadows, wondering whether they concealed her aunt's secrets. The rich fragrances of saffron, cinnamon and myrrh surrounded her. This seemed to be less a place for Hada to sleep than to hoard the things precious to her: bunches of pungent dried herbs hanging on hooks; spices sealed in jars or overflowing from woven reed baskets.

A dusty beam of light from a narrow slit in the wall slashed across Hada's face, revealing the fury in her eyes. "The fault is not in you, but in your god!" Her cleft lip quivered. Nara had never seen her so distressed. "The priests of Gath would have you pray to *Dagon* for a son? Fools! What does a god of war know about creating life? He can only destroy it!"

Nara stared at her in shock. "How can you speak such blasphemy?" Hada had always offered her motherly comfort, but now she was revealing a part of herself that she had always kept hidden. Wondering whether she had been wrong to trust her, Nara said, "Only Dagon and his host rule over us in Gath. They have since time began."

Hada sighed. "Yes, that is the first thing every Philistine child learns. It is a lie."

"A *lie*?"

Hada's sad eyes took on a distant stare, as if peering back in time. "Once, long ago, when I was a child, the golden altar atop the South Citadel was hallowed to a different deity, a powerful deity: *Ashdoda*."

"Ashdoda . . ." Nara had never heard the name, and yet, when she spoke it aloud, it seemed strangely familiar.

"Dagon is a male god." Hada pointed to the bruises on Nara's arms and shoulders. "He brings only pain and death." She reached into a bowl of dried rose petals and crumbled them between her fingers. "Dagon cannot make a single flower blossom or feed one hatchling in a nest of doves." She waved a hand toward the pungent herbs in her chamber. "I surround myself with these to remind me of the fruitfulness of the earth and the fertility that only Ashdoda can bring. Only she is the giver of life. Only she can make barren women fertile and deserts bloom. My beloved, only she can get you with child."

Nara examined the confusion of jars and baskets. "Show me a graven image of Ashdoda and I will pray to her."

"Alas, I do not have one. Such an idol is the rarest of treasures." Hada hesitated, as if unsure where to begin. "Long ago, enthroned in her silver citadel on the moon, Ashdoda wept. Her tears rained down upon us from the sky. They were the priceless gifts of her love. Her tears fell to earth as fiery stones. Our ancestors carved each stone into Ashdoda's likeness."

"What became of them?"

"When the male priests of the male god, Dagon, seized power, they set out to destroy all the graven images of Ashdoda. To worship the goddess—even to speak her name—was punished with death. Almost all her believers were slaughtered." She lifted her chin proudly. "A few of the faithful survived."

Nara spoke slowly, knowing the weight of her words: "You are one of them?"

Hada embraced her. "I have waited so long to tell you this!" Nara leaned closer and her aunt pressed her split lip against her cheek. "A handful of women, believers in the goddess as I am, escaped from Gath. They call themselves the daughters of Ashdoda."

"Where did these women go?"

"They live in hiding as hunted fugitives. If the Philistines ever find them, they will destroy them. The daughters of Ashdoda took with them the last graven image of the goddess, which was carved from one of her tears from the heavens long ago. That idol can get you with child and give Goliath a son."

"Then I must find it."

"You cannot. But there is a woman who may be able to go out and fetch it for us—"

"That cannot be," Nara interrupted. "No woman of Gath is allowed to leave the city walls without a man to escort her."

Hada slid open the bolt and led her out of the chamber, carefully shutting the door behind them. Blinking in the glare of the courtyard, she said, "I have a cousin, a woman of Gath, who comes and goes with her husband through the Gates of Glory to gather firewood outside the city walls." She lowered her voice. "He has fallen deathly ill. I know she bribes the guards to let her pass alone through the gates to perform her task. I will ask her to take our plea to the daughters of Ashdoda. If they are as compassionate as they are devout, they will give my cousin the sacred idol to bring to you."

Nara whispered, "But you said that in Gath to possess an idol of Ashdoda is punished by death."

"That is so. But if you are to get with child and save yourself from Goliath's fury, it is a risk you must take."

Nara eyed the cage of woven twigs in the courtyard. She heard the wings of the doves imprisoned within it, fluttering, restless. "I fear there is no time left for a miracle."

Hada's cleft lip parted. Nara understood that it was not quite a smile, only a wisp of hope. "There is always time for a miracle if the goddess wills it. If your prayer pleases her, she can get you with child tomorrow." She cupped her chubby fingers tightly together. "But in order to pray for such a miracle, you must clasp her sacred likeness in your hands."

Chapter 37

Tobiah, Saul's advisor, had revealed the secret location to him. Even so, it took Jonathan far longer than he had expected, scrambling up and down the rocky slopes in the sweltering heat. When, at last, he crept through a narrow passage flanked by tall limestone slabs, two sentinels stepped out to block his path.

"I must see Amariah."

Few of his people were granted an audience with the high priest of the Israelites. But Jonathan saw that the men-at-arms recognized him and feared arousing his notorious temper. They escorted him past the gleaming white Tabernacle sheltering the Holy Ark, which was nestled in the shadows among jagged boulders. Outside the canopy, a handful of lesser priests and acolytes chanted prayers.

Amariah, high priest and heir to the line of Aaron, sat apart, warming himself in a pool of sunlight while all the others kept to the shade in the heat of the day. How different he was from the Philistines' high priest in Gath, Jonathan thought. When he had glimpsed Dalziel leading Goliath and his bride in the procession to the temple of Dagon, the high priest looked arrogant and crafty, a man to be feared. But the high priest of the Israelites was bent over, as if from bearing the crushing burden of the Holy Ark. The fair skin of his forehead was blistered from shepherding the most sacred of treasures from one desolate hiding place to another. His eyes were glazed with an overwhelming sadness, his beard a pale, faded red, like the last embers of a dying fire.

Though Amariah's white robe was threadbare, Jonathan noticed that the silver breastplate hanging around his neck had been carefully polished. It gleamed brightly, as if to offer proof of his shining faith. Jonathan knew the breastplate was studded with twelve jewels—beryl and jasper, emerald and ruby—one for each of the twelve tribes. But as he walked closer, he noticed the priest had removed two of the jewels: one clear and sparkling, the other blood-red.

Amariah was casting the two stones down onto the flat surface of a granite slab that glistened in the heat. The old man appeared mesmerized by the pattern of colored light spun by the whirling jewels. They rolled to a stop. He studied them where they lay, as if to divine their meaning, and furrowed his brow. He scooped up the two stones and forcefully cast them down again. Once more, he shook his head in seeming helplessness.

The high priest was so consumed with his task that he did not at first notice his visitor. He looked up, startled to see Jonathan standing before him. "Son of Saul, what has brought you here?" His tone was courteous, respectful, but not friendly.

"I come for your wisdom."

"Forgive me, but wisdom is something you have never sought from me before. It seems you would rather face death in battle from Philistine iron than kneel with me before the Holy Ark in prayer and reflection."

Jonathan pointed to the two stones in Amariah's hands. "You are the only one who can cast the Urim and Thummim. I remember, as a boy, watching you use them before my father for acts of prophecy, to see beyond—"

"I see nothing!" Amariah interrupted him bitterly. "The Urim and Thummim are silent." As if they were a mere annoyance, he hastily fitted the two jewels back into his glittering breastplate.

Jonathan spoke with the firm voice of a king's son: "The stones tell you nothing because the future is not yet decided. But with your help, we can assure what will come to pass."

"With my help? Whatever help you want of me, son of Saul, I have nothing to offer. I am one who has been humbled and dishonored."

"Dishonored? My father has entrusted you to watch over the Holy Ark, our most precious treasure. What greater honor—?"

"And a greater excuse to be rid of me!" Amariah snapped. "Saul assigned me this task to keep me away from his court in Gibeah, so he can ignore my priestly counsel and act on his own godless whims. He has reduced me to being custodian of the Ark, nothing more."

Jonathan suspected that Amariah's dour, self-pitying eyes concealed a secret. "Growing up in the palace, I heard it whispered that you are also entrusted with something else of great value from the Early Times."

"There is nothing more," he muttered.

Jonathan persisted: "From the time when Joshua led our people . . ."

The high priest ran a feeble hand across his closed eyes. When he opened them, Jonathan saw that the old man had decided to tell the truth. "Yes, I safeguard the treasures of Joshua for the final battle at the End of Days, when our people face utter destruction."

"That time has come. That is why you must give them to me." Jonathan noticed that Amariah's fingers hovered uncertainly over his breastplate. "Do not look to the stones to make the decision for you. It is one only you can make."

He saw that the high priest was weakening, beads of sweat running down his brow. "I cannot give those treasures to your father. It is not God's will for him to make use of them. He is no longer worthy in the sight of the Almighty."

"I do not want them for my father. I want to give them to another . . ."

"Samuel's chosen?" Amariah spoke the words with a serpent's hiss. "You would give them to the shepherd anointed by the mad prophet?"

"You know of David?"

"Yes, I have ways to learn such things from the court at Gibeah." Amariah tugged at his beard so hard that he winced. "Samuel claims to hear the voice of God, but he never seeks my guidance. He is deaf to my wisdom!"

"I will not defend Samuel, but I speak for the one he anointed. I believe in David, enough to give up my own claim to the throne for him."

"The son of Jesse. . . . He has never come to ask for my blessing. I doubt he even respects the Commandments in the Holy Ark!"

Jonathan's voice hardened: "Joshua's treasures are meant for David. He needs them to face Goliath."

"*Goliath*?" For the first time, Amariah cracked a smile, his laughter as bone-dry as a cough. "The shepherd is mad! And Samuel was madder still to anoint him!" He shook his head. "Impossible! I cannot do what you ask. If the king finds out that I helped David—"

"Saul will not find out." I am quick to anger, Jonathan thought, but I am clumsy at the art of persuasion. He forced himself to kneel down humbly before Amariah. "Only with the power that brought our past victories can we shape our future. And only David can use that power to save our people."

Amariah bristled. "Our people are past saving."

"Tell me where you have hidden Joshua's treasures!"

Jonathan sensed that Amariah was probing him with his gaze, searching for what he might find in his heart. It was as if the priest discovered something unexpected there, something more than the brutal soul of a hot-tempered warrior. He lowered his voice so the other priests and acolytes would not overhear him. "I will tell you where to find Joshua's treasures. But against Goliath, I fear even they will not be enough."

Chapter 38

"We should not have come," Nara whispered to Hada.

The marble steps of the Well of Blessings shimmered in the morning light. When she was a child, the lowly daughter of a blacksmith, she had never imagined she would be allowed to visit this gathering place for the wives of the rich and powerful of Gath. The pristine water of the well gushed from the beaks of four gilded eagles and was said to flow directly from the spring where the god Dagon himself drank.

Like the other common people of the city, Nara's father had been forced to use the crumbling well in the market, where peddlers washed the dust of the Spice Road off their donkeys and butchers rinsed the blood of pigs from their hands. Since marrying Goliath, however, she had often come with Hada to the Well of Blessings, where she had been warmly received.

Today, as usual, she saw that the wealthy women had come here to trade gossip and flatter each other on their finery, their carefree laughter mingling with the placid murmur of the fountain. She always felt ill at ease in this place where she knew she did not belong, but today, she felt cold terror.

"They will see that I deceive them," she whispered. "They will see I am no longer with child."

"No one will know." Hada eyed the billowing cloak that concealed her niece's belly. "They will be too busy vying for your favor."

No sooner had she spoken, than Nara was immediately surrounded by women fawning over her as the wife of Goliath, soon to be the mother of his son. In their garish robes of ruby red and emerald green, their wrists tinkling with gold jewelry, the wealthy women of Gath showered her with honeyed words. She was deaf to their flattery. Her father had taught her, "Praise that does not come from the heart is as worthless as rust." Her halting words of thanks were met with gracious smiles, as if she spoke with the eloquence of a high priest. Though they called her "sister," Nara distrusted them.

"We run too great a risk coming here."

"It must be tonight," Hada said. "Only when the moon is full and Ashdoda's silver citadel is in its full glory can she answer your prayers. But first, you must have a graven image of her to clasp in your hands."

Nara noticed that two guards clutching spears were standing in the shade of a nearby archway. Were they watching her? She nervously studied the women gathered at the well. Handmaidens braided the hair of their mistresses with golden threads, while servants scooped sparkling water from the well with silver ladles.

"Has she come yet?"

"She will come," Hada said.

As Goliath's wife, Nara had learned to walk over to the side of the Well of Blessings shaded by acacia trees, which was reserved for women of privilege. Her aunt left her and joined the servants and handmaidens gathered in the harsh glare on the other side of the well. She saw how Hada, self-conscious because of her cleft lip, scorned because she was barren, felt more at ease conversing with these humble women. Nara knew that unlike their mistresses, the servants would not judge her.

Hada's tongue flicked restlessly through the cleft in her lip as she scanned the crowd. From the other side of the well, Nara caught sight of a gaunt young woman in a threadbare robe bearing a heavy bundle of firewood on her shoulders. A life toiling in the harsh sun had ravaged her face, leaving it wrinkled beyond her years. Eyes lowered, she cautiously approached the handmaidens at the well.

Nara saw that the two guards had stopped talking. They had spotted the intruder. Clearly, this woman did not belong in such elite company. Nara held her breath as Hada gradually made her way over to the stranger. If the guards saw her speaking with this outsider, she feared that her aunt might fall under suspicion. But to Nara's relief, the two women did not exchange a word. As if by accident, Hada brushed against the bearer of the kindling. Then the stranger was gone.

It all happened so quickly that only now did Nara realize what had taken place. The intruder had slipped Hada an object that she now concealed in the folds of her robe. The guards had gone back to talking with each other, apparently unaware of the act.

As soon as she could without drawing attention to herself, Hada rejoined Nara on the shaded side of the well. Her pudgy fingers secretly pressed something into the broad palm of her niece's hand.

The stone feels as warm as a living thing.

Nara clasped it tightly. Awed to be holding one of Ashdoda's precious tears at last, she could not resist opening her fingers and peering down at it: The stone had been carved into a round figure with full breasts and broad hips. It seemed to glow softly, as though burnished by the touch of the countless women who had clasped it in supplication. She furtively ran her thumb across Ashdoda's face. If the graven image ever had eyes, a nose and mouth, they had been rubbed off long ago by the fingers of women seeking its blessing.

Suddenly, Hada whispered, "Give it back to me!"

She snatched the idol out of Nara's hand and hastily withdrew to the far side of the well, losing herself among the servants and handmaidens.

Nara realized that her aunt had reason to panic. Temple guards with spears and shields were advancing rapidly down an alleyway into the square. There could be no doubt now that they were coming for Hada.

"Seize her!" It was the voice of a young man, a voice that Nara recognized.

Arjun.

Though dressed as a servant, he spoke with authority. The commander who accompanied him nodded to one of his men, who grabbed Hada by the shoulders. Nara understood now that Arjun had betrayed them, a spy planted in Goliath's household by the priests. She blamed herself for being as blind to it as Hada had been.

"Search her," Arjun said.

The men sprang into action as if the order had been given by the commander himself. One of them rifled through the folds of Hada's robe. It sickened Nara that Arjun seemed to take pleasure in tormenting an old woman who had only treated him with kindness. The guard triumphantly pulled out the object hidden in her robe and raised it for all to see: the likeness of the goddess, carved from one of Ashdoda's tears. He handed it to Arjun, who held it warily between his fingertips, as if it was something too unclean to clutch tightly in his fist.

At the sight of the graven image, a fearful hush fell over the wealthy wives of Gath. Nara realized that this object, so holy to Hada, was obscene to them. Averting their eyes, they backed away from it, for to gaze on an image of Ashdoda was forbidden.

Impatient, the commander clapped his hands for the men to set to work. Two guards bound Hada's wrists tightly behind her with leather thongs. With the blades of their javelins, three more men set about digging a shallow pit beneath the acacia trees at the edge of the courtyard. At first, Nara did not understand—she had grown up in the refuge of the forge, sheltered from Philistine cruelty—but from the way the women around her whispered fearfully to each other, she dreaded what was about to take place.

For a few moments, she only heard the javelins scraping out the dirt. Her hands bound behind her back, Hada silently watched them. To Nara's surprise, her aunt looked upon the men not with hatred, but with pity.

When they had finished digging, a voice broke the silence.

"For what you have done, you will be punished."

In his shimmering white robe, Dalziel, the high priest, emerged suddenly out of the alleyway leading from the temple, as if he had been urgently summoned here. His face cold and gray as marble, Dalziel studied the idol in Arjun's hand with contempt. He turned to the women. "All the graven images of Ashdoda in Gath were destroyed by the priests long ago." He pointed at Hada. "This woman has brought one into the city and betrayed us!"

Dalziel snatched the idol from Arjun and placed it on a marble step of the Well of Blessings. A guard gave him a heavy iron mace. Nara watched as Dalziel grasped the handle with both hands. His spindly arms raised it high above his head.

He brought the mace down hard.

The holy stone, the last priceless tear of a goddess that had seemed so eternal to Nara, shattered into dust before her eyes. In that moment, she felt that her hope of bearing a son for Goliath was shattered along with it.

At the sight of the idol's destruction, Hada's eyes filled with tears. Nara understood that her aunt did not weep for her own fate, but for all the miracles that the idol would never bring to pass.

The high priest beckoned for two of the men to drag over a bulging ox-leather sack. They emptied it out before him, a score of black stones clattering onto the tiles of the courtyard. Nara observed that all of them were obsidian, their edges chipped to make them as sharp as spear points.

Dalziel spoke harshly to the wives at the well, as if they were all guilty. "Because Hada's wickedness is a stain on every woman of Gath, it will be for you to carry out her punishment."

The temple guards roughly shoved Hada into the pit, then set to work burying her up to her waist in dirt. Nara saw that though her aunt's soiled cheeks were streaked with tears, she raised her head high, showing no fear.

"Who else in Gath worships Ashdoda?" The high priest asked

Hada. "Tell me and I may spare you."

"No one." Trapped in the pit, Hada held her torso upright, her shoulders back. "I am the last daughter of Ashdoda in Gath." She avoided looking in her direction, Nara knew, for fear of betraying her.

Dalziel glared at the women standing before him. "Any one of you who does not throw a stone will be punished as Hada is punished."

Nara watched with disgust as each woman dutifully knelt down and picked up a sharp stone.

How eager the good wives of Gath are to please him! These privileged women have never bloodied their hands to chop off the head of a chicken or gut a pig, but they do not hesitate to take a good woman's life.

All of them held a stone now. All but Nara. She felt the harsh gaze of Arjun and Dalziel upon her, waiting to judge her a traitor, but the urge to rescue Hada was overwhelming. Nara clenched her fists tightly at her sides, fighting a battle with herself. She knew she was stronger than Dalziel's men, but they were armed with swords, spears and javelins. Even so, she was seized by the impulse to fight them, to prove her love for Hada, though it would cost her life.

As if sensing her niece's thoughts, Hada met her gaze. Slowly but firmly, she shook her head. Nara understood that her aunt was telling her, "Do not save me."

Hada says I must live and so I will live. I must live to avenge her.

Nara forced herself to lean down to pick up a stone. In her shame, it felt almost too heavy to lift. Holding it, she forced herself to stand shoulder to shoulder with the other women, who faced Hada at a distance of seven paces.

I am one of them now. I am one of the executioners.

Dalziel clapped his hands together once. The women let out a shrill cry. With the rattle of the gold and silver bracelets on their wrists, all of them threw their stones at once.

Nara hurled her stone along with all the rest, but she aimed far over Hada's head, deliberately missing her.

If all the others do the same, my aunt will be spared.

But she saw the other women were terrified of the high priest, fearful they too would be accused of worshipping Ashdoda. In their cowardice, they summoned all their strength to hurl their stones at the helpless target. So many struck Hada at once—the harsh thud of rocks striking flesh—that Nara realized each woman could convince herself that her stone was not the one that had ended Hada's life. But Nara knew the truth.

You are all killers.

Before Hada's bloodied torso slumped over, the light in her eyes was snuffed out.

"Such is the fate of all who turn away from Dagon to worship Ashdoda, goddess of women and of weakness," Dalziel said.

Nara's heart cried out at the terrible crime that had been committed. She longed to run up and kneel beside her beloved aunt, to embrace her in the ever-widening pool of blood where she lay. But though she grieved for her, Nara knew she could not weep in view of the priests, or she too would be condemned. The guards dragged Hada's lifeless body out of the pit and threw it onto a donkey cart.

"She will not be consecrated on a pyre to be sent to the High Places," Dalziel said. "Instead, her body will be thrown into the charnel pit."

Nara knew of that foul-smelling trench where the carcasses of goats and oxen were dumped, along with the corpses of common criminals. Fighting back tears, she watched the donkey cart creak down the alleyway.

Hada, you were the most honorable of women, but Dalziel has denied your soul its rightful journey to the High Places. Forgive me, my beloved aunt. Know that I will avenge you.

Once Dalziel's men had left, servants set to work scrubbing the blood from the tiles with water from the well. Then, with their hands, they scooped the dirt back into the hole that Dalziel's men had dug. Soon, Nara thought, there will be no sign of the murder that took place here.

The women of privilege had already returned to their gossip. As for the Well of Blessings, she saw that its pristine water flowed, untainted, as before. She thought bitterly, these pampered women do not have a drop of blood on their robes or on their hands. They will always have life served to them with a silver ladle. In her grief, she left the women at the well and walked down the alleyway toward her dwelling.

In Hada, I had more than a beloved aunt and true friend. In Hada, I had a loving mother. She sacrificed her life to bring me a holy idol beloved by women. That gift is gone forever. The promise it carried is lost. What hope is there for me now?

Chapter 39

"Where are we going?" David jogged down the dusty path to keep up with him.

"To see a great wonder."

He was wary of Jonathan's "wonders." Was this another one of his wild schemes, as misguided as his foolhardy attempt to murder Goliath on his marriage day? Reluctantly, he followed Jonathan away from the poisoned well, until the walls of Gibeah vanished from sight. The rocky hills of open country stretched before them.

"And what is this great wonder?"

Jonathan answered his question with one of his own: "What is the holiest treasure of our people?"

"The Ark of the Covenant," David said.

"I am about to show you a treasure that rivals the Holy Ark, and this one will save your life!"

David realized that the barren plot of ground where Jonathan had brought him had once been an olive orchard. The trees had been uprooted, the adjoining barley fields sown with salt. He saw the skeletons of slaughtered goats. Jackals had cracked the bones in their jaws for the marrow, and a raucous flock of crows squabbled over the scraps.

Beyond the ravaged field, they approached the walls of an Israelite farmer's stone dwelling gutted by fire. The blood of a pig was smeared on the charred doorpost. The animal's carcass, crawling with maggots, lay splayed across the threshold. Defiled. David knew no Israelite would ever dwell here again.

"You said you would show me a great wonder," he said. "I see only the fruits of wickedness."

Jonathan smiled mysteriously. "Sometimes, the holiest things are hidden in the least holy places."

David followed him beyond the charred dwelling, to a crag

overlooking a steep ravine. A faint sound rose from below, a sweet melding of voices. David recognized it now. Israelite priests were chanting, their fervent prayers rising to the heavens.

"Where have you taken me?"

"The Philistines expect us to hide the Ark of the Covenant at a sacred site. Instead, Saul commands his priests to conceal the Ark near the last dwelling that the Philistines have defiled, because the enemy will not return there soon." Jonathan laughed. "My father may be mad, but he is sometimes wise!"

David peered over the cliff. Israelite sentries with spears blocked the narrow footpath that wound into the ravine. The men recognized Jonathan and stood aside to let them pass. Nestled in the hollow at the base of the cliff, David caught sight of a shimmering white canopy. A handful of Israelite priests stood vigil before it.

"Is this the Tabernacle?"

"Yes, the great tent that shelters the Holy Ark." Jonathan said.

David gazed at it in silent wonder. The tent curved so gracefully, it looked to him more like a vessel for the Great Sea than a shelter for the most hallowed of treasures. Perhaps this was so, he thought, because, like a great vessel, the Tabernacle must protect the Ark in every port and weather every storm.

"How long has the Tabernacle been kept hidden here?" he asked.

"By my father's order, only a week. It never stays in the same place for more than one Sabbath. Before the next, the Tabernacle will be moved to protect it from capture by the Philistines."

David felt irresistibly drawn to the Tabernacle and started down the trail toward it. Jonathan grabbed his arm. "I did not bring you here for this. Along with the Ark, there is something else of great value that we move from place to place."

"What can that be?"

"In case the Ark is ever lost to us, this treasure is kept hidden at a safe distance from it."

Jonathan led him along a jagged shale outcropping. The chanting of the priests faded into the distance. The ravine where the Ark was hidden vanished behind them. At last, he stopped and looked around him. "Amariah told me it would be here." He pointed to a small mound of dirt nearby. "There!"

Puzzled, David said, "It looks like a shallow grave."

"You will see it is not." Jonathan knelt down and clawed away at the dirt with his fingers. He beckoned for David to help him. "The Commandments in the Ark of the Covenant tells us what is righteous. But we also need the weapons to fight what is wicked, as you will fight Goliath. I brought you here to arm you for that battle."

Together, they labored to scrape away the layer of packed dirt. In the unforgiving heat, it was slow, arduous work. Impatient, Jonathan unsheathed his sword and stabbed at the stubborn earth.

The tip of his blade thudded against something hard. David saw the blade had struck a plank of weathered cedar. Jonathan swept away the dirt with his hand, revealing what looked like an ancient chest. Unlike the exquisitely crafted Ark of the Covenant, which was graced by two golden seraphs, it seemed this had been hastily hammered together from rough-hewn planks.

"This is a fragment of a city gate," Jonathan said, as if reading David's thoughts.

"An Israelite city?"

"No, an enemy city in the Early Times, one even more infamous than the Philistine city of Gath.

David could think of only one such city, but it existed so long ago, it seemed impossible that any relic from that day could have survived. "Jericho?"

Jonathan ran a finger along the coarse grain of the weathered wood as if reading the past of his people. "It is said that the Holy Scrolls tell the story. When Joshua led our people into the Promised Land of Canaan, he attacked the enemy stronghold of

Jericho. Our priests blew rams' horns to bring down the city walls. But it was the sword of Joshua, blessed by the Almighty, which killed our enemies. It was the sword of Joshua that led our people to victory in countless battles. He triumphed because his sword and shield were hallowed by God."

As if he thought David would not believe what he was about to say next, he met his gaze firmly with his own. "Joshua's sword and shield were forged of *iron*."

"But only the Philistines know how to make weapons of iron!"

"In Joshua's time, the secrets of forging swords and shields of the deadly metal were known to our people," Jonathan said. "But over the generations, the Philistines killed off all of our blacksmiths. Our knowledge of the secrets died out. Today, the mysterious art of working iron is jealously guarded by the Philistines and kept from us. That is why we lack blades of iron to defeat them . . ."

David looked down at the weathered coffer, understanding. "Until this moment."

Jonathan nodded. "Joshua led our men to topple the mighty walls of Jericho. With what I am about to give you, it is your destiny to topple Goliath."

He leaned over to pry open the chest with his sword, but spotted something at his feet. "The seal is broken!"

David saw that fragments of an ancient beeswax crest lay scattered in the dust. Jonathan forced the tip of his sword under the lid and twisted it. The weathered planks resisted, then gave way. The rusty hinges creaked open.

The coffer was empty.

As if to convince himself that the treasure was gone, Jonathan ran his hand along the inside of the musty chest.

"Stolen by the Philistines?" David asked.

"If they had stolen them, they would have trumpeted it to the world."

David hesitated before saying it: "Your father . . ?"

"The high priest, Amariah, fears my father more than he fears the Almighty. He must have warned Saul that I wanted Joshua's treasures for you. My father had his men seize them."

David had not said the words before: "Saul wants Goliath to kill me."

Chapter 40

Tonight, as every night, Goliath's foul breath, the coarseness of his touch, afflicted Nara. Tonight, as every night, he performed his duty and forced her to suffer on the marriage bed. His cold indifference told her that this was a hollow ritual. His cruelty told her that he no longer believed she could give him a son.

He dozed fitfully, threatening to awaken at any moment. Nara lay beside him in bed with her eyes open. When she closed them, she saw Hada's lifeless face, bloodied by the hail of stones. It grieved her that she had not been able to cradle her aunt in her arms at the moment when her spirit departed.

Hada, you cared for me selflessly, guided me with gentleness and understanding. You were taken from me when I needed you most. If you were still alive, what would you have me do?

The sapphire radiance streaming through the bedchamber window told her the full moon had risen. Ashdoda's silver citadel shimmered in its full glory. It must be tonight, Hada had said. Only tonight could her prayers to the goddess be answered.

I must pray to Ashdoda, but how? Dalziel crushed the holy idol of the goddess into dust. But Hada told me that unless I hold the graven image in my hands, Ashdoda will be deaf to my entreaties.

And yet, if the goddess is as compassionate as Hada said, she may take pity on me. I must throw myself on Ashdoda's mercy.

First, she would have to escape from Goliath. He dozed restlessly, the hilt of his unsheathed dagger within easy reach on the floor beside him. His body sprawled across most of their immense bed. She feared he would sense her movements, and forced herself to wait for his uneven breathing to slow to the steady rhythm of heavy sleep.

Soon the moon will go down. My chance will be lost.

* * *

Nara could wait no longer. Cautiously, she raised her body from the bed and lowered her feet to the floor. Three long steps and she reached the door. Outside, the deserted courtyard was shrouded in shadows. The servants had retired to their quarters, but she knew they could all too easily be awakened.

She crept over to the ladder that led to the roof of her bedchamber. As she climbed the shaky rungs, they creaked underfoot, threatening to snap under her weight. She heard the rasp of Goliath's snoring from below. At last, she pulled herself up and clambered onto the roof.

Standing there under the heavens, she had expected to be bathed in moonlight. Instead, the sky suddenly darkened. As heavy as Goliath's hand, a cloud blotted out the silver citadel of the moon.

If Ashdoda is so compassionate, so loving, how can she turn her back on me now?

Swiftly, like a glittering sword unsheathed, the moon flashed from behind the clouds, dazzling in its brilliance. Ashdoda's silver citadel shimmered above her. Its radiance filled her with hope, but she feared that it would quickly fade away. Clasping her hands before her, she knelt down awkwardly in the moonlight.

"Ashdoda, goddess of women, for a fleeting moment today, I held one of your precious tears in my hand. I felt your life-giving warmth. Now, though your likeness has been taken from me, I implore you to hear my prayer. I beg you to give me the seed of new life. For the good of my people, help me conceive a son by Goliath."

She feared her prayer was not enough to win Ashdoda's blessing and felt she had to offer her more. "Answer my entreaty, and this I swear to you upon my life: I will raise my son to have the compassionate heart of a daughter. I will raise my son to heal instead of kill. No matter what befalls me, I promise to live and die in your service. Only help me to get with child tonight."

She remained motionless on her knees, her hands folded before her in supplication, and waited for an answer from the heavens. Her rapid breathing grated harshly in her ears, so loud that she worried it would drown out Ashdoda's gentle voice if the goddess whispered a reply.

Holding her breath, she strained to listen. No night birds sang. Even the dogs in the dwellings of Gath were silent. Suddenly, like a slap in the face, a gust of wind rose up and smothered the moon with clouds, quenching its radiance. Nara feared that her audience with Ashdoda was over.

The goddess is deaf to my prayers. I am unworthy of her.

Her eyes filled with tears. Suddenly, she glimpsed flashes of light.

Sparks were showering down from the sky, as if from an anvil of the gods, embers cascading from the heavens onto the distant hills.

She rubbed her eyes, fearing they deceived her. Then she remembered what Hada had told her, and the awareness filled her with wonder.

Ashdoda is weeping.

She felt blessed to witness this miracle. Gazing out over the city, it seemed to her that all the other Philistines of Gath were blind to it. This late at night, those who were still awake were confined to their dwellings, captives of their petty fears and cramped lives. None of them was gazing up into the skies in search of wonders. On the lofty ramparts, the sentinels were scanning the shadowy plain below, ever watchful for Israelite marauders. They were too consumed with their narrow task, she thought, to raise their eyes to the glittering firmament.

If we are not ever-vigilant for miracles, how will we know when one is upon us? Ashdoda has given me a sign. The goddess has spoken.

She remembered how Hada had told her, "In ancient times, Ashdoda's tears rained down upon the earth as fiery stones. Our priestesses carved them into idols to honor her, for what can be more holy than Ashdoda's tears of compassion?" Here and now, for a reason Nara did not understand, this miracle from ancient times was once more taking place before her eyes.

Why does Ashdoda weep? Does she weep for my suffering? Does she grieve for the murder of my beloved Hada?

Her aunt had told her that only one of the ancient stones remained, and Nara had watched Dalziel crush it to dust. She believed that these fiery stones, newly fallen from the heavens, once again brought the power of Ashdoda's magic.

If I can possess these stones . . .

She dared to hope that their sorcery could bring her a son. But first, she would have to locate the stones in the darkness, which would take another miracle. How could she find the hot tears of Ashdoda that were lost in the vastness of the night?

Her eyes strained to probe the shadows. She glimpsed a light flickering in the black void beyond the city walls: On a distant hilltop, a tree had been set ablaze by the fiery stones.

The flaming branches mark the place where Ashdoda's hot tears streaked to earth. As long as the tree burns, I have a beacon to guide me. But I must reach it quickly, before the flames die. Once the tree crumbles to ashes, the holy stones will be lost forever among all the stones of the earth, like raindrops lost in the Great Sea.

* * *

The murky streets of Gath were deserted. If one of the sentries on the parapets looked in her direction, Nara knew she would be discovered. She crept from one shadowy doorway to the next. It was difficult for a woman her size to move with stealth, but as silently as she could, she guided her ungainly body through the narrow alleyways.

She stole past modest dwellings where Philistine families dozed peacefully. She envied them their small and simple lives.

If only my life could be so small and so simple, a life embraced by children, sheltered by the arms of a loving husband. Instead, I must set out alone into the night.

At last, the Gates of Glory loomed before her. The bronze rosettes that studded the doors gleamed in the moonlight like the teeth of a giant beast. Above the gates, six sentries stood watch. If they heard her trying to unbolt the gates, she knew she would be an easy target for their spears.

There was only one other chance left for escape: a place shunned by the living, a place she loathed. She rushed through the night toward it.

* * *

Sheathed in ancient bronze, the Gates of Eternity were blackened and scarred, as if ravaged by the torrent of grief that had flowed through them over the generations. Nara had avoided this place ever since her brother, Jadan, was carried through these gates on his shield, his throat pierced by an Israelite javelin. Among the living, only the bereaved came to these portals of the dead.

It was forbidden for those who still drew breath to walk out of these gates, for fear it would bring a curse upon them. Tonight, she had no choice. As she had guessed, the Gates of Eternity were not as heavily guarded as the Gates of Glory. Only two sentinels stood on the parapet.

The iron lock on the gates was obscured in the darkness. She knew how it worked—she had once helped her father repair the weathered hasp on his anvil—but it would test her strength to pry it open.

Above her, footsteps rang out. Along the top of the parapet, a thickset sentry clutching a spear made his rounds, marching closer. If he looked down, he would spot her. She clung to the shadows, motionless as an idol of stone. When he had walked past, she wedged her fingers between the heavy iron hasp and the door.

She pulled. The bolt slid clear.

Chapter 41

David penned his flock safely for the night beside his father's dwelling in Bethlehem, but he could not sleep. His mind teemed with questions.

Without the sword and shield of Joshua, how can I fulfill the promise of my anointing? How can I do battle with Goliath and triumph over him?

He wandered away from his home and plunged into the darkness. The dim stars overhead shed no light, taunting him. He felt lost, as if he was once more threading his way into the labyrinth of thorns where Samuel found refuge. Tonight, in the labyrinth of darkness, there was no way out. He could no more reach beyond this moment to grasp his future than he could have stretched out his arms in the thorn thicket without impaling his hands on the spines.

In that moment of despair, he bore witness to the sight: Fiery stones fell from the heavens, raining earthward. He gaped up at them in wonder, unable to believe what he saw. An instant later, on a distant hill, a tree burst into flames.

A story that his mother had told him flashed through David's mind: Moses the Lawgiver once beheld a burning bush. The Most High spoke to him from the flames.

The Almighty has never spoken to me. Tonight, from this tree blazing in the distance, will I hear His voice at last?

He felt uneasy to be setting out alone, plunging deep into the darkness without his flock. It was his duty to look after them, but they also protected him. Their bleating alerted him to human marauders or wild predators stalking in the shadows. Venturing so close to Philistine land, he knew that tonight his survival might depend on just such a warning.

* * *

In the distance, the burning tree shimmered like a beacon. He quickened his pace toward it, swallowed up in a sea of shadows. Menacing, indistinct shapes loomed before him, the phantoms that prowled in the night. He heard the strident cries of unknown birds of prey circling overhead and smelled the foul odor of carrion.

The goal seemed beyond his reach. The burning branches flickered before his eyes, fading along with the promise they held. He knew he had to hurry. When the beacon of flames died, his chance to commune with the Almighty would be lost forever.

In his haste, he stumbled in the darkness, his knees bloodied by shards of flint, his arms stung by nettles. He wished he had a torch to light the way, but realized it would only alert Philistine marauders lurking in the shadows and draw them to him. Scrambling up a slope that bristled with thorn bushes, he slipped on loose pebbles and fell, then pulled himself back to his feet and rushed ahead. Only the thud of his tread and the rasp of his breathing broke the silence. For an uneasy moment, the flaming tree vanished behind a ridge. It seemed that he had lost his way.

He rounded a ridge strewn with boulders and the acrid odor of charred wood stung his nostrils. The burning oak stood before him, its stark branches raised to the heavens like the fingers of a scorched hand. Only a few of the boughs were still aflame.

I will hear the voice of the Almighty at last.

He gazed into the dying flames of the branches for a sign, strained with his mind and with his heart to grasp the holiness of the moment. At first, he heard nothing. Then, from the other side of the tree, he heard the rustle of movement.

A woman.

She was crouched down on her hands and knees in the shadows at the foot of the blackened oak, groping frantically through the steaming ashes. It seemed she was searching for something.

Gazing down on her from the hillside, he could only make out a few details in the firelight: The woman's hair was elaborately braided in the Philistine manner. Her fine linen robe and intricately stitched sandals told him she must be one of the privileged of Gath.

He spoke to her in the Philistine tongue, which he had learned from other shepherds. "I am David, the youngest son of Jesse of Bethlehem." He stepped out of the darkness, revealing himself to be young and unarmed, but kept his distance.

"I see an Israelite before me," she replied with contempt. "And so, I see a coward."

She stood up. To David's amazement, she was the tallest woman he had ever seen. It seemed impossible to him, and yet . . .

"I know who you are," he said.

That the two of them faced each other alone, here and now, he knew was a miracle. It seemed all the more remarkable to him when he spoke the words aloud: "You are the wife of Goliath."

She did not deny it. Despite the strength of her powerful legs, he saw that her knees were unsteady. Tears glittered in her eyes.

"Why have you come here?" she asked.

"Once, our Lawgiver, Moses, heard the voice of the Almighty from a burning bush. When I saw the tree on fire, I came here, hoping to hear His voice."

"Alas," she said, mocking him, "once again, your invisible God has failed you. The burning tree did not speak!"

"The tree did not speak, but the Almighty has spoken," he replied. "He has brought the two of us together."

"And why would your God do such a thing?" she asked with disdain.

"That is a mystery I do not understand." He smiled gently. "The Almighty gives me much to ponder."

"You Israelites spend too much time pondering and not enough time fighting fearlessly in battle. I despise you for your weakness." Her voice hardened. "And I despise you for taking my brother's life."

"I regret that your brother died." He saw that his sympathy for her grief surprised her. "Your brother did not die by my hand. I am a shepherd. I have never killed a Philistine. I have never killed any man."

"A Philistine would be ashamed to admit such a thing," she said scornfully. "The priests of Dagon teach us that a man who has not slain an enemy in battle is not a man."

He frowned. "Then I am fated to become a man all too soon."

"And who is it you plan to face in combat," she asked with a disparaging smile, "a child or an old woman?"

"Goliath."

She burst into laughter. "Wretched shepherd, you have stood under the sun too long. It has melted your mind as a furnace melts copper."

Studying her more closely, he saw the Philistine woman's arms were soiled to the elbow from searching through the ashes, her fine robe torn as if she had run all the way from Gath.

"Perhaps I am mad," he said, "but it was madness for you to come here. Why would the wife of Goliath leave the safety of Gath and risk walking here, alone, at night?" She squirmed under his probing gaze, but he continued relentlessly. "There can only be one reason. You search for the fiery stones that fell from the sky. You believe there is sorcery in them."

"Yes, I came for the holy stones," she said defiantly, "but I did not find them." She wiped the back of her hand across her eyes, unwittingly smearing gray ash on her cheek.

He saw that she avoided his gaze, struggling to hide the despair in her eyes. "Look about you," he said. "There are no holy stones here."

"Or did you steal them? Israelites are born thieves!"

"I have no use for stones. To pray to stones is idolatry." He spoke to her slowly, as if instructing a child: "There is only one God. The Almighty. All other gods are but hollow statues that will soon crumble to dust. You might as well pray to a dead dog, for all the good your stones will do you!"

The pain on her face told him how deeply his words hurt her. He regretted that he had spoken harshly, telling her of things too foreign for her to understand. He examined her now with fascination, not as a Philistine, not as an enemy, but as a riddle to be solved. "Why, I ask myself, does the wife of Goliath, the mightiest warrior in Gath, need these stones so desperately that she risks her life to find them?"

Nara pressed her lips tightly together, as if she feared betraying the truth. He continued with cold logic. "What is required of Goliath's wife? Only one thing: to bear him sons. And despite the joyful proclamations of your priests, it must be that *the bride of Goliath is no longer with child."*

She flinched as if he had struck her. This Philistine woman, so much taller and stronger than he was, seemed so pitiable to him that he felt the overwhelming urge to comfort her. He started down the hillside toward her, but before he reached the place where she was standing, the last flames on the branches died. He was swallowed up in darkness. He realized she had fled into the night.

Our meeting was ordained by the Almighty, but I failed to grasp its meaning. Now it is too late. The Philistine woman has returned to her world and I have gained no understanding. I will not have another chance. I failed to grasp the divine purpose that brought us together from our warring peoples to meet here in this miraculous moment. For that failure, I will pay a heavy price.

Chapter 42

Her grimy face streaked with tears, Nara scrambled down the faint trail that she hoped would lead her back to Gath. The moon was only a memory. She felt as if Ashdoda had abandoned her.

A glance back at the hilltop revealed that the burning oak had been reduced to a blackened skeleton. Its promise had died along with the flames. She brooded that she was returning home empty-handed. She stumbled, fell against a boulder, tearing her robe, but groped her way forward into the darkness. Despite her disappointment at her failure, it was a relief to leave the brash young Israelite behind. His words probed too deeply, she thought. They wounded her because they forced her to face the truth: Ashdoda's holy stones had been denied to her.

The Israelite had scorned her sacred idols as worthless and called worshipping them an act of folly. She refused to accept such blasphemy. Her people, any people, were only as mighty as the gods they worshipped, the gods who watched over them. What power could the Israelites' invisible Almighty have, she thought, if He took no earthly form, if it was forbidden to carve His likeness in stone? No wonder the shepherd's people were so easily crushed in battle.

The Israelite was right about one thing. It was reckless for me to come here tonight. But it is madness for him to think that he can fight Goliath. Before the shepherd can unsheathe his sword, he will fall dead from my husband's spear.

And what of my own fate? How long will Goliath let me live if I fail to bear him a son? Whose head will he chop off first, the Israelite's or my own?

* * *

It was the coldest hour of the night. The charred oak was lost in the darkness behind her and she had not yet caught sight of the walls of Gath. Hope had deserted her and with it, the desire to defend herself. She was no longer vigilant for threats in the shadows. If this was her time to be taken, she would accept her fate.

I am doomed. Without a child in my belly, I am condemned to die at Goliath's hand.

She had to return before he awoke at dawn, but the trail back to Gath seemed longer and more tortuous than it had been on the way there. She feared she had lost her way.

A ghostly figure loomed before her.

Was it a spirit? She knew that the night held phantoms. She had heard that sometimes the vengeful souls of the dead stalked their prey in the darkness. But in her despair, she did not fear the fury of the dead as much as the wrath of the living. Unwavering, she advanced toward it.

The gaunt apparition blocking her path was a woman. Her emaciated face was ageless, so pallid that it seemed to glow. Her wild silver hair smelled like the acrid tanneries of Gath. Necklaces gleamed around her withered throat, but instead of the baubles of silver or gold favored by Philistine women, this stranger wore rough beads of carved olive wood, horn and bone, and amulets stitched from dried seed pods and dyed dove feathers. Her loose-fitting garment was sewn from scraps of leather instead of loom-woven fabric. It reminded Nara of the ragged clothing of the mad women who crouched in the dust of the spice market, shouting curses at the sun.

"If you are a demon or a thief, I have nothing to offer you," Nara said.

"I am Keturah," the woman replied, her voice so soft, so fragile, that it took Nara by surprise. "I am not here to take, but to give." She cradled a wrapped bundle in her arms as tenderly as if she held a swaddled infant. "Nara of Gath, your prayers have been answered."

"You know my name?" This stranger must be a witch, Nara thought. How else can this be?

"Your departed aunt Hada was one of us. She was much beloved. All of us mourn her fate."

Nara could not imagine the plump, motherly Hada having anything in common with this lost soul. "No one mourns her more than I do," she said warily, and strained to look into the stranger's eyes. They glowed softly, like the beads shimmering around her neck. Nara found no menace in them, only a sorrow that spoke of how much she had lost.

"Take what I have brought you." Keturah placed the small bundle into her hands.

Nara unfolded the rough-spun cloth to see what was nestled inside: five black stones, smooth and round, each no larger than a fig, each remarkably heavy for its size. She understood now why they had been so carefully wrapped: The newly fallen stones were as hot as bread pulled fresh from Hada's oven, too hot to hold in her bare hands.

"Tonight, when the stones fell from the sky, the daughters of Ashdoda rejoiced," Keturah said. "We rushed to the burning oak and gathered the stones before others could come to steal them. The stones are yours now. They must be kept out of the hands of men."

"Thank you for this precious gift." Nara clutched the bundle in her arms and murmured a silent prayer of thanksgiving.

The tears of the goddess will perform the greatest of miracles. They will grant me a son.

She pressed the wrapped stones tightly to her chest and drew strength from their warmth, as if from the embrace of Ashdoda herself.

"Hada told us that you are Goliath's wife, but that in your heart you are one of us, a daughter of Ashdoda," Keturah said. "In your aunt's name, for all of us, I ask you to do what must be done."

"What must I do?"

"Return to your dwelling in Gath. Tomorrow, when the moon rises, kneel beneath its radiance. Arrange these five sacred stones into a crescent before you. Pray to them. If the goddess smiles upon you, you will become heavy with child."

"But why would you have me bear Goliath a son if the priests of Dagon are your enemies?"

"You must give him a son," Keturah said. "If you fail, the priests will find another woman who can. Without you as his mother, Goliath's son will grow up with the cruel heart of his father. He will hunt down the last of us and destroy us. But if *you* bear Goliath a son, you will lead him down the path of compassion."

"So long as Goliath lives, so will his wickedness," Nara said.

"Goliath is not a god. He will not live forever. And when Goliath dies, the Philistines will be defeated. The power of the priests will crumble. On that day, the daughters of Ashdoda will be free to return to Gath at last. All the Philistines will look to your son to found a kingdom of peace and forgiveness, and to rule justly over it."

I was wrong to doubt the goddess. I was always part of Ashdoda's plan. Her tears fallen from the heavens hold a bright promise. Their power for good can bring about wonders beyond my imagining.

But the stones weighed heavy in her arms. She saw in Keturah's mournful eyes that she feared for her. In the darkness, her ageless face looked as white as sun-bleached bone.

"Do what you must, Nara, but be vigilant," Keturah said. "Or Hada's fate will be your fate."

Chapter 43

Before the last stars in the eastern sky were snuffed out, Nara approached the walls of Gath. She cradled the holy stones in her shawl as tenderly as if she held a newborn child.

With their sorcery, I will soon bear Goliath a son.

The sentinel at the Gates of Eternity had yet to make his final rounds for the night. The massive bronze doors were unbolted, as she had left them. She pried them wide enough to force herself inside. From there, she made her way silently through the murky alleyways toward her dwelling. So far, she had not been seen. Ashdoda is with me, she thought.

When she slipped into the bedchamber, Goliath was snoring loudly. It seemed he had not awakened since she had left. She yearned to lie down with the precious bundle in her arms, but did not dare to run the risk. Instead, she slid the stones beneath the heavy oak platform supporting the immense bed. Then she pulled off her torn robe and, with water from a clay jug, washed the grime from her arms and legs. Weary, she lowered herself onto her side of the marriage bed.

Sleep was impossible. The new day was already here, the rising sun tinting the granite walls of the city as pink as an infant's cheek. It weighed on her that she would not be able to draw upon the sorcery of the stones until this new day ended and night fell.

* * *

She awoke, blinking in the glare of morning. To her relief, Goliath had already set out with his men. She would have to wait until after sunset to pray to Ashdoda's stones, but she could not risk leaving them here in the bedchamber. She knew the high priest might have planted more spies like Arjun in her household.

She decided to hide them in the granary chamber, an airless storage compartment only visited by the lowliest female servants. Since this week's flour had already been milled and brought to the cooking tent, there was no reason for anyone to set foot inside the chamber for wheat or barley before nightfall. The small room was next to the ladder that led to the roof. She reasoned that after the moon rose, she could safely retrieve the stones there, without having to risk carrying them all the way from her bedchamber.

By mid-morning, the servants were all distracted by their chores in the cooking tent. She decided this was the time to act. Clutching the precious bundle, she hurried across the sunbaked courtyard, careful not to awaken the doves that dozed fitfully in their cage of cedar twigs.

The hinges of the granary door resisted, then creaked open. In the stifling heat of the chamber, the air was heavy with the smell of yeast. Awkward in the cramped space, she stooped down among the baskets of grain.

Where to hide the stones? There was no time to decide. She heard a man's heavy footsteps close at hand, followed by the clatter of iron. Through a crack in the door, she caught sight of a javelin, the tip so massive it could only belong to Goliath. Had he come home early?

She held her breath and waited for the footsteps to pass. They did not. The door creaked open.

"My beloved daughter!"

To her relief, it was her father Ezel, clad in his ragged ox-leather apron, his unkempt gray beard reeking of charcoal. She realized that despite his new wealth and position, he could not resist working with his hands in the heat of the forge, as he had all his life. "I have brought your husband a javelin that I hammered out for him on my anvil." The weapon was so heavy that he seemed relieved to set it down beside the baskets of barley. Stretching his sore arms, he studied her, crouched before him.

"Why do I find Goliath's wife in a place only visited by the lowliest servants?"

She tried to stuff the secret bundle into a sleeve of her robe without him noticing, but he playfully grabbed it from her. "Does a daughter keep secrets from her own father?"

He opened the folded cloth and saw what was concealed inside. "These stones do not honor Dagon," he murmured.

Was that suspicion in his voice? Nara had never been able to lie to her father, but she feared telling him the truth. He had taught her that for a Philistine to worship any god but Dagon and his attendant deities was punishable by death.

"Father, I pray you will understand . . ." She could not say more.

Ezel leaned closer to her and ran his callused hand tenderly along her cheek. She tried to look away, but he caught the desperation in her eyes.

"You have lost your child," he said gently.

"The son I carried in my womb . . ." Her voice faded. She dreaded his reaction. "I must do anything I can to get with child."

She feared he might strike her. Instead, he reached out to embrace her where she knelt beside him. She was so much larger than he was that he hugged her awkwardly, as a boy might hug his mother. But he spoke to her as her father: "I mourn your loss. I will not betray you. I know why your aunt Hada was put to death." He eyed the bundle before him. "I know there is magic in these stones."

"You know of the goddess? I thought she was known only to women!"

"Ashdoda." He said the word softly. It sounded blasphemous on her father's lips, a forbidden name that she had never heard him speak before. "For a woman to bring forth life is her divine purpose. It is only right that you should turn to Ashdoda now."

"But all my life you spoke only of Dagon!"

"The cruel god of our people does not hold sway over the heavens and the earth. He only rules a corner of it. If he reigned over all things, why were my beloved wife and son taken from me? There are many fearsome gods in the High Places. All are worthy of worship except one: the Almighty of the Israelites. For no man can pray to a God who forbids idols made in his own image. Without idols, how can one worship Him?"

He furrowed his brow and winced, as she knew he always did in the forge when faced with a problem he could not solve. "If Ashdoda's stones can bring you a son, you must pray to them. But how can you, without being discovered?"

"Tonight, I will climb to the roof of our dwelling. Beneath the moon, I will pray to the stones. And if I am judged worthy, I will receive Ashdoda's blessing."

"I will keep watch so no one discovers you at prayer," he said.

"I am blessed to have a father who risks everything to help his daughter."

"If you fail to bear a son, the priests will do away with me too, for my daughter will have shamed Goliath."

"I will not shame you *or* Goliath," she said with fresh hope. "I will bear him a son."

"I ask only one favor in return." He pressed her large hand between both of his. "Ashdoda's holy stones are known to possess potent magic. Whetting the blade of any sword, even a blade of copper, on one of the stones, will endow it with the deadly power to vanquish the enemy. After you pray to the stones, after they get you with child, allow me to borrow them to sharpen the blades of the weapons in my forge. The magic of the stones will make me first among blacksmiths in all of the five Philistine cities."

She embraced him. "The stones of Ashdoda will bless both of us."

Chapter 44

David picked up a stone from the dust. His tunic stank of ashes from the charred oak the night before. The odor reminded him of the ashes of mourning his mother had worn after two of his brothers were slain in battle by the Philistines.

It was fated for me to meet the wife of Goliath. That moment might have brought miracles, but I failed to grasp its meaning. Now my chance has passed. Will I ever have another?

Standing alone with his flock, he felt the harsh glare of the morning sun like a judgment upon him. He untied the strip of leather from his belt.

I use my sling not to hunt but to seek. With it, I attempt the impossible. With it, I seek to know the unknowable.

He understood that a stone thrown by a mortal man could never strike the sun. That made no difference to him. He believed that simply in the attempt, he could find secrets unseen by mortal eyes, as a falcon hunts for a blind master.

He slipped the stone into the pouch of his leather sling. He whirled the sling around his head once, twice, three times. He listened until the blur of the leather strips through the air sounded like a harsh winter wind.

Then, with a snap of his wrist, he let it fly.

One moment, the stone was an earthly thing within his grasp. The next, it flew as if endowed with a life of its own. He squinted into the distance to trace its path, hoping to lose sight of it in the sun's brilliance.

The stone dropped quickly to earth. He shielded his eyes with his hand and scanned the dusty plain, searching for the place where it had fallen. Another failure, he thought. I am no closer to a revelation.

But to his astonishment, at the very place where the stone had landed, a figure appeared.

Najab, the lanky young Nubian, his shaved black head gleaming, advanced over the hill toward him. David recognized him from the market in Gibeah. Cloaked in a faded indigo robe, the trader led his string of five donkeys heavy-laden with what looked like their usual burden of iron ingots for the forges of Gath.

The Nubian is a heathen, a foreigner, an idol-worshipper, David thought. There could be no one less likely to be sent as a messenger by the Almighty. But he had learned that often the truth comes from the place where he least expected it. Najab's sudden appearance was a strange coincidence. He asked himself, what is a coincidence but a miracle we mortals do not yet understand?

The gangly Nubian took long, confident strides toward him on bare feet thick with calluses. To David's relief, he halted his string of donkeys a prudent distance from the flock. Whenever their paths crossed at the crowded well in Gibeah, Najab's ill-tempered beasts bullied David's docile sheep, nipping at their flanks.

"My Nubian friend!" David held out his goatskin of water to him as was the Israelite custom. "I know we have had our quarrels. Let us put them behind us."

"The quarrels were between my donkeys and your sheep, not between us!" Najab grinned good-naturedly, speaking the Israelite tongue with his strange clucking accent.

He accepted David's goatskin of water, but though his lips were parched, he did not drink from it. Instead, he poured a stream into the gaping mouth of his lead donkey. "Forgive me, but my beloved Shaya needs the water more than I do." David saw how the Nubian took pleasure in watching the animal gulp its fill.

Najab pointed to the sling in David's hand. "You hurled a stone in our direction. Were you aiming at my donkeys, or the fleas that ride on them?"

David smiled. "I hope your donkeys and their fleas will forgive me. They were not my target."

"What *was* your target?" Najab waved a gangly arm across the vast emptiness that surrounded them. "I see no wild creatures worth hunting."

"I aim at the sun," David said, realizing the Nubian could not possibly understand.

Najab laughed scornfully. "No wonder you Israelites cannot defeat the Philistines." He threw up his hands. "You aim for the impossible! And when you miss, you spend an eternity trying to explain why!"

"I know I can never hit the sun, and yet I throw the stone," David said, struggling to put his thoughts into words. "I do it to force my heart to stretch beyond what is small and mean and narrow, to attain something more, a glory worthy of the Almighty."

"You go to such lengths to seek out your God!" Najab scoffed. "For my gods, I only have to do *this*!" With a thumb, he rubbed the twisted snakes carved into the flesh of his forearm. "I carry my graven idols with me. They are always there to hear my prayers and give me comfort." His tone softened as he handed back the goatskin of water. "Jonathan told me you rescued him from Gath. For that, I honor you." He placed his hand over his heart. "But he also told me you plan to face Goliath in battle." His eyes narrowed. "Even my most slow-witted donkey knows that is folly!"

"It is only folly because I do not yet have the weapons I need." David said. "To kill Goliath, I must have a sword and spear of iron equal to his."

Najab arched an eyebrow. "And how do you intend to find such iron weapons? The Philistines have kept the secrets of working iron from your people for generations. Even your Almighty God cannot give those secrets to you!"

David felt compelled to confide to this foreigner something he would not have told his own flesh and blood. "Last night, I saw a tree burst into flames on a distant hill. I believed it was a sign from the Almighty. I was certain He would speak to me."

"And did he?" Najab asked dubiously.

"When I reached the tree, I met a Philistine woman." David paused, knowing the seeming absurdity of what he was about to say: "She was the wife of Goliath."

The Nubian grunted in disbelief. "This cannot be!" But he saw on David's face that it was so. "Why would the wife of Goliath leave Gath to go there, of all places, and at night?"

"She came seeking holy stones fallen from the sky." David sighed, reluctant to admit failure. "The Philistine woman and I parted ways. She never found her stones and the Almighty never spoke to me."

A fly landed on Najab's arm. "Ah, but your God *did* speak to you!" He swatted the insect with a precise slap of his hand. "Your Almighty spoke, but you were deaf to Him!" He broke into a sly smile and ran his fingers along the intertwined snakes carved into his forearm. "All the secrets of making blades of Philistine iron stood before you, but you let them walk away!"

"You speak in riddles!" David said in exasperation.

Najab pointed at his heavy-laden donkeys. "For years, like my father before me, I have brought iron ingots to the forge of Ezel, master blacksmith of Gath. When his son was killed in battle, Ezel taught his daughter, Nara, the mysterious arts of shaping the black metal . . ."

"But women are forbidden to work in the forge!"

"To satisfy the Philistines' hunger for weapons, Ezel had no choice. He has kept Nara's labors a closely guarded secret to this day. But I visited Ezel's forge often. He is my friend. I know the truth. No one else can know. For Nara has become Goliath's wife."

David wrapped the leather sling around his fist so tightly that it hurt. "What if the Philistine woman did know the mysteries of working iron? What good does all that do me now? I will never cross paths with her again. A thunderbolt does not strike twice in the same place."

Najab shook his head. "If your Almighty is as almighty as you say, then His lightning can strike a thousand times on a donkey's whisker!"

David was about to kneel down to pick up another stone, but thought better of it. He tucked his sling back into his belt.

The sun has climbed too high. The time for casting stones today is past.

The sun is hopelessly beyond my reach. As out of reach as the moment when Goliath will fall dead at my feet.

Chapter 45

At sunset, Goliath returned from battle, drunk on the butchery of war. After carousing with his comrades in arms, he toppled onto the marriage bed, reeking of barley beer. A moment later, he was snoring loudly.

Slipping on her robe of fine white linen, Nara crept out of the bedchamber. To her relief, the servants had retired to their quarters for the night. The shadowy courtyard was deserted. She unbolted the front door, alerting her father that it was safe to enter. Careful not to rouse the doves sleeping in their cage, she slipped into the granary chamber and retrieved the bundle of stones from the basket where she had hidden them.

Clutching his sword, Ezel stood watch at the foot of the tall ladder as she climbed it. The wooden rungs creaked under her weight, threatening to awaken Goliath. At last, holding the stones, she pulled herself up onto the roof and stepped into the sapphire radiance of moonlight. She felt as if she was floating in the luminous waters of a sacred sea. When she glanced over the edge, Ezel nodded to her that all was quiet below.

She knelt down beside the rain cistern and pressed the bundle of stones tightly against her womb, feeling their warmth flow into her. With the reverence of a priestess, Nara placed the five sacred stones in a crescent on the roof before her, as Keturah had instructed. She admired how, bathed in moonlight, the arc of stones radiated a pale blue glow. Lifting her eyes to the moon, she imagined the goddess, on her glittering silver throne, gazing down mercifully upon her.

"Forgive me, holy Ashdoda," she whispered, her hands clasped before her in prayer. "I do not know the words to the ancient chants, but I beg you to hear my plea. You, who have the power to nurture all growing things, help the seed that Goliath has planted within me to take root. With your blessing, I will bear a son for my people. Goliath acts with the cruelty of men, but I pledge to raise my son to act with a woman's compassion. I will raise my son so that, out of his love for you, he will heal instead of kill."

She fell silent and stared intently at the sacred stones spread out on the roof, waiting for a sign from the heavens. She did not have to wait long.

The stones trembled, as if possessed with life. It seemed that her prayers were answered.

But she saw now that this was no miracle. The five stones did not quiver because of some force from the heavens. The roof was shaking beneath her feet. From below, she heard the clash of iron blades and Goliath bellowing in rage. She peered over the edge and saw him throw her father against the wall. Ezel groaned and fell to the ground.

Goliath did not climb the ladder, rung by rung. Instead, in his fury, he hauled himself up, using only the strength of his powerful arms. He landed heavily on the roof, a javelin clutched in his fist.

"You betray me!"

Lunging toward her, he kicked aside the five black stones and sent them tumbling down into the courtyard. "You pray to Ashdoda behind my back!"

He struck her hard across the face. She tasted blood in her mouth and staggered backward. She knew that another blow with equal force would kill her.

"Nara!"

It was her father, struggling to climb the ladder. She saw now that Goliath's javelin had gashed his chest, but Ezel pulled himself onto the roof to defend her, sword drawn.

Goliath spat on him. "You help my wife pray to a goddess of women and weakness. *That* is why Dagon denies me a son!"

Goliath seized Ezel by the throat, tightening his grip with his massive right hand. Nara struggled to wrench her father free, but her strength was no match for Goliath's. A single swipe of his left hand knocked her down, her body striking the roof with such force that she feared it would collapse beneath her.

Clutching Ezel by the neck, Goliath lifted him into the air: "Pray to your goddess now, old man!"

Her father could neither cry out nor beg for mercy. Nara scrambled to her feet and lunged for Goliath. It was too late.

"Fly to Ashdoda!"

Goliath hurled Ezel over the edge. For an instant, her father's body flashed in the moonlight, then plunged into the shadowy courtyard below. He crashed into the birdcage of woven cedar twigs. The doves burst free, soaring skyward, white wings vanishing into the night.

Nara peered down into the murky courtyard. Ezel lay motionless on his back, a pool of blood widening from the spot where his head had struck the tiles.

"Your father's body will be thrown into the charnel pit," Goliath said. "There he will rot beside your worthless aunt Hada and all in Gath who are to be despised."

She felt the overwhelming urge to kill him, but knew she was not strong enough.

And yet, Goliath is mortal. Only let me live long enough to see him die.

She clambered awkwardly down the ladder to the courtyard where Ezel lay. His eyes gazed, unblinking, at the moon. She cradled him in her arms, pressed her cheek against his coarse beard with its familiar scent of charcoal and smelted iron. She remembered what he used to tell her each night as a child: "There is nothing on earth as eternal as the anvil of a blacksmith. There is nothing on earth as eternal as my love for you." She murmured a prayer under her breath: "May my father's soul find refuge in Ashdoda's silver citadel, among the few men with the courage to die for the goddess of women."

The holy stones Goliath had kicked from the roof lay

scattered around her in the courtyard. None had shattered, but with her father's death, it seemed they no longer glowed with the sapphire radiance of the moon. She glanced back at Goliath, who glared down at her from the roof. "The goddess will make you pay with your life," she said.

He drew back his javelin. "Yes, someday I will die. If I displease Dagon, someday an enemy as mighty as I am may chop off my head with a great sword of hammered iron. But no woman will ever defy me!"

He hurled the javelin down at her.

She sidestepped, but not quickly enough. The point struck her forehead a glancing blow, before the javelin clattered onto the tiles. Goliath pulled his dagger and strode over to the ladder leaning against the far end of the roof. Before he could reach it, she ran over and threw all her weight against it.

The ladder tottered, then fell with a crash.

Goliath was stranded on the roof. He bellowed for help. She heard the voices of guards in the nearby garrison, then the clatter of their swords and spears echoing down the alleyway as they ran toward the dwelling. Fearing they would burst in at any moment, she scrambled to gather up the five sacred stones from the courtyard.

Fists pounded on the heavy front door. Clutching the stones awkwardly in her arms, she ran across the courtyard and escaped through the servants' passage into a back alleyway.

I will not die tonight. I will not be denied a daughter's vengeance. When Goliath perishes, I will witness it with my own eyes.

* * *

In the jagged shadows of the city ramparts, she struggled to force open the Gates of Eternity as she had once before. She wrenched the bolt clear and strained to pry the bronze doors wide enough to wedge her body through. Weary and wounded, cradling the holy stones in her arms, she felt her strength ebbing. She knew that, at any moment, Goliath's men would shout for the sentries to seal off the city, trapping her inside Gath.

With a final lunge, she squeezed her body through the narrow opening and forced herself out, into the void of the night.

Trumpets blared from the ramparts. The barking of dogs, the clamor of men, told her they were coming after her. A chill wind cut through her fine linen robe. Her forehead throbbed, bloody from the gash of Goliath's javelin. She vowed not to look back toward Gath. Her beloved father and Hada were dead. No one of her flesh and blood lived there now. Gath was a city filled with enemies.

Where can I go? The night when the holy stones fell from the sky, I had the burning oak to show me the way. Now I have no beacon to guide me. Ashdoda has deserted me. Even the moon and stars deny me their light.

At least, Goliath can no longer punish me. That I ever dreamed of bearing him a son fills me with disgust. I will not spawn a race of monsters.

The snarling of dogs grew louder, her pursuers relentlessly closing the distance. Her forehead pounded from her wound. She clutched the stones tightly. With each step, they weighed heavier in her arms. So far, these gifts of Ashdoda have been more a curse than a blessing, she thought, but she would never surrender them.

They are seeds to bring forth miracles. They are my hope for deliverance.

With the back of her hand, she wiped away the trickle of blood seeping from her forehead. Exhaustion bore down on her. Her body had become a painful burden that all her strength could not drag forward. Soon, she lacked the stamina to put one foot in front of the other. The path veered uphill and she struggled to keep her balance, but her ungainly height made that impossible.

Forcing herself ahead, she knew that her heart should be beating rapidly, but it seemed that it, too, was slowing down.

Two more heartbeats. One more heartbeat . . .

Her knees buckled. In her last conscious moment, she thought, better to die like this, alone and free. Better to die here in this desolation than to be dragged back to Gath and stoned to death.

Her body crashed down onto the hard earth. Though her eyes were shut, she sensed her enemies closing in, surrounding her, rejoicing that they had seized her at last. The blood pounded in her head, drowning out their voices.

Chapter 46

Her mind swam out of the depths. At first, Nara's blurred senses could find no clue to where she was. Her wounded forehead throbbed. She tried to open her eyes, but something moist covered them. She breathed in a pungent, unfamiliar smell. At first, she thought the Philistines had thrown her into the charnel pit of Gath. But no, she realized that the scent she struggled to identify did not come from rotting flesh, but from fragrant herbs unknown to her.

What she had first thought was blood oozing from her forehead, she now understood was a moistened poultice wrapped in comfrey leaves. A hand deftly removed it. Nara opened her eyes and recognized Keturah, the pale woman who had given her the holy stones the night before. She examined Nara's wound and tenderly placed a fresh poultice on her brow.

"You must rest."

She realized they had changed her out of her bloodied linen robe into a simple black garment of coarse wool. Looking around her in the twilight, Nara found she was lying on a rough-woven straw mat inside a cave. The boulders at its mouth glistened with droplets from what seemed to be an underground spring. The glow of resin torches revealed that the cave walls were daubed with images of the moon in its changing phases, from narrow as a dagger blade to round as a melon.

"You are safe," Keturah said. Nara did not believe her.

She saw that deep within the cave, a fire flickered weakly. Unlike the bitter scent of iron and charcoal that she knew from her father's forge, this smoke smelled sweet with the fragrance of birch and cedar. Most of it swirled out of the cave mouth into the night sky, but some of it lingered, a gentle haze veiling a group of kneeling women. What had at first sounded like a howling wind, she realized was the chanting of their voices. She could not understand their words, which echoed off the smoke-blackened walls.

Slowly, her eyes adjusted to the gloom. The women prayed before a graven image of Ashdoda that was as tall as Nara herself. The full breasts and broad hips of the idol were identical to those carved into the tear of the goddess that Hada had pressed into her hand, the sacred stone that had brought about her aunt's death. She glimpsed only a faint outline of a face cut into the stone, the delicate features of a benign deity. She marveled that, long ago, this massive graven image had somehow been moved in through the narrow cave mouth. A cleft in the granite overhead revealed the night sky. The moonlight that filtered down endowed the statue with the soft glow of life.

Nara saw that the women who knelt before the idol wore loose-fitting cloaks of rough-spun flax. For adornment, they had fashioned necklaces from bird feathers, seed pods, and pebbles of quartz and amber. Their arms were marked with symbols depicting the phases of the moon, echoing the images daubed in fruit pigments on the cave walls.

An old woman placed a lily as an offering into Ashdoda's outstretched hand. A maiden stepped forward from the group and kissed its foot. Nara guessed that the youngest who had taken refuge here had been discarded by their Philistine husbands when they were unable to bear sons.

Keturah removed the compresses from Nara's forehead and offered her a simple wooden bowl. "This will give you strength."

Nara sat up and lifted it cautiously to her lips: cold barley porridge sweetened with honey. Grateful, she gulped it down. When she had finished, she asked, "Why did you bring me here?"

Keturah lowered her eyes modestly. "Zelmai will speak with you."

She nodded in the direction of the elderly woman who had been leading the others in prayer. Among the Philistines of Gath, such toothless crones had nothing more to do all day than gossip in the spice market, Nara thought. But from the way the women bowed their heads reverently as Zelmai passed among them, it seemed she had the authority of a high priestess. Her spine warped with age, she shuffled over to where Nara lay.

The old woman placed her warm palm to Nara's gashed forehead, then, with a finger, checked the pulse at her throat. Zelmai smiled gently, as if recognizing a familiar face. "Yes, I see her in you." Her mouth was webbed with wrinkles, but her eyes burned brightly. She delicately traced the tip of her finger down Nara's nose, lips and chin. "You are your mother's daughter."

"You knew my mother?" Nara could not connect this outcast to her life in Gath.

"I was with her on the day she perished," Zelmai said with pride.

"That cannot be. My father and my aunt Hada said she died giving birth to me."

"She did not die in childbirth." The old woman tenderly brushed a strand of hair from Nara's face. "When your mother gave birth to your brother, Jadan, her firstborn, there was great rejoicing. But she could not get with child a second time. I secretly gave her a graven image of Ashdoda to help her conceive again. She soon became heavy with child. But an enemy of your father, a rival blacksmith, betrayed her for possessing the holy idol. The priests sentenced her to death."

"Then how was I born?"

"Your mother was soon to give birth. Your father begged the priests to wait and see whether the infant would be a boy who could fight for Gath. Instead, you were born. They took it as proof that your mother had betrayed Dagon." Her eyes met Nara's. "Your mother was stoned to death. It was the same fate her sister Hada would later suffer."

"I was raised on lies," Nara said bitterly.

"Your father and aunt lied to protect you. The priests wanted you put to death, along with your mother. But such was your father's love for you, he told them that if you were killed, he would take his own life. The warriors of Gath needed the iron swords he hammered out in his forge. They could not let him perish. And so they let you live."

"I owe my father my life," Nara said sadly. "And in the end, he gave his life for me."

Zelmai slipped her small white hands, like two doves, into Nara's broad palm. "As a bird returns to its nest, you have come home at last to join us."

"I cannot join you." She tried to pull herself up and winced from her throbbing forehead. "By helping me, you have all put yourselves in grave danger. The Philistines are hunting for me. If they find me here . . ."

"The Philistines of Gath are always hunting for us," the old woman broke in. "They have never found us. Here we have all we need to live." She nodded toward the water dripping down the cave wall. "We drink from a pure underground spring. At night, we gather plants for food . . ."

She stopped and cupped a hand to her ear: The shouts of men, the barking of dogs, rang out in the distance.

"I beg you, listen to me!" Nara's voice resounded off the cave ceiling. The women stopped chanting and turned toward her. "They are coming for me. As surely as they will kill me, they will kill all of you. You must leave at once!"

"We are as one with this holy place," Zelmai said, eying the graven image of Ashdoda. "We will not abandon it." She folded her hands calmly before her.

Nara struggled painfully to her feet. "I have brought destruction to all who loved me—to my mother, my aunt and my father. You must go!"

"We trust in our goddess to defend us," Zelmai said.

"Against the Philistines, that is not enough. You must take up weapons . . ."

"We have none." The priestess smiled. "If we shed blood as wantonly as men, why should the goddess bless us? Ashdoda will only watch over us if we love peace as she does."

Nara saw the serenity on the faces of the women and feared for them. Outside, the barking grew louder. "I will draw their dogs away, so you are not discovered." She picked up the five stones from the straw mat beside her. "Take the tears of Ashdoda. You will need their sorcery."

The priestess accepted them and embraced her. "Your gift will be a blessing for us."

Her legs unsteady, Nara walked over to the cave mouth and peered into the darkness. She heard the voices of the Philistines advancing closer. She clambered out through the cave mouth and breathed in the chill night air. The clatter of swords and spears, the snarling of dogs in the shadows, were almost upon her.

I will sacrifice myself so the daughters of Ashdoda may live. My death will have meaning, even if my life did not.

A hand seized her arm.

Chapter 47

"Come with me." David beckoned Nara to follow him down a steep gully hidden behind a thicket of thorn bushes. The path narrowed. She struggled to force her awkward body between the boulders to keep up with him.

"Why are you here?" she whispered, wary of him.

"I went out alone tonight, seeking a sign from the Almighty. I heard the shouts of the Philistines hunting for you. I knew there was one place you might take refuge."

"You knew of the cave?"

"Once, searching for a lost lamb, I came upon it. The women begged me not to reveal their hiding place. I never have."

"They trusted you," she said. "Why should I trust you now?"

He paused on the trail and looked up at her. "Because the foe of your enemy is your friend."

He glanced back at the silhouettes of the Philistines in the distance. Their lead dogs were yelping excitedly. The soldiers pulled at their tethers, struggling to control them as they reached the boulders at the cave mouth. Twenty more in the raiding party ran up, swords drawn. David and Nara watched as they plunged into the cave and vanished from sight.

Echoing from the depths, the barking of the dogs deepened into guttural snarls. And yet, they heard no screams. The glow from the mouth of the cave flared up and was quickly snuffed out.

"We must go now," he said. She did not move. After what she had seen, he realized she could not so easily turn her back on the women. "It is too late to save them. But there is still time to save yourself."

"The Philistines were coming for *me*," she said. "I should have died with them."

"No, your life was spared for a reason." His words coaxed her to follow him deeper into the gorge.

"The women believed they were secure in their holy place," she said sadly.

"There is no cave on earth deep enough to escape the wickedness of men."

He guided her along a rugged path overgrown with the twisted roots of dead oaks. Splinters of flint, sharp as knives, cut Nara's ankles. Suddenly, they heard the barking of the Philistines' dogs closer than before.

"They are back on your scent," he said.

"Where can we go?"

"To a safe place."

He led her hastily down a trail dense with undergrowth. She was forced to tear out brush by the roots to follow him. When she stumbled and fell, she did not pull herself back to her feet, but crouched, breathless, on the ground. "I left them the sacred stones," she said, fighting back tears. "I thought Ashdoda's magic could protect them . . ."

"The stones are worthless. Ashdoda could not even save the poor souls who devoted their lives to her!" He could see that his harsh words had wounded Nara. "Do not feel shame to weep before me," he said gently. "I wept when my brothers died at the hands of the Philistines."

But she did not weep. It seemed to David that for her, the time for weeping had passed. He watched as, with fresh determination, she climbed slowly back to her feet and forced herself to follow him. He moved effortlessly through the darkness, but she was so tall and awkward that each step was difficult, the steep trail crumbling underfoot. She bent down to wedge her body through a cleft between boulders.

"Why do you risk your life to help me?" she asked, fighting to catch her breath. "An Israelite does not rescue a Philistine out of simple kindness. What will you ask of me in return?"

David did not tell her. She would find out soon enough.

Chapter 48

The clouds on the horizon reddened at sunrise like blood seeping from a wound. David knew the risks of bringing Nara to this outlying Israelite encampment beyond Gibeah.

"My people must not catch sight of you." He beckoned for her to crouch down in the brush beside him. "The Israelites grieve for many killed by Goliath's sword. They will try to do you harm." He did not tell her that he was also in danger. If they saw him helping a Philistine, the Israelites would put him to death as a traitor. He pressed a finger to his lips for Nara to keep still, but she snapped dry twigs underfoot.

I am used to shepherding my obedient flock. Now I must shepherd an unpredictable Philistine who holds my life in her hands.

She whispered, "If it is so dangerous for me here, why have you brought me?"

To answer, he beckoned her to follow him behind a granite slab at the edge of a cliff. From there, they could peer down into the Israelites' encampment undetected. Her lips tightened with distaste. He realized the sight of his people repelled her. Some were gaunt from hunger. Their clothes were ragged and, lacking sandals, many walked barefoot on the flinty earth. The women and girls bore unglazed clay jugs on their shoulders. Without a well from which to draw pure water, they were forced to fetch it from a muddy stream.

Nara winced at the smell of rancid goat that drifted toward them. In the ravine below, Israelite women roasted scraps of meat over dying coals. "Your people live like savages," she said. "I pity them."

"They are not savages and they are not to be pitied." He stifled the anger in his voice, but felt the chasm that separated them.

"If your God is so much more powerful than our gods, why

are your people poor, while we Philistines prosper? Why do your women wear rags, while the women of Gath wear fine linen woven with threads of gold?"

"Our prophets tell us, 'Who is the wealthy man? He who is happy with what he has.'"

"What he has?" she scoffed. "And what do you have that makes it worth living in squalor?"

David was surprised to hear the chanting of voices. Attracted to the sound, he led Nara away from the cluster of ragged goatskin tents with their feeble cooking fires, to the brink of a narrow gorge. He saw that the trail that led down the steep slope was guarded by four Israelite sentries, and beckoned for her to keep out of sight. Beyond the guards, he glimpsed the curved canopy of a broad tent that he had seen only once before, when he was searching with Jonathan for Joshua's sword and shield.

The Tabernacle. As he looked down on it in the early morning light, the pale white canopy seemed to glow softly from within, as if it radiated the glory of the Ark that it enshrined. He saw that the chanting that had drawn him here came from the Israelites who knelt before it: men, young and old, with women at a respectful distance behind them—mothers, wives, daughters. All were consumed in prayer.

"The Tabernacle holds the Ark of the Covenant, our greatest treasure." He pointed to the entrance of the tent where white-robed priests stood their vigil. "I did not know this would be here. I believe it was fated by the Almighty that the Tabernacle was moved to this place so I could show it to you. So you could see it with your own eyes and understand."

"I understand nothing." Nara shook her head, puzzled by the sight. "Our gods dwell in temples of gold. Why does your God inhabit so humble a place?"

"He does not live there. The Tabernacle protects the Ark that holds the Tablets of His Law. These Commandments tell us how to lead our lives as we must."

She was struggling to make sense of it. "The Laws from your God . . . Is their purpose to smooth out the rough road of life?"

"No, His Laws are difficult because they are good, and good because they are difficult."

"How can something that makes each day of your life a trial be a blessing?"

He struggled to put it into words. "The Law dares us to be more than we are, perhaps more than we can ever be. The Law challenges us to lift our souls up to the High Places. It is easier to kill a man than to forgive him. And yet, only by acts of forgiveness can we be true to the Almighty."

He saw that he had done little to dispel her confusion. "If your Ark is so precious," she asked, "why is it kept so far from Gibeah?"

"To protect the Ark from capture by the Philistines, the priests move it from one site to another. Sometimes they stop near small encampments like this one. It allows our scattered people to draw strength from it." He pointed beyond the men in prayer beside the Tabernacle, to the wives and mothers kneeling further away, cradling infants in their arms. Widows, their foreheads marked with ashes, their garments torn in grief, clasped their hands together and raised their voices to the heavens in lamentation.

"These women mourn their loved ones killed by Goliath and his men," David said. "They pray that no more will die."

"Sorrow is the bond that unites all women," Nara said, and swept her hand across her eyes. He saw that the grief of the Israelite widows had rekindled her own. "These women weep the same tears as the widows of Gath." She cut herself short and looked at him with suspicion: "Why did you bring me here?"

"So you would accept us for who we are."

His words sparked her anger. "You think you can make me into one of you? I would never belong to your tribe. I see only a wretched people who suffer greatly!"

"I ask only that you listen."

"I will not listen," she said defiantly. "The Laws of your God are foreign to me."

"The Laws may seem foreign. But my people. . . . Did you not say that sorrow is the tie that binds all women?"

She nodded reluctantly. "That is true."

"And is there not one thing that all widows hunger for?" He had sensed that hunger in her, recognized it smoldering in her eyes. "It is not gentle and it is not womanly, but every widow would sacrifice her life for it above all else."

A dark understanding passed between them. She uttered the word: "Vengeance."

* * *

They set out once more. Now that the last shadows of night had vanished with the rising sun, he knew that the Israelite sentries could spot them at any moment. It troubled him that he had to be as wary of his own people as she was. He led Nara quickly away from the encampment, into the barren desolation.

When they were out of danger, he stopped and turned to her. "I need your help."

He saw that she was fighting a battle with herself, torn about how to answer him. At last, she said, "I know only one thing: I must avenge the murder of my father, my mother and my beloved Hada . . ."

"And I must avenge the killing of my two brothers. I must avenge the deaths of all of my people that Goliath has taken from us—"

"No," she stopped him, as if knowing what he was about to say. "Goliath has already slain too many. I will not help send you to your death."

He chose his words carefully. "If the Almighty wills it, I will die. But would you not risk your life to kill Goliath?" She nodded reluctantly. "Then how can you deny me the chance to risk mine?"

Chapter 49

David saw that Nara was puzzled by the sight. The thing that he had taken her all this way to see was nothing more than two upthrust boulders with a scorched, blackened slab of rock placed flat across them.

She bent down and discovered that charcoal had been heaped between the two boulders. Enclosed by the slab that lay across them, they formed a primitive furnace. A crude bronze hammer and tongs leaned against a waist-high block of granite that served as an anvil.

"*This* is your forge?"

He heard pity in her voice. Or was it contempt? "It is good for nothing more than mending blades of copper or bronze," he said. "We are ignorant of the art of working iron. For generations, the Philistines have kept the secrets of the black metal from us." He proceeded with care. "The Nubian trader says you know those secrets. He says your skill at the anvil rivals your father's."

"Najab!" She shook her head in disgust. "My father's trusted friend spies for the Israelites!"

He pressed: "Did he speak the truth?"

Pride crept into her voice. "I am the only woman in Gath who knows how to work iron."

He pointed out a stack of heavy gray stones, each as big as his fist, beside the makeshift forge. "On his way from the smelting pits of Timna, Najab secretly sold these iron ingots to Jonathan." He picked up one of them. "Use your skill with the forge. Make me weapons of iron. I swear on the lives of all who have fallen that I will use them to slay Goliath."

"I would gladly hammer out the iron blade that chops off Goliath's head," she said. "But I cannot. You lack the one thing I must have."

"Do not tell me you need the blessing of your father's false god." As soon as he spoke, he regretted the contempt with which he had said it.

"I do not need the blessing of a god. I need the handiwork of men. There is a device that has been handed down from father to son by Philistine blacksmiths over countless generations. No Israelite has ever seen this contrivance. No Israelite even knows it exists. Only a few master blacksmiths in Gath have the knowledge to construct it. My father made me swear to never speak its name, but I do now: The Serpent's Tongue."

"The Serpent's Tongue." He repeated the words without understanding their meaning.

"My father taught me how to use it. A Philistine blacksmith would die before betraying its secrets."

He watched, puzzled, as she picked up one of the Israelites' makeshift tools, which looked to him like two sheep's bladders stitched together. "This is a crude bellows used by your people. They pump it to raise the heat of the flames so the furnace can melt copper or bronze." She threw it back into the dust. "It is useless to melt iron. That deadly metal must be brought to a far greater heat."

"But how does the Serpent's Tongue. . ?"

"It alone can force the flames of the furnace to burn hot enough to melt iron. Without it, the stubborn metal cannot be shaped on the anvil to forge invincible blades of war. The Serpent's Tongue is forked like a two-headed viper, which allows it to goad the flames to a fierce heat. It is worked with the legs, rather than the arms, to give it much more force. Thanks to the Serpent's Tongue, Goliath's iron blades do not bend or break like lesser metals. His sword shatters the weak copper blades of your people."

"It seems you know Goliath's weapons well."

"I hammered out the sword and spear my father presented to him as my dowry." She frowned at the thought. "It was my love-gift to Goliath before I knew the wickedness in his heart."

"And now you will hammer out a blade of iron to kill him."

She turned her back on the crude forge. "You do not have a Serpent's Tongue. Without it—"

"Then we must get one."

At first, she did not reply, deep in thought. When she spoke, he heard the doubt in her voice. "There is a Serpent's Tongue in my father's forge. My father kept it hidden. But I worked at his side. I know where it is . . ."

He stopped her. "If you are saying that to fetch the Serpent's Tongue, I must enter Gath and go to your father's forge . . ."

"No, you would be quickly captured and killed. But there is one man who might do this for me."

Chapter 50

"Goliath killed your father, my beloved friend." Najab ran a sweaty palm over his shaved head so that it gleamed like polished obsidian. "Now you would have Goliath kill me too!"

The Nubian seemed as eager to be rid of Nara as he was to deliver his mangy donkeys from the swarm of flies that afflicted them. Outside Gibeah, sheltered from the heat of the day beneath a copse of cedars, he plucked burrs from the muzzle of one, whispered comforting words into the ragged ear of another, and pried out a pebble wedged in the hoof of a third. Finally, seeing Nara would not leave him in peace, he blurted out, "Yes, what you say is true. I can run faster than the wind. If I could, I would dash all the way to Gath in the blink of an eye to fetch the thing you seek. But it cannot be."

She saw that she had thrown him off-balance and pushed harder. "Did my father Ezel not treat you fairly all his life? Did he not pay you well?

"Yes, and I weep for your father!" He licked his lips, uneasy where she was leading him. "When I delivered ingots to his forge, he did me many kindnesses. While the other blacksmiths of Gath fed my darlings straw, he fed them barley. While the others treated me like a slave, he bade me sit with him in the coolness of the evening to sip honey wine. And in return, because you were his daughter, I brought you gifts."

She nodded. "I remember. A crystal of quartz, an ox-horn comb, a scarab beetle green as an emerald. I prized them highly." She skewered him with a look. "But because you gave me gifts, you thought I would not notice . . ."

He squirmed under her gaze. "Notice what?"

"My father trusted you. He never counted the number of iron ingots you brought him because he always took you at your word."

"A man's word is his most precious jewel," he replied, but he ran a nervous thumb along the snakes carved into his forearm as if to keep them from biting him.

"I used to watch you unload the ingots from your donkeys. I was only a child, but I was old enough to count."

He bit his lip. "Yes, it is true . . ." He let out a heavy sigh. "I did your father a grave injustice. I gave him fewer ingots than he paid me for."

"*Many* fewer."

"Yes, many fewer." He studied her, puzzled. "You knew this, and yet, you never told your father. Why?"

"Children are selfish. I feared that if I told him, you would be angry and stop bringing me gifts. In that, I failed my father. But you did far worse. You betrayed his trust. It is bad enough to wrong a man while he is alive, but you failed to make amends after his death."

Najab plucked a cockroach off the back of his lead donkey. He crushed the insect thoughtfully between his thumb and forefinger. "Yes, I wronged him." He furrowed his brow. "I wronged him, but now it is too late."

"It is not too late. As his flesh and blood, I have the power to forgive you on his behalf, if you do as I ask. If you refuse, the curse of my father's spirit will cripple you so you hobble like a lame donkey."

He saw there was no escape. Placing his right hand over his heart, he murmured the words that she had been waiting to hear. "I will go to Gath. I will enter the forge of your father, but . . ." He stopped. "Once I go inside, how will I find the treasure I seek?"

"Go to the furnace. On the right corner, near the top, there is a loose block of granite. Pry it out. Inside the hollow, you will find the Serpent's Tongue. Bring it back to me and I will make weapons of iron to punish Goliath for his wickedness."

With a broad grin, he patted the intertwining snakes on his arm. "Upon all my gods, I will go to Gath and find what you seek."

After thanking him, Nara rejoined David, who had been watching them from the shade of a cedar nearby. When she glanced back at Najab, his smile had faded. She saw he was afraid.

* * *

Crouched together behind boulders on a steep slope, Nara and David surveyed the desolate plain. In the distance, the Nubian led his caravan of five donkeys along the windswept trail toward Gath. David saw that, as usual, the dusty animals were heavy-laden with iron ingots for the forges of the Philistines. The donkeys moved so slowly in the afternoon heat, it seemed they hardly moved at all. Najab walked impatiently beside them.

"Look at him," David said. "His heart and soul ache to run. Instead, he must crawl along at the pace of his most slothful donkey."

"May Najab's gods, my goddess Ashdoda, and your invisible Almighty all work together to hasten his safe return."

"No," David replied with the stubborn certainty of his people. "Only the Almighty need help Najab. All other gods are the dreams of fools."

"Do not offend those foreign gods," she warned. "Even if they are only dreams, they rule the minds of those who worship them."

The rising wind stung David's face with sand from the desert beyond. He gazed into Nara's eyes, seeking to read her thoughts. He did not like what he found there: her foreboding that even if Najab returned with the Serpent's Tongue, even if she hammered out deadly weapons of iron for him, he was still doomed to die at Goliath's hand.

Chapter 51

"When the sun reaches its peak, I will return from Gath with the Serpent's Tongue. Meet me at the shrine hallowed to my gods. If I do not return, know that I have failed. Know that we will only meet again in the world to come."

The Nubian had instructed David to follow the dry riverbed that cut like a scar across the jaundiced land from Gibeah toward the Great Sea. On the desolate trail, he passed towering termite mounds and a thicket of withered tamarisk trees. How strange, he thought, that Najab worshipped the creature that the Almighty had damned for all eternity. His father, Jesse, had told him how God punished the serpent in Eden:

"Cursed are you above all cattle, and above all wild animals. Upon your belly you shall go, and dust shall you eat all the days of your life."

Tending his flock, David had watched newborn lambs, the most innocent of creatures, die from the venom of adders. He had seen a beloved old shepherd, moments after he was bitten by a viper, gasp his last breath. What drove serpents to commit such acts? he wondered. Other animals killed for food, but it seemed that snakes killed out of a wickedness only rivaled by man's.

Even now, in the midday sun, he saw no sign of the holy site that was to be their meeting place. "How will I know when I arrive there?" he had asked Najab.

"You will know when you come upon it," was all the Nubian would say.

* * *

David heard a faint hissing. At first, he thought it was only the wind raking through the withered, ankle-high grass. Ahead, he glimpsed what looked like a water hole, a welcome sight to a thirsty traveler in this parched, barren country. He took a few more steps. The hissing grew louder. He wondered: Without so much as a heap of stones to mark it, could this be Najab's shrine?

Only when he reached the brink of the pit did he discover what lurked in its depths: a seething multitude of snakes, their forked tongues darting. He saw how the water from a dying spring allowed the creatures to nest and breed among the rocks, even as it lured their prey to come and drink. How many snakes there were, he could not say. It was impossible to tell where one ended and another began, as if they were the intertwining coils of a single writhing serpent. The gleaming silver scales, the flicking tongues, the threat of their venom, fascinated yet repelled him. If this was the Nubian's shrine, he saw no holiness here.

At the far rim of the pit, Najab stepped into view. His face was haggard, his indigo cloak dusty and torn. "Do you have it?" David asked.

Najab flashed a triumphant smile. David followed him over to his five donkeys, which were tethered nearby. Najab untied a burlap sack from the back of Shaya. "Behold the treasure I risked my life to steal!" With a flourish, he opened the sack to reveal the precious object.

The Serpent's Tongue was an intricate device of wood and bronze like none David had seen before. It was fashioned from two leather bladders linked by an elaborate system of bronze tubes to a forked snout. The bladders were attached to wooden levers wide enough to be pumped by the feet. He realized how, as Nara had told him, this enabled the snout of the serpent to blow powerful blasts of air, bringing the flames of the furnace to the intense heat needed to melt iron.

"May the Philistine woman use this to forge the sword that chops off Goliath's head!" Najab said.

"You have my deepest thanks."

"I am not the one to thank." The Nubian led David back over to the brink of the pit. "It is time for both of us to express our gratitude to my gods, who make all things possible."

David was mesmerized by the glistening scales in the pit below. "To pray to my God, we lift our eyes to the heavens," he said. "To pray to yours, you look down into the mud."

Najab bristled. "You Israelites imprison your God in a coffin you call your 'Ark' or shackle Him in the stale parchment of your Holy Scrolls. We worship our gods where they live, nestled in the womb of the earth, from which all life flows." He clasped his hands before him in prayer. "We exalt the only creatures that defy death, for the oldest of their kind shed their skins to become young again—"

The harsh braying of Najab's donkeys interrupted him. The skittish animals tossed their heads and pawed the ground.

A man emerged from among them. He was tall and lean, wearing the dented bronze breastplate of a hardened Israelite warrior. His right hand was missing three fingers. To secure his grip on his sword, the hilt had been lashed tightly to his wrist with a leather strap. David recognized him: Shodok, the commander who had spoken out against Saul in Gibeah.

"How did you know we would come here?" David asked.

The commander smirked. "At the stables in Gibeah, one of my men overheard Najab chattering to his four-legged concubines."

"I can keep secrets from my fellow men," Najab murmured in shame, "but not from my lovelies!"

The crunch of dirt underfoot, the glint of blades, alerted David that two of Shodok's men had crept up on them from behind, swords drawn. Both wore leather wristbands with crude wooden amulets dangling from them. *They might call themselves Israelites*, he thought, *but they are pagans. They have known the Almighty and forsaken Him.*

"I am unarmed," he said, as Shodok and his men advanced toward him. "What threat am I to you, that you would harm me?"

"A mortal threat," Shodok said. "I have learned that Samuel anointed you to rule after Saul. If my men hear of this, some will choose to follow you as their king, instead of me. That must not happen." He leveled his sword point at Najab's throat. "Give me the Serpent's Tongue."

"What good is it to you?" David asked. "No Israelite knows how to use it."

"I am told you have a Philistine woman versed in its secrets of forging iron. If a woman can learn them, my own blacksmith in Gibeah, gifted at working copper and bronze, can easily master them. With iron blades, my men will crush Saul and those who still follow him."

He lunged forward to snatch the Serpent's Tongue from Najab, but the Nubian clutched the device close to his chest. One of Shodok's men thrust out with his sword, nicking Najab's arm. Bloodied, the Nubian lost his grip on the Serpent's Tongue. It dropped onto the rim of the pit. He dove for it, but the dirt crumbled beneath him.

David saw that Najab was hanging over the edge of the pit by one hand, his feet dangling—and the Serpent's Tongue was wobbling precariously, threatening to topple into the pit.

Najab or the Serpent's Tongue. There was only time for David to save one of them.

Without hesitation, he reached down, seized Najab's hand, and pulled him up to safety.

The Serpent's Tongue plummeted toward the snakes. Shodok lunged out to grab it in midair, but lost his footing. He fell into the pit, the device shattering on the rocks beside him.

Gazing into the depths, David watched the precious fragments of the Philistine device vanish, lost along with Shodok's body beneath the writhing coils.

Seeing their master's fate, Shodok's men fled.

Chapter 52

Sweltering in the heat, Jonathan and Michal were stacking charcoal and kindling into the makeshift forge formed by the three blackened stone slabs. Nara carried over a heavy armful of ingots. As David scrambled down the barren hillside toward them, he saw they were working too hard to notice him.

All that remains is for me to bring them the Serpent's Tongue. If only I had it to give them . . .

When David drew closer, Jonathan caught sight of him. "I rejoice that you have come back!" He rushed over and embraced David, then offered him a goatskin of water. David took a few hasty gulps. He saw that Michal's eyes shone with joy at his safe return.

Nara blurted out the question on all their minds: "Did Najab do as he promised?" She nodded toward the Nubian, who was approaching them with his string of donkeys.

"Yes, but we were ambushed by Shodok," David said.

"He had to choose between a treasure and your humble servant," Najab said with a grin, as he joined them. "I am blessed that David chose one who is no more worthy than his donkeys!"

Nara could hardly bring herself to say the words. "The Serpent's Tongue was *lost*?"

"Destroyed," David said. "I had no choice."

Nara slumped down on a boulder. "To sacrifice a man's life for a device made of wood and metal would have been wrong . . ."

"No better than idolatry," David said.

She nodded, accepting the merit of what he had done, but she could not hide her disappointment that the Serpent's Tongue was lost.

"The Almighty has spoken." Jonathan nodded in Nara's direction. "It was not God's will for the Philistine woman to forge blades of iron for you."

"It is not as easy as you think to know God's will," David cautioned.

But Jonathan's mind raced ahead. "Now, without the Serpent's Tongue, you can follow only one path: You must claim the iron sword and shield of Joshua!"

"But they are lost! When we opened the coffer—"

Jonathan broke in with the brashness that David so distrusted: "My father must have hidden them from you. He must know where they are."

"He will never tell us."

"He will never tell *you*. But I am his own flesh and blood." Jonathan added, with supreme self-confidence, "I will persuade him! The next time I see you, I will have Joshua's sword and shield in my hands." With a cocky wave, he set out toward Gibeah.

"I too must take my leave." Najab embraced David in gratitude. He bowed to Michal and Nara, touching his hand to his heart in respect. Then he rejoined his donkeys and, clucking his tongue, poked them with his staff. Grudgingly, they plodded down the dusty trail with him.

Michal beckoned to Nara. "Come with me. I will find a safe place for you to take refuge . . ."

"No, I will stay here for now. I have been running for too long. After I have rested . . ." Nara stopped, uncertain what she would do next.

"I will send a handmaiden to fetch you before sunset," Michal said. "You will not be forgotten."

David gazed at the blackened boulders of the makeshift furnace that had been so carefully prepared with charcoal and iron ingots.

It mocks me, proof that I have failed. An iron blade will never be forged here. I will never have the sword I need to fight Goliath.

He realized Michal had been watching him, and read the worry on her face. "Where will you go now?" she asked. "What will you do?"

He turned in the direction of Bethlehem. "It is time for me to listen to the counsel of my wisest advisors."

"Your father? Your brothers?"

He laughed. "No, the sheep in my flock."

"Your sheep are wise?"

"Yes, wise because they force me to think for myself!"

As David walked away, he did not confide his secret wish to her, his secret hope that alone in the silence, he might hear the whispered words of the Almighty at last.

Chapter 53

Jonathan watched night tighten its grip on Gibeah. At any moment, he expected the thunderclap of the gates of the city being slammed shut and bolted until dawn. And yet, even now, he hesitated outside the walls. Despite his boast to David, he did not know whether he could persuade Saul to give him the sword and shield of Joshua. He dreaded facing his father. He feared Saul's rage.

He forced himself to walk toward the gates of the city. Gazing through the great portals, he saw the humble mud-brick dwellings were plunged into darkness. It saddened him that so few of his people could afford oil for their lamps.

He was surprised to hear footsteps approaching. His sister rushed toward him out of the shadows. "I am coming with you," she said.

"I am Saul's eldest son and his favorite. What makes you think you can convince him to tell you where he has hidden Joshua's sword and shield, if I cannot?"

"You will speak to his mind," she said. "I will speak to his heart."

Though he frowned to show his displeasure, he was secretly pleased that Michal had joined him. It was safer this way. He did not want to face his father alone.

When they entered the gates together, he felt the sentries on the parapets staring down at them. Michal noticed it too. "They have never seen the son and daughter of the king enter the palace side by side," she said.

He knew it was true. The two of them were opposites: He was a hunter, a fighter, a hot-headed taker of risks, while she was a gentle peacemaker: "For the first time, we have a common cause."

"May it not be the last," she said.

Brother and sister quickened their pace across the courtyard. At the portal to the palace, the guards recognized them and pushed open the doors. Their steps echoed hollowly down the murky, torch-lit corridor, on the way to Saul's bedchamber. They passed sullen guards with spears, watching them.

"Saul fears his own people as much as he fears the Philistines," he said.

"There will never be enough guards to protect our father from himself."

The gold-etched doors to the king's bedchamber burst open. Tobiah rushed out and shut the doors tightly behind him. "You should not have come. You cannot see him!"

"We must," Jonathan said.

"You place your lives at risk!"

"Our father will not harm us," Michal said.

Tobiah wrung his hands. "Saul has changed much since your last visit."

The delicate notes of a lyre rippled from within the king's bedchamber. "Once, David played for Saul in this very place," Michal said. "This music does not rival his." Even so, Jonathan found the melody calming, the touch of the player's fingers on the strings gentle but assured.

With a crash, the music was cut short. Through the massive oak door, they heard Saul shouting in fury.

The guards wavered in fear, but Jonathan seized the gilded handles and threw the doors wide. Fragments of ivory from a smashed lyre were scattered across the floor of the bedchamber. He saw that the slender young servant who had played it, cowered in a corner, hands clasped before him, begging for mercy. Saul raised his sword high, the blade gleaming crimson in the torchlight, as if it had already shed blood.

Jonathan stepped between them. "Enough!" He grabbed his father's arm. Saul's face was gaunt, his eyes fevered. Tobiah was right that my father has changed, Jonathan thought. The evil spirits have returned with a vengeance.

Michal rushed over to the terrified youth. "Go!" Too frightened to speak, he scrambled to his feet and fled the room.

The sword wavered in Saul's hands. His eyes snapped back into focus. He blinked, startled to see Jonathan and Michal standing before him. The sword slipped from his fingers and clattered to the floor.

"My beloved son and daughter. . . . The evil spirits afflict me again. This time, music cannot keep them at bay!" In despair, he gazed down at the scraps of ivory strewn before him. "They said this lyre held powers of sorcery, but it is worthless!"

"Father, a lyre does not possess magic," Michal said gently. "It is the one who plays it." She reached out to take his hand, but he stiffened and backed away.

"Only David had the power to rid you of demons with his lyre," Jonathan said.

"Yes, and now I know why. David is a demon himself!" Saul eyed the two of them suspiciously. "Of course! That is why you came here together. Who else could have sent you?"

"David did not send us," Jonathan said. "We came to ask a favor on David's behalf."

"Why should I help this shepherd who has turned my own son and daughter against me, this usurper who would steal my throne?"

Jonathan did his best to stifle his anger. "Samuel has announced it is the will of the Almighty for David to rule after you. So it must be."

"The old prophet is mad," Saul scoffed. "How else could he anoint a shepherd to follow a king?"

"Whether or not you think Samuel is mad, David is the prophet's Chosen. And now, his Chosen is determined to face Goliath in battle."

"More madness!" Saul burst into a shrill laugh. "Then let him die quickly at Goliath's hand!"

Michal knelt before him. "Father, we ask your help so David can defeat the Philistine, so our people can have peace at last."

"How can I believe a word you say?" he replied. "Even a blind man could see you are bewitched by him!"

She lowered her eyes modestly. "I know only that I have a deep respect for David. And I know that without your help, he will die." Her eyes glistened and she wiped them with the back of her hand.

"Dry your tears," Saul said. "They will not melt my heart! David has cast his spell over you! You surrender to his lies as readily as the evil spirits surrendered to the music of his lyre!"

"For the good of our people, he must defeat Goliath," Jonathan said. "He can only do this with weapons sacred to the Israelites. You taught me that Joshua's sword and shield were forged of iron in the Early Times, before we lost the secrets of working the black metal. I have opened the ancient coffer that once held them. The coffer is empty."

Saul's eyes widened in amazement. "Empty? That cannot be!"

Is he deceiving me? Jonathan wondered. Saul is cunning. If he had stolen Joshua's treasures, he would never admit it. Jonathan proceeded with caution, knowing his father's violent temper was even more unpredictable than his own. "I came to you because I thought that in your wisdom, you would know where they are."

"You think *I* stole them? I do not plunder the treasures of my own people!" Saul threw back his shoulders and thrust out his chin, struggling to regain his regal bearing. "That the weapons have vanished is not an act of men. It is a sign from God!" He grasped Jonathan by the shoulders and peered into his eyes with the fervor of one possessed. "This proves the Almighty does not favor David for the throne. It proves He wants to see David die so *you*, my son, can be king!"

Jonathan was about to object, but he saw he was too late. Though they still stood face-to-face, the king had suddenly left them, retreating back into his own world, his eyes lost in a vacant stare.

"It is best you leave now!" Tobiah ushered Jonathan and Michal out into the corridor, seemingly relieved that their meeting had ended without bloodshed. Jonathan glanced back through the open door: His father knelt on the floor, eyes closed, hands clasped above his head. "At last, after far too long, he prays," the king's advisor said. "It means Saul has found fresh hope!"

Yes, Jonathan thought, Saul has found fresh hope that soon David will die.

* * *

Side by side, brother and sister walked down the dim corridor that led away from the king's chamber. After their shared defeat, they moved at a slower pace. Neither spoke, the only sound the hollow echo of their feet on the cold stone floor.

"All my life, I feared my father's lies," Jonathan said at last. "It is worse now, when I know he is telling me the truth."

Michal nodded. "He believes the sword and shield of Joshua vanished through an act of the Almighty."

What if Saul is right? Jonathan thought. What if God Himself is bent on David's destruction?

They emerged into the cold night air of the shadowy palace courtyard. Now that their visit to their father had ended in failure, his mind groped for another plan. He peered up into the sky, searching for answers. The heavens glimmered faintly overhead, as murky as the ill-lit dwellings of Gibeah. A man of action, he was never more miserable than in these moments when he was forced to face uncertainty.

I can no more foretell what will come tomorrow than I can read the stars. If the heavens hold a message from the Almighty, it is hidden from me.

He shoved past the two sentries at the outer palace doors.

They lowered their spears meekly before him. Brother and sister no longer walked side by side, but kept their distance. Jonathan realized that the bond that had united them in their plea before Saul was broken. He was dispirited, but he noticed that Michal suddenly moved at a brisk pace, as if with fresh purpose.

Though he feared she would see his question as a sign of weakness, he asked, "Where are you going?"

"To find the sword and shield of Joshua."

"But . . . where?"

"A place where you are forbidden to go."

Chapter 54

Before Goliath, there were other giants. David's father had told him so: "Back in the Early Times, before the Great Flood," Jesse had said, "the Evil Ones walked the earth and afflicted our people."

Because David knew that he must soon face the Philistine, he had come with his flock to this long-dead place where giants once ruled, in search of understanding. It was said that the toppled thicket of strangely shaped pillars of stone survived from the distant days of Noah. David's sheep nibbled at the patches of grass among them. He took comfort that, even here, they could find enough to stave off their hunger.

That is also why I have come, to satisfy a hunger of a different kind.

All his life, he had found a wisdom in silence that he could not find in words, a wisdom he could not even find in the music of his lyre. And yet, today, the silence suffocated him. He felt trapped among the cold gray shafts that jutted skyward like shattered columns. He could find no clear passage through them. He had lost his way.

Without warning, Samuel loomed before him. True to the unsettling nature of the prophet, he appeared suddenly, a stark presence standing rigidly upright among the tilted granite spars, his face the same deathly gray as the stone.

"How did you know where to find me?" David asked.

"I knew you would bring your flock to a place that others avoid." With his one good eye, Samuel studied the hyacinths, crocuses and black mulberry that thrust up between the jagged stumps of stone. "Other shepherds shun this place like death itself, but you know that even here new life grows."

"To find life where there is death. In these times, that is what we all must do."

"That is your gift," the prophet replied. "So it is that our people must find food for the spirit in a desolation where it seems there is none." With his one good eye, he surveyed the toppled oblong spars. "Do you know what these are?"

"They say that in the Early Times these were once mighty oaks, but that with the Great Flood, the Most High transformed them into stone."

Samuel shook his head. "The truth is more wondrous than that, and more terrible. These were not trees. They are all that remains of the Evil Ones. Yes, the giants in the Early Times were even mightier and more fearsome than Goliath. For their wickedness, they were swept away in the Great Flood. The Almighty turned their bones to stone."

David studied the splintered shafts. He thought he could discern fragments of immense skulls. The sharp, jagged slabs could have been the giants' teeth and the massive columns could have been the bones of their arms and legs.

"In the Great Flood, all the Evil Ones did *not* die," Samuel said. "Goliath descends from their unholy race. If he brings forth sons and founds his own dynasty, he will restore their wicked kingdom to rule the earth."

David was troubled by his words. "If the Almighty is all-powerful, how can He allow the seed of Evil to blossom in our own time?"

"Because it is upon each of us, in his own generation, to fight wickedness," Samuel said. "How else can we prove our righteousness before Him?" While the prophet's blind eye stared coldly ahead, David felt the good one studying him with compassion: "I come to you because I have received a revelation from the Almighty."

It was what David had hoped for. "An omen?"

"No," the prophet muttered with annoyance. "I did not hear a portent in the clucking of ravens, or see a vision in the embers of a dying fire. I beheld Him in all His glory. I heard the words from His lips:

'When the sun rises tomorrow in the Valley of Elah, David, son of Jesse, must do battle with Goliath. Either David will kill the Philistine, or David will perish. And on the outcome will hang the fate of the world.'"

David was overwhelmed by the awareness that the time of waiting was over. Without hesitation, he said, "I am ready to face him."

Samuel did not look convinced. "If you are to triumph, you must fight him as a king fights. You must think and act like a king. Only then will you be worthy to become one."

"But I do not have the weapons of a king," David objected, his voice betraying his uneasiness. "I had thought the Serpent's Tongue could fashion me a sword of iron to rival Goliath's. That chance is lost. And when I sought out the hallowed sword and shield of Joshua, they had vanished."

The prophet's blind eye, the sickly yellow of curdled milk, transfixed him. "You must use what you have, not what you wish for!"

Chapter 55

After David and Najab had returned empty-handed, and joined Michal, Jonathan and Nara at the makeshift forge, they had split up, fate leading them down different paths. Only Nara had stayed behind. Perhaps it was the familiar smell of the ingots, or the scent of charcoal from the crude furnace, but somehow this place calmed and comforted her. Lying down on a patch of grass in the shadow of the smoke-blackened stones, she had fallen into a deep sleep.

She awoke to a revelation.

Though I cannot make David weapons of iron, I can still help him to slay Goliath. I do not yet know how. I will only know when I set eyes on David once more.

She had to find him, but knew she could not do this by herself. By good fortune—or, as she would later believe, by destiny—she waylaid Najab on the trail outside Gibeah. When she explained all that was at stake, he felt honor-bound to guide her. "If I can track down one lost donkey in the Great Desolation," the Nubian had said, "I can easily track down David with a flock of sheep!"

Najab had kept his word. He had sniffed the wind and tirelessly examined hoofprints in the dust. At last, they had crept silently into the labyrinth of stone where Samuel faced David beside his flock. She had found that one enormous quartz shaft had split down the middle into a deep trough. It allowed her to crawl, unseen, closer to them, close enough to overhear the prophet's words.

Huddled beside her, Najab translated in whispers. She heard Samuel tell David that the time had come to face Goliath. And she heard the prophet's parting words: "You must use what you have, not what you wish for."

It seemed to her that David did not understand the meaning of Samuel's words. But Nara believed she understood. It compelled her to act.

Careful to not be seen by David, she led Najab away from the labyrinth of stone. "The prophet said, 'Use what you have,'" she said to him. "It means that instead of wishing for a sword of iron, David can use a simple blade of Israelite copper to slay Goliath!"

"An empty hope," Najab said. "Against Philistine iron, such a crude blade would surely bend and break."

"No, my father taught me that even copper blades, when whetted with Ashdoda's holy stones, are more deadly than iron. I must fetch the stones from Ashdoda's cave."

"What if the Philistines have destroyed them?"

"I know in my heart that my goddess has left them there for me to bring to David."

"You have little time. David will face the Philistine at dawn."

"Then I must get them now!"

In her excitement, she took long, rapid strides away from him, down the dusty path. Najab watched her lope into the distance. She had said that Ashdoda's cave was on Philistine land, and he wanted to tell her that he feared for her. But it was too late. She was gone.

His hand crept over to his arm, and his fingers slid down the intertwining snakes carved there. He prayed that in this strange and foreign land, the merciful gods of his own distant people might see fit to watch over her.

Chapter 56

Growing up in Gibeah, Michal had been taught that the Mikveh was the most serene of places, its purifying waters a refuge for contemplation when an Israelite maiden attained womanhood. Yet now, as she stepped into its perpetual twilight, this was a place she feared.

A willowy servant girl knelt respectfully before her, then returned to pouring water from an alabaster pitcher over hissing coals. Before Michal's eyes could penetrate the dense shroud of steam, she heard a harsh voice.

"Why have you come?"

It was her mother, Ahinoam, hidden in the mist.

As if addressing an invisible spirit, Michal said, "I come to purify myself in these waters."

Her mother's voice replied coldly, "This holy pool is fed by an uncorrupted spring that flows directly from the Garden of Eden. It is rich in blessings. As daughter of the king, it is your privilege to bathe here. Instead, you have always chosen to visit the Mikveh of the common people, which is built of mud bricks and fed by a cistern of rainwater."

"May it please you that I have come here at last." Michal did not give the reason she had avoided this place for so long: She would not risk being naked and defenseless in the domain of this woman she so distrusted.

Peering through the steam as she approached, Michal saw that her mother was naked, seated on a marble step of the pool as if it was her throne. Ahinoam's belly was flaccid, her breasts sagging, her hair wild. To Michal, she looked more like a pagan sorceress than a queen. She knew Ahinoam's power no longer flowed from her beauty, but from her knowledge of dark palace secrets—profane, unspoken things. Though the immersion pool could hold twenty women, she saw that Ahinoam was alone. Michal knew that, at her whim, the wife of the king could exclude all others.

Ahinoam studied Michal with suspicion. "My daughter, you enter the holy Mikveh, yet you do not remove your robe for the bath." Ahinoam beckoned to a figure emerging from the mist. "Cael will prepare you for immersion."

Michal saw that her mother's attendant had powerful shoulders and sinewy arms. Her hair was cut as short as a man's, and she wore a white shift knotted around her waist. Her gray eyes were stern and probing. Michal felt herself being judged, as Cael must judge every woman whose body she purged of all that was unclean.

Michal hesitated, reluctant to enter the holy waters. But she knew that to escape her mother's suspicion, she must undergo the ritual immersion. She dutifully removed her robe and stood exposed before her.

"We face each other in our nakedness, a mother and daughter," Ahinoam said. "And yet, you hide your true motives. You cannot deceive me. I know why you have come. First you went to Saul and now you come here, seeking the sword and shield of Joshua." Michal realized that despite their hatred for each other, her mother and father were united in their resolve to assure Jonathan the throne.

Ahinoam nodded to Cael and she set to work, scrubbing Michal's shoulders, back and hips, her arms and legs, with a coarse cloth and soap made of boiled animal fat and ashes.

She scours my skin harshly, as if she thinks that to purify me, she must inflict pain.

"You have come here in vain," Ahinoam said. "Like Saul, I believe the sword and shield of Joshua vanished by the will of the Almighty. It is proof of God's plan for my beloved Jonathan, not David, to be king."

Cael finished grooming Michal for the sacred bath, untangling the knots from her lustrous black hair with an ivory comb. She sprinkled fragrant myrrh on her neck and shoulders from an alabaster vial.

"It is time to send the shepherd back to his sheep," Ahinoam said. "Time for you to stand by your brother as the rightful heir to the throne." She spoke the words benignly, but Michal sensed an underlying threat.

How different she is from my father, Saul. He is overcome by murderous rages, but it is when Ahinoam seems most benevolent that she is most to be feared.

"I will not abandon David," Michal said firmly. "My brother, Jonathan, will not abandon him. David will be king."

Ahinoam climbed out of the pool. The slender servant girl dried her with a linen cloth and helped her into her robe. "You have been readied for the sacred immersion," Ahinoam said to Michal. "May you find the truth in these holy waters, even if it is not the truth you seek." She abruptly left the Mikveh with the servant girl close behind.

Alone now with Cael, Michal descended the three marble steps into the warm waters of the pool. She felt the attendant's scornful gaze examining her naked body.

In Cael's eyes, I am a callow maiden, a virgin who is scarcely a woman, while Ahinoam has given Saul six children.

The attendant followed her silently into the pool and glided toward her through the water. As Cael approached, Michal noticed a small bronze key dangling around her neck on a silver chain. She did not know what the key unlocked, only that here in the Mikveh, it was as much a sign of Cael's authority as Saul's gold signet ring was in his palace.

Michal sank up to her neck in the ritual bath. Her face flushed from its warmth, but the water did nothing to soothe her. Its gleaming surface felt as sharp as a knife blade against her throat. The attendant fanned out Michal's long black hair in the water. "I will see to it that not a strand escapes the sacred immersion," Cael said.

Her strong hands gently pressed down on Michal's shoulders. Shutting her eyes, she held her breath as Cael pushed her head beneath the surface. The water closed over her, engulfing her in silence. She knew that this moment of complete immersion was meant to be a time for serene and holy thoughts, but that was impossible. Her heart was filled with anger at her mother.

The only way I will find peace is to leave this place.

She lifted her head against Cael's hands, signaling that she was ready to come out—but Cael did not release her, shoving her head deeper under the water.

Frantic, Michal struggled to force her head up. Cael twisted her long hair and thrust her deeper. Starved for air, she struck out with her fists, but Cael's sharp fingernails dug into her shoulders, holding her beneath the surface. Bubbles streamed from her nose and mouth. Her vision blurred. She reached out to wrap her fingers around Cael's neck, but it was no use. The attendant was too strong for her.

Her last breath spent, Michal shook her head violently, tearing her long hair out of Cael's grasp. Flailing out for something to cling to, her fingers grabbed hold of the silver chain hanging from Cael's neck. She clutched the bronze key and twisted the chain tightly around the attendant's throat.

Cael choked, trying to tear off the chain that strangled her. Michal felt Cael's grip on her neck loosen. Seizing the moment, she raised her head above the water. Gasping for breath, Michal let go of Cael's chain and scrambled up the wet steps, out of the pool. Her bare feet slipped on the slick marble. She fell to her knees.

Suddenly, Cael lunged out of the water. She grabbed Michal's ankle and dragged her back toward the pool. Michal tore her foot free, kicked the attendant hard in the face, and broke clear of her grasp.

On the rim of the pool, she spotted the massive alabaster pitcher used to pour water on the hot stones. She strained to grasp the handle, but at first the vessel seemed too heavy to lift. She seized it with both hands and raised it up. As Cael pulled herself out of the pool, Michal brought it down hard on her head.

With a groan, the attendant collapsed, face down, in the water.

Michal fought to catch her breath. Her bloodied shoulders stung where Cael's sharp nails had clawed at her. She looked down at the attendant floating motionless in the water.

Do I have it in my heart to let her drown?

No, she knew she could not take a human life. Summoning what was left of her strength, she climbed back into the pool, grabbed Cael, and dragged her over to the edge. She lifted her body out of the water, onto the marble rim, and pressed her ear to Cael's mouth. She was still breathing, unconscious, but alive.

Michal stood up unsteadily, shivering from a chill. She knew there could be no doubt that Cael had acted on her mother's orders. If Ahinoam believed that Michal was helping David, that Michal stood in the way of Jonathan becoming king . . .

My mother is even capable of plotting the murder of her own daughter.

The awareness filled her with disgust, but she shed no tears. She harbored no illusions about her mother's love. Jonathan, and only Jonathan, had always ruled Ahinoam's heart. As the youngest, and a girl, Michal had been raised by lowly handmaidens, while her brother was lavished with Ahinoam's love. In Jonathan, her mother perceived all the strengths that Saul lacked, a young king who would find glory where Saul had found only disgrace.

But what drove my mother to have me killed here, today? Ahinoam is not afflicted with madness like my father. She needs a cold-blooded motive for murder. Could it be that she fears what I might discover here?

Her restless gaze played across the row of jars cluttering the edge of the sacred pool. The fragile vessels of carved alabaster contained costly fragrances: hyacinth, rose and frankincense to cleanse the spirit; rare, sweet-smelling floral essences unknown to her, hoarded by Ahinoam and her inner circle.

She noticed that one detail was not as it should be: The precious vessels should have been safeguarded within the cabinet beside the sacred pool. Instead, the ritual jars and vials of fragrance were haphazardly scattered in front of the cabinet doors. Strange, she thought, that they had not been locked away as prudence demanded. Stranger still, the doors to the cabinet had not been left open, awaiting the return of the vessels. The doors were shut.

What if the cabinet held something more precious than sacred vessels for the ritual bath?

Kneeling beside Cael where she lay, unconscious, Michal unfastened the chain from around her neck and removed the bronze key. Her wet fingers fumbled with it, trying to insert the tip into the lock of the cabinet door, but she was badly shaken and her hands trembled. The key failed to catch. At first, she thought it did not fit. Then the key seized hold. A turn of her wrist, and the lock clicked.

The hinges of the inlaid cabinet doors creaked open. Inside, she beheld the luster of ancient iron. She had never seen these objects before, but she knew what they must be. Priceless things. Hallowed things.

The sword and shield of Joshua.

She marveled how, in those distant Early Times, her people knew how to forge weapons of iron, an art long lost to them. Joshua's sword had a short broad blade. It was not massive like those wielded by Goliath's men, and yet, she believed it was invincible, blessed with the divine power that enabled Joshua to conquer the armies of Canaan.

Ahinoam is cunning, she thought. My mother knows how precious the sword and shield would be to any man who covets the throne, so she hid them in the one place men are forbidden to enter. Michal guessed that even Saul did not know that his wife had plotted the theft from the buried coffer. Ahinoam trusted no one but herself to keep Joshua's ancient treasures out of David's hands, to ensure his destruction by Goliath.

Michal told herself that the sword and shield of Joshua would be David's salvation. Despite its age, the gleaming blade showed not a fleck of rust, as if it had been waiting for generations to be carried into combat for one final victory. She judged that the weapon would fit David's hand as snugly as if it had been forged only for him.

Yielding to temptation, she allowed herself to clutch the hilt of the sword tightly, and imagined the iron blade dripping with Goliath's blood.

Chapter 57

At dusk, Nara crossed the steep gorge that marked the boundary to the Philistines' domain. She knew that somewhere in the wasteland that stretched before her, a ravine concealed the mouth of Ashdoda's cave. And within the cave, she was certain the holy stones were hidden. When David's blade was whetted on the stones of Ashdoda, Nara was sure that it would acquire the power of her sorcery. Then, even if his sword was forged of crude Israelite copper, it would deliver the full force of Ashdoda's vengeance. If the shepherd was to kill Goliath, she was convinced it was the only way.

* * *

Three stunted cedars hunched like vultures against the night sky. Below them, from the cave mouth, came a faint glow. Nara feared that since slaughtering the daughters of Ashdoda, Philistine soldiers might still be posted there, lying in wait for any believer who would return.

A hooded figure crouched in the gap between the boulders. Nara was relieved to see it was not a Philistine, but one of Ashdoda's faithful, her face pale as the moon. Closer now, she recognized the gaunt woman who had first entrusted her with the newly fallen stones.

"Keturah!" Nara embraced her. "I was sure they had killed you."

"They killed many of us. But we endure." Keturah beckoned to a gangly younger woman to take up her post as sentinel at the cave mouth, then led Nara down through the passageway into the cavern.

After the slaughter that had taken place here, she expected to be overwhelmed by the stench of rotting corpses. But in the dim glow of oil lamps in niches on the walls, she discovered that the bodies of the Philistines' victims had all been removed.

Like a flower sprouting out of charred earth, the faith in Ashdoda blossoms around me.

Wearing tattered robes, a score of women—both fresh-faced maidens and rheumy-eyed crones—knelt in prayer before the massive idol of Ashdoda. She sensed that the goddess was gazing down benevolently upon them. The graven image of black obsidian had been mutilated by the Philistines, the arms hacked off, the face scarred. And yet, it seemed to her that the women worshipped the idol more fervently than ever. The cave echoed with their whispered entreaties, some in the Philistine tongue, others in languages alien to her. They had kindled sprigs of sage and balsam that smoldered like incense, filling the air with a delicate fragrance.

Peering into the shadows, Nara recognized the images daubed on the cave walls in ocher and indigo pigments that depicted the phases of the moon. Since her last visit, the pictures had been spattered with rust-colored blotches—the blood of the martyred women, she guessed, who had been slain here by the Philistines. The worshippers seemed too caught up in prayer to notice the ungainly figure who knelt down beside them. To Nara's surprise, she recognized a few faces from her last visit.

"Some of you escaped. How?"

"We hid where they could not follow." Keturah stepped over to an ox hide daubed with an image of the full moon, which hung on the cave wall. She pulled the hide back, to reveal it was a flap concealing a shadowy crawlspace.

"Our tunnels lead all the way to safety on the far side of the ravine. They were too narrow for the Philistines to enter and pursue us."

"And when the men finally left?"

"We returned. We knelt before our murdered sisters and wept. When night came, we buried our dead outside the cave, beneath the blessings of the moon."

Keturah bowed her head reverently before the mutilated idol. Nara saw that she grieved over its wounds as if it was a living thing. "Our graven image of Ashdoda has survived a terrible ordeal. She cries out for our healing love. That she has suffered so terribly makes us all the more faithful to her."

Nara searched for a face among the worshippers. "Where is Zelmai? I must speak with her."

Keturah lowered her eyes. "Zelmai's spirit has departed for the High Places." She pointed up at a cleft in the cave ceiling, through which Nara saw a sliver of moonlight. "Her soul abides in the Silver Citadel with Ashdoda now."

It was as Nara had feared. "The sacred stones . . . I entrusted them to her . . ."

Sensing her distress, Keturah spoke gently: "When we returned here and found Zelmai among the dead, we searched everywhere for the stones. We knew they were precious beyond price. But despite all our efforts, we never found them. They must have been destroyed by the Philistines."

How could Ashdoda allow me to come all this way in search of the stones, yet deny them to me now?

Nara clasped her hands before the obsidian goddess: "Guide me to the five holy stones. Only they will allow me to avenge the killing of your daughters. Though David is an Israelite and not one of us, when I give him the stones, he will bring you sweet vengeance."

She held her breath and listened. The goddess did not reply. She heard only the murmured entreaties of the women around her.

Then, a piercing cry.

The scream came from the sentinel at the cave entrance. Torn from their prayers, the women responded as one. Without exchanging a word, they stood up and made their way deeper into the cave. She watched Keturah scurry into the shadows with them and lift the ox-leather flap hanging on the cave wall. The old woman helped the others, one by one, crouch down and enter the hidden crawlspace leading into a narrow tunnel.

From outside, beyond the cave walls, Nara heard muffled noises: the snarling of dogs; the clatter of swords; commands shouted in the Philistine tongue.

"Come with us!" Keturah said.

"I cannot go with you."

Keturah lowered her eyes sadly, understanding. Nara's hips and shoulders were much too broad for her to escape with them into the cramped crawlspace. The shouts of the Philistines rang out, closer now, resounding off the cave walls.

"Hurry!" Nara squeezed Keturah's hand in farewell, then lowered the flap to conceal her, as the old woman escaped with the others deep into the tunnel.

I am fated to remain here, alone and unarmed, to face the Philistines. The holy stones, and the hope their magic offered me, are lost forever.

Seeking wisdom from the goddess, she ran the palm of her hand along the obsidian stump that had once been Ashdoda's right arm. The stone was cold and dead to her touch.

Even here, in her own shrine, the goddess offers me no comfort.

She looked back toward the cave mouth. Silhouetted by the torches of the men outside, a Philistine cast a giant shadow.

He has come for me, Goliath himself.

Chapter 58

It was not Goliath. She saw now that the shadow belonged to the one who, after her husband, was the most hateful of men.

Arjun. In the dim light, she recognized his rotten teeth and crooked nose. He wore the gold-hemmed linen robe of an acolyte of Dagon.

Arjun has the force of Evil in him, as David has the force for Good.

"I knew you would return," Arjun said. "I begged the priests to let me lie in wait here, so I could kill you myself."

Nara eyed him with contempt. "I invited you into my household, but you betrayed my trust. You spied for the priests and had my beloved Hada stoned to death. But you will not take my life."

He unsheathed a curved sword of iron. She judged the blade was long enough for him to slash her before she could seize him. "Goliath will reward me for your head." He bared his rotten teeth. "He despises you because you disgraced him before his own men."

She edged away from him until she could go no further, her back pressed against the massive graven image.

His blade sliced through the air.

She twisted out of its path. The cutting edge whooshed past her arm and clattered off the obsidian idol, striking sparks.

In the instant it took him to steady the blade, she slid behind the idol. He pulled back his sword, poised for his next thrust. Before he could take one step closer, she threw all her weight against the carved block of stone. From the base of the graven image, she heard a sharp crack, followed by a groan, as if a great tree had been torn from its roots.

The idol was tilting. Thrown off-balance, Arjun staggered backward.

Nara hurled her shoulders against the obsidian figure once

more. It shuddered for a moment, then toppled. There was no time for Arjun to leap out of the way.

The idol crashed to the ground with such force that Nara feared the cave would collapse around her. The fine powder of shattered stone engulfed her and she shielded her nose and mouth with her robe, gasping for breath.

At first, after the dust settled, she saw no sign of Arjun. Then she noticed something protruding from beneath the toppled block of obsidian: the bloody fingers of his hand.

Nara was repelled by what she had done. She had never killed a man. In Gath, they had taught her that to slay an Israelite was praiseworthy, but to slay a Philistine was a crime punished by death. And yet, she felt no remorse. She remembered how Arjun had betrayed her aunt to the priests, how Hada had fallen, bloodied, under a hail of stones.

This is more than vengeance. It is justice.

Only now did she realize the price she had paid. The fallen idol that had crushed Arjun blocked the cave mouth.

She was trapped inside.

Chapter 59

Outside the cave, the Philistines struggled to move the toppled idol that sealed it shut. She heard them cursing as they grappled with the massive block of obsidian, unable to dislodge it.

"The goddess took her vengeance on Arjun!" one of the soldiers said in panic.

"We must return to Gath before Ashdoda takes her revenge on *us*!" another muttered.

She listened until their voices faded and died away in the distance. All she heard now was the nervous cadence of her breathing and the steady drip of water trickling down the cave walls.

By now, the daughters of Ashdoda have fled down tunnels too narrow for me to enter. They are safe, but for me, there is no escape.

Only one oil lamp in the cave had not been snuffed out. In its dim glow, the fallen idol of Ashdoda looked immense and immovable.

How cruel, that the goddess I have prayed to so fervently, the goddess I have risked everything to serve, now seals my fate.

To escape, she knew she must somehow push the graven image far enough away from the cave mouth for her to squeeze through. She seized hold of the cold stone head of Ashdoda, threw all her weight against it. Impossible. Her knees buckled and she collapsed to the cave floor, overcome by her helplessness.

I have sacrificed my life for nothing. I have brought David no closer to killing Goliath. I placed all my hopes in Ashdoda and the goddess has betrayed me.

As if to punish her for the blasphemous thought, the flame of the last oil lamp flickered out.

Ashdoda has smothered me in darkness.

She ran her hands along the fallen body of the graven image, trying to find comfort there. Her fingers touched the scars where the Philistines had mutilated its obsidian arms, and moved down the idol's legs. Feeling their way in the darkness, her hands stumbled across something unexpected: a chiseled groove at the base of the pedestal. She inserted her fingers into the groove and pulled. A wooden compartment slid open. She groped blindly inside.

Though she could not see them, she felt their warmth: Ashdoda's stones. She pulled them out, her trembling hands counting them, one by one. They were there, all five. This must have been Zelmai's final act, she thought. The priestess must have hidden them here, moments before they killed her.

Ashdoda plays a cruel trick on me. I have the stones I came for, but what good are they to me now?

She shut her eyes and struggled to imagine the goddess gazing down on her with compassion from her silver citadel of the moon. She whispered into the suffocating darkness, "Blessed Ashdoda, are these not your tears?" She clasped them tightly against her heart. "Do they not possess your powerful sorcery? Then, I pray you, help me now. I do not plead for my own life. But help me to use these stones to save David. Help me to wreak your vengeance on Goliath."

Her words were swallowed up in cold silence. She feared that the time for prayer was over. Her eyes had been closed to summon Ashdoda into her heart. Now she opened them.

Did her sight deceive her?

After spending so long in near total darkness, her eyes detected a faint glow. She saw now that it came from above, filtering down through a narrow fissure in the cave ceiling. She remembered how Zelmai had pointed out the cleft that allowed moonlight to shine down on the idol's face.

That can be my way out. My escape will not come from prayers to a goddess, but from my own strength.

She slipped the five stones into the pockets of her robe. First, she had to leap up and grab a handhold on the slippery cavern wall. Several times, she tried and failed. Finally, the fingers of her right hand seized hold of a nub of stone. Her left hand found another. Slowly, painfully, she pulled herself upward.

Near the top of the wall, she lost her footing. Slipping backward, she wedged her fingers into a crack in the granite. Her feet dangled helplessly. She strained to reach above her, to slide her hand into the cleft glowing with moonlight, but a chunk of stone crumbled away in her fingers.

She fought to grab another handhold.

At last, pulling herself up with both arms, she forced her body through the opening in the cave ceiling, thrust herself outside into the cold night air. She fell backward, sweaty and exhausted, onto the moist earth. Her muscles were sore, her shoulders and legs badly bruised. But she was alive.

She felt among the folds of her robe: The holy stones were still there, all five of them.

My journey to Ashdoda's cavern was ordained in the High Places. I was destined to face Arjun. If I had not toppled the idol to crush him, how could I have found the stones hidden inside its base? Only I was tall and strong enough to pull myself out, to escape and bring the stones with me. . . .

Her knees unsteady, she forced herself to stand up. Her ribs ached with each breath.

Now it is for me to make sure the stones reach David in time.

Why do I risk my life for one who belongs to an enemy tribe, one who worships an enemy God?

She knew she did not do it out of anything so foolish and fragile as the love of a woman for a man. To her, coy smiles and tender embraces were as worthless as rust. No, she thought, this is a passion that the Philistine tongue has no word to describe. It is the eternal bond between two mortals who share a common enemy—and will sacrifice their lives to destroy him.

PART III

Chapter 60

"I almost gave up hope of finding you."

Her black robe drawn tightly around her, Michal could have been any one of the countless young widows of Gibeah. David only recognized her when she pulled the mantle from her head, her profile dimly outlined in the darkness. Facing her in this no man's land, surrounded by the vastness of the night, he felt that both their lives were at risk.

"How did you know to look for me here?"

"Najab told me you would pass this way. He said that when he was with the Philistine woman, he heard Samuel tell you that tomorrow you must face Goliath in the Valley of Elah."

"Why did you risk coming here?"

"I found the weapons the Almighty intends for you: the sword and shield of Joshua."

He stared at her in disbelief. "Jonathan and I searched for them. They were gone!"

"Stolen. My mother, Ahinoam, hid them, to keep them from you. I gave them to Jonathan. He has taken them to Elah and will wait there for you at our father's tent."

"But Saul will never allow me to use them!"

"My father will yield to the will of his favorite son, as he has so many times before."

David sensed the doubt in her voice. "It is not so easy to predict what Saul will do, even if he is your father."

She pressed ahead: "Jonathan will see to it that you receive Joshua's sword and shield. Trust him as you would trust me."

"I trust him completely." He felt that he had many things to say, but feared saying too much. He longed to pledge himself to her, but knew this was not the time to speak of matters of the heart. He said simply, "You must go. Return to the safety of Gibeah. Know that I will not forget your kindness."

She lowered her eyes modestly. He sensed that they both found the shadows of night a blessing, because they veiled emotions better left unseen and unspoken. For an instant, they stepped closer, so close that their lips touched. Yet so tender was it, so fleeting, that at first he was not certain whether this was a kiss or only his bold imagining of one. It was as if the meeting of their lips was not driven by their shared desire, as if it was brought about by a sudden upheaval of the earth beneath their feet.

Dizzied, he pulled away from her. A cold wind blew between them, like an iron blade forcing them apart. He knew that the deepest feelings were also the most fragile. To say goodbye would only remind them that they might never see each other again. Without a word of farewell, they turned and went their separate ways.

David looked back and watched Michal setting out for Gibeah, until she vanished in the darkness. The road to the Valley of Elah stretched out before him. He studied the eastern horizon and wondered whether he already saw the first dim hint of dawn. No, he guessed he had misjudged the time. It was still the dead of night, but how soon before dawn came? Now that Michal was gone, he struggled to purge the tenderness from his heart.

What use to me is compassion, what use is gentleness, when everything in heaven and on earth hinges on my killing Goliath?

Chapter 61

At the foul-smelling livestock pens outside the walls of Gibeah, drunken traders from Israelite villages and distant lands dozed, side by side, in the open air. If Najab had joined them, they might have offered him a swig from their jug of barley beer. Instead, Nara saw that he was curled up in a cramped stall, finding comfort in the dusty warmth of his five donkeys. The Nubian lay motionless in the moldy straw, his tongue lolling from the side of his mouth.

She prodded him in the ribs. He squirmed and opened one bleary eye. At the sight of her, he sat bolt upright. "Daughter of Ezel!"

She knelt in the straw beside him and lowered her voice, fearing she would awaken the men dozing nearby. "I have them." From the sleeve of her robe, she removed a stone and held it up between two fingers. It glowed in the murky light like a jewel.

Awestruck, he examined the stones as she pulled them out, one by one. "The tears of a goddess!" He weighed each of the round black stones in the palm of his hand. "I can feel the magic in them."

She sighed. "A magic I cannot give to David. It seems he has already set out for Elah."

He furrowed his brow and stroked his fingers along the snakes carved into his forearms, seeking answers. Finding none, he shook his head solemnly. "David's fate is now in the hands of the gods."

"No, his fate is in *our* hands!"

Najab's eyes narrowed with suspicion. "The last time you came to me, you asked me to risk my life in the city of the Philistines. What is it you ask of me now?"

"I ask for your help. I am viewed as the enemy. But you are a trader known to both Israelites and Philistines. They will let you pass freely through their battle lines . . ."

He laughed nervously. "To carry your holy stones to David, would you have my donkeys sprout wings like eagles?"

"Your donkeys cannot fly. But you, Najab, can *run,* fast enough to reach Elah in time to give David the stones."

He shifted his weight uneasily from one wide, callused foot to the other. "You say this, and yet, you have never seen me run . . ."

"When you delivered ingots to my father in Gath, you often boasted you were the fastest creature with two legs upon the earth."

He chewed his lip, his mind scrambling for excuses. "The distance to Elah is too great! To get there by dawn . . ." His eyes darted over to the leaden horizon. "Who knows how soon the sun will rise?"

"Najab, you must help me. Without the sorcery of the stones, David will die." Her voice hardened. "If he perishes because you refused to help him, your spirit will be shunned in the High Places when your own time comes."

He glanced over at his donkeys, as if seeking their support, but the animals turned their backs on him. He ran his fingers once more along the snakes carved into his forearms, but they brought him no comfort.

At last, he nodded. "I will go." He groaned as he rose to his feet. She stood up beside him. He looked up at her and pressed his right hand to his heart. "I will not do this for your gods, or for the Israelites' invisible Almighty—not even for my own beloved deities who reside in the High Places. I will do this because at the pit of vipers, David saved my life. Now it is upon me to save his."

She handed him the five stones. "When you give these to David, tell him he must sharpen his blade on them."

"David does not carry a sword."

"Then you must lend him yours." She pointed to the weapon in its shabby scabbard, which hung from Najab's belt.

"But mine is only made of copper."

"With the power of Ashdoda's sorcery, even your copper blade can slay Goliath."

One by one, he slipped the stones into a goat-leather pouch and knotted it to his belt. "Trust that I will do everything you ask."

He took leave of his donkeys, one by one, stroking the right ear of each for good luck. Then he patted the flank of Shaya, his favorite, and checked the feeding trough. "My lovelies will have enough barley and water until I return."

He stretched one sinewy leg, then the other, to loosen his thigh and calf muscles. "Nara, daughter of Ezel, I have known you since you first held a broom to sweep your father's forge. I know you well. I understand how much you hate Goliath and how much you wish to see him die at David's hand. Promise you will not follow me to Elah to bear witness, even from a distance. If the Israelites do not kill you, the Philistines will!"

She pressed her right hand to her heart. "I swear I will not follow you. I have seen enough of the cruelty of men."

The Nubian bowed to her once more, then turned and broke into a run, loping away from the livestock pens with a graceful stride, his bare feet falling silently, barely touching the dark earth. She noticed that, wisely, he did not take the road—he knew it was not the shortest way to the Valley of Elah—but cut across the broken, desolate land.

As soon as he vanished from sight, she realized she had not told him the truth.

I promised Najab I would not go to Elah. It is a promise I cannot keep. I must watch David whet Najab's sword on Ashdoda's stones. I must watch his sword cut off Goliath's head.

She set out, walking at a brisk pace. As Najab had done, she left the road, veering across the rugged plain. It was a long distance—she knew she must conserve her strength—but she broke into a run. Breathing hard, her heart pounding, she moved without Najab's natural grace. She stumbled, fell to her knees, then pulled herself back to her feet and set off again, taking broad strides into the night.

Najab warned me it is too dangerous to go to Elah, that if either side sees me they will kill me. And yet, I will go, I must go, to bear witness. David's struggle is my struggle, and I will not abandon him. If David is wounded, I will feel the blade of Goliath's sword as if it pierced my own flesh. And if David dies, I will rend my clothes and weep, as a Philistine woman in Gath weeps for her beloved, when he is carried home on his shield through the Gates of Eternity.

Chapter 62

The birds did not sing at dawn. David wondered whether they kept silent for fear of what this day would bring.

At first light, he reached the Valley of Elah, where the Israelite and Philistine battle lines faced each other across the barren land. The black smoke of the Israelites' cooking fires drifted toward him, smelling as bitter as defeat. He had decided to bring food to his brothers, and carried with him a coarse-woven bag holding parched grains, flat loaves of bread, and cheeses. A small kindness, he thought, but if the worst happens, it will be the last gift I can give them.

He passed the young boys who minded the donkeys. Like David, they did not carry swords and were considered unfit for battle. A few of them hungrily eyed the sack on his shoulder, suspecting it held food, and seemed tempted to snatch it from him.

The sight of his people tore at David's heart. They crawled out of their ragged tents, rubbing the sleep from their eyes, as if the night had tormented them with spiteful dreams. The Israelites had been beaten down, their bodies scourged and their spirits crushed. Their wounds were still raw, but he knew these men awoke to yet another day that would bring either disgrace or death. Many leaned, dispirited, on their spears. A few chanted half-hearted prayers into the wind, as if believing that their God was deaf to their pleas.

Their faith is as shabby as their tunics. Is this all the devotion that the Almighty can inspire? If so, our God is as toothless and feeble as the Philistine priests claim.

It troubled him to see that many of his own people wore small, crudely carved idols on leather thongs around their wrists and necks. No doubt, if they thought their invisible Almighty had failed them, these men would turn to such false gods. How desperate my people must be, he thought, how feeble their faith, for them to resort to this!

He shouldered his way through a surly throng of battle-scarred men twice his age, the only one who was unarmed, without a helmet, shield, or sword. His brothers were not to be found. Some men choose to be heroes and lead their people into battle, he thought bitterly. My brothers would rather hide among a pack of cowards to save their skins.

At last, he caught sight of them: Eliab, the firstborn, Abinadab and Shammah. Like the other Israelites, with their crude spears and torn ox-hide shields, they looked disheartened and afraid. They may claim to be warriors, he thought, but in their hearts they are already vanquished.

"Greetings, my brothers!" he called out.

Eliab, the eldest, eyed the sack of food suspiciously. "Did our father tell you to bring this to us?" David nodded. If he told them the truth, he thought, that he brought it to them out of simple kindness, they would see it as a sign of weakness.

"You are lazy as a dog that sleeps all day in the sun!" Abinadab grumbled.

Though they treat me like a servant, I forgive them. Now is the time for forgiveness. This may be the last time we will see each other in this life.

His brothers ripped open the sack of food. As Eliab, Abinadab and Shammah devoured the parched grain, loaves and cheeses, he looked on them with compassion.

When Samuel anointed their youngest brother as God's Chosen, was that not reason enough for them to hate me? Now they are forced to risk their lives for a king they do not respect, and an invisible God they believe has abandoned them.

"To be our servant is your true calling," Abinadab mumbled with his mouth full.

"Yes, and to mind the sheep!" Instead of offering David the last scraps of bread and cheese, Shammah threw them to a mongrel sniffing at his feet.

David was no longer paying attention to his brothers. He listened to the rising morning wind.

Why do I not hear His voice? The Most High spoke to Abraham and Moses. He speaks to the prophet Samuel. May he speak to me now, to guide me through the final moments before I face Goliath.

He strained to hear the voice of the Almighty. He heard only the sullen murmuring of fearful men.

Chapter 63

Nara ran swiftly across the shadowy, unforgiving land. It seemed to her that Ashdoda smoothed out the rocky path, lengthened her stride, and hastened her every step. She arrived in the Valley of Elah sooner than she had imagined possible, as the sun gleamed, red as a rusty shield, on the horizon. She felt no weariness, only joy to have made it there in time.

Her stride slowed as she approached the battle line. Careful to stay out of view, she skirted the Philistine camp, where well-fed donkeys were tethered beside orderly rows of tents. Slipping behind a grove of gnarled oaks, she clambered up the steep slope overlooking the Philistine line. She took cover in a boulder outcropping, hidden from the eyes of the sentries.

Like every child in Gath, she had grown up hearing tales of the Philistines' prowess in war, but this was the first time she saw them arrayed for battle. They sharpened their gleaming iron swords on whetstones, confident that armed with invincible weapons of the black metal, they would follow Goliath to certain victory.

Without the blood of warriors flowing in his veins, can David fight Goliath and live?

Among the hundreds of Philistines below, she recognized no one. It was as if, along with their shields and helmets, the men of Gath wore masks, transformed into faceless killers. The crimson battle standards billowed in the morning breeze. The wind brought with it the scent of pork roasting over Philistine campfires. She had been told that her people cooked pigs near the Israelite lines to sicken the enemy with the odor of the creature they loathed.

Mingled with the pungent scent of pork, she breathed in the fragrance of frankincense. The Philistine priests had carried a fierce graven image of Dagon with them from Gath. Carved of cedar, it stood taller than a man, with ivory fangs and blood-red rubies for eyes. As if he sensed the importance of this day, the High Priest Dalziel himself had come to bless the Philistine host. She watched as he swung a smoking censer of beaten silver, leading the men in prayer with the age-old chant: "Victory above all things." She saw how her people drew strength from the idol of Dagon.

I know why David's tribe suffers so terribly: They have no idols to protect them. Without a fierce likeness of their God to confront Dagon, from what source can the Israelites draw their strength?

There was still no sign of Najab. For David to have time to whet his sword with Ashdoda's magic, the Nubian had to be here now with the holy stones. Where was he? Had he been waylaid—or killed—on the trail to Elah?

She heard a crash of thunder.

Chapter 64

The thunder did not erupt from the heavens. Gazing across the Valley of Elah, David saw that, in the distance, the Philistines were pounding their swords against their shields, a storm of iron clashing against iron. They heralded the arrival of the leader that he knew they both feared and loved, the one for whom they would gladly die.

For the first time, David saw Goliath.

It is true, all of it, just as the stories say: The Philistine stands head and shoulders above all other men. He has the thick, shaggy mane of a lion and a beard as wild as brambles in a ravine. The Philistine's hairy arms and legs of knotted muscle are massive as the limbs of a giant oak. His face is inscrutable as a mountain crag, but hidden beneath his heavy brows, his eyes smolder with menace.

David understood how the sight of the Philistine filled his brothers with terror, but he neither feared nor hated Goliath. In this moment, he was overcome with wonder, as if he bore witness to a heartless force of nature—a whirlwind, an inferno, a plague of locusts that blotted out the sky.

One can cower before so powerful a force, or one can defy it.

Goliath marched toward the front of the Philistine battle line with long strides, towering over his men, who parted before him like the sea. The warriors of Gath now beat their swords against their shields at a rapid pace, the rhythm building, David thought, to keep up with the pounding of their hearts. Watching them, he understood that to the Philistines, Goliath was more than their commander. They shouted out their praise as if the god Dagon himself had come down to earth and walked among them.

In the glare of the rising sun, Goliath's bronze helmet, coat of mail and greaves blazed with a blinding radiance. He raised his massive iron sword, a weapon so heavy that David guessed only

Goliath had the strength to lift it with one hand. He wondered what the Philistines would say if they knew that Goliath's sword was hammered out by a woman? And what would they say if they knew that this woman, Goliath's wife, was now bent on his destruction? Would their idol crumble before their eyes?

If they knew the truth, the Philistines would see Goliath as I do, for what he is: a man as mortal as any other—a man who is lesser, not greater, than other men. A man who does not deserve to live.

The clatter of metal on metal reached a crescendo. Goliath stepped through their ranks to stand alone in front of the Philistine host. He gazed across the open field toward the battle line of his enemies.

Even from this great distance, David heard Goliath bellow out to the Israelites in their own tongue:

"Am I not a Philistine and are you not servants of Saul? Choose a man for yourselves and let him come down to me. If he is able to fight with me and kill me, then we will be your servants. But if I prevail against him and kill him, then you shall be our servants and serve us. I defy the ranks of Israel this day; give me a man, that we may fight together."

Surveying the Israelite battle line, David saw that his people were stricken with cowardice. No doubt, he thought, his brothers were paralyzed with dread like all the rest.

Cowardice runs in their blood, the same blood that flows in my veins.

The awareness filled him with shame. In their dwelling in Bethlehem, he had overheard his brothers whisper that for forty days, Goliath had issued this challenge without a single Israelite daring to face him in battle. My people dishonor themselves as they dishonor their God, he thought.

I will face Goliath to pay homage to all those who have fallen, and to prepare the way for all those not yet born. I must do this because it is my destiny. For that, I am blessed.

He made his way through the ranks of dispirited men. They

lowered their eyes in disgrace and grudgingly moved aside to let him pass. He reached the front of the Israelite battle line, but he did not stop there. He took three paces in front of his people and stopped, alone in the no man's land that separated him from Goliath.

David raised his fist above his head to say, "I accept your challenge."

From Philistine and Israelite alike, he was met by scornful laughter. But he saw that Goliath's face betrayed no emotion, ponderous as an idol of granite. The Philistine raised his heavy fist high above his head, announcing that he would fight the Israelite to the death.

A hush settled over the Valley of Elah. David understood that this was the time set aside for the Philistines to invoke the power of their god Dagon, and for the Israelites to pray to their invisible Almighty. He knew that this time was crucial for him. As he had promised Michal, he must hurry to Saul's tent to claim the sword and shield of Joshua that Jonathan had brought him—and hope that Saul did not thwart their plan.

As he walked among his people, on his way to the king's tent, he saw that no one prayed for him to prevail over the Philistine. They turned their backs as he passed, as if he was already dead.

He caught sight of Saul's tent, ornamented in faded gold leaf, on a knoll well behind the Israelite front line. He guessed that the king had commanded that it be pitched at so great a distance so he would not have to witness the cowardice of his men. Outside the tent, five sentries stood guard with spears. There was no sign of Jonathan.

What if he failed to bring Joshua's sword and shield? If I go to the king's tent, will Jonathan be there to give me what I need, or will I find myself trapped and at Saul's mercy?

He felt the Israelite host watching him with contempt. "The king will never let you fight on our behalf!" Eliab, his oldest brother, yelled out at him.

"Why should Saul place the fate of our people in your hands?" Shammah jeered, and the others laughed.

David was surprised to see a lanky, familiar figure weaving through the hostile throng toward him: Najab, his shaved head gleaming in the sun. It seemed that the Nubian had lurked among the Israelites, biding his time, waiting for the right moment to approach.

"The gods have taken pity on me. I found you!" In gratitude, Najab stroked his fingers along the snakes carved into his arm.

"Why have you come?"

The Nubian untied the goat-skin sack from his belt and opened it. He spoke under his breath, so the Israelites would not overhear him: "These are the stones of Ashdoda, entrusted to me by the Philistine woman." He gripped the hilt of the sword that hung from his belt. "When sharpened with Ashdoda's sorcery, even my copper blade can kill Goliath."

David handed the sack back to him. "Leave the stones there." He pointed to a dry creek bed in the distance that was strewn with pebbles.

"The stones will be lost there!" Najab protested. "How will you know which ones possess Ashdoda's magic?"

"I will know," David said. "Now do as I ask. Then leave here and save yourself."

"As you wish."

Reluctantly, the Nubian carried the sack over to the dry creek bed. David watched him kneel down and empty out Ashdoda's five stones among hundreds of others. Then David hurried up the narrow path toward the canopy edged in peeling gold leaf, where the banner of the Lion of Judah flew. With scant time left for him to retrieve the sword and shield of Joshua, he believed that everything depended on what he would find there.

Five sentries with spears blocked his path. Beyond them, he saw someone emerging from the shadows of the tent—not Jonathan, but Saul, wearing a faded robe stitched with silver threads. He shuffled over like an old man, as if, David thought, he had aged years in a matter of days.

With a stiff nod of his head, the king ordered the guards to let him pass. He spoke coldly: "Son of Jesse, I saw you accept Goliath's challenge. I do not like to watch any man perish, not even a lowly shepherd. Today you will die."

David heard someone approaching from behind him. He turned and saw Jonathan, holding a sword and shield in his hands. "David will fight Goliath on behalf of our people," he told his father. "I have brought him what he must have to ensure his victory." His eyes met Saul's defiantly. "With or without your blessing."

The king did not hesitate with his answer: "My son, if this is your wish, then let it be so. The son of Jesse may have Joshua's sword and shield, and my blessing to fight Goliath on behalf of our people."

David was surprised by the king's sudden show of support. "Thank you for believing in me. I will not disgrace you."

Saul's jaw stiffened, his right hand twitching on the hilt of his jeweled dagger. "Know that I only give my blessing so you will face Goliath in battle, nothing more. When he has your head, I will finally be rid of you." He turned to Jonathan. "My son, you will see for yourself. Even bearing the hallowed sword and shield of Joshua, David will die. Then you will finally accept that it is your destiny to be king, and the mad prophet, Samuel, will be powerless to stop it." He withdrew into the shadows of the tent.

"Do not listen to the rantings of an old man," Jonathan said. He led David beyond the shade of the gilt-edged canopy, into the morning glare. As Jonathan brought the sword and shield out into the sunlight, David realized they were like none he had seen before. The glittering blade had the luster of an unfamiliar metal that he knew must be iron. He admired its craftsmanship, from a time when the Israelites still possessed the secrets of working the black metal. When he lifted the massive oval shield, which was simply etched with silver, it seemed strong yet remarkably light. He marveled at how these holy relics had acquired a rich patina across the generations, as if burnished by their ancient glory.

"Take them, my friend," Jonathan said. "Joshua carried them into battle. They are blessed by the Almighty. They will bring you victory over Goliath." He helped David ease the leather strap of the shield over his left arm, then pressed the hilt of the sword into his right hand. "If my sister could see you now, she would rejoice that a shepherd has become a warrior."

It thrilled David that Joshua himself had once carried this sword into battle. He grasped the hilt of the weapon and weighed it in his hand, then ran his thumb lightly along the cutting edge of the iron blade. Even after countless generations, it was so sharp that it drew blood.

"Who can say how many Canaanites fell before this sword at Jericho?" Jonathan said. "This blade won the Promised Land for our people. Today, you will use it against Goliath to reclaim our lost glory."

David knew that he should feel blessed. He knew that he should accept these gifts and thank his beloved friend, who, with Michal, had gone to such lengths to arm him for battle. And yet, he felt a twinge of doubt. It was not the voice of the Almighty that he heard, but a whisper from within himself.

He asked Jonathan, "If the Israelites see me clutching Joshua's sword and shield, how will they look upon me?"

"They will see that you bear the noble history of our people with you into battle."

Even as Jonathan spoke, David felt the sword and shield afflicting him like a crushing weight. "Our history is a heavy burden to carry on my shoulders. I do not want to be dragged down by the folly of old illusions and forsaken dreams." He glanced at Saul, who was watching him with suspicion from the shadows of the royal tent.

If I carry the burdens of the past with me, it will make my shoulders as stooped and my heart as heavy as Saul's. Instead of being weighed down, I want to be lifted up.

He said to Jonathan, "I cannot cloak myself in past glory. I cannot use old weapons to defend old ways. It is not for me to fit into the mold of those who came before me, but to break it."

"What will you do?"

He heard the anguish in Jonathan's voice and felt how deeply his friend feared for him. "If I am to become king, I must be a different leader than Joshua. I must be a different ruler than Saul. If I am to be king, I cannot be what I am not. If I am to lead, I must follow my own path."

"But Samuel said you must fight as a king fights!"

David looked into his friend's eyes, hoping that in his love for him, Jonathan would accept his decision. "This is what I have come to understand: Before I can be worthy of becoming a king, I must accept that at heart I am a shepherd. To be true to myself, I must act as a shepherd."

He pulled off the glittering shield and handed Jonathan the iron sword, a shepherd once more.

David saw that despite his misgivings, his friend understood that it was impossible to dissuade him from the path he must take. Jonathan embraced him, then walked to the edge of the knoll. He announced to the Israelite host arrayed below: "David, son of Jesse, has my blessing, and the blessing of my father, Saul, our king, to face Goliath in solitary combat on behalf of our people. And may the Almighty bring David a swift and certain victory."

The restless Israelite multitude did not cheer Jonathan's words, but muttered resentfully, a roiling sea of discontent. David thought, they must believe that Saul's consent for me to fight on behalf of our people is further proof of his madness. He realized that despite Jonathan's show of confidence in him, his friend feared that today he would die by Goliath's sword.

Jonathan made the announcement out of love, to show the world his belief in my destiny—even if, at this moment, he secretly doubts it.

David walked resolutely away from Jonathan and the royal tent. He knew now what he must do.

* * *

From her high vantage point on the windswept slope above the Philistine battle line, Nara gazed across the barren field at the Israelite host. In his amber tunic, the color of a barley field at harvest, David stood out against the gilded canopy of Saul's tent. She had been overjoyed by Najab's arrival, and had watched him present the stones of Ashdoda to David. She had been troubled when David refused them, gesturing for the Nubian to place the stones in the creek bed, but quickly understood the wisdom in it. This way, no one would suspect the power of the stones until David could retrieve them at the right moment and put them to use.

She rejoiced when Jonathan offered a sword and shield to David, realizing that the son of Saul had somehow found Joshua's lost treasures. David's Almighty has smiled on him, she thought.

All he must do now is whet the iron blade of Joshua's sword with the stones of Ashdoda . . .

To her alarm, David handed the sword and shield back to Jonathan and walked away.

Has he turned his back on his own destiny? Has he decided not to face Goliath after all? If David is a coward, I have gravely misjudged him.

But she saw now that she had been mistaken. David was not fleeing the Valley of Elah. He was walking resolutely over to the creek bed where Najab had dropped Ashdoda's sacred stones among countless others. She saw David kneel down and pick up one stone. Then he selected another and another, carefully weighing each one in his hand until he had gathered five from among the hundreds scattered at his feet. She strained to see which stones he had chosen, but at so great a distance, it was impossible to tell.

I know in my heart that he has picked up Ashdoda's holy stones, the ones Najab brought him. But he has no sword to sharpen with them. What good is their magic to him now?

David slipped the five stones into his shepherd's pouch. Then she saw him pull out a long strip of leather that he kept tied to his belt. She recognized it as his sling. It is hardly a weapon, she thought. It is little more than a child's toy . . .

It cannot kill a man, much less Goliath. But if David can hurl one of the five holy stones with his sling, that single stone will possess the full force of Ashdoda's vengeance.

Chapter 65

David pushed his way through the Israelite host. The men had scoffed in disbelief when Jonathan announced that Saul had given his blessing for a shepherd to fight Goliath, but they were powerless to defy the king. David saw the anguish on their faces, the certainty that once Goliath chopped off his head, the Philistines would slaughter or enslave all of them.

He emerged from among his people to stand alone on the barren plain that separated him from the enemy. The Valley of Elah fell silent.

Goliath bellowed out, *"Am I a dog, that you come to me with sticks? Come to me, and I will give your flesh to the birds of the air and to the beasts of the field."*

David replied, *"You come to me with a sword and a spear, but I come to you in the name of the Lord of Hosts. This day the Lord will deliver you into my hand."*

The Philistines jeered him, their taunts drowning out his words.

The sun bore down on the vast desolation that separated the two men. Goliath took a decisive step forward. As one, the Philistines let out a mighty shout. The Israelites were mute, as if they believed this moment sealed their fate.

The roar of the Philistines echoed among the distant hills and faded away into an uneasy stillness. The wind that hissed through the tall grass dwindled and died.

Goliath marched relentlessly toward David, his footfalls heavy upon the earth, his sword in one hand, his spear in the other. Then, while he was still far from him, Goliath stopped.

David realized that the Philistine had cunningly positioned himself. Despite the distance, Goliath had the strength to hurl his spear and strike him. But at this range, it would be impossible for a stone from David's sling to reach the Philistine.

I do not know whether my task can be achieved, only that it is for me alone to make the attempt.

He watched Goliath judge the distance to his target, as calm as a priest poised to sacrifice a lamb on an altar. Overhead, vultures circled on wings as gray as the smoke from funeral pyres, impatient for the Philistine to be done with him.

Goliath drew back his spear.

Even now, David did not move.

The thick sinews of Goliath's right arm glistened like bands of the black metal, stretched taut. He pivoted his body, poised to put his full weight into the throw.

David did not wait for death to come. He pulled out a stone from his shepherd's bag and weighed it in his hand. Before the ponderous muscles of Goliath's shoulder could flex to hurl his spear, David deftly slipped the stone into his sling.

He spun the strip of leather above his head—one, two, three times.

He listened until the whoosh of the leather spoke with the voice of the whirlwind.

With a snap of his wrist, he sent the stone into the sky.

I see that against all the laws of heaven and earth known to me, the stone takes flight like a living thing. Is this the work of the Almighty? Or have I found a boundless strength within me that I never knew existed? Perhaps they are one and the same.

In the instant after the stone was no longer his, when it soared from the leather into the air, David shut his eyes. He knew that some acts must be felt with the heart before they can be seen. His childhood dream flashed through his mind:

The cave held a priceless treasure. An unearthly radiance glowed from within its depths, a promise of unimagined wonders yet to come. But an immense boulder blocked the cave entrance.

At last, he understood: The boulder that stood between him and deliverance for his people, the boulder that had seemed so immense, so immovable, was a stone small enough to fit into the palm of his hand.

It was the stone that he had hurled at Goliath—the stone that, at that very moment, struck the Philistine's brow.

The sharp impact of the blow echoed across the Valley of Elah. Then a shroud of silence settled over the assembled host. Neither David nor Goliath moved. The shepherd held his sling, empty in his hand. Goliath towered before him, clutching his sword and spear.

David felt as if they had both succumbed to a powerful spell—as if they might remain poised like this for eternity, good and evil hanging in the balance.

Then Goliath fell.

When David heard the Philistine's body strike the ground, he believed the echo resounded beyond the assembled armies, beyond Gath, traveling all the way to the far-flung Philistine cities of Gaza, Ashkelon, Ashdod and Ekron. And he believed the sound traveled farther still, to the remotest corners of the world. When Goliath fell, David imagined that the echo rippled across time, into the future and beyond, all the way to the outer ramparts of eternity.

What was the sound? He knew it was louder than the thunder of a mighty oak crashing to earth. When Goliath's body struck the ground, David heard the groan of the boulder rolling from the mouth of the cave in his dream. And now that the boulder had moved away at last, he sensed a warm radiance shining forth from within its depths.

He felt that when he hurled his stone, he at last touched the sun. In this single act, he discovered a promise beyond anything he had imagined, a hope he could not put into words.

Until now, the Israelites had been spellbound, unable to speak or move. Suddenly, like embers seemingly dead that burst into flame, they erupted in a deafening roar. Voices long mute with despair sang praises to heaven. David glanced back at the royal tent: Saul and Jonathan fell to their knees, hands clasped in prayers of thanksgiving.

And the Philistines? It seemed to David that they too had been struck by his stone and rendered speechless. They gaped in disbelief, refusing to accept that their invincible leader, the one who had always towered above them, now lay lifeless in the dust.

David turned his back on the Philistines, in their panic, and on his own people, in their rejoicing. He walked away from them, across the hard and barren earth, to the place where his enemy had fallen.

He stood over Goliath and gazed down in wonder at what he had done. Though his fellow Israelites filled the air with songs of jubilation, he felt no joy.

Is this how it feels to kill a man?

He realized that to take a life violated the holiest of God's Commandments. It was wrong to destroy anything that God had made. David expected to be overcome with remorse, as he had been when he was forced to kill a sick old ram to put it out of its misery. But he felt no regret at Goliath's death.

Wickedness must be destroyed. Tear it out by the roots, or it will spread like a plague, engulf the earth like a pestilence.

He knelt down beside Goliath's sword that lay in the dust. The hilt was so wide that David could barely wrap his fingers around it. He doubted he could lift the massive iron weapon off the ground.

But the cheers of the Israelites endowed him with a strength that he never knew he had. Slowly, steadily, with both hands, he raised the weapon. When he had lifted it high over his head, he allowed his left hand to drop, so that he only held the sword with his right. He pointed the blade to the sky to catch the sun, and the Israelite multitude raised their swords to capture David's reflected glory.

Then, as if the final judgment came as a thunderbolt from the heavens, the blade flashed downward. Goliath's head rolled away from his body and came to rest, face-down in the dust.

David tightened his grip on Goliath's sword and gazed at the iron blade dripping with Goliath's blood. Nara had told him that she had hammered out this blade for her dowry, with her own hands.

The Philistine woman is here with me now. She has wreaked her vengeance.

He reached down and dug his fingers into Goliath's tangled mane, which was matted with sweat, dust and blood. He struggled to lift the massive head high enough for all to see: Goliath's eyes glittered, unblinking, gazing out upon the world with the bitter wisdom of the dead.

He is Goliath no more. The Philistine's head is the head of a man. But his body lying in the dust is the body of a beast.

* * *

The Israelite host in the Valley of Elah joyfully beat their spears on their shields, shouting David's name. Their king sought refuge inside his tent. David realized that Saul might still sit on the throne, but that from this moment forward, he was the one who ruled the hearts of his people. From the awe on their faces, it seemed the Israelites believed that since he could slay Goliath, he had the power to defeat Death itself. That he was a shepherd, the youngest son of Jesse, untrained in the skills of war, made this day all the more miraculous. His people saw it as proof that he was the Chosen of the Almighty.

David carried Goliath's head in one hand, his sword in the other, and the jubilant Israelites parted ranks before him. He made his way up the hill to the royal tent and stopped before the gilt-edged canopy. Jonathan was waiting to greet him. "I honor you, as you honor us with what you have done," he said. Instead of embracing David, he knelt humbly at his feet.

Assailed by the voices of the multitude crying out David's

name, Saul emerged from the tent. David saw not victory, but defeat, in the king's eyes—the somber awareness that Samuel had been right; that David, not his son Jonathan, was God's Chosen for the throne.

David presented the bloodstained trophy to the king, who accepted it with trembling hands. Even in death, Goliath's cruel, unblinking eyes, his open jaws with their jagged teeth, possessed a fearsome power.

Chapter 66

From the hilltop, Nara watched the Israelites crowding around David, shouting his name with the same blind loyalty that her people had once showered on Goliath. The Philistines fled in confusion. Their cumbersome helmets, heavy coats of mail, and swords of iron weighed them down in their headlong rout. Blinded by panic, they knocked over the graven image of Dagon, splintering the cedar idol under their feet, grinding its ruby eyes and ivory teeth into the dust. Even Dalziel, the high priest, abandoned his shattered god, soiling his pristine white robes as he fled in terror.

The Israelites pursued the Philistines into the distance, until the dust cloud raised by their flight veiled the shame of their defeat. Nara could no longer see her people, but she could still hear their desperate pleas for mercy. The rout dwindled to a stain on the horizon, the cries of battle lost in the wind.

In the Philistines' panic to save their own skins, Goliath's body was forgotten, as if all that mattered to her people was that he was dead and David was victorious.

The Israelites see this miracle as proof of the power of their Almighty. I know that is not so. It was not the invisible God of the Israelites who struck down Goliath. I know it was Ashdoda.

A sacred stone from the goddess had taken flight from David's sling to kill the Philistine. Even on the field of battle, Dagon's domain, she had witnessed how Ashdoda's sorcery had defeated her enemy.

The gift of the goddess, the holy stone that killed Goliath, had been forgotten by both sides. But Nara did not forget. She vowed that the killing stone must not be lost in the dust. It was too holy, too precious, too potent for that. Ashdoda's gift had worked a miracle. If it could slay Goliath, what other wonders could it perform?

I must reclaim it. I must grasp the killing stone in my hand.

She scrambled down through the boulders on the high slope, past gnarled oaks, until she stood on the barren plain. Moments before, a thousand men had watched Goliath fall here in the dust. A thousand men had gasped in wonder. Now the field was deserted, forsaken by both Israelite and Philistine. All was silent, except for the sigh of the wings of vultures circling overhead.

Goliath's headless body lay on its back, naked in the dust. The Israelites had stripped it of its glittering coat of mail and greaves, trophies to be prized. The blood dripping from his severed neck soaked the ground. She took pride that a blade of her own making had chopped off Goliath's head. But she did not come here to rejoice in her vengeance.

The killing stone. Where is it?

Her hands groped among the sharp blades of sun-scorched grass near Goliath's body, but found nothing.

Then she caught sight of it—the only stone large enough for David to have hurled from his sling. It was stained with blood.

The killing stone. I must have it.

Before she could take a step closer, vultures swooped down on Goliath's corpse. Reeking of carrion, their flapping wings blocked her way. The scavengers hissed and lunged at her with their sharp, hooked beaks. She saw that they glared at her with the red eyes of Dagon.

For years, Goliath left the flesh of the Israelites on the battlefield for the vultures to devour, she thought. Now the vultures feast on him. But even that will not be the end of Goliath's disgrace. After the vultures gorge themselves, and the maggots have their fill, jackals will crush his bones in their jaws to suck out the marrow.

In the vultures' frenzy, the stone vanished into the dust beneath their talons. She feared she had lost it forever. Then, through the blur of thrashing wings and tearing beaks, she caught sight of the bloodied stone. She could wait no longer. She had to seize it now.

She charged toward the scavengers. They lashed out at her with their hooked beaks, driving her back. In fury, she raised herself to her full height and rushed at them again, shouting and waving her arms.

Startled, the vultures gave ground. The stone lay in their midst. Lunging out, she snatched it from the dust.

The vultures engulfed Goliath's body once more, their wings shrouding the feast from her eyes. Nara was deaf to the sound of tearing flesh and breaking bones as they ripped Goliath apart. The fate of his corpse no longer mattered to her, for she clasped the prize tightly in her fist.

She had no doubt that this was the killing stone. It was still wet with Goliath's blood. Only now, when she examined the stone more closely, did Nara discover the true wonder and the true mystery of that day. The awareness struck her with such force that she sank to her knees.

The sacred stones, Ashdoda's tears fallen from the heavens, are round. This stone that killed Goliath is flat. The sacred stones are black as the night sky, but this stone is brown as the dust. David did not choose one of Ashdoda's tears, the sacred stones that fell from the heavens. He chose a stone from the earth. The goddess did not slay Goliath. Ashdoda did nothing to vanquish the Philistine's wickedness.

This cannot be. It cannot be. And yet, it is so.

Goliath was slain by some other force, one beyond my understanding. What gave the killing stone its deadly power?

She knew she must find the answer.

Until now, she had kept out of sight. But she had to hear the truth from David's lips. Despite the danger, this would be her last chance. Now that he was the victorious hero of the Israelites and she was one of the vanquished, she feared she would never be able to approach him again.

* * *

In search of David, Nara followed the Israelite host as they pursued the Philistines with a vengeance. She kept low, her black robe wrapped tightly around her.

I am yet another widow in mourning. But unlike other widows, I do not weep. I rejoice.

She exulted that the iron blade she had hammered out for Goliath in her father's forge was now in David's hands, defending his life. And yet, it grieved her that the blade was shedding Philistine blood. She prayed that her people would not stand and fight the Israelites. Better for them to flee and rejoin their wives and children inside the gates of Gath, than die here for Dagon, the cruel god who had betrayed them.

Ahead of her, among the advancing Israelites, she caught sight of the royal standard emblazoned with the Lion of Judah. David must be there, she thought, and ran toward it, heedless of the clash of swords and the cries of dying men.

Caught up in their pursuit of the fleeing Philistines, at first the Israelite soldiers ignored her. But it soon grew difficult for her to keep a safe distance from the thrusting spears and slashing blades. She feared she would be killed in the blind fury of battle. Philistine bodies were strewn on the ground before her. She tried not to gaze down at them, dreading that she would see the faces of men she had known in Gath. Stepping over a corpse, she stumbled and fell to her knees.

When she looked up, three Israelites stood over her, their spears pointed at her throat.

"She is a Philistine," one of them said. "Kill her."

Nara clutched the stone tightly in her fist.

I will die, and never know the secret of the killing stone.

Chapter 67

"Spare her."

The spear points that hovered at Nara's throat quickly withdrew. The men bowed their heads respectfully to the one who had spoken. David's tunic had been torn by Philistine iron, his arms stained with Philistine blood. His right hand still clutched Goliath's sword. If the burden of carrying the massive weapon wearied him, he did not show it.

"My men almost killed you." He lifted his hand, inviting her to stand up, even though it meant she looked down at him. "It is good that I was nearby."

"I thought you would be over there." She pointed to the crest of the hill, where Jonathan held the banner of the Lion of Judah, overlooking the advancing Israelites.

"Why should I stand apart from my men? I belong with them, to make sure they are merciful as well as brave." He frowned, and spoke to the soldiers who had threatened Nara. "If we are as cruel as the Philistines, why should the Almighty grant us victory over them?" He turned back to her. "Though it is the way of your people to put their prisoners to the sword, we must not. The Almighty will judge us more by how many lives we spare than by how many we take."

He stepped closer to her. "You ran a great risk to find me. Why?"

She reached into a fold of her robe and pulled out the blood-stained stone. "I found this beside Goliath's body. It is the stone that killed him."

He stared at her in disbelief. "You risked death to bring me *this*?"

She boldly returned his gaze. "Yes, I came because I must ask you a question." She held out the killing stone. "You chose this from the creek bed. It is not one of the holy stones of Ashdoda that I had Najab bring to you."

"That is true," David said.

"Najab told you of the power of Ashdoda's stones, but you chose not to use them."

"That is also true."

"You could have used Ashdoda's sorcery. You could have hurled one of her stones with your sling . . ."

"And yet, I did not." He spoke to her gently, as one explains a simple truth to a child. "I could not use the stones of Ashdoda. I did not want anyone to believe the sorcery of a pagan goddess enabled me to kill Goliath. Instead, the miracle had to come from the humblest of things that the Almighty can create. It had to show the power of a God of small things, as well as of great ones, for the Almighty is the one God of all things."

"But the stones of Ashdoda are holy!" she protested.

"Yes they are holy." He took the killing stone from her and dropped it to the ground among countless others. "*All* stones are holy. So is every mountain and every cloud in the sky, every locust and every blade of grass. All things that live, no matter how humble, are holy, as are all things that have died, and all things that have never drawn breath, for all are the handiwork of God."

She pondered his words. "Then what is unholy?"

"The evil that one man does to another out of hate." The sadness in his eyes overcame him and his voice softened. "The evil that fevers the minds of men in war."

He saw she was struggling to make sense of all that she had suffered. "I thought I was helping you by giving you Ashdoda's stones. Now you say it was folly."

"No, you helped me more than you know," he said. "When Najab offered me Ashdoda's stones fallen from the sky, I finally understood the truth, that I must use a stone from the land of my people in my sling to kill Goliath. I realized that I could only kill him with the weapon of a shepherd, as I must be a shepherd to watch over my people."

"Your people . . ." She eyed David's men, who stared at her with suspicion. "They see me as the enemy, and my own people see me as a traitor. I cannot remain here, but I have nowhere to go."

"You will stay." It was not a request. It was a command. "This is where you belong."

"But I am not one of your tribe!"

"Nara of Gath, you have suffered much," he said. "Your father and your beloved aunt were murdered, and you have been cast out by your own people. You were born a Philistine, but your suffering has made you one of us."

"But even if I join you, what purpose can I serve?"

"A noble purpose: to work the black metal, iron, as only you among us can."

She turned the thought over in her mind. "I grew up in my father's forge. He taught me the secrets of the Serpent's Tongue. My father's was destroyed, but I believe I can fashion another. It will not be easy. It may take weeks or even longer . . ."

"It will not take as long as you fear," he said.

He saw how his confidence in her rekindled her belief in herself. She lifted her head and drew herself up to her full height. "With the Serpent's Tongue, I will make you swords and spears to use against the Philistines."

"You will make more important things than weapons of war," he said. "Someday, we will live with the Philistines in peace. Then you will use your hammer to beat iron swords into plowshares for the planting, and scythes for the harvest—"

"David!"

It was Jonathan, beckoning to him from the crest of a distant hill. The son of Saul waved the banner of the Lion of Judah above his head: "Come lead us!"

David saw that his people were impatient, hungry for him to take command. "I will come!" he called back.

For a moment, caught up in his thoughts, he turned away from the carnage of battle and gazed into the brilliance of the sky, peering into the High Places. In that moment, David understood that the Almighty of his people was more than a God who issued Commandments chiseled into cold tablets of stone. He understood that the Almighty also gave His wisdom as blessings, as the rain is a blessing to parched earth, and lilies are a prayer written on a barren slope in spring.

Author's Note

As one who has spent much of his adult life making documentary films, I have learned that often what is not recorded by the camera is more revealing than what is. I brought that mind-set with me when I decided to explore the clash of David and Goliath. This watershed event, one of the world's most beloved stories, is only a few pages long in the Old Testament (I Samuel, Chapter 17). In fact, the story is so familiar, each of us feels we own it. So I chose to take my version of the Biblical story that I have "owned" since I was a child, and bring it to life through my own lens.

Beginning with the Biblical text, I set out to write a novel based on the narrative I imagined between the lines, to discover what mysteries and surprises might be hiding there. My purpose was to broaden the scope of the story—to take a look with a wide-angle lens. I also wanted to focus on the minds, motives and hearts of some of the Bible's most fascinating figures, along with characters—male and female—I created. I sought to do it while remaining faithful to the spirit of the original.

For the sweeping panorama, I decided to add the dimension of the Philistines themselves, using the latest research as well as my own imagination. Archaeologists accept that Goliath's city of Gath actually existed. The Bible says the Philistines were formidable warriors. It also indicates that they had forbidden the Israelites to learn the secrets of how to work iron. As a result, when they faced the Philistines in combat without iron weapons, the Israelite soldiers were at a deadly disadvantage.

Except for their mastery of iron, the arch-enemies of the Israelites were depicted in the Old Testament as crude barbarians. I was surprised to learn that the latest archaeological discoveries tell a different story. In digs at sites such as Beth Shemesh and Ashkelon, in what is now Israel, artifacts have revealed that the Philistines were an advanced, sophisticated people. They were accomplished builders, skilled makers of wine and olive oil, and adept with the loom and the pottery kiln. Because history is written by the victors, the Bible gives the Israelites the last word, and only in modern times has the truth come to light.

Another dimension of the panorama I developed in the novel is that just as the Israelites believed profoundly in their God, so other peoples of the time fervently worshipped their own gods. Archaeological evidence shows that the Philistines worshipped the mighty god Dagon, which in my novel I chose to depict as a god of war. There is also evidence that the Philistines had worshipped a mother goddess. I depict her in my novel as Ashdoda, goddess of the moon, representative of other female deities from the eastern Mediterranean. I also added the cult of an animistic serpent god, such as might have been worshipped by foreign traders traveling through David's world.

In addition to imagining a panorama of gods and peoples, I wanted to focus intensely on key players in the drama. For the characters who are well-known, I sought to portray them in a way faithful to the Biblical accounts: dangerously unstable King Saul; his son, the impulsive Jonathan; and, of course, David the shepherd hero.

Among lesser known Biblical characters, I found Saul's youngest daughter, Michal, who would become David's first wife, especially fascinating. She is the only woman in the Old Testament of whom it is explicitly said that she loves a man. (I Samuel 18:20 "Now Saul's daughter Michal loved David.") Though Michal will never bear David a child, later in the Bible she will save his life, helping him to escape from Saul's assassins (I Samuel 19:11). Certainly, Michal's actions in my novel illustrate her heartfelt devotion to him.

Another important Biblical character I decided to include was David's mother. Surprisingly, her name is not even mentioned in the Old Testament, though it is given as Nitzevet in the Talmud. Despite her omission from the Biblical account, I wanted to show how I believe that her influence on David could have been significant.

Into this story renowned for depicting one lone hero, I introduced other, unexpected heroes. Among them is Najab, a Nubian, who could have come from the land south of Egypt that is known today as Sudan. I wanted to show that such an adventurous trader might have enriched the texture of life in the land of the Israelites, as well as, in my novel, helping David's cause.

Nara, the "Philistine woman" of the title, is a pivotal figure in the novel. In fact, I was so intrigued by the notion of a female Philistine hero, that Nara was the first character I conceived. While Goliath the Philistine is one of history's most despised villains, I wanted to show that this much-maligned people also could have fostered heroes. And why not a woman? A blacksmith's daughter, because of her remarkable height and strength, Nara is chosen to become Goliath's wife. Later, ironically, she will become David's ally and forge the sword that chops off Goliath's head.

Nara is the only woman who comes to know both David and Goliath and to experience firsthand the clash of their cultures. She is also caught up in the worship of Ashdoda, the goddess revered by the female outcasts of Gath. Though she experiences the conflicting worlds of three different gods and feels alien from all of them, Nara ultimately takes refuge among the Israelites. When, at the end of the novel, David invites Nara to settle with them, it is a hopeful step toward peace and understanding between their peoples. Perhaps only an outsider like Nara, the wife of the killer Goliath, could be the blacksmith David chooses to beat swords into plowshares.

By their actions in my story, Najab and Nara, both outsiders and non-Israelites, help make it possible for David to triumph over Goliath. The bravery of these characters does not diminish

David's heroism. It only makes us value it more.

David is one of the most inspiring figures in the Old Testament, the leader who united his nation, wrote immortal psalms and conquered Jerusalem. He is the king from whose line will spring the Messiah. But David's moral weaknesses will have devastating consequences later in his life, when he seduces Bathsheba and brings about the death of her husband, Uriah the Hittite. In *David and the Philistine Woman,* I wanted to tell the story of David when he was uncorrupted, a young man finding his way, a shepherd seeking to grasp his destiny. Even then, he was a human being with weaknesses as well as strengths.

Unlike Moses or Abraham, David, as depicted in my novel, never hears the voice of God. He must seek out that voice in his own heart. Perhaps that is the spark that kindled my passion to tell this story in the first place. Like David, in our troubled world, we must do the right thing without hearing a divine voice to direct our actions. I wanted my novel to show that what links people of goodwill is not so much the god they worship—Najab, Nara and David each have their own—as it is their bond of common humanity and shared compassion.

By the end of the novel, David learns that whether or not it is ordained in heaven, nothing of value is achieved in our world unless it is done by human hands. When, at last, David hurls the stone, he watches it soar and thinks to himself:

I see that against all the laws of heaven and earth known to me, the stone takes flight like a living thing. Is this the work of the Almighty? Or have I found a boundless strength within me that I never knew existed? Perhaps they are one and the same.

It is for each of us to judge with our own conscience how far we can hurl the stone and what our target must be.

Paul Boorstin
http://www.paulboorstin.com

About the Author

Paul Boorstin is an award-winning documentary filmmaker and screenwriter whose work has appeared on Discovery, A&E and the History Channel, as well as on NBC, ABC and CBS. A resident of Los Angeles, he has traveled around the world making documentaries for National Geographic. His screenplays have been produced as motion pictures by Paramount and 20th Century Fox. He is also a blogger for the Huffington Post and a contributor to the *Los Angeles Times*.

Book Group Discussion Topics

1. Discuss the stages of awareness that David goes through as his character develops in the novel.
2. What does the novel say about the relationships between fathers and mothers and their sons and daughters?
3. The relationships between siblings is important in the novel. What are other examples in the Bible of siblings helping or hurting each other?
4. The novel portrays worshippers of four gods: the Philistines' Dagon; the goddess Ashdoda; a serpent deity; and the Israelites' Almighty. Discuss how these gods, the ways they are worshipped—and the values of the worshippers—differ.
5. Discuss how the author depicts David's character and the world he lived in. How does this differ from your perception of David and his world before reading the novel?
6. At the end of the novel, why does David choose not to use either Joshua's sword and shield, or Ashdoda's stones, when he finally faces Goliath?
7. As women of their time, how do Ahinoam, Nitzevet and Hada attempt to fulfill their own ambitions through the lives of those they have raised?
8. In the novel, what is the role of the Philistine priests? The Israelite priests? How do they differ?
9. How and why is the secret of making iron a key element in the story?
10. Several places in the novel, the author describes Israelites who worship idols along with the Almighty. Why did these Israelites do so?
11. Do you think that at the end of the story, Nara will stay with the Israelites, as David requests? That she will worship Ashdoda or the Israelites' Almighty?
12. Read the story of David and Goliath as it unfolds in the Bible

(I Samuel, Chapter 17) and discuss how it may have inspired the author's retelling of it.

Top Hat Books

Historical fiction that lives.

We publish fiction that captures the contrasts, the achievements, the optimism and the radicalism of ordinary and extraordinary times across the world.

We're open to all time periods and we strive to go beyond the narrow, foggy slums of Victorian London. Where are the tales of the people of fifteenth-century Australasia? The stories of eighth-century India? The voices from Africa, Arabia, cities and forests, deserts and towns? Our books thrill, excite, delight and inspire.

The genres will be broad but clear. Whether we're publishing romance, thrillers, crime, or something else entirely, the unifying themes are timescale and enthusiasm. These books will be a celebration of the chaotic power of the human spirit in difficult times. The reader, when they finish, will snap the book closed with a satisfied smile.
If you have enjoyed this book, why not tell other readers by posting a review on your preferred book site.

Recent bestsellers from Tops Hat Books are:

Grendel's Mother
The Saga of the Wyrd-Wife
Susan Signe Morrison
Grendel's Mother, a queen from Beowulf, threatens the fragile political stability on this windswept land.
Paperback: 978-1-78535-009-2 ebook: 978-1-78535-010-8

Queen of Sparta
A Novel of Ancient Greece
T.S. Chaudhry
History has relegated her to the role of bystander, what if Gorgo, Queen of Sparta, had played a central role in the Greek resistance to the Persian invasion?
Paperback: 978-1-78279-750-0 ebook: 978-1-78279-749-4

Mercenary
R.J. Connor
Richard Longsword is a Mercenary, but this time it's not for money, this time it's for revenge…
Paperback: 978-1-78279-236-9 ebook: 978-1-78279-198-0

Black Tom
Terror on the Hudson
Ron Semple
A tale of sabotage, subterfuge and political shenanigans in Jersey City in 1916; America is on the cusp of war and the fate of the nation hinges on the decision of one young policeman.
Paperback: 978-1-78535-110-5 ebook: 978-1-78535-111-2

Destiny Between Two Worlds

A Novel about Okinawa

Jacques L. Fuqua, Jr.

A fateful October 1944 morning offered no inkling that the lives of thousands of Okinawans would be profoundly changed—forever.

Paperback: 978-1-78279-892-7 ebook: 978-1-78279-893-4

Cowards

Trent Portigal

A family's life falls into turmoil when the parents' timid political dissidence is discovered by their far more enterprising children.

Paperback: 978-1-78535-070-2 ebook: 978-1-78535-071-9

Godwine Kingmaker

Part One of The Last Great Saxon Earls

Mercedes Rochelle

The life of Earl Godwine is one of the enduring enigmas of English history. Who was this Godwine, first Earl of Wessex; unscrupulous schemer or protector of the English? The answer depends on who you ask…

Paperback: 978-1-78279-801-9 ebook: 978-1-78279-800-2

The Last Stork Summer

Mary Brigid Surber

Eva, a young Polish child, battles to survive the designation of "racially worthless" under Hitler's Germanization Program.

Paperback: 978-1-78279-934-4 ebook: 978-1-78279-935-1 $4.99 £2.99

Messiah Love

Music and Malice at a Time of Handel

Sheena Vernon

The tale of Harry Walsh's faltering steps on his journey to success and happiness, performing in the playhouses of Georgian London.

Paperback: 978-1-78279-768-5 ebook: 978-1-78279-761-6

A Terrible Unrest

Philip Duke

A young immigrant family must confront the horrors of the Colorado Coalfield War to live the American Dream.

Paperback: 978-1-78279-437-0 ebook: 978-1-78279-436-3